SPACE WARPED

Written by **Hervé Bourhis**

Drawn by **Rudy Spiessert**

Colors by **Mathilda**

Cover by **Rudy Spiessert**

Translation: **Dan Heching** (Issues 1-2)
Edward Gauvin (Issues 3-6)
Americanization: **Kevin Church**
Letters: **Deron Bennett**

Editor: **Dafna Pleban**
Original Showcase Editor: **Lewis Trondheim**
Design: **Carol Thompson**

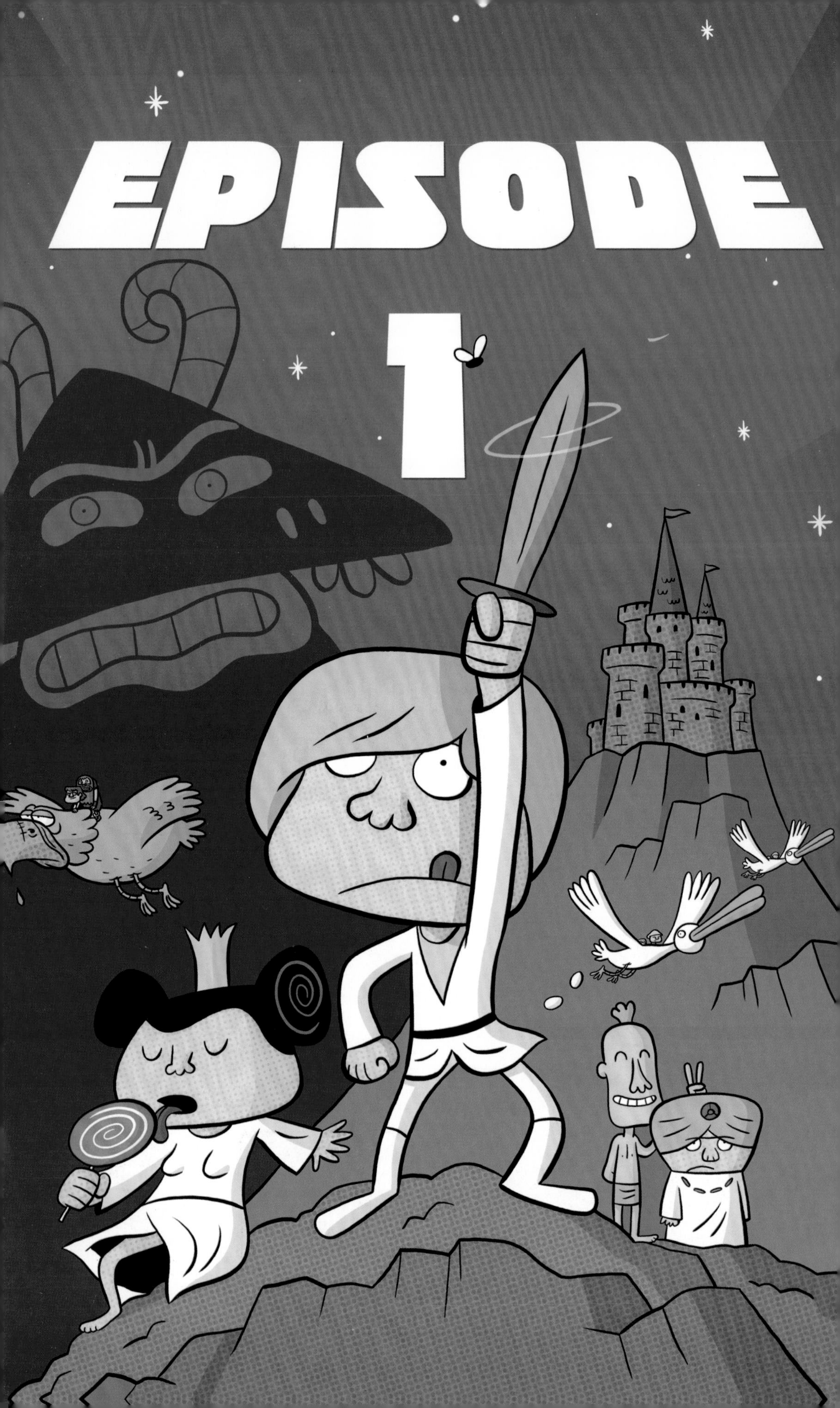
EPISODE
1

far away, in a land long ago...

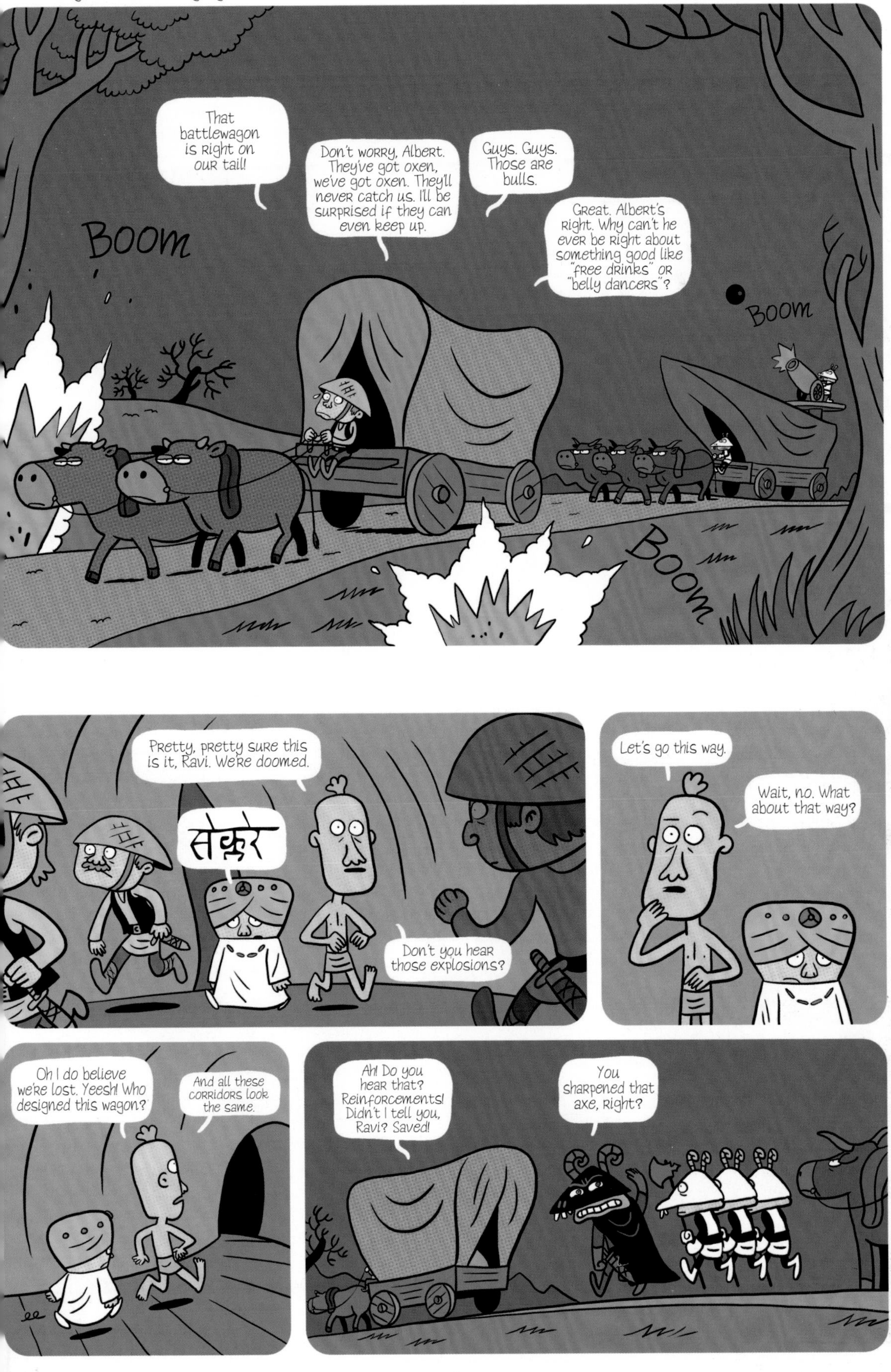

That battlewagon is right on our tail!
Don't worry, Albert. They've got oxen, we've got oxen. They'll never catch us. I'll be surprised if they can even keep up.
Guys. Guys. Those are bulls.
Great. Albert's right. Why can't he ever be right about something good like "free drinks" or "belly dancers"?
Boom
Boom
Boom
Pretty, pretty sure this is it, Ravi. We're doomed.
सेक्रेर
Don't you hear those explosions?
Let's go this way.
Wait, no. What about that way?
Oh I do believe we're lost. Yeesh! Who designed this wagon?
And all these corridors look the same.
Ah! Do you hear that? Reinforcements! Didn't I tell you, Ravi? Saved!
You sharpened that axe, right?

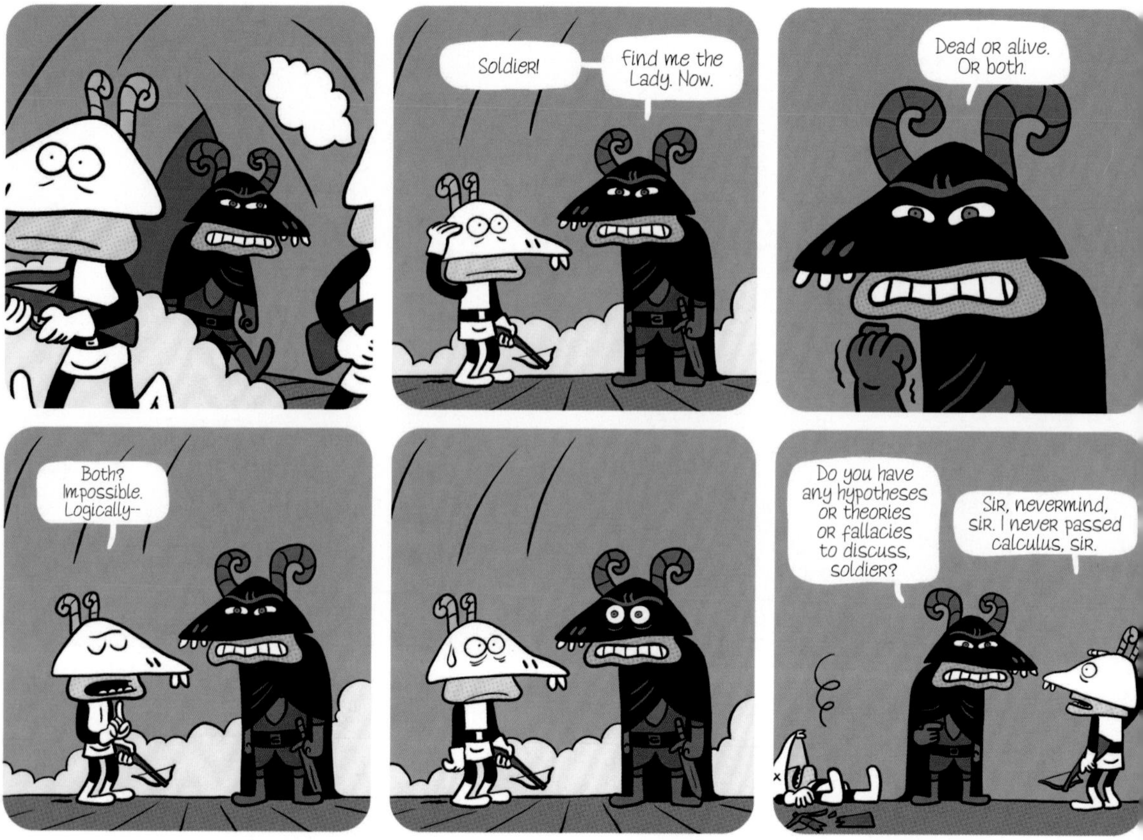
Soldier!
Find me the Lady. Now.
Dead or alive. Or both.
Both? Impossible. Logically--
Do you have any hypotheses or theories or fallacies to discuss, soldier?
Sir, nevermind, sir. I never passed calculus, sir.

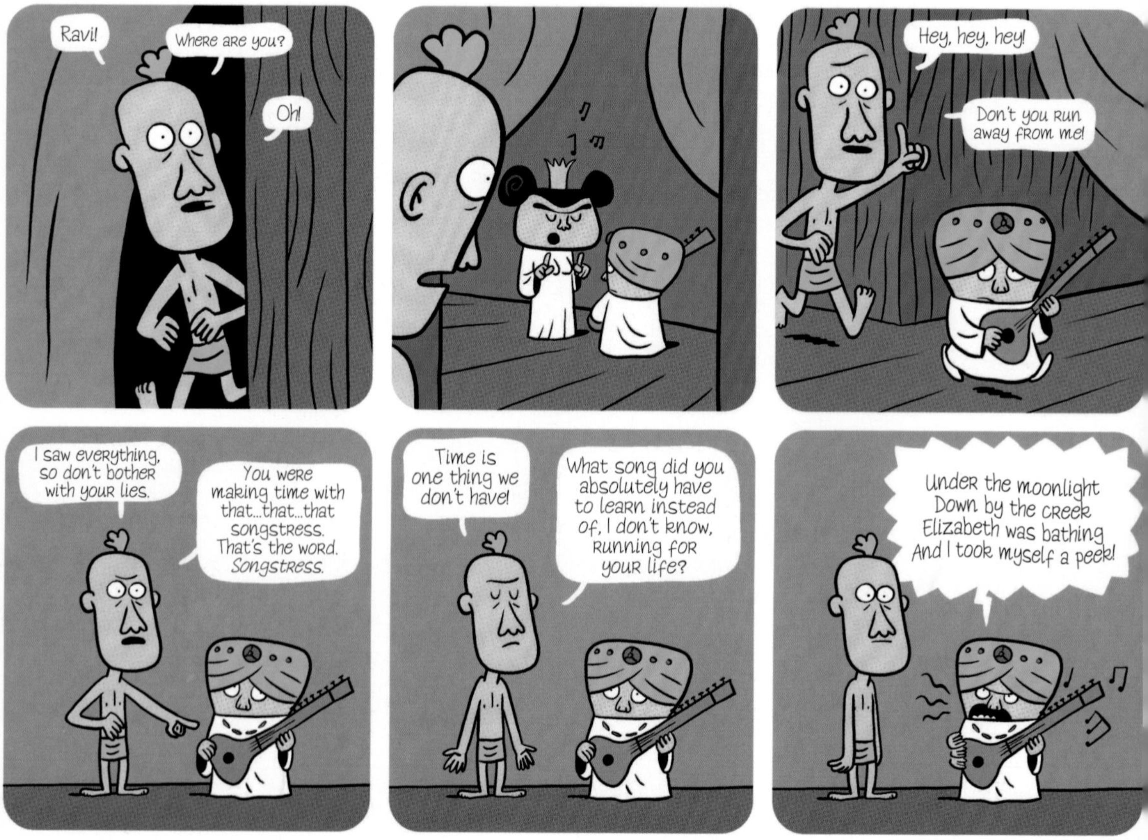
Ravi!
Where are you?
Oh!
Hey, hey, hey!
Don't you run away from me!
I saw everything, so don't bother with your lies.
You were making time with that...that...that songstress. That's the word. *Songstress.*
Time is one thing we don't have!
What song did you absolutely have to learn instead of, I don't know, running for your life?
Under the moonlight
Down by the creek
Elizabeth was bathing
And I took myself a peek!

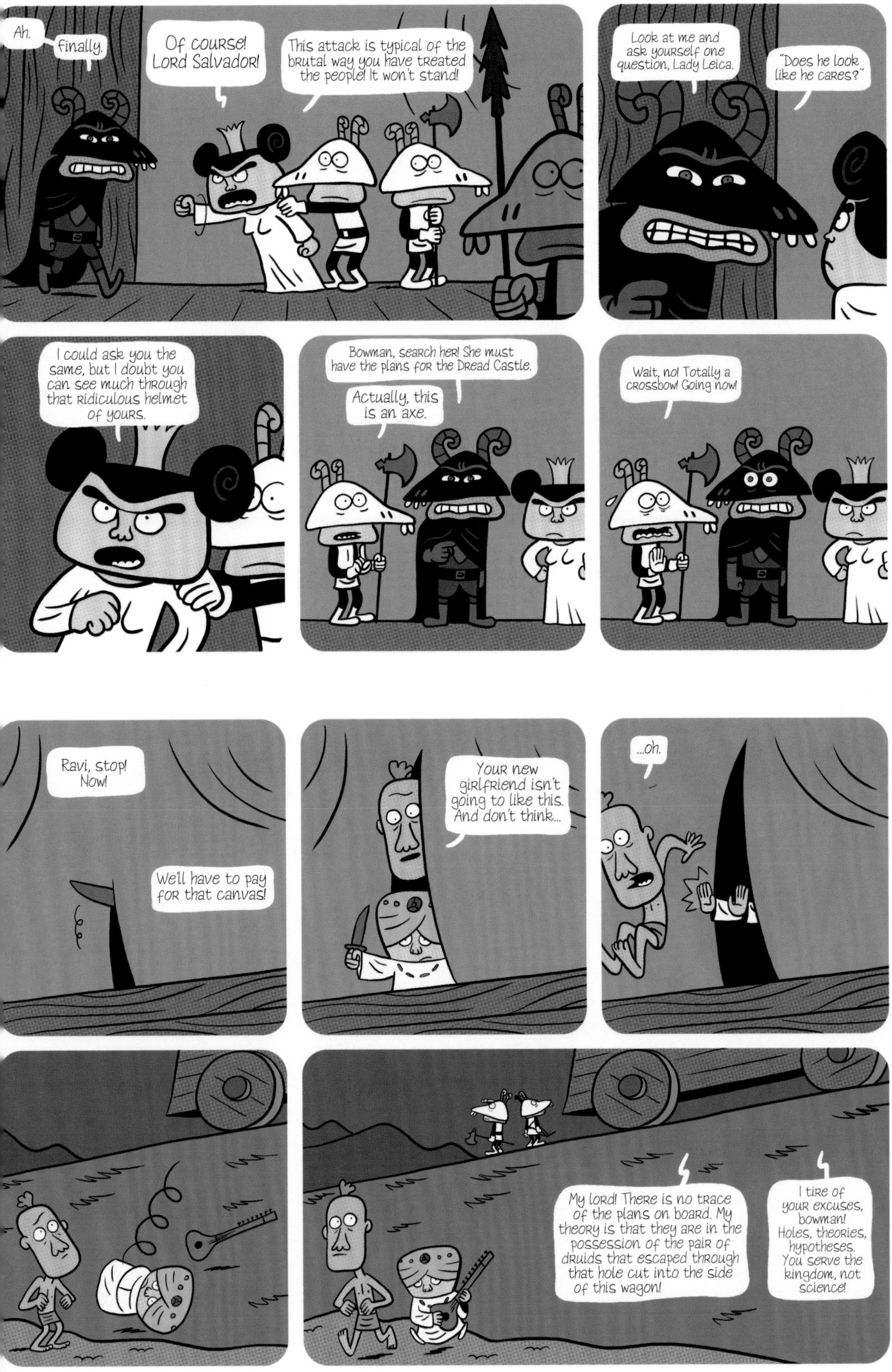
Ah.
Finally.
Of course! Lord Salvador!
This attack is typical of the brutal way you have treated the people! It won't stand!
Look at me and ask yourself one question, Lady Leica.
"Does he look like he cares?"
I could ask you the same, but I doubt you can see much through that ridiculous helmet of yours.
Bowman, search her! She must have the plans for the Dread Castle.
Actually, this is an axe.
Wait, no! Totally a crossbow! Going now!
Ravi, stop! Now!
We'll have to pay for that canvas!
Your new girlfriend isn't going to like this. And don't think...
...oh.
My lord! There is no trace of the plans on board. My theory is that they are in the possession of the pair of druids that escaped through that hole cut into the side of this wagon!
I tire of your excuses, bowman! Holes, theories, hypotheses. You serve the kingdom, not science!

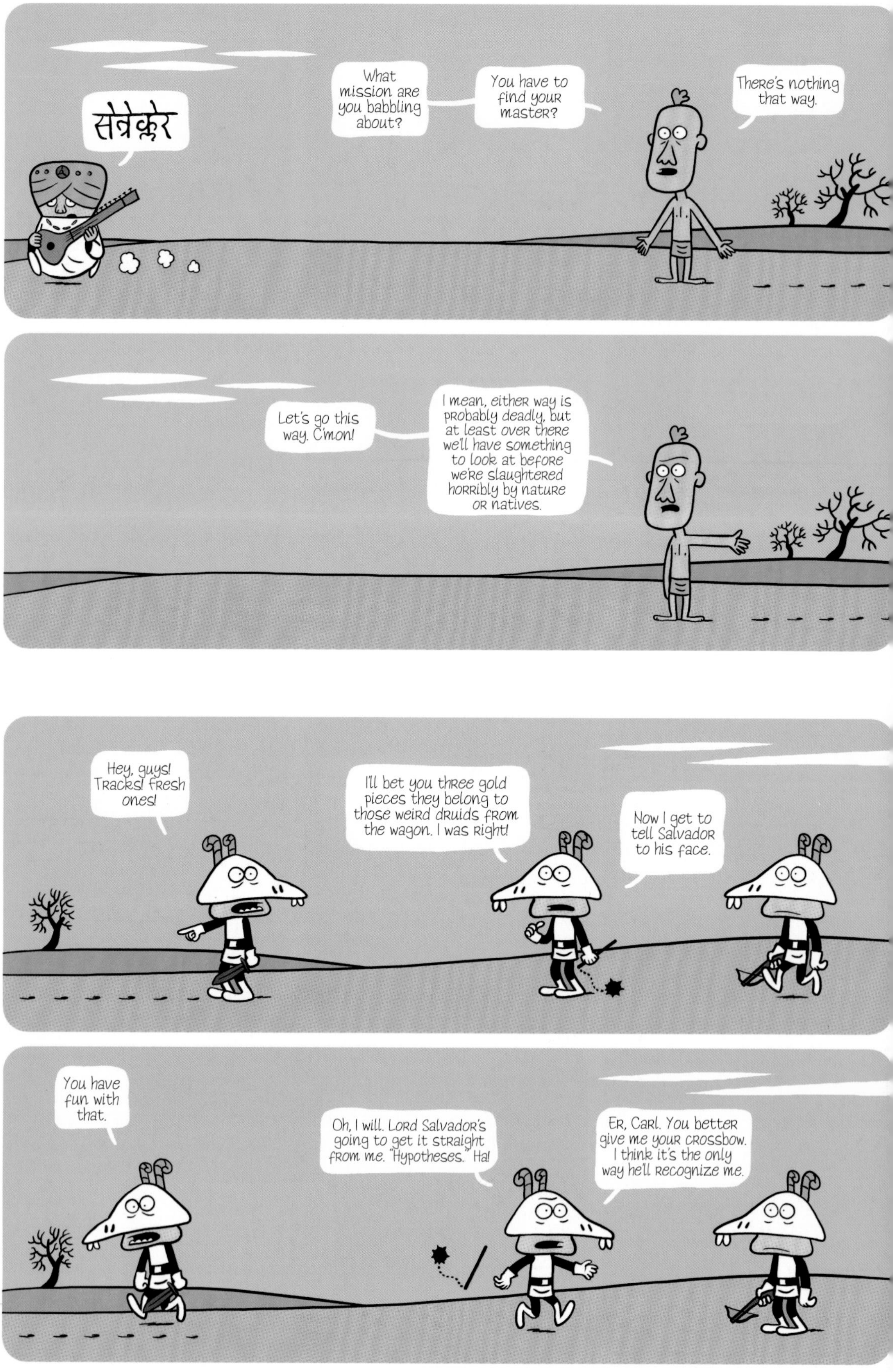
सेत्रेक्लेर
What mission are you babbling about?
You have to find your master?
There's nothing that way.
Let's go this way. C'mon!
I mean, either way is probably deadly, but at least over there we'll have something to look at before we're slaughtered horribly by nature or natives.
Hey, guys! Tracks! Fresh ones!
I'll bet you three gold pieces they belong to those weird druids from the wagon. I was right!
Now I get to tell Salvador to his face.
You have fun with that.
Oh, I will. Lord Salvador's going to get it straight from me. "Hypotheses." Ha!
Er, Carl. You better give me your crossbow. I think it's the only way he'll recognize me.

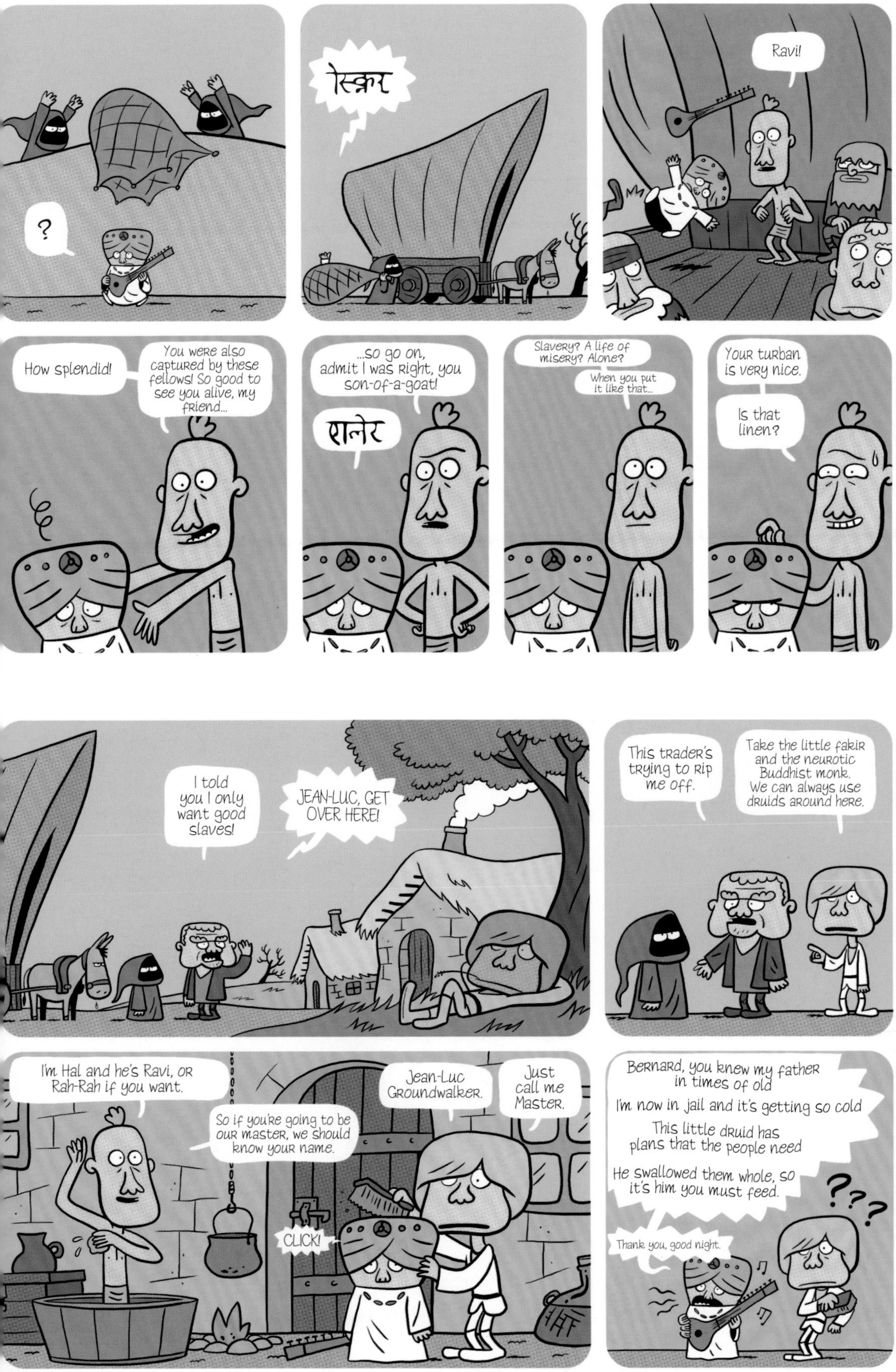
?
Ravi!
How splendid!
You were also captured by these fellows! So good to see you alive, my friend...
...so go on, admit I was right, you son-of-a-goat!
Slavery? A life of misery? Alone?
When you put it like that...
Your turban is very nice.
Is that linen?
I told you I only want good slaves!
JEAN-LUC, GET OVER HERE!
This trader's trying to rip me off.
Take the little fakir and the neurotic Buddhist monk. We can always use druids around here.
I'm Hal and he's Ravi, or Rah-Rah if you want.
So if you're going to be our master, we should know your name.
Jean-Luc Groundwalker.
Just call me Master.
CLICK!
Bernard, you knew my father in times of old
I'm now in jail and it's getting so cold
This little druid has plans that the people need
He swallowed them whole, so it's him you must feed.
Thank you, good night.
???

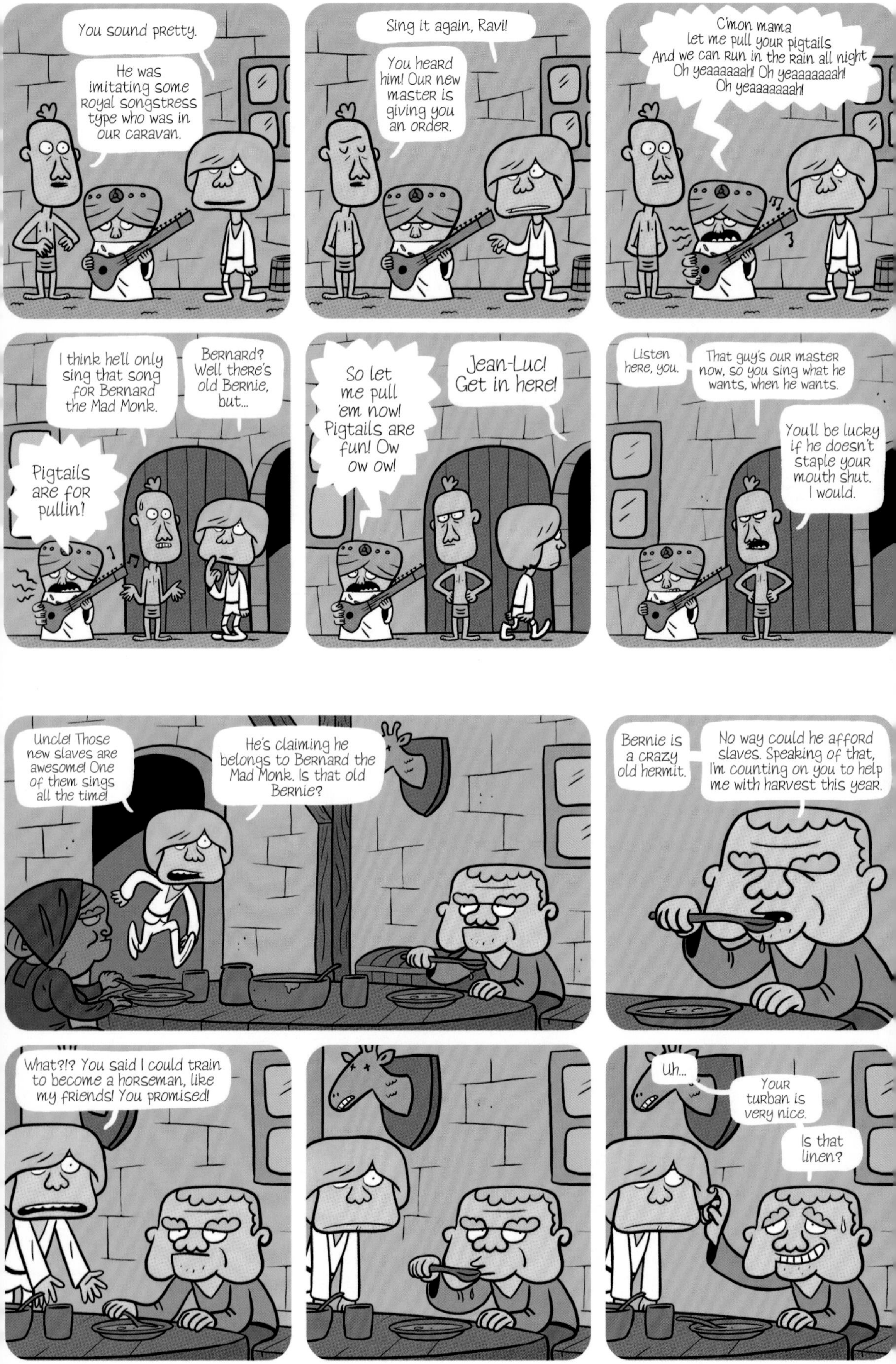

You sound pretty.
He was imitating some Royal songstress type who was in our caravan.
Sing it again, Ravi!
You heard him! Our new master is giving you an order.
C'mon mama let me pull your pigtails And we can run in the rain all night Oh yeaaaaaah! Oh yeaaaaaaah! Oh yeaaaaaaah!
I think he'll only sing that song for Bernard the Mad Monk.
Bernard? Well there's old Bernie, but...
Pigtails are for pullin'!
So let me pull 'em now! Pigtails are fun! Ow ow ow!
Jean-Luc! Get in here!
Listen here, you.
That guy's our master now, so you sing what he wants, when he wants.
You'll be lucky if he doesn't staple your mouth shut. I would.
Uncle! Those new slaves are awesome! One of them sings all the time!
He's claiming he belongs to Bernard the Mad Monk. Is that old Bernie?
Bernie is a crazy old hermit.
No way could he afford slaves. Speaking of that, I'm counting on you to help me with harvest this year.
What?!? You said I could train to become a horseman, like my friends! You promised!
Uh...
Your turban is very nice.
Is that linen?

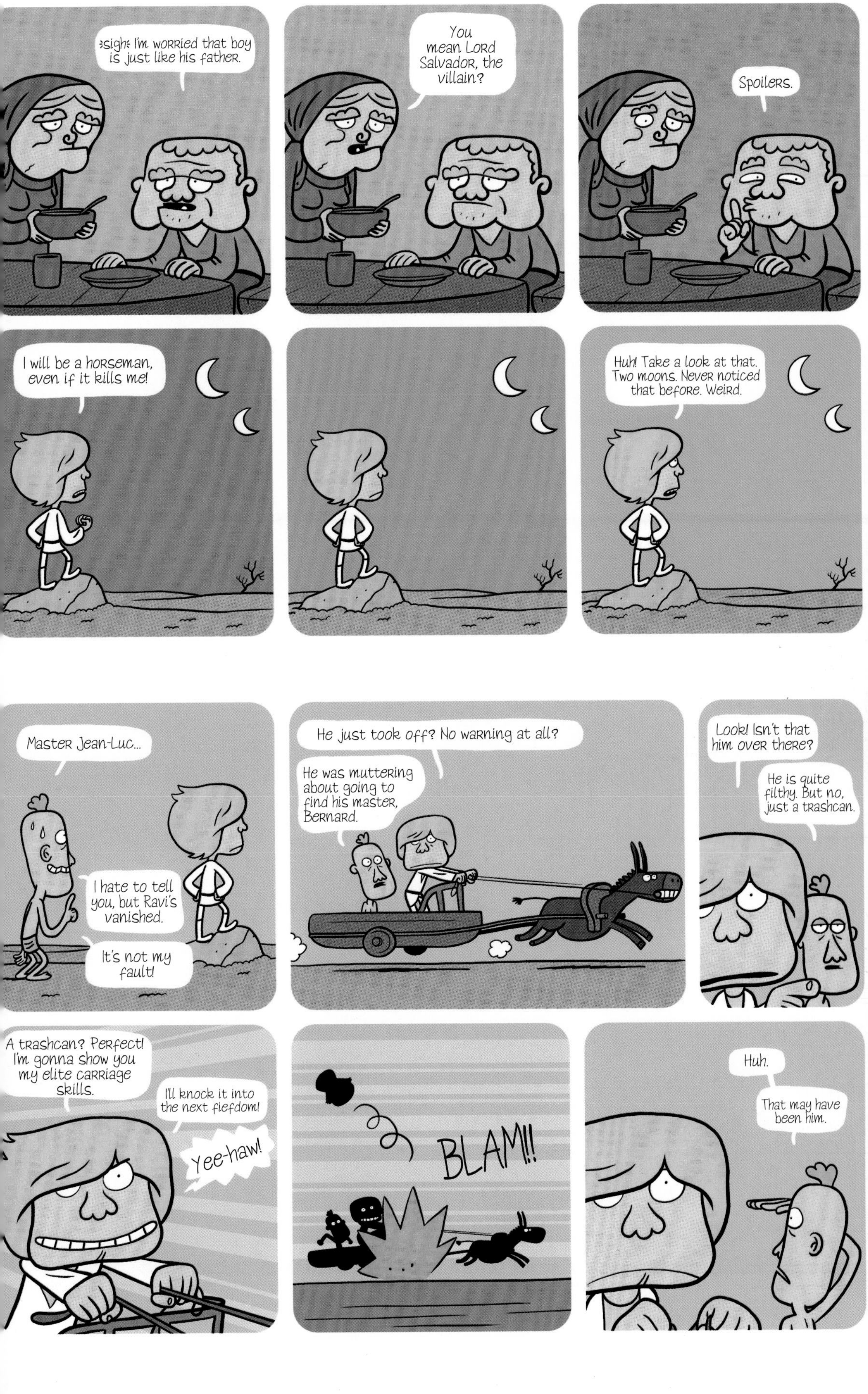
:sigh: I'm worried that boy is just like his father.
You mean Lord Salvador, the villain?
Spoilers.
I will be a horseman, even if it kills me!
Huh! Take a look at that. Two moons. Never noticed that before. Weird.
Master Jean-Luc...
I hate to tell you, but Ravi's vanished.
It's not my fault!
He just took off? No warning at all?
He was muttering about going to find his master, Bernard.
Look! Isn't that him over there?
He is quite filthy. But no, just a trashcan.
A trashcan? Perfect! I'm gonna show you my elite carriage skills.
I'll knock it into the next fiefdom!
Yee-haw!
BLAM!!
Huh.
That may have been him.

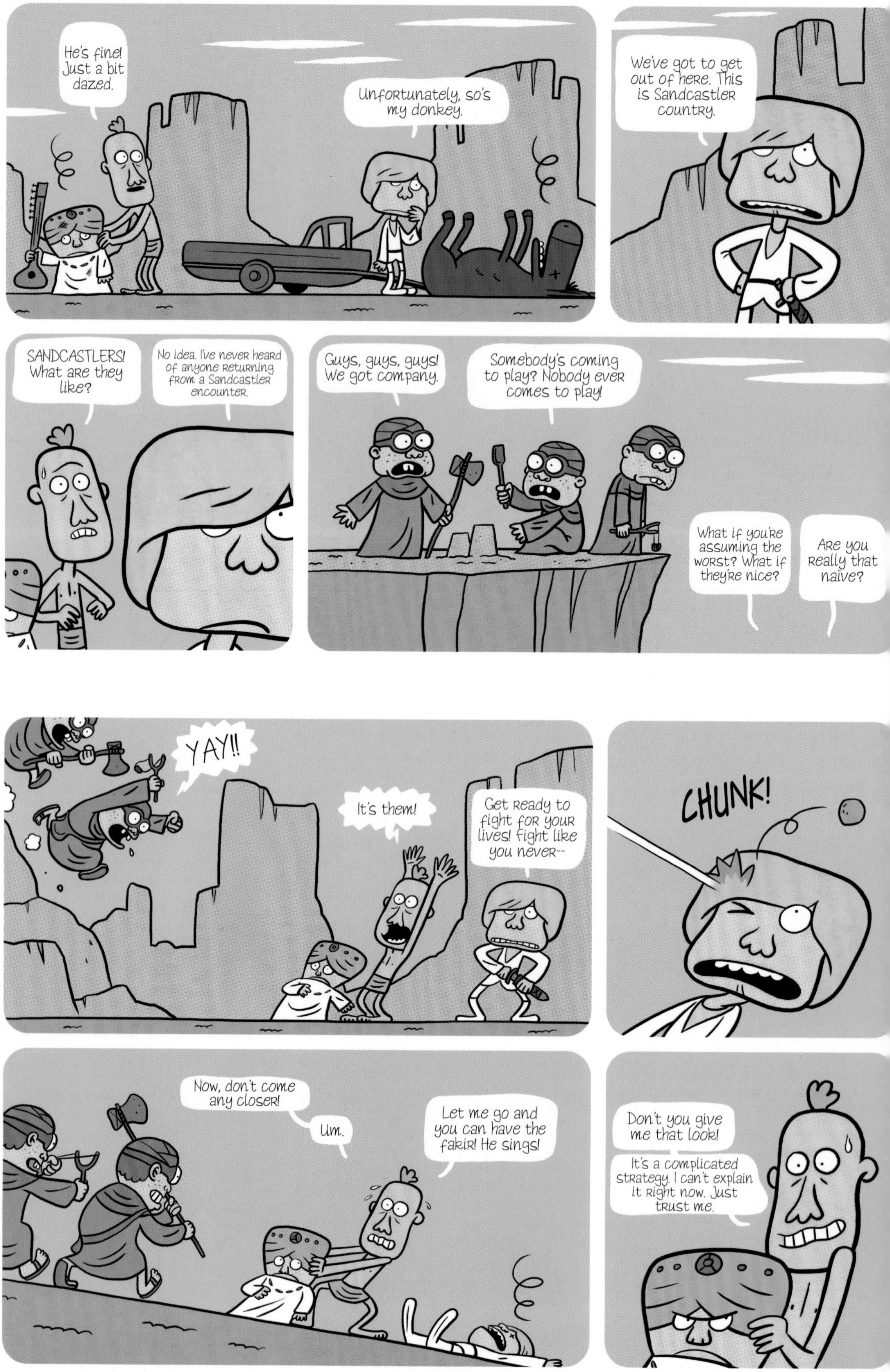
He's fine! Just a bit dazed.
Unfortunately, so's my donkey.
We've got to get out of here. This is Sandcastler country.
SANDCASTLERS! What are they like?
No idea. I've never heard of anyone returning from a Sandcastler encounter.
Guys, guys, guys! We got company.
Somebody's coming to play? Nobody ever comes to play!
What if you're assuming the worst? What if they're nice?
Are you really that naïve?
YAY!!
It's them!
Get ready to fight for your lives! Fight like you never--
CHUNK!
Now, don't come any closer!
Um.
Let me go and you can have the fakir! He sings!
Don't you give me that look!
It's a complicated strategy. I can't explain it right now. Just trust me.

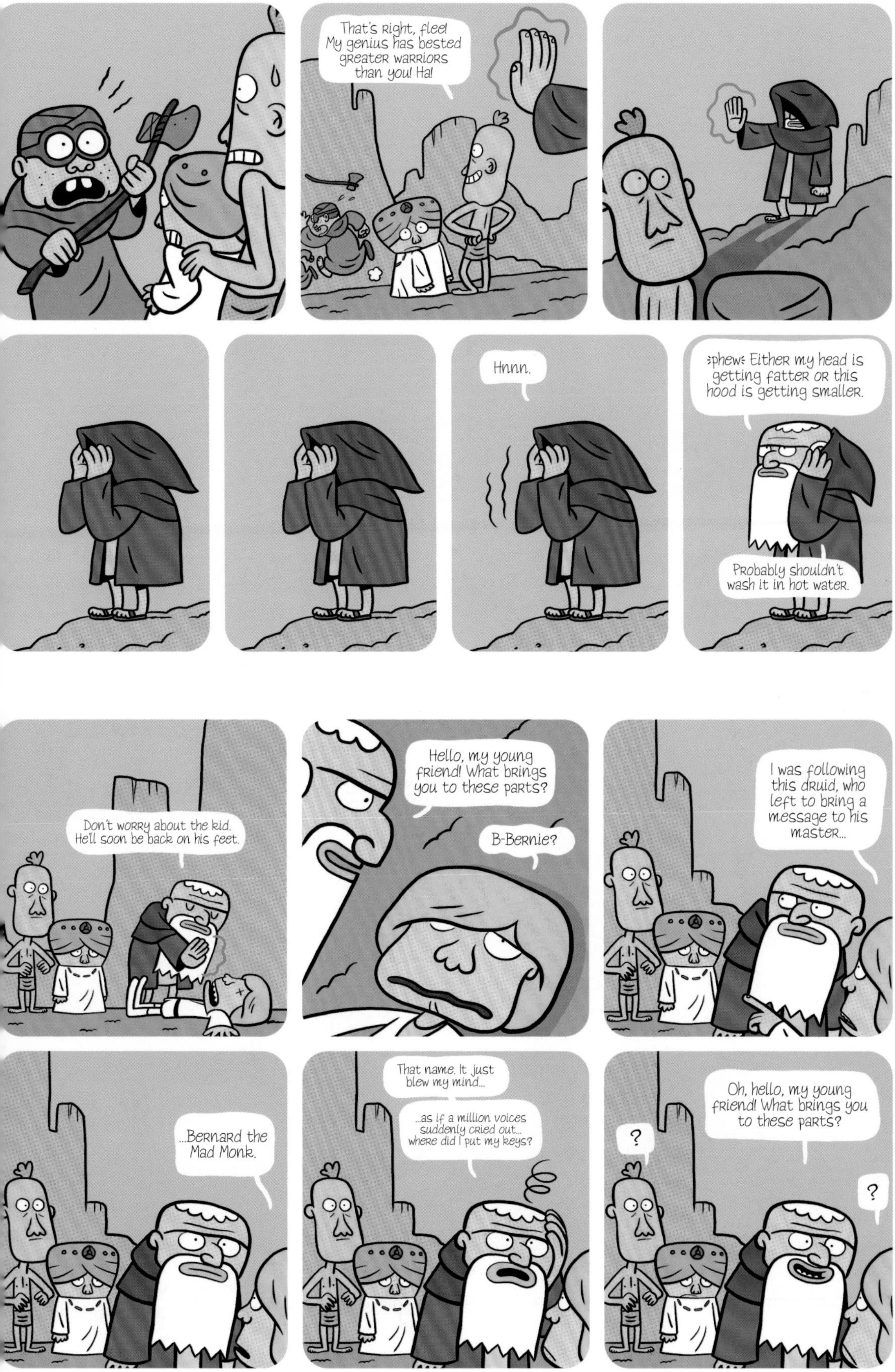
That's right, flee! My genius has bested greater warriors than you! Ha!
Hnnn.
:phew: Either my head is getting fatter or this hood is getting smaller.
Probably shouldn't wash it in hot water.
Don't worry about the kid. He'll soon be back on his feet.
Hello, my young friend! What brings you to these parts?
B-Bernie?
I was following this druid, who left to bring a message to his master...
...Bernard the Mad Monk.
That name. It just blew my mind...
...as if a million voices suddenly cried out... where did I put my keys?
?
Oh, hello, my young friend! What brings you to these parts?
?

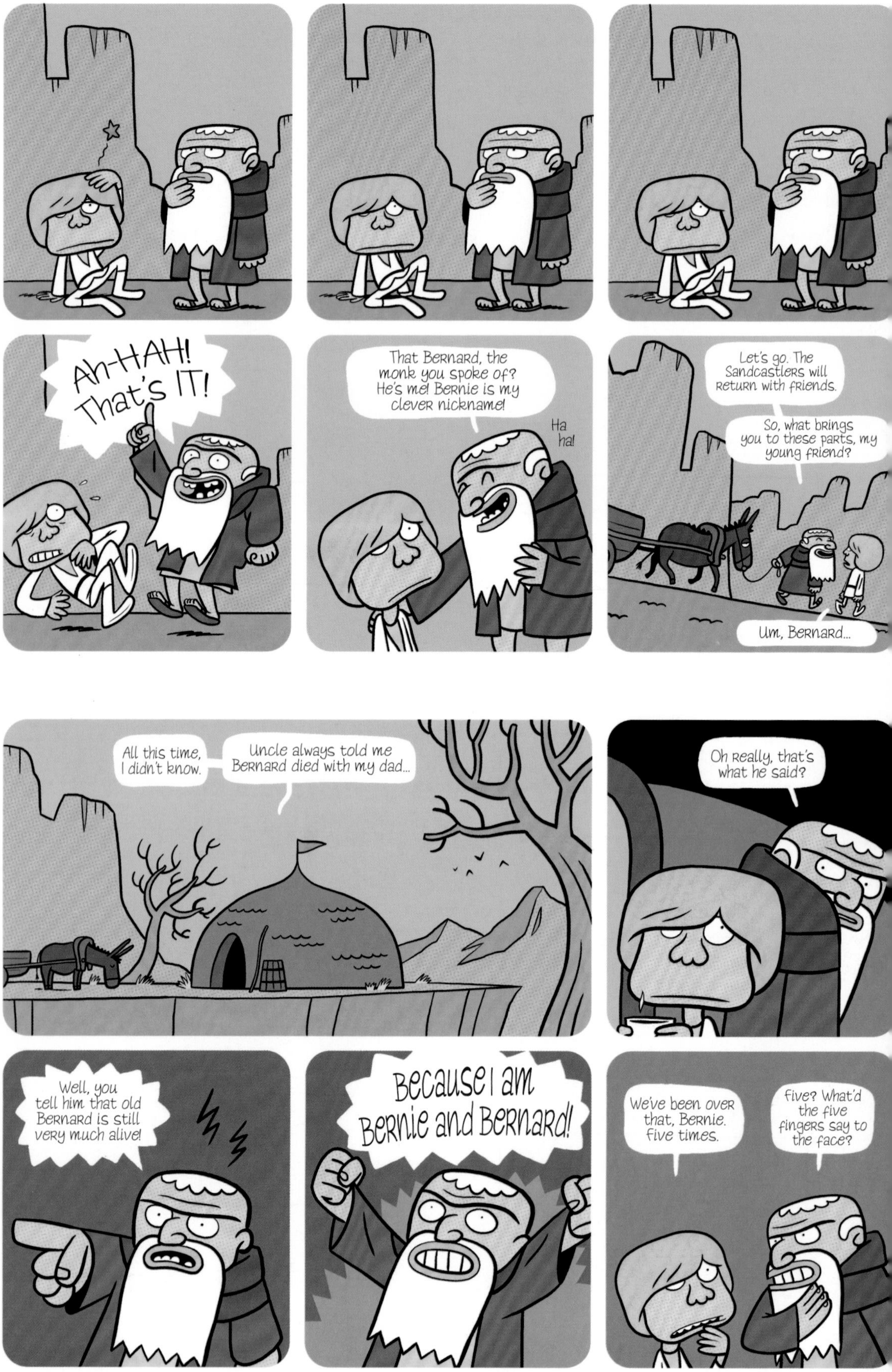
Ah-HAH! That's IT!
That Bernard, the monk you spoke of? He's me! Bernie is my clever nickname!
Ha ha!
Let's go. The Sandcastlers will return with friends.
So, what brings you to these parts, my young friend?
Um, Bernard...
All this time, I didn't know.
Uncle always told me Bernard died with my dad...
Oh really, that's what he said?
Well, you tell him that old Bernard is still very much alive!
Because I am Bernie and Bernard!
We've been over that, Bernie. Five times.
Five? What'd the five fingers say to the face?

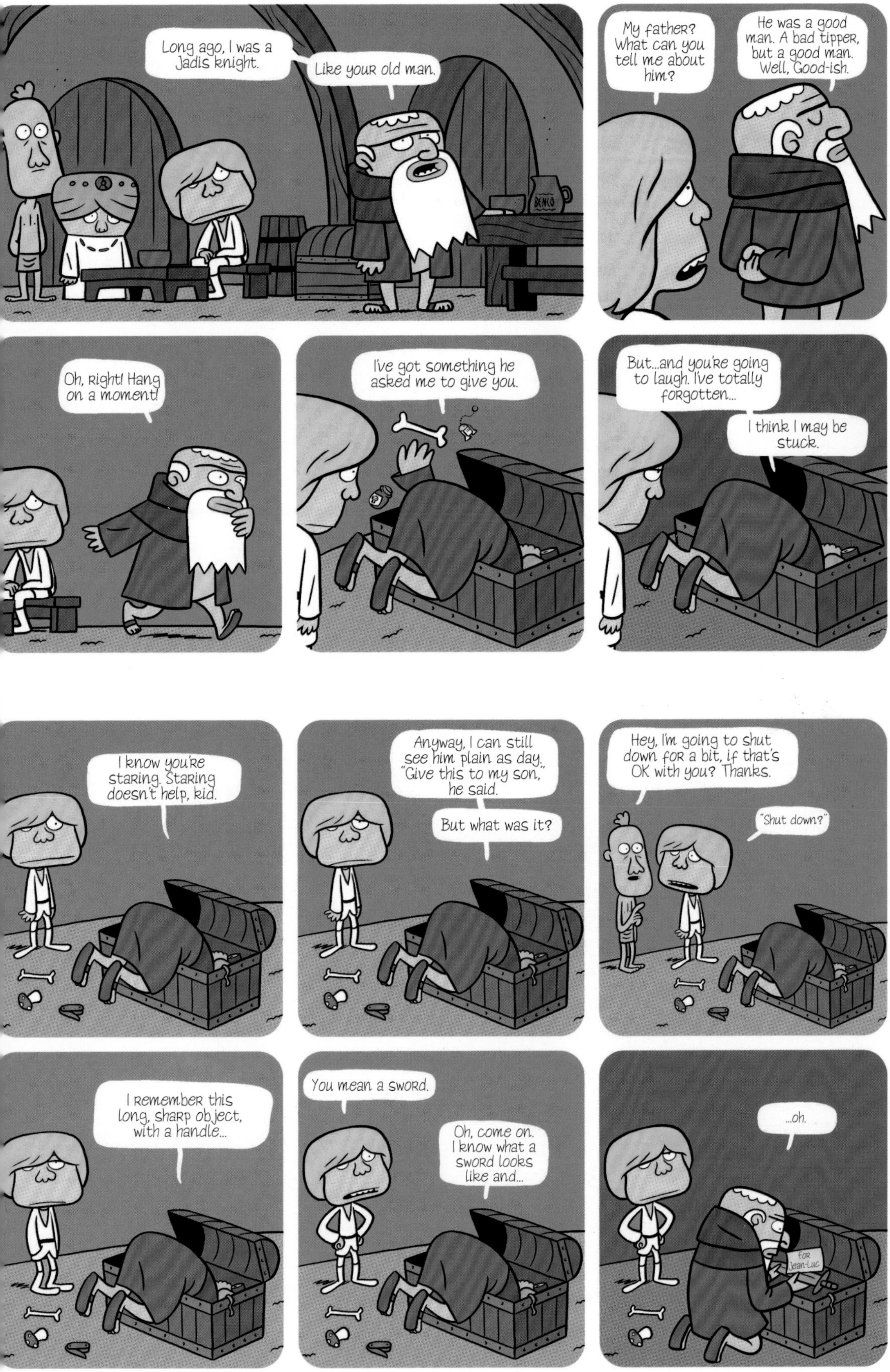
Long ago, I was a Jadis knight.
Like your old man.
My father? What can you tell me about him?
He was a good man. A bad tipper, but a good man. Well, Good-ish.
BENCO
Oh, right! Hang on a moment!
I've got something he asked me to give you.
But...and you're going to laugh. I've totally forgotten...
I think I may be stuck.
I know you're staring. Staring doesn't help, kid.
Anyway, I can still see him plain as day. "Give this to my son," he said.
But what was it?
Hey, I'm going to shut down for a bit, if that's OK with you? Thanks.
"Shut down?"
I remember this long, sharp object, with a handle...
You mean a sword.
Oh, come on. I know what a sword looks like and...
...oh.
For Jean-Luc

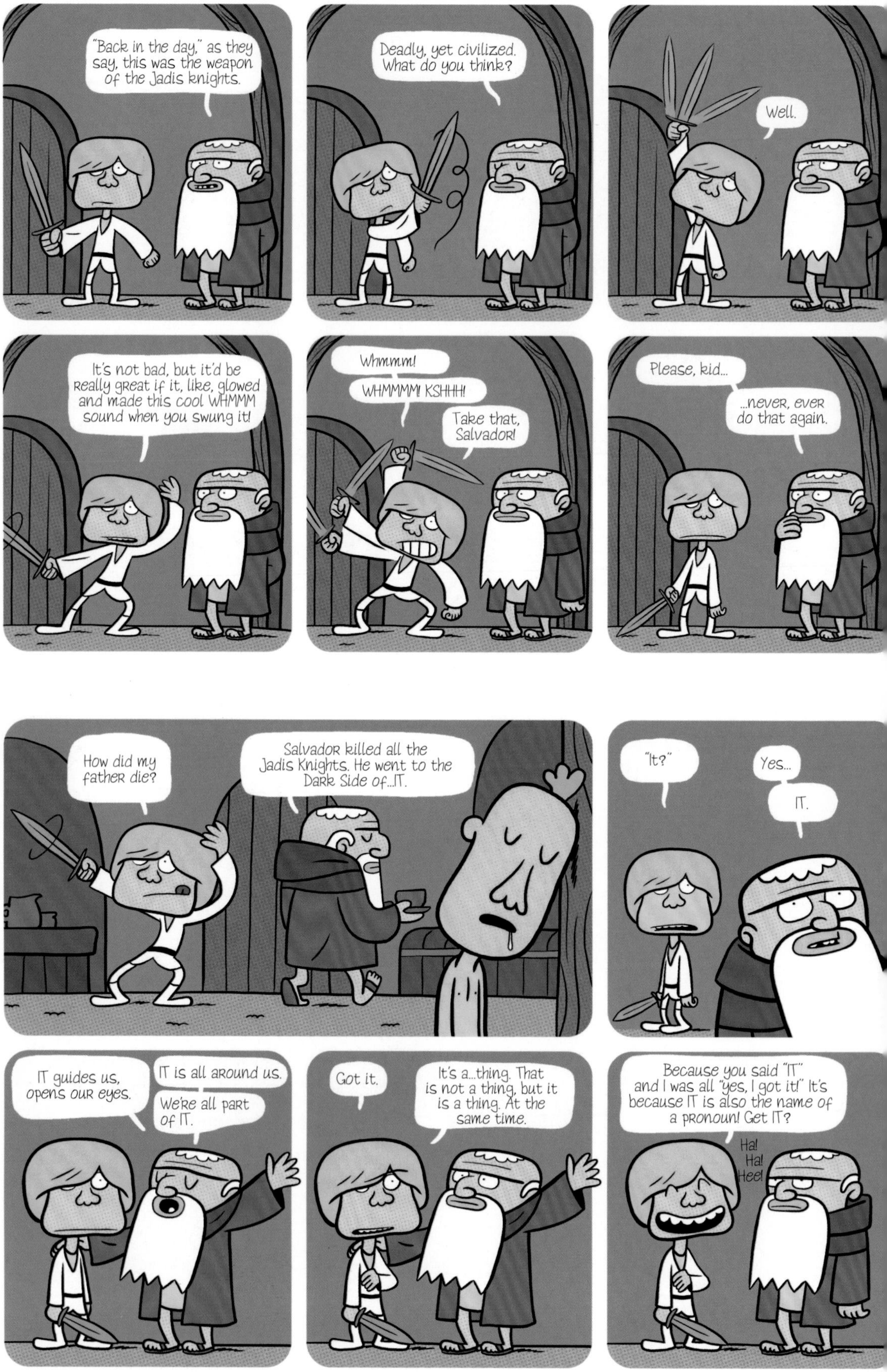

"Back in the day," as they say, this was the weapon of the Jadis knights.
Deadly, yet civilized. What do you think?
Well.
It's not bad, but it'd be really great if it, like, glowed and made this cool WHMMM sound when you swung it!
Whmmm!
WHMMMM! KSHHH!
Take that, Salvador!
Please, kid...
...never, ever do that again.
How did my father die?
Salvador killed all the Jadis Knights. He went to the Dark Side of...IT.
"It?"
Yes...
IT.
IT guides us, opens our eyes.
IT is all around us.
We're all part of IT.
Got it.
It's a...thing. That is not a thing, but it is a thing. At the same time.
Because you said "IT" and I was all "yes, I got it!" It's because IT is also the name of a pronoun! Get IT?
Ha! Ha! Hee!

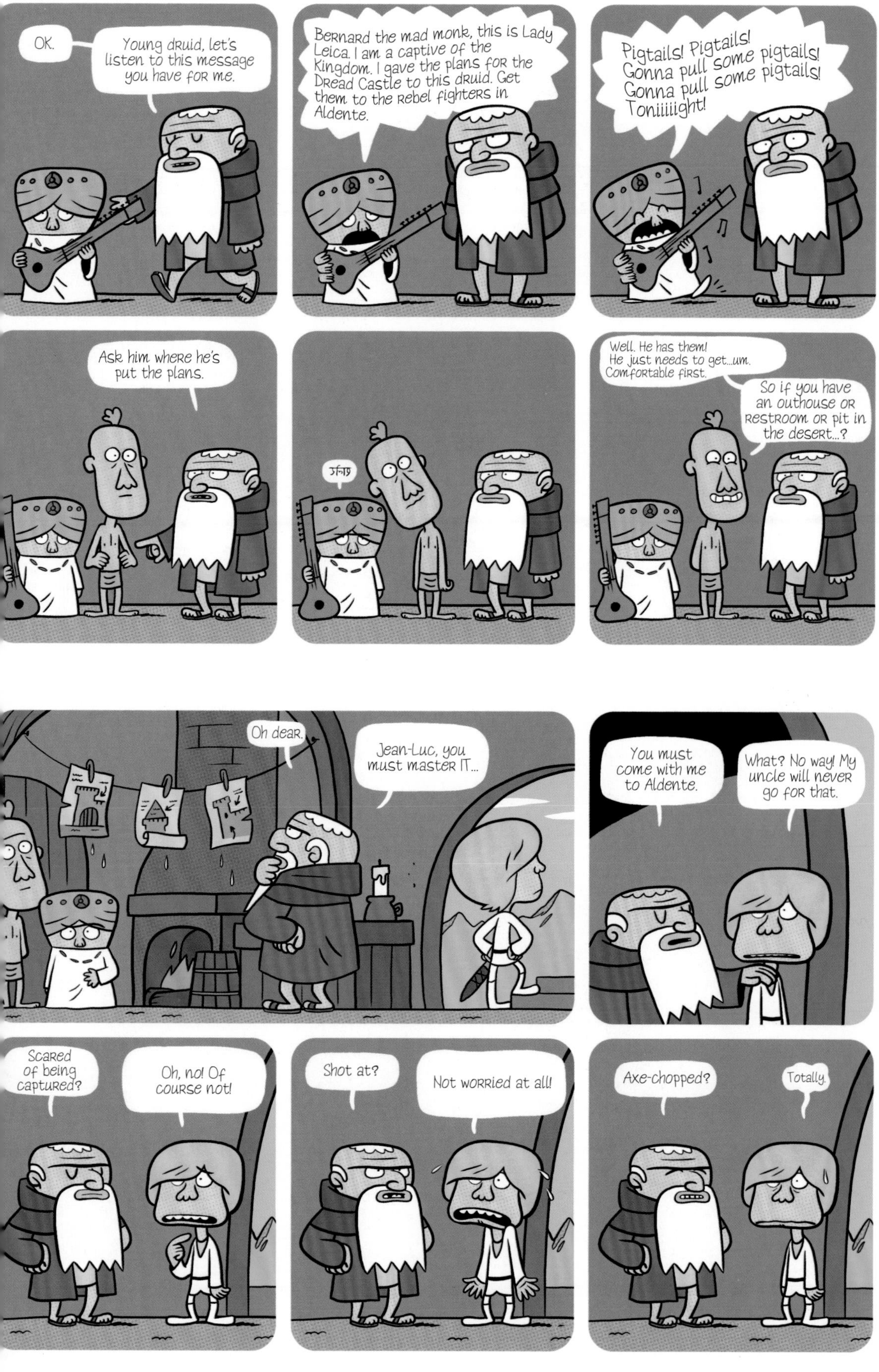
OK.
Young druid, let's listen to this message you have for me.
Bernard the mad monk, this is Lady Leica. I am a captive of the Kingdom. I gave the plans for the Dread Castle to this druid. Get them to the rebel fighters in Aldente.
Pigtails! Pigtails! Gonna pull some pigtails! Gonna pull some pigtails! Toniiiiight!
Ask him where he's put the plans.
Well. He has them! He just needs to get...um. Comfortable first.
So if you have an outhouse or restroom or pit in the desert...?
Oh dear.
Jean-Luc, you must master IT...
You must come with me to Aldente.
What? No way! My uncle will never go for that.
Scared of being captured?
Oh, no! Of course not!
Shot at?
Not worried at all!
Axe-chopped?
Totally.

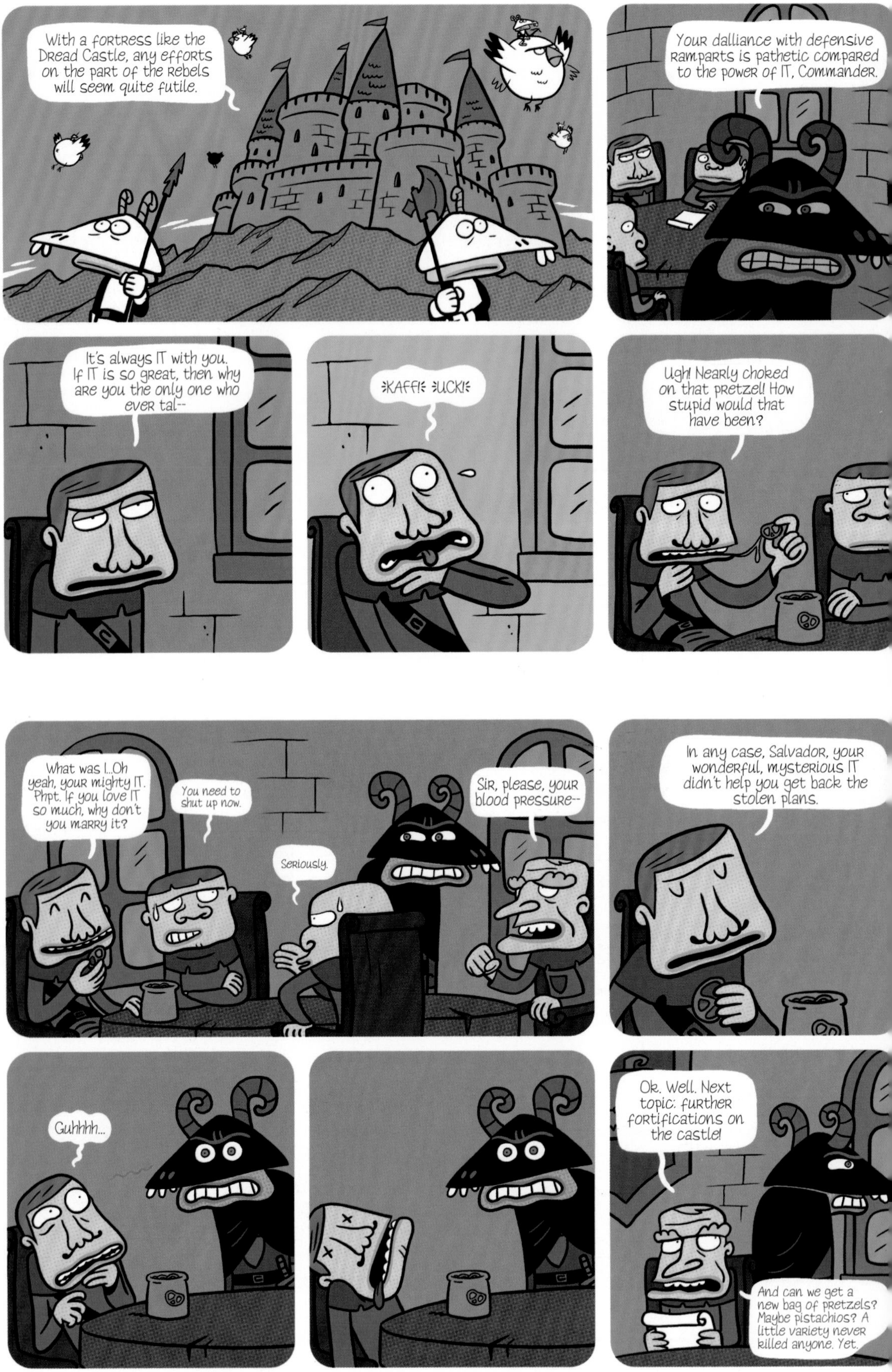

With a fortress like the Dread Castle, any efforts on the part of the Rebels will seem quite futile.
Your dalliance with defensive ramparts is pathetic compared to the power of IT, Commander.
It's always IT with you. If IT is so great, then why are you the only one who ever tal--
KAFF! *UCK!*
Ugh! Nearly choked on that pretzel! How stupid would that have been?
What was I...Oh yeah, your mighty IT. Phpt. If you love IT so much, why don't you marry it?
You need to shut up now.
Seriously.
Sir, please, your blood pressure--
In any case, Salvador, your wonderful, mysterious IT didn't help you get back the stolen plans.
Guhhhh...
Ok. Well. Next topic: further fortifications on the castle!
And can we get a new bag of pretzels? Maybe pistachios? A little variety never killed anyone. Yet.

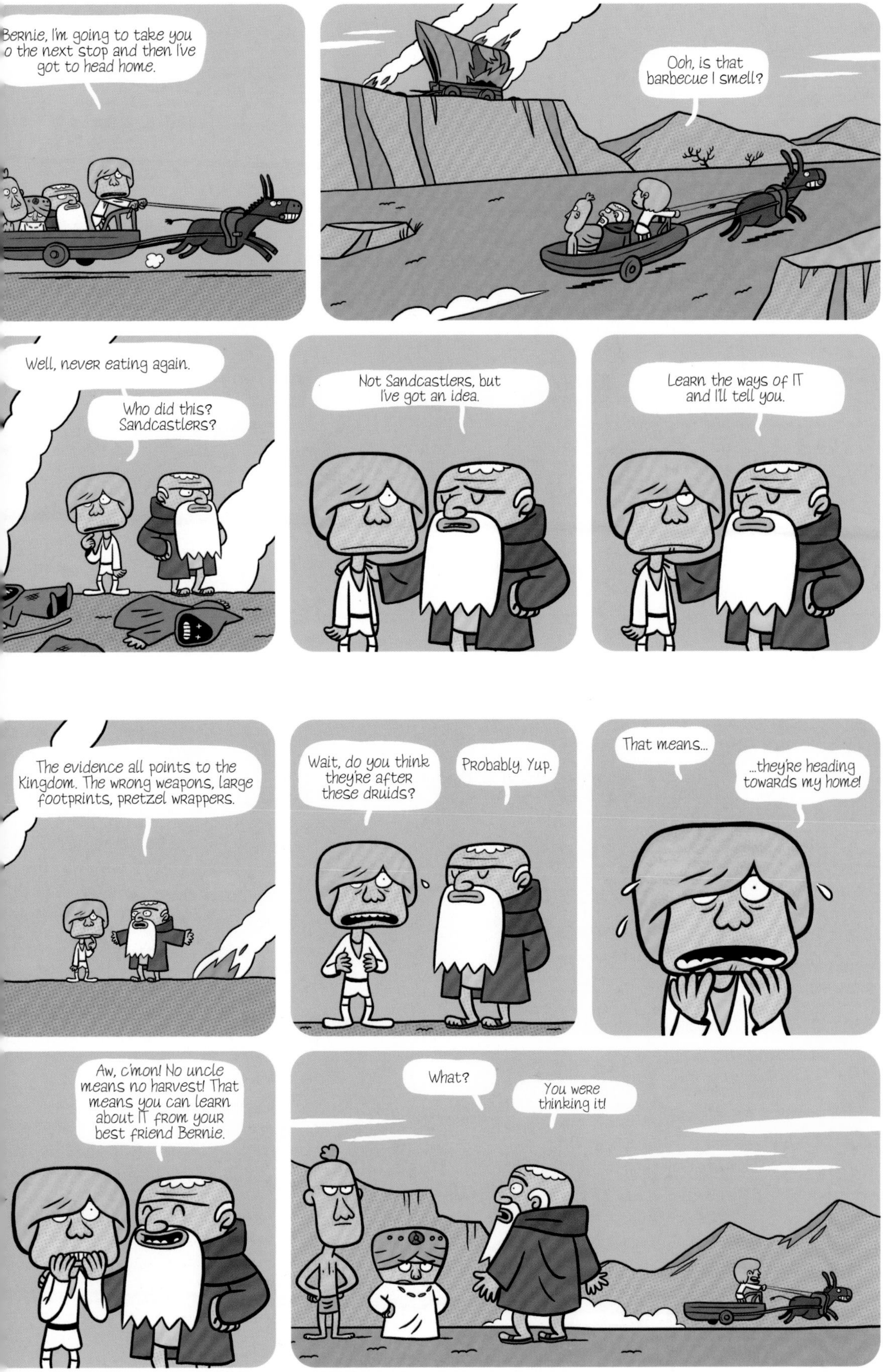
Bernie, I'm going to take you
o the next stop and then I've got to head home.
Ooh, is that barbecue I smell?
Well, never eating again.
Who did this? Sandcastlers?
Not Sandcastlers, but I've got an idea.
Learn the ways of IT and I'll tell you.
The evidence all points to the Kingdom. The wrong weapons, large footprints, pretzel wrappers.
Wait, do you think they're after these druids?
Probably. Yup.
That means...
...they're heading towards my home!
Aw, c'mon! No uncle means no harvest! That means you can learn about IT from your best friend Bernie.
What?
You were thinking it!

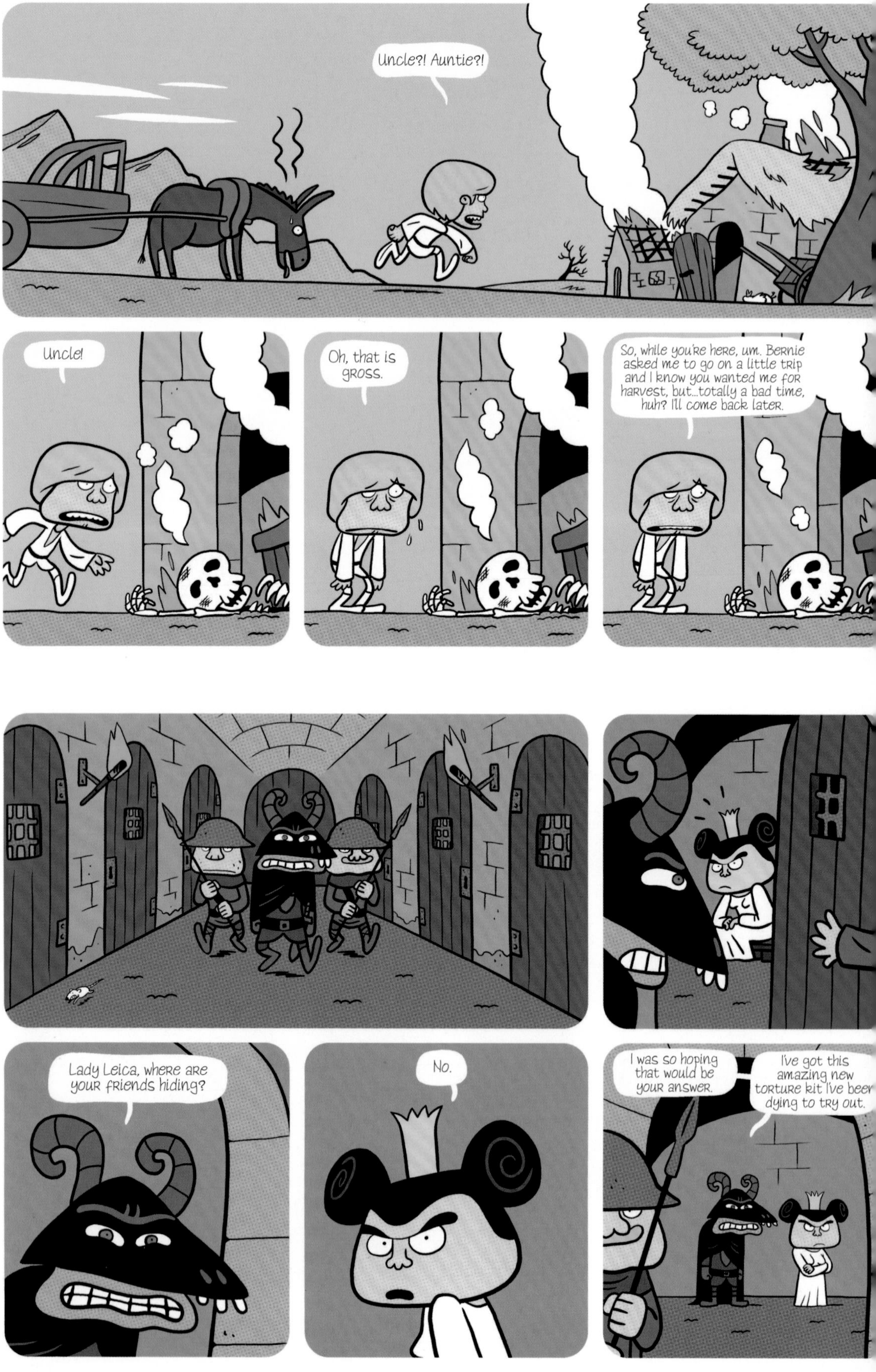
Uncle?! Auntie?!
Uncle!
Oh, that is gross.
So, while you're here, um. Bernie asked me to go on a little trip and I know you wanted me for harvest, but...totally a bad time, huh? I'll come back later.
Lady Leica, where are your friends hiding?
No.
I was so hoping that would be your answer.
I've got this amazing new torture kit I've been dying to try out.

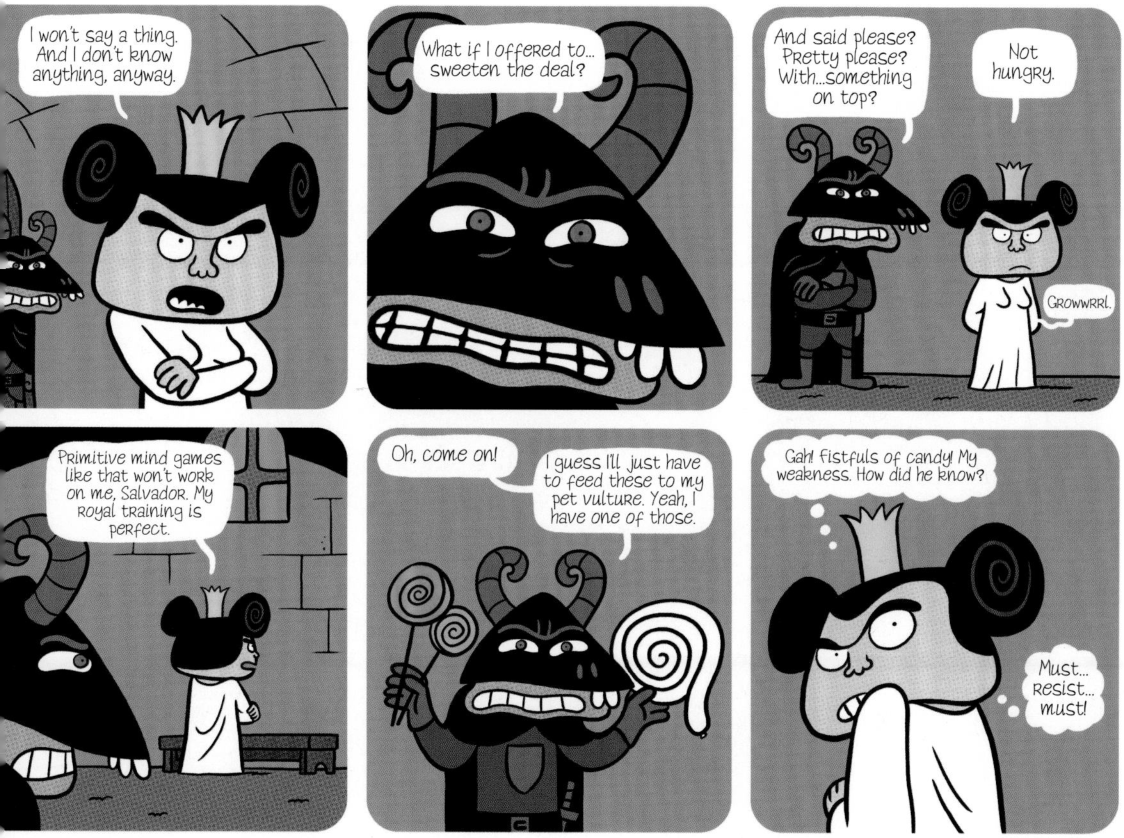
I won't say a thing. And I don't know anything, anyway.
What if I offered to... sweeten the deal?
And said please? Pretty please? With...something on top?
Not hungry.
GROWWRRL.
Primitive mind games like that won't work on me, Salvador. My Royal training is perfect.
Oh, come on!
I guess I'll just have to feed these to my pet vulture. Yeah, I have one of those.
Gah! Fistfuls of candy! My weakness. How did he know?
Must... resist... must!

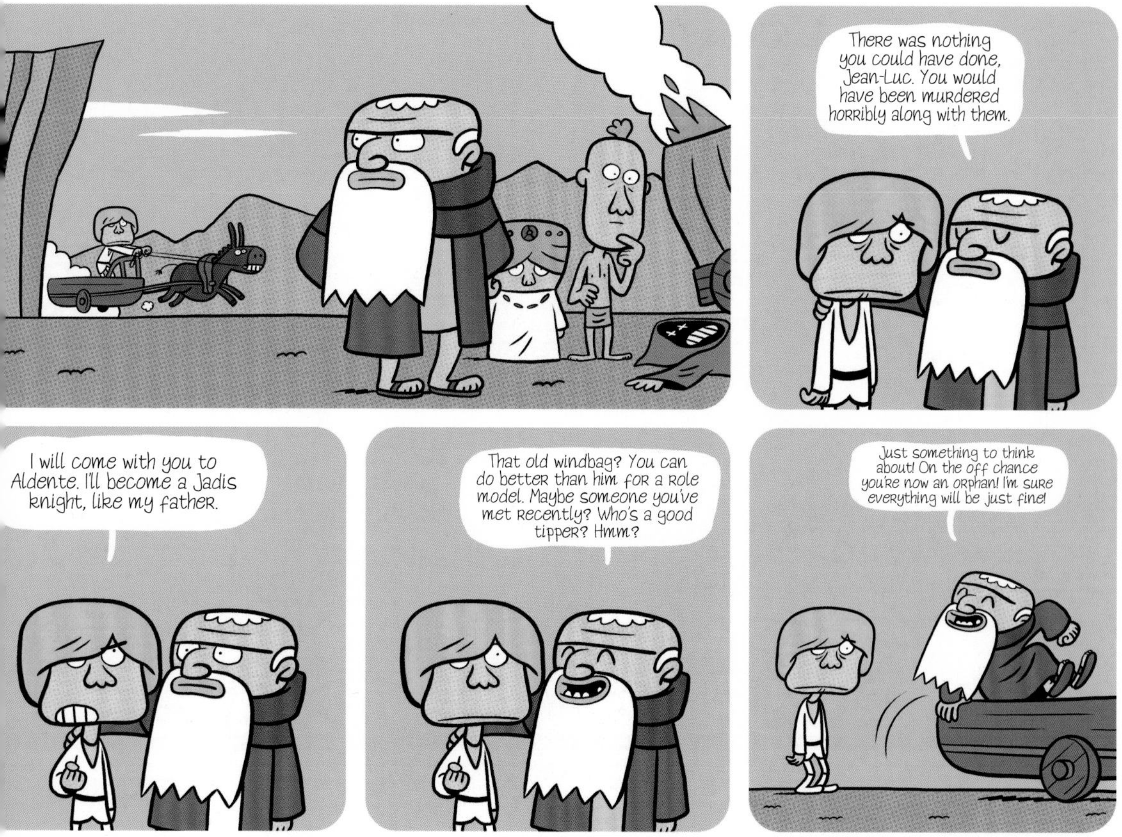
There was nothing you could have done, Jean-Luc. You would have been murdered horribly along with them.
I will come with you to Aldente. I'll become a Jadis knight, like my father.
That old windbag? You can do better than him for a role model. Maybe someone you've met recently? Who's a good tipper? Hmm?
Just something to think about! On the off chance you're now an orphan! I'm sure everything will be just fine!

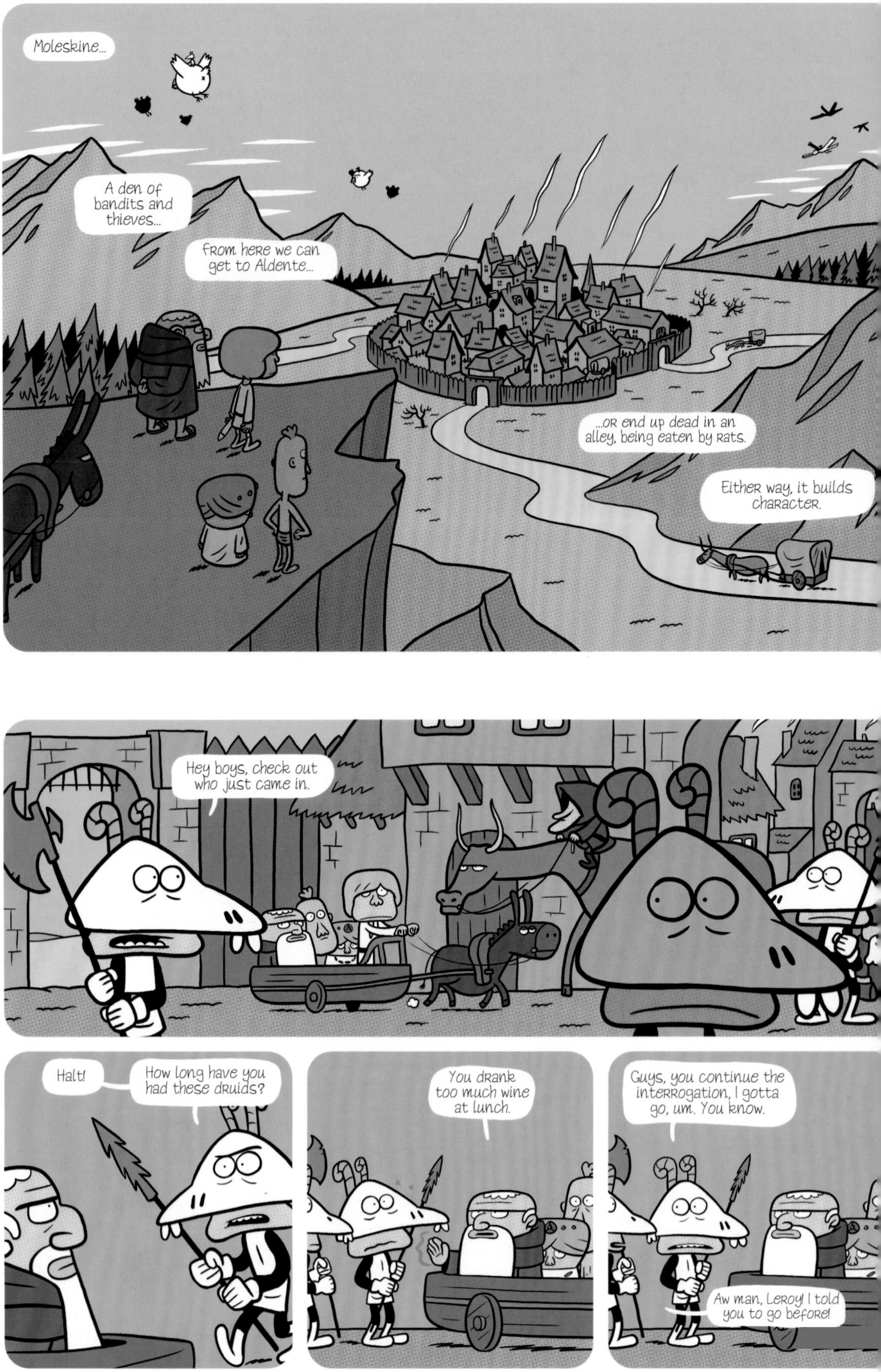
Moleskine...
A den of bandits and thieves...
From here we can get to Aldente...
...or end up dead in an alley, being eaten by rats.
Either way, it builds character.
Hey boys, check out who just came in.
Halt!
How long have you had these druids?
You drank too much wine at lunch.
Guys, you continue the interrogation, I gotta go, um. You know.
Aw man, Leroy! I told you to go before!

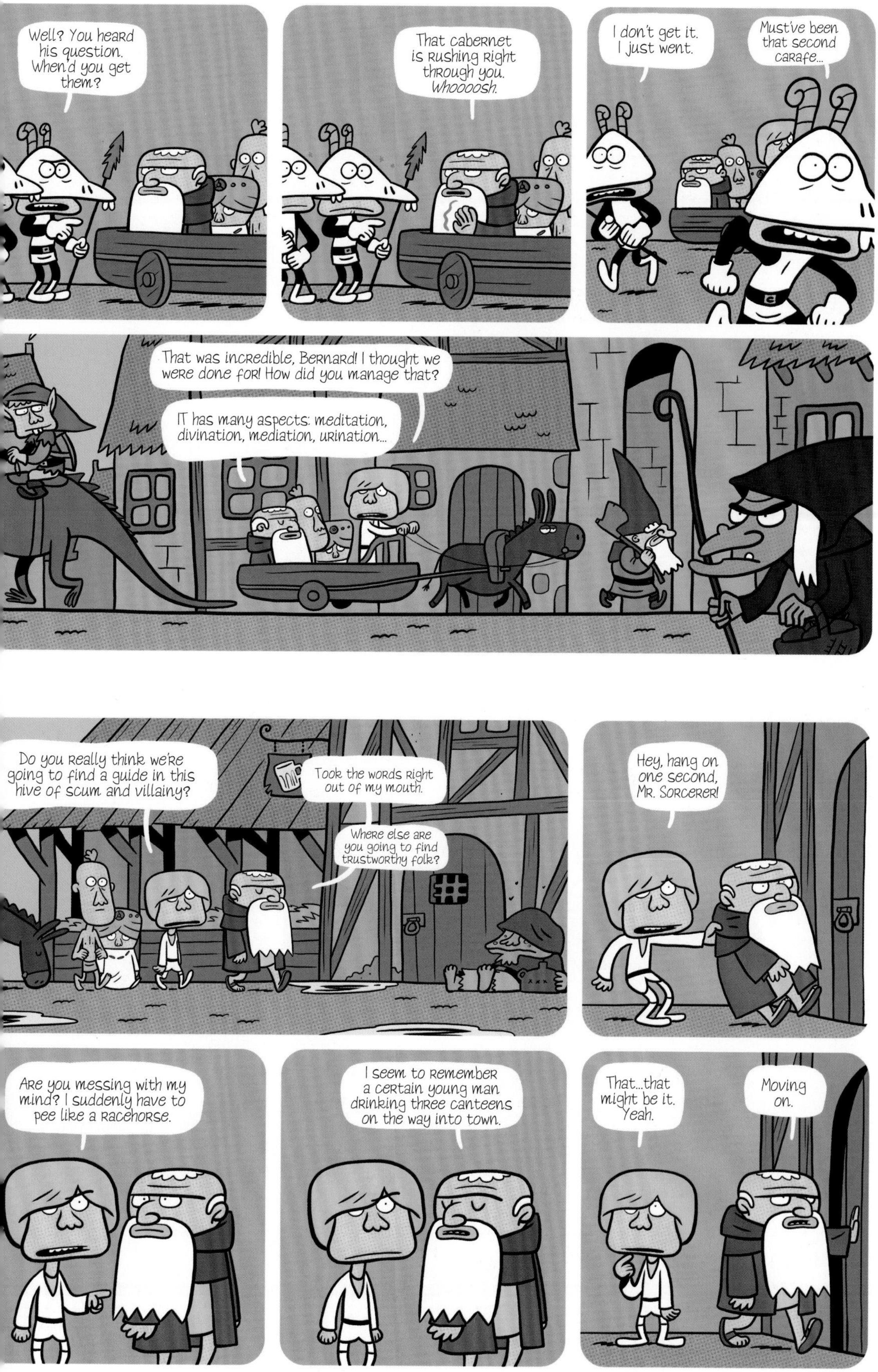
Well? You heard his question. When'd you get them?
That cabernet is rushing right through you. Whoooosh.
I don't get it. I just went.
Must've been that second carafe...
That was incredible, Bernard! I thought we were done for! How did you manage that?
It has many aspects: meditation, divination, mediation, urination...
Do you really think we're going to find a guide in this hive of scum and villainy?
Took the words right out of my mouth.
Where else are you going to find trustworthy folk?
Hey, hang on one second, Mr. Sorcerer!
Are you messing with my mind? I suddenly have to pee like a racehorse.
I seem to remember a certain young man drinking three canteens on the way into town.
That...that might be it. Yeah.
Moving on.

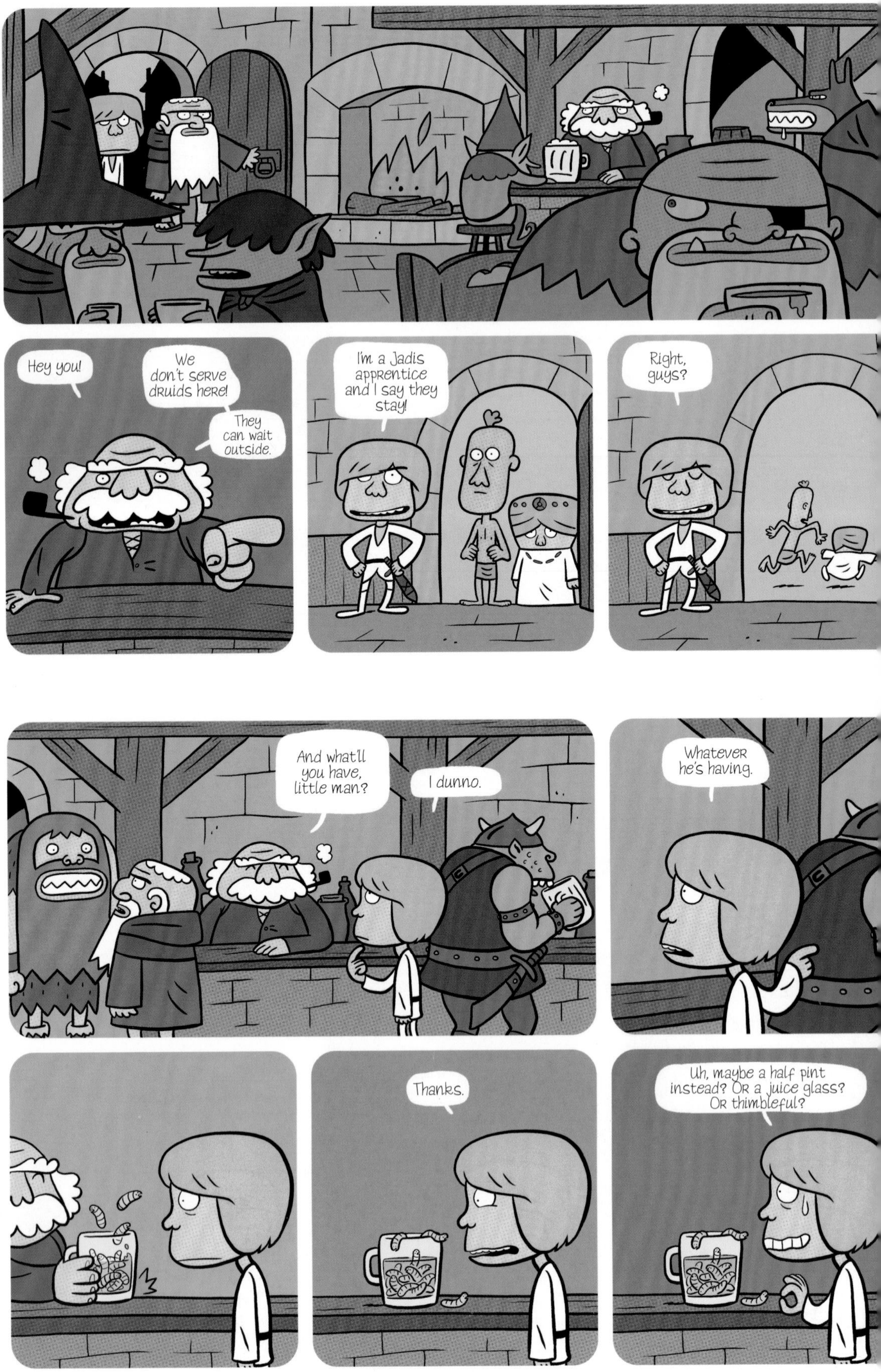
Hey you!
We don't serve druids here!
They can wait outside.
I'm a Jadis apprentice and I say they stay!
Right, guys?
And what'll you have, little man?
I dunno.
Whatever he's having.
Thanks.
Uh, maybe a half pint instead? Or a juice glass? Or thimbleful?

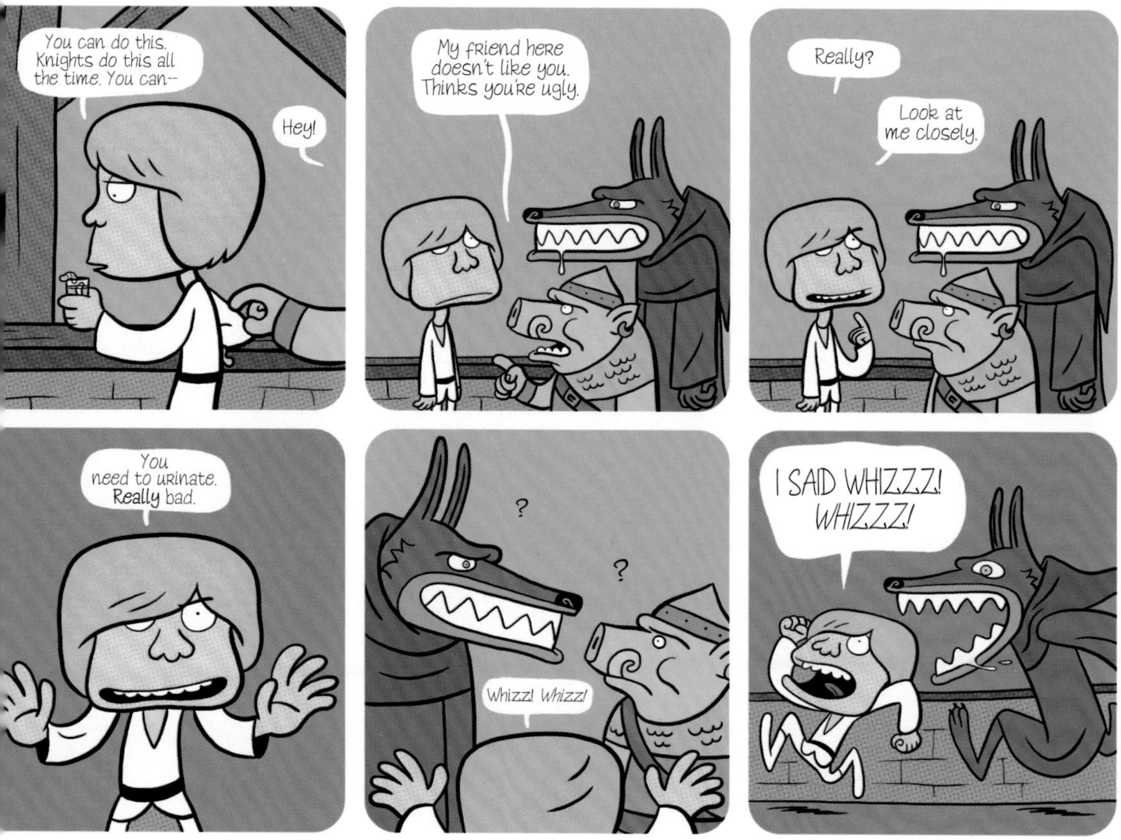
You can do this. Knights do this all the time. You can--
Hey!
My friend here doesn't like you. Thinks you're ugly.
Really?
Look at me closely.
You need to urinate. **Really** bad.
?
?
Whizz! Whizz!
I SAID WHIZZZ! WHIZZZ!

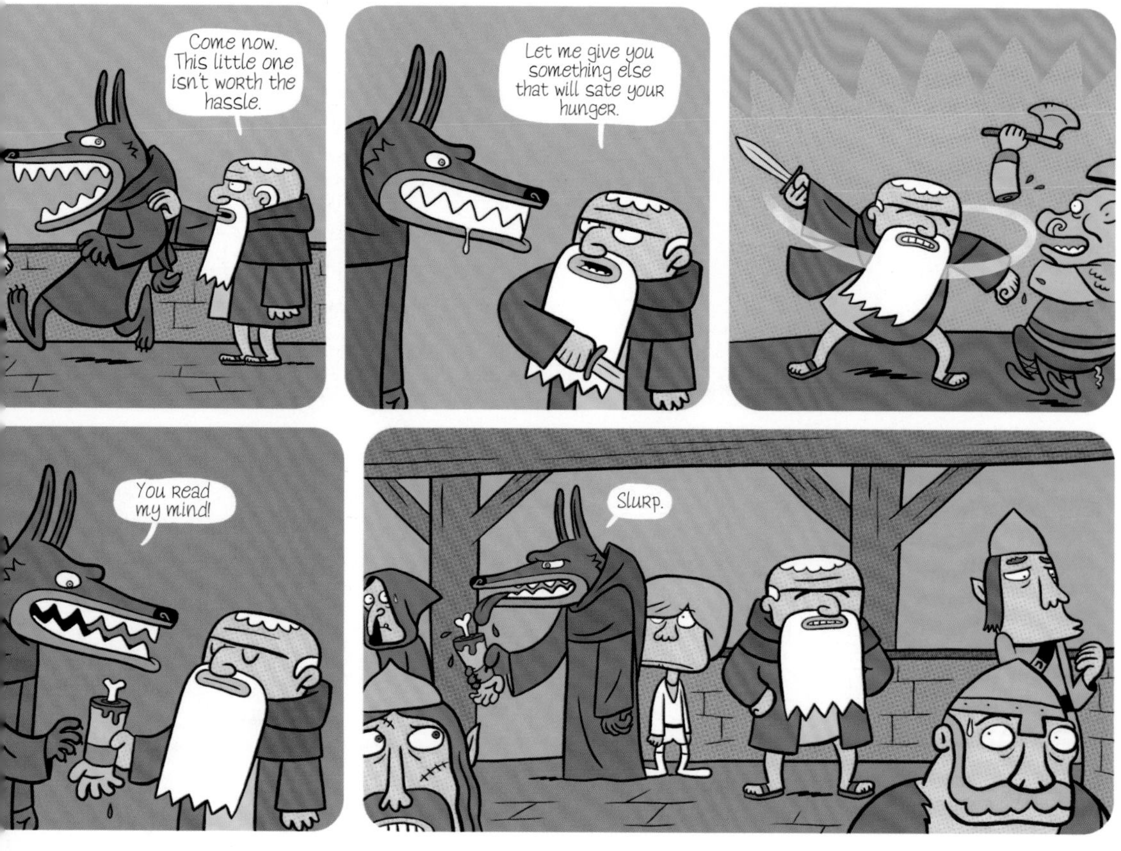
Come now. This little one isn't worth the hassle.
Let me give you something else that will sate your hunger.
You read my mind!
Slurp.

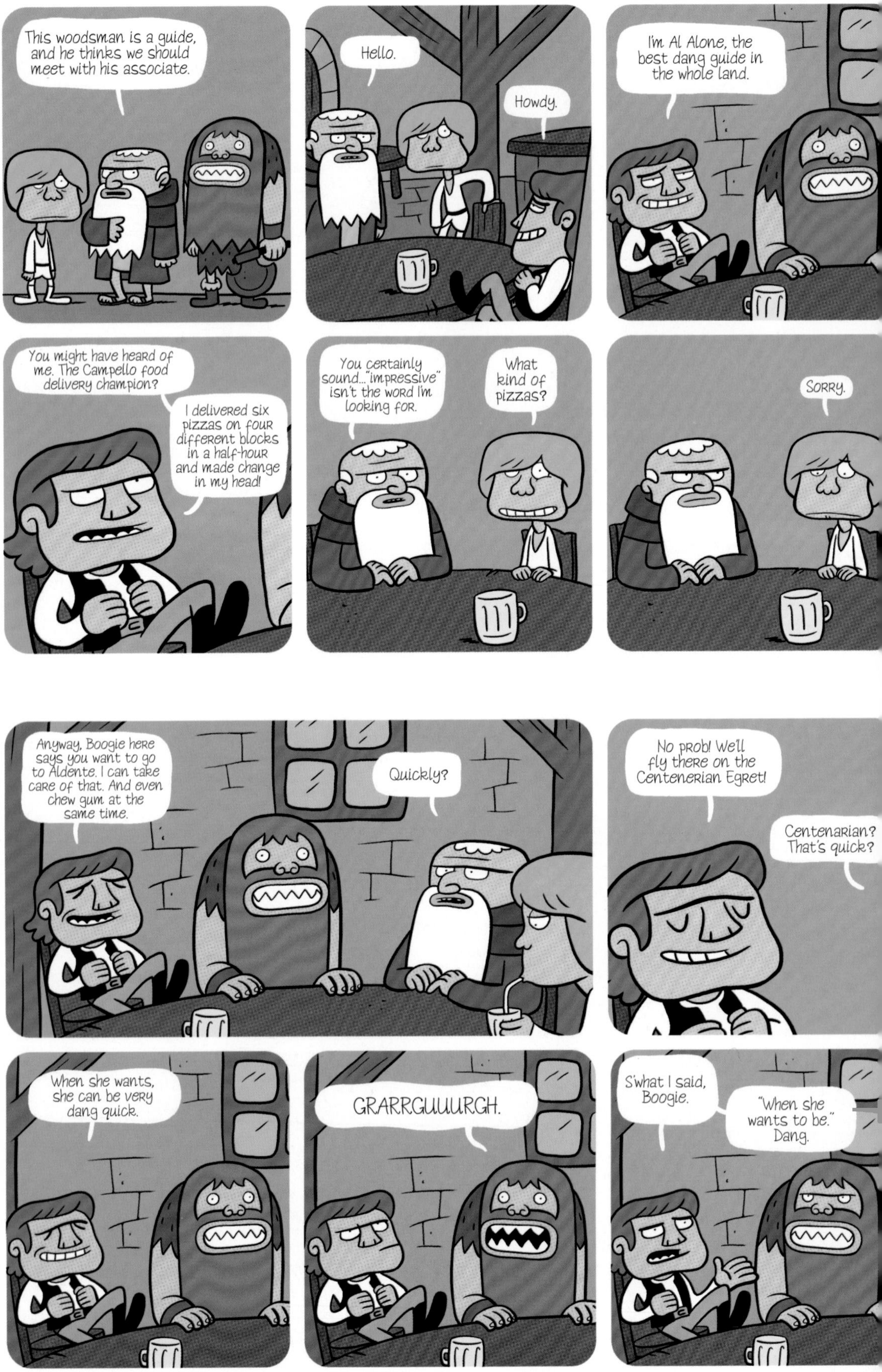

This woodsman is a guide, and he thinks we should meet with his associate.
Hello.
Howdy.
I'm Al Alone, the best dang guide in the whole land.
You might have heard of me. The Campello food delivery champion?
I delivered six pizzas on four different blocks in a half-hour and made change in my head!
You certainly sound..."impressive" isn't the word I'm looking for.
What kind of pizzas?
SORRY.
Anyway, Boogie here says you want to go to Aldente. I can take care of that. And even chew gum at the same time.
Quickly?
No prob! We'll fly there on the Centenerian Egret!
Centenarian? That's quick?
When she wants, she can be very dang quick.
GRARRGUUURGH.
S'what I said, Boogie.
"When she wants to be." Dang.

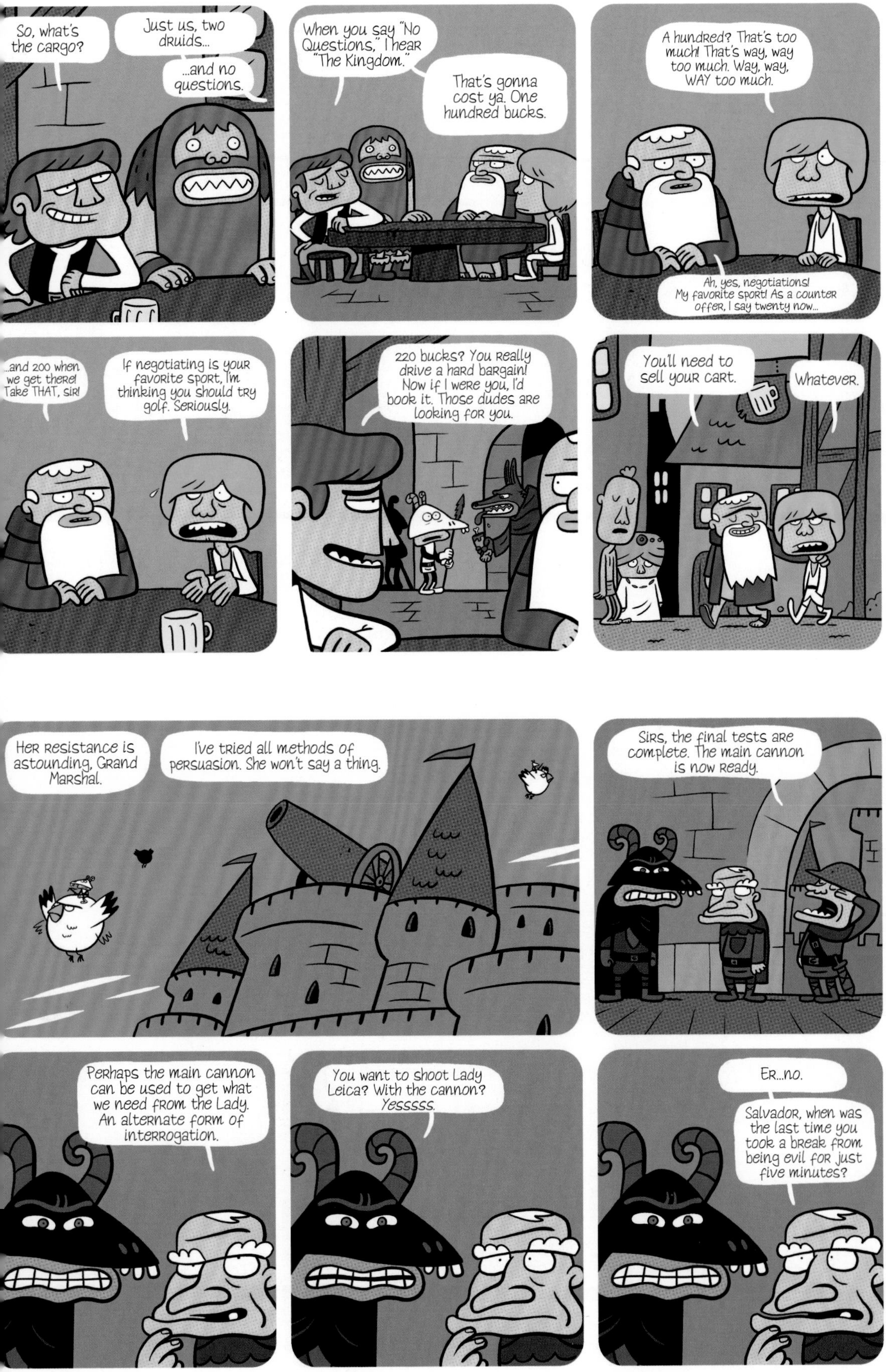

So, what's the cargo?
Just us, two druids...
...and no questions.
When you say "No Questions," I hear "The Kingdom."
That's gonna cost ya. One hundred bucks.
A hundred? That's too much! That's way, way too much. Way, way, WAY too much.
Ah, yes, negotiations! My favorite sport! As a counter offer, I say twenty now...
...and 200 when we get there! Take THAT, sir!
If negotiating is your favorite sport, I'm thinking you should try golf. Seriously.
220 bucks? You really drive a hard bargain! Now if I were you, I'd book it. Those dudes are looking for you.
You'll need to sell your cart.
Whatever.
Her resistance is astounding, Grand Marshal.
I've tried all methods of persuasion. She won't say a thing.
Sirs, the final tests are complete. The main cannon is now ready.
Perhaps the main cannon can be used to get what we need from the Lady. An alternate form of interrogation.
You want to shoot Lady Leica? With the cannon? *Yessss.*
Er...no.
Salvador, when was the last time you took a break from being evil for just five minutes?

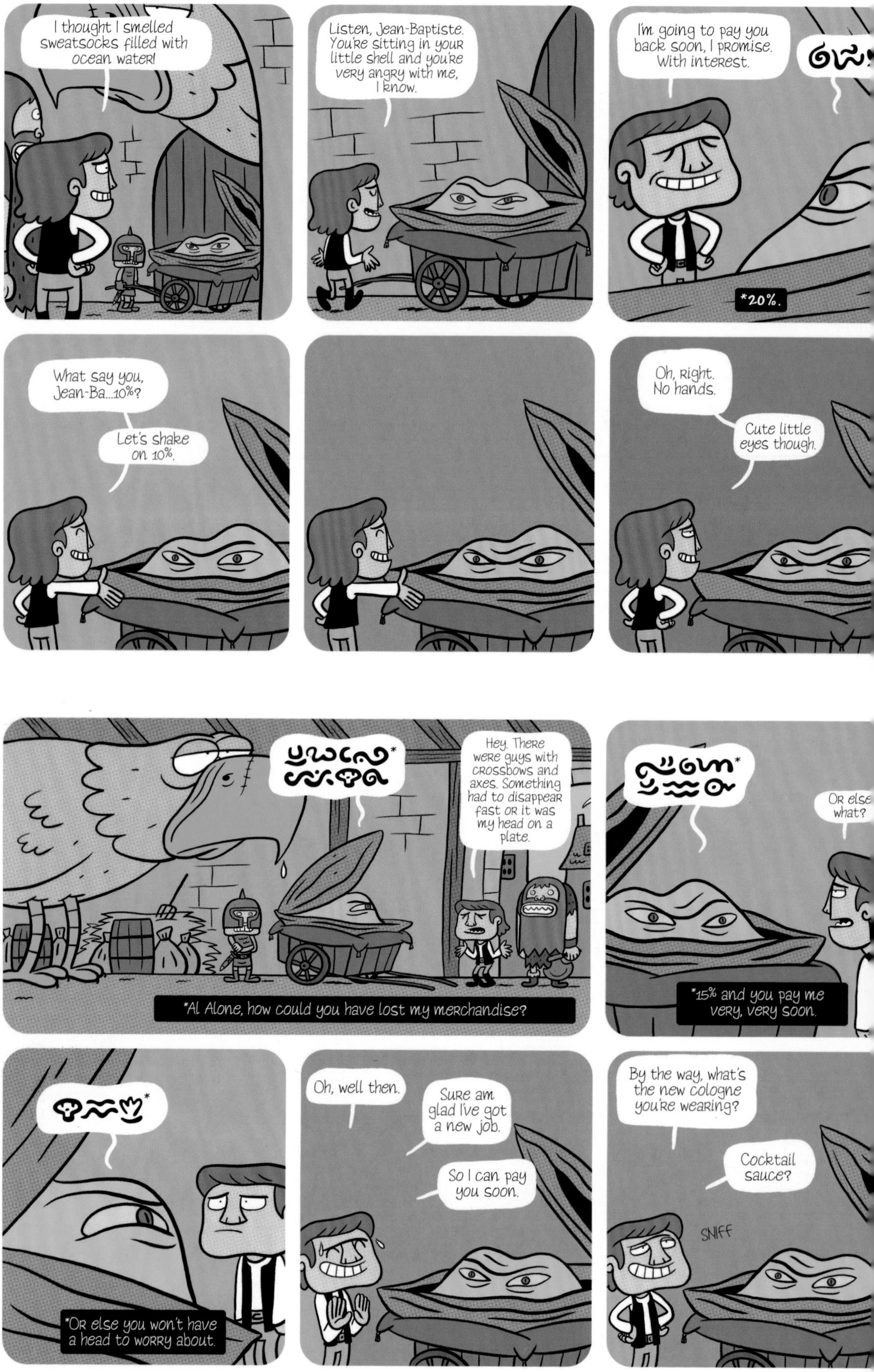
I thought I smelled sweatsocks filled with ocean water!
Listen, Jean-Baptiste. You're sitting in your little shell and you're very angry with me, I know.
I'm going to pay you back soon, I promise. With interest.
*20%.
What say you, Jean-Ba...10%?
Let's shake on 10%.
Oh, right. No hands.
Cute little eyes though.
*Al Alone, how could you have lost my merchandise?
Hey. There were guys with crossbows and axes. Something had to disappear fast or it was my head on a plate.
Or else what?
*15% and you pay me very, very soon.
*Or else you won't have a head to worry about.
Oh, well then.
Sure am glad I've got a new job.
So I can pay you soon.
By the way, what's the new cologne you're wearing?
SNIFF
Cocktail sauce?

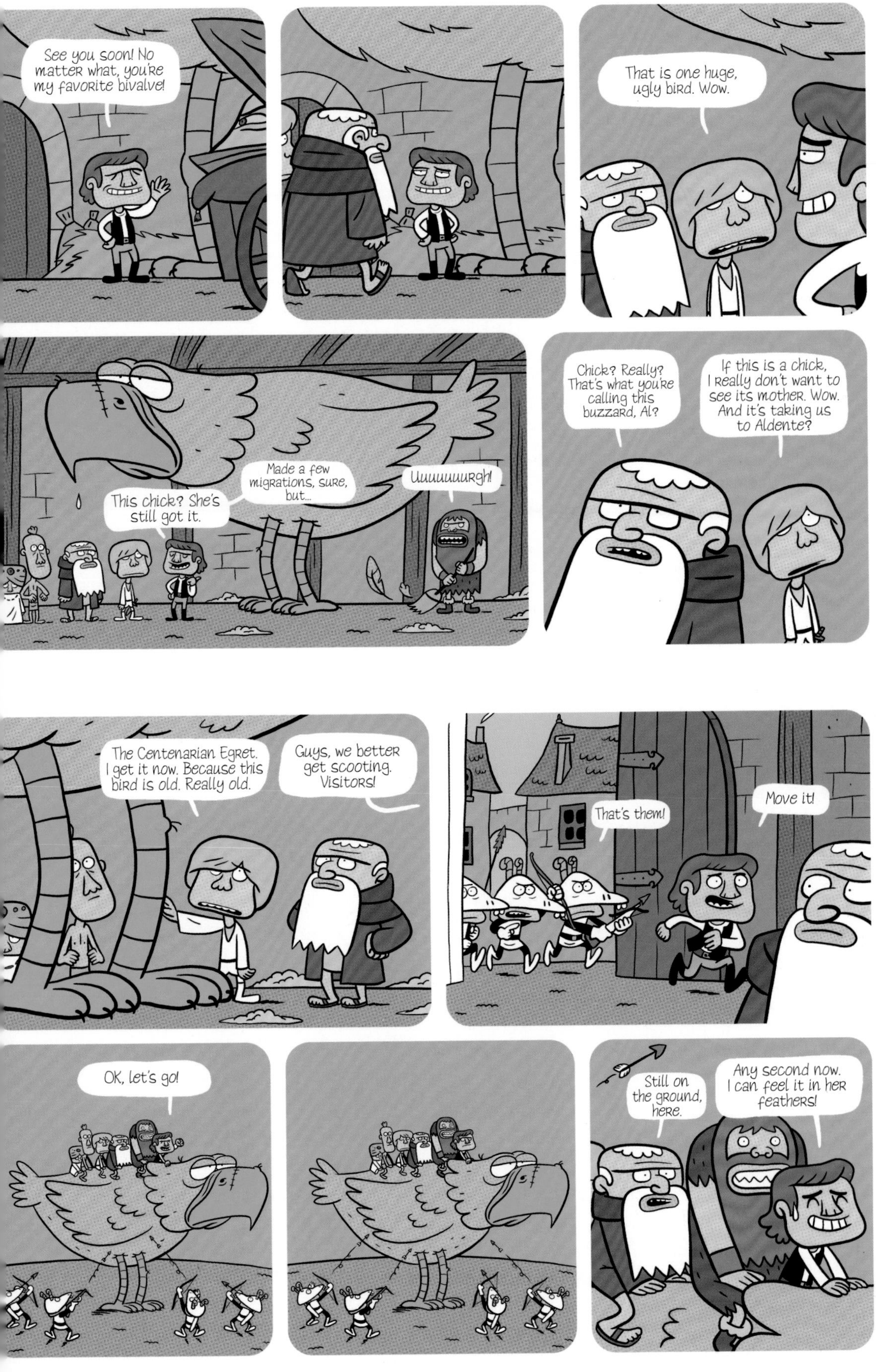
See you soon! No matter what, you're my favorite bivalve!
That is one huge, ugly bird. Wow.
This chick? She's still got it.
Made a few migrations, sure, but...
Uuuuuuuurgh!
Chick? Really? That's what you're calling this buzzard, Al?
If this is a chick, I really don't want to see its mother. Wow. And it's taking us to Aldente?
The Centenarian Egret. I get it now. Because this bird is old. Really old.
Guys, we better get scooting. Visitors!
That's them!
Move it!
OK, let's go!
Still on the ground, here.
Any second now. I can feel it in her feathers!

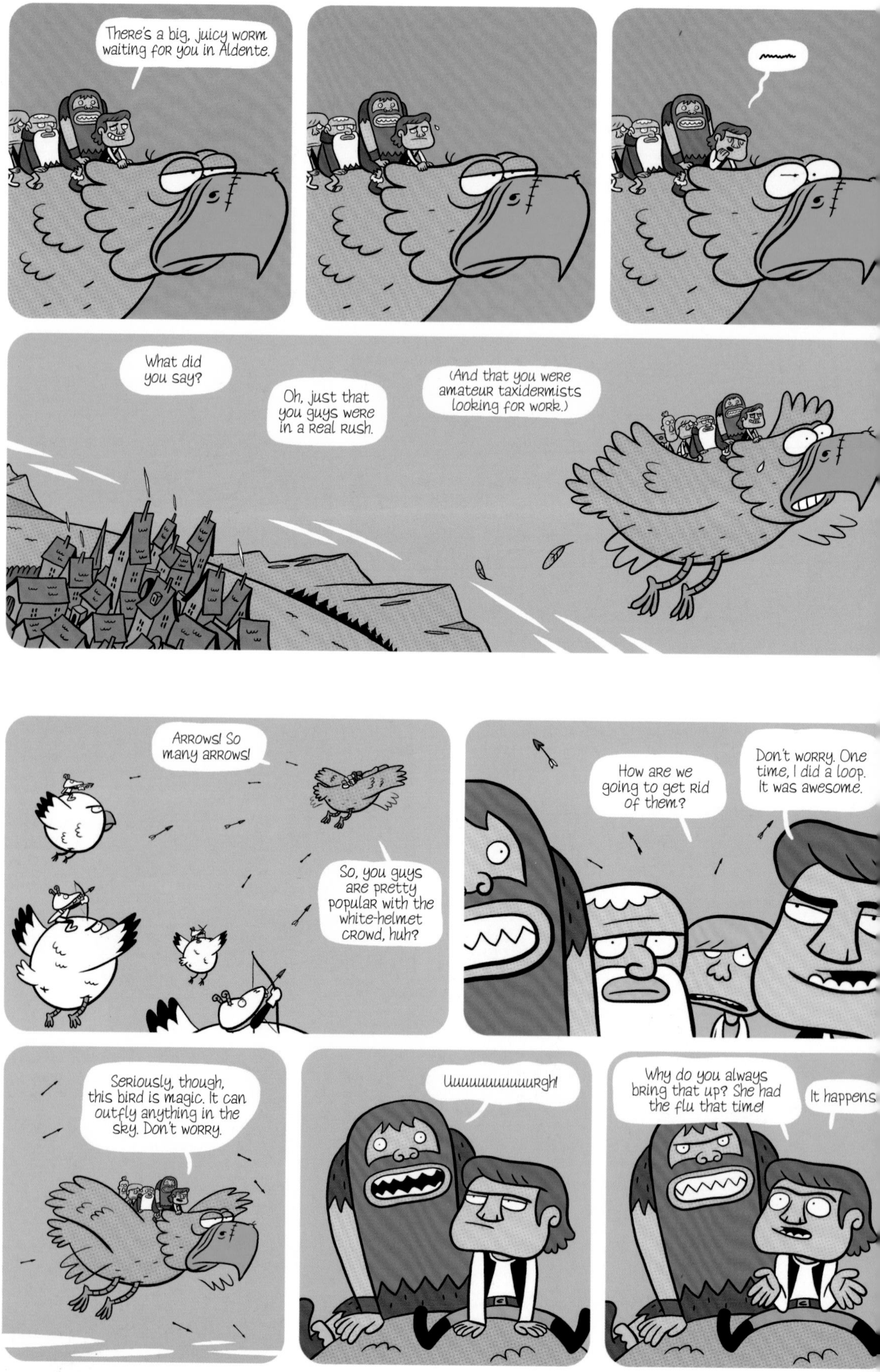
There's a big, juicy worm waiting for you in Aldente.
What did you say?
Oh, just that you guys were in a real rush.
(And that you were amateur taxidermists looking for work.)
Arrows! So many arrows!
So, you guys are pretty popular with the white-helmet crowd, huh?
How are we going to get rid of them?
Don't worry. One time, I did a loop. It was awesome.
Seriously, though, this bird is magic. It can outfly anything in the sky. Don't worry.
Uuuuuuuuuuurgh!
Why do you always bring that up? She had the flu that time!
It happens

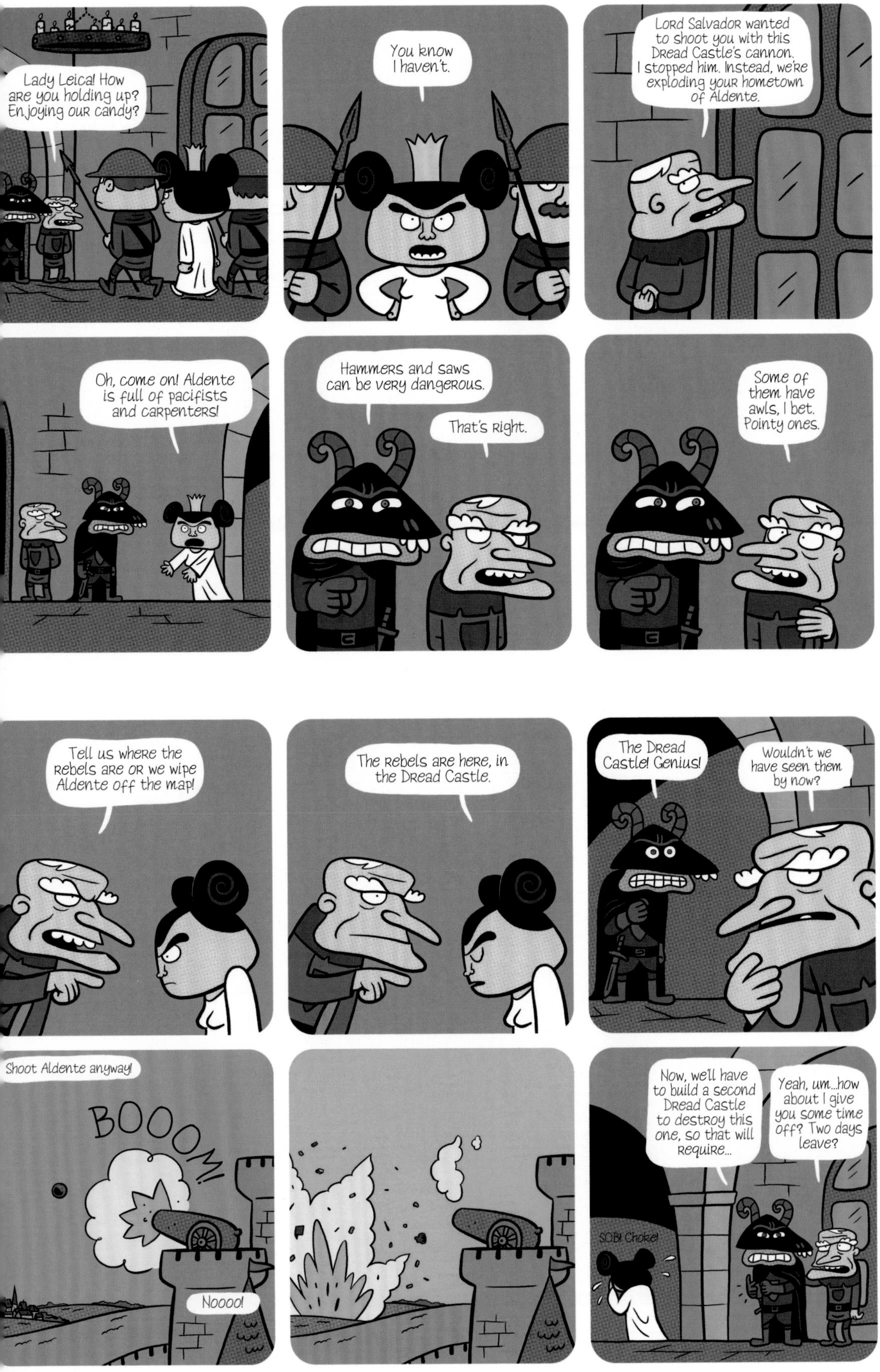

Lady Leica! How are you holding up? Enjoying our candy?
You know I haven't.
Lord Salvador wanted to shoot you with this Dread Castle's cannon. I stopped him. Instead, we're exploding your hometown of Aldente.
Oh, come on! Aldente is full of pacifists and carpenters!
Hammers and saws can be very dangerous.
That's right.
Some of them have awls, I bet. Pointy ones.
Tell us where the rebels are or we wipe Aldente off the map!
The rebels are here, in the Dread Castle.
The Dread Castle! Genius!
Wouldn't we have seen them by now?
Shoot Aldente anyway!
BOOOM!
Noooo!
Now, we'll have to build a second Dread Castle to destroy this one, so that will require...
Yeah, um...how about I give you some time off? Two days leave?
SOB! Choke!

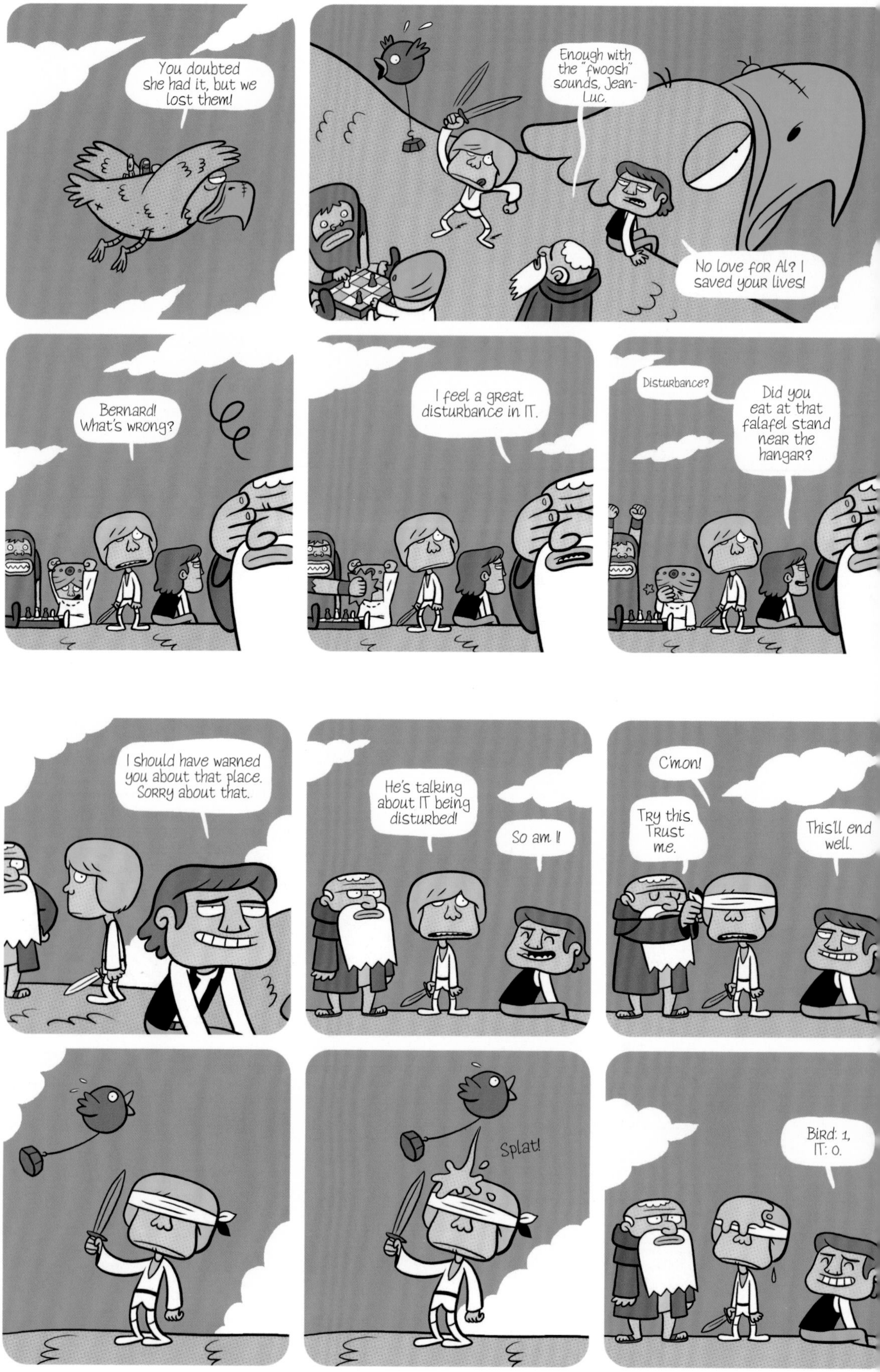
You doubted she had it, but we lost them!
Enough with the "fwoosh" sounds, Jean-Luc.
No love for Al? I saved your lives!
Bernard! What's wrong?
I feel a great disturbance in IT.
Disturbance?
Did you eat at that falafel stand near the hangar?
I should have warned you about that place. Sorry about that.
He's talking about IT being disturbed!
So am I!
C'mon!
Try this. Trust me.
This'll end well.
Splat!
Bird: 1, IT: 0.

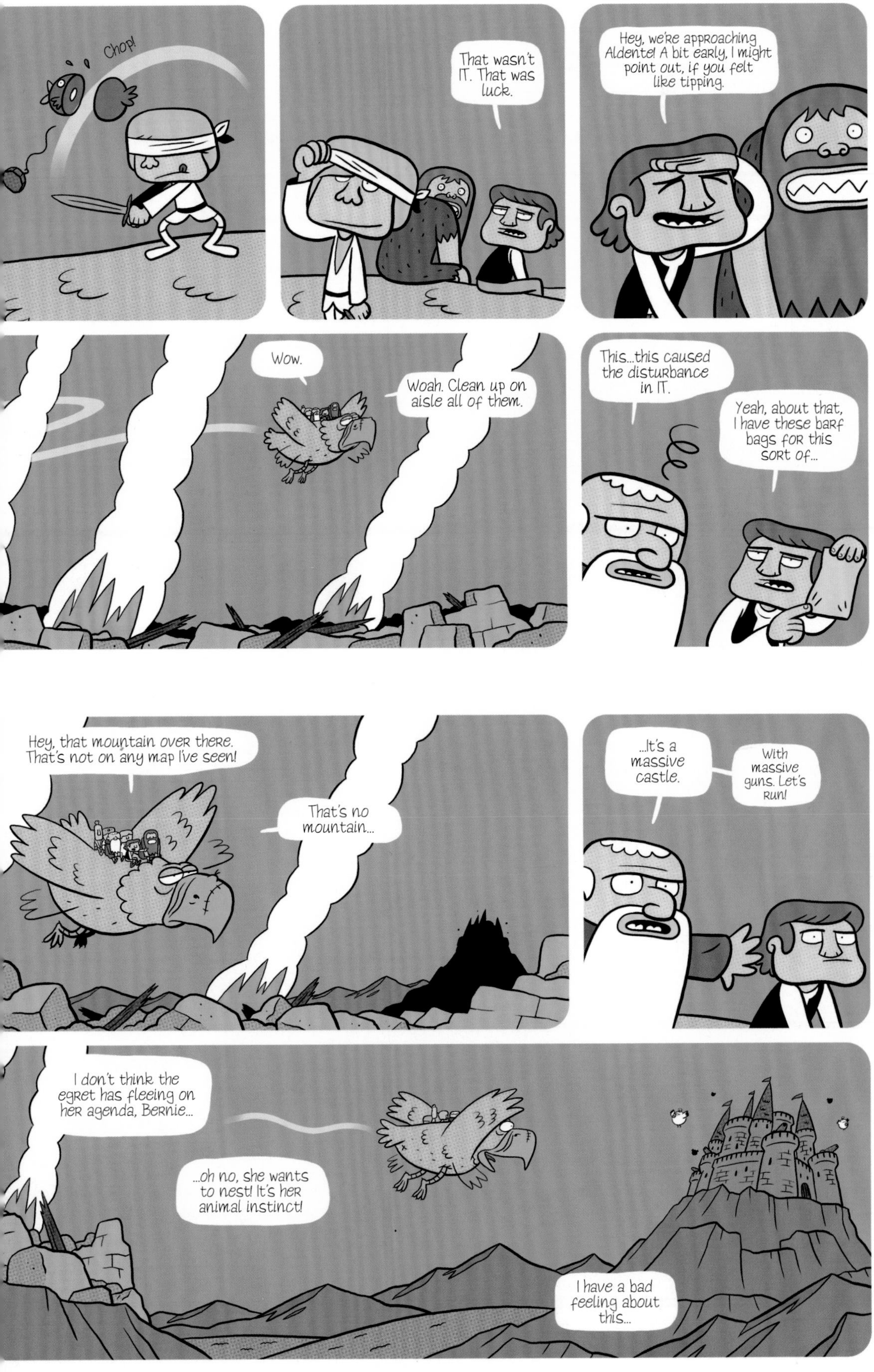
Chop!
That wasn't IT. That was luck.
Hey, we're approaching Aldente! A bit early, I might point out, if you felt like tipping.
Wow.
Woah. Clean up on aisle all of them.
This...this caused the disturbance in IT.
Yeah, about that, I have these barf bags for this sort of...
Hey, that mountain over there. That's not on any map I've seen!
That's no mountain...
...It's a massive castle.
With massive guns. Let's run!
I don't think the egret has fleeing on her agenda, Bernie...
...oh no, she wants to nest! It's her animal instinct!
I have a bad feeling about this...

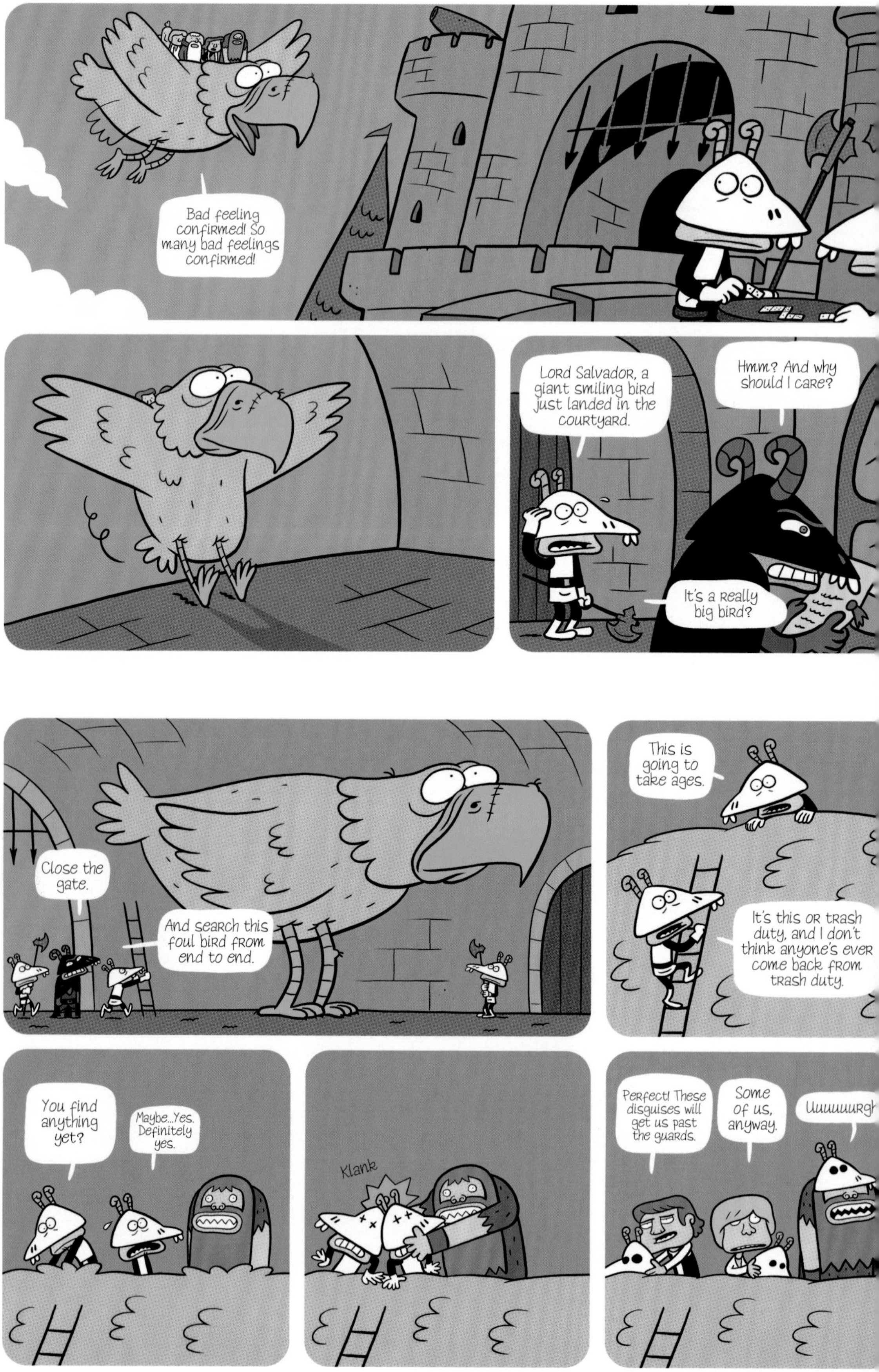

Bad feeling confirmed! So many bad feelings confirmed!
Lord Salvador, a giant smiling bird just landed in the courtyard.
Hmm? And why should I care?
It's a really big bird?
Close the gate.
And search this foul bird from end to end.
This is going to take ages.
It's this or trash duty, and I don't think anyone's ever come back from trash duty.
You find anything yet?
Maybe...Yes. Definitely yes.
Klank
Perfect! These disguises will get us past the guards.
Some of us, anyway.
Uuuuuurgh

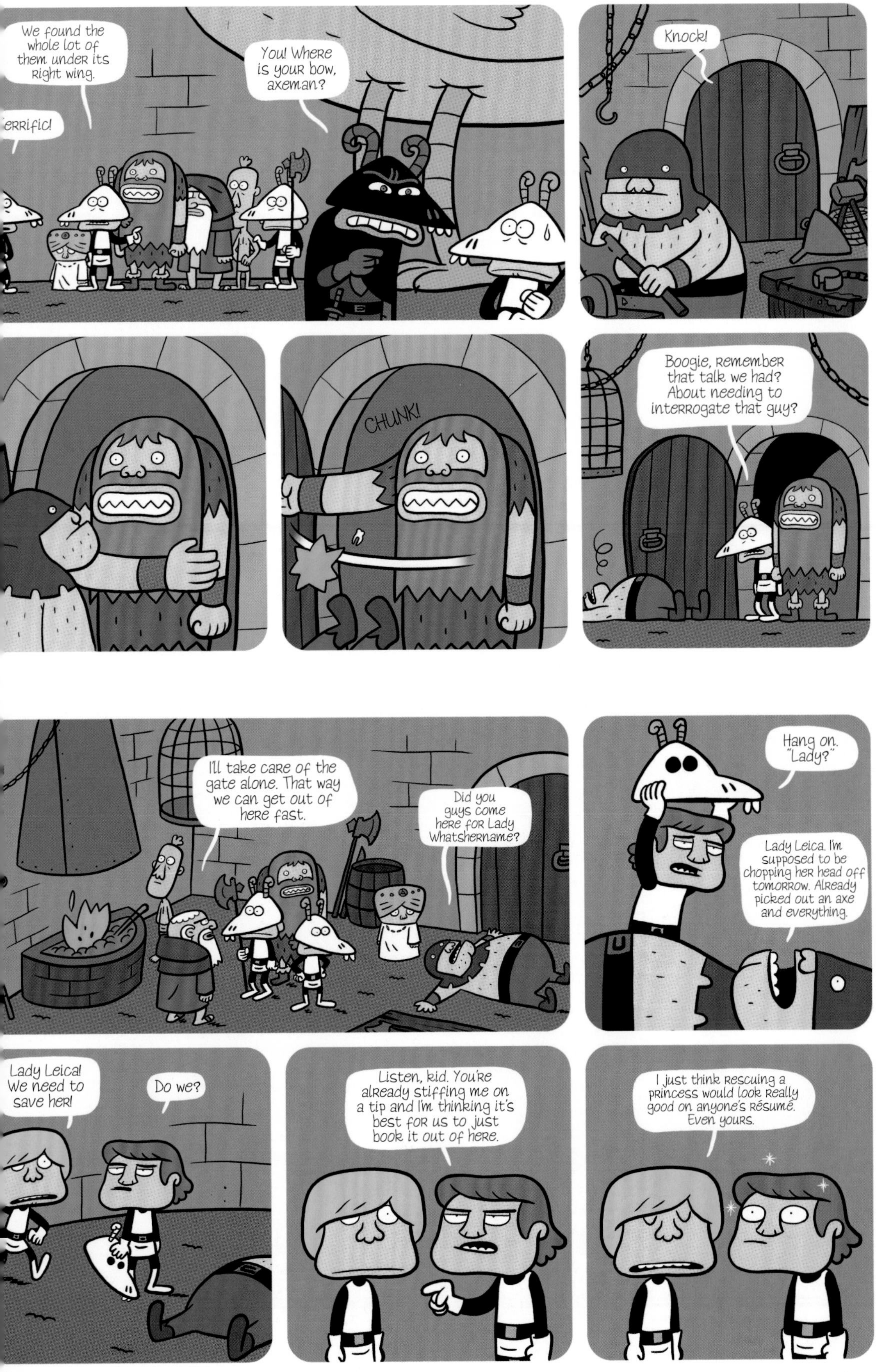
We found the whole lot of them under its right wing.
erRific!
You! Where is your bow, axeman?
Knock!
CHUNK!
Boogie, remember that talk we had? About needing to interrogate that guy?
I'll take care of the gate alone. That way we can get out of here fast.
Did you guys come here for Lady Whatshername?
Hang on. "Lady?"
Lady Leica. I'm supposed to be chopping her head off tomorrow. Already picked out an axe and everything.
Lady Leica! We need to save her!
Do we?
Listen, kid. You're already stiffing me on a tip and I'm thinking it's best for us to just book it out of here.
I just think rescuing a princess would look really good on anyone's résumé. Even yours.

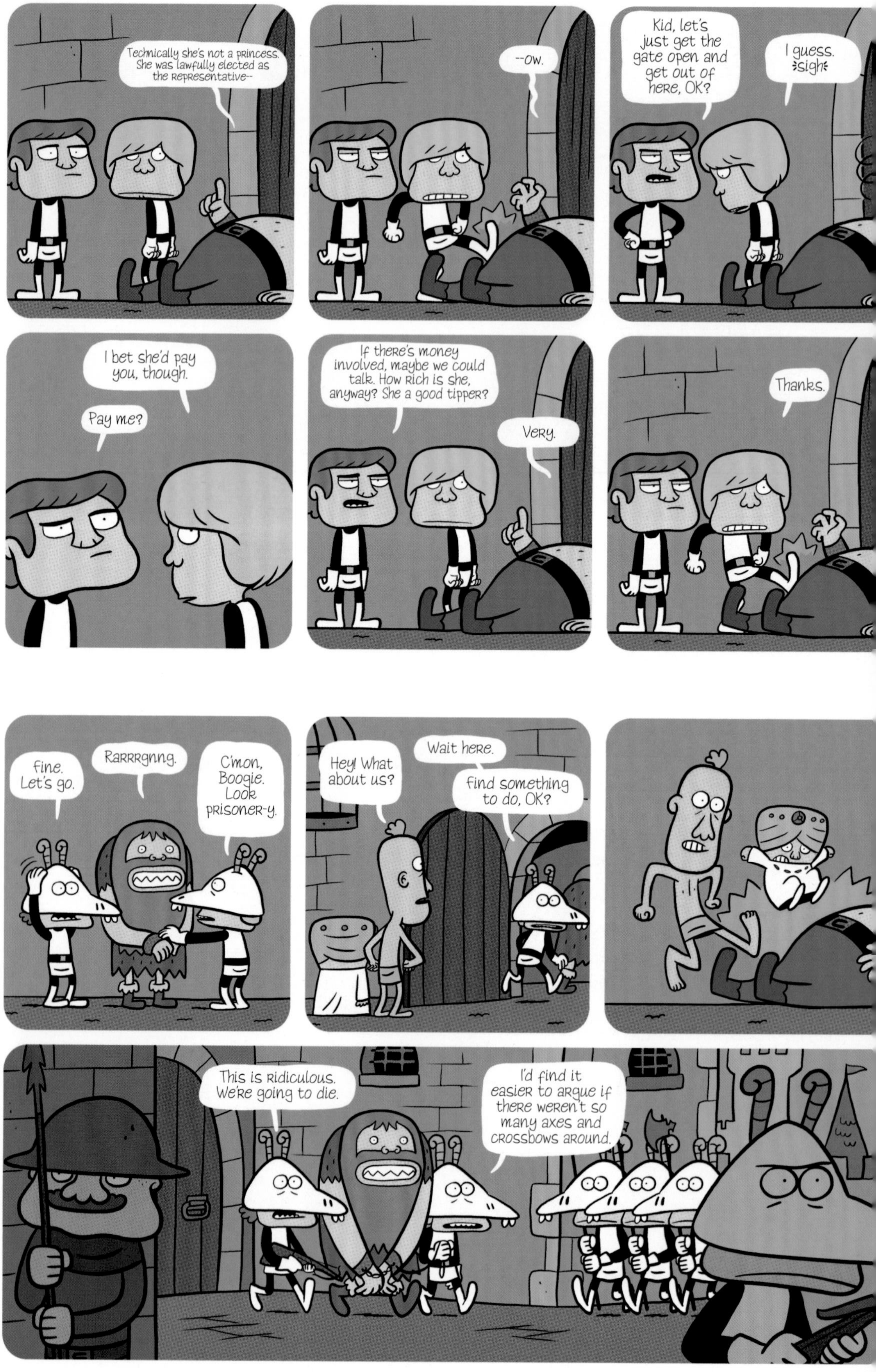
Technically she's not a princess. She was lawfully elected as the representative--
--ow.
Kid, let's just get the gate open and get out of here, OK?
I guess. ≯sigh≮
I bet she'd pay you, though.
Pay me?
If there's money involved, maybe we could talk. How rich is she, anyway? She a good tipper?
Very.
Thanks.
Fine. Let's go.
Rarrrgnng.
C'mon, Boogie. Look prisoner-y.
Wait here.
Hey! What about us?
Find something to do, OK?
This is ridiculous. We're going to die.
I'd find it easier to argue if there weren't so many axes and crossbows around.

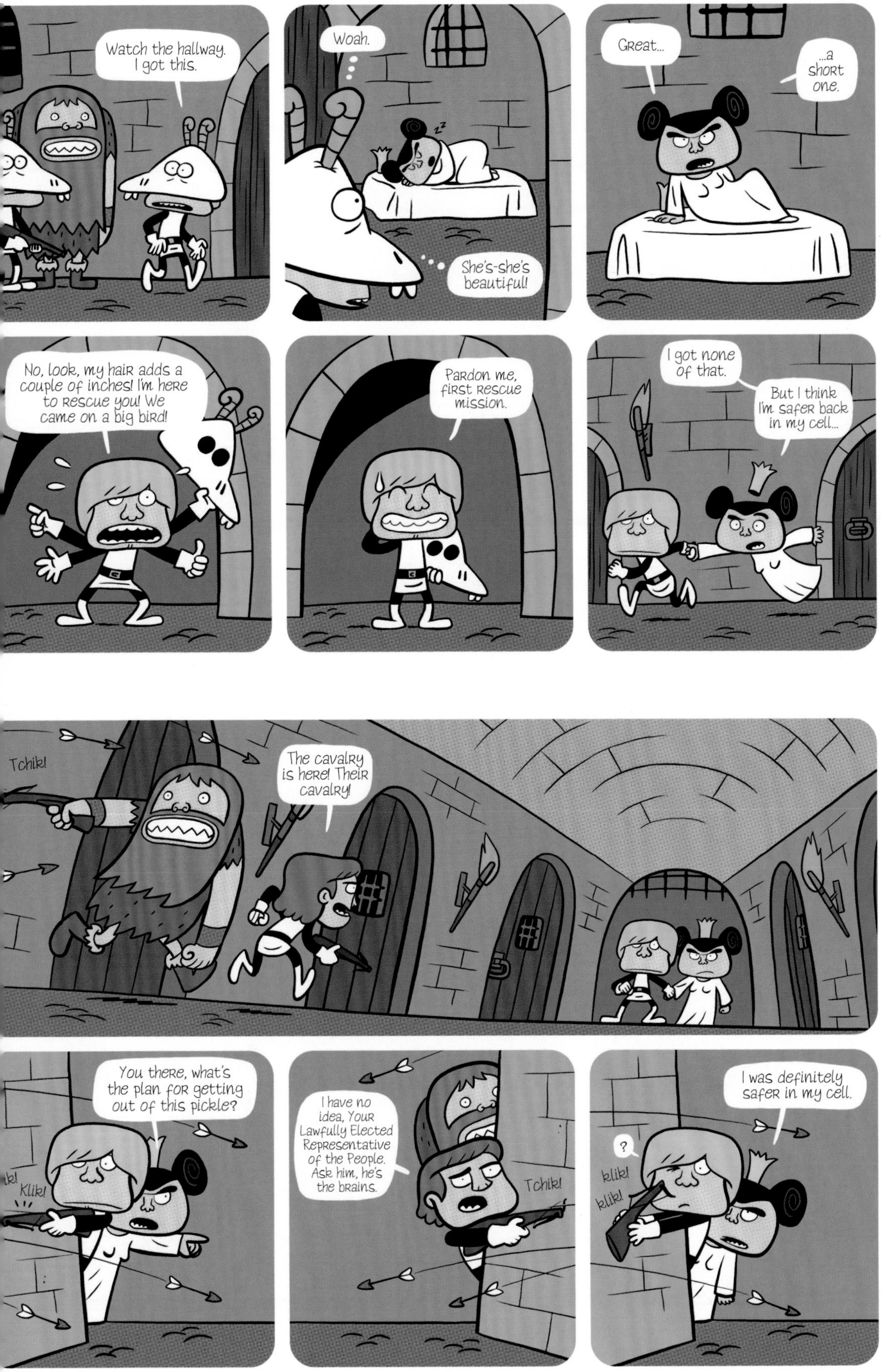
Watch the hallway. I got this.
Woah.
She's-she's beautiful!
Great...
...a short one.
No, look, my hair adds a couple of inches! I'm here to rescue you! We came on a big bird!
Pardon me, first rescue mission.
I got none of that.
But I think I'm safer back in my cell...
Tchik!
The cavalry is here! Their cavalry!
You there, what's the plan for getting out of this pickle?
Klik!
I have no idea, Your Lawfully Elected Representative of the People. Ask him, he's the brains.
Tchik!
I was definitely safer in my cell.
?
klik!
klik!

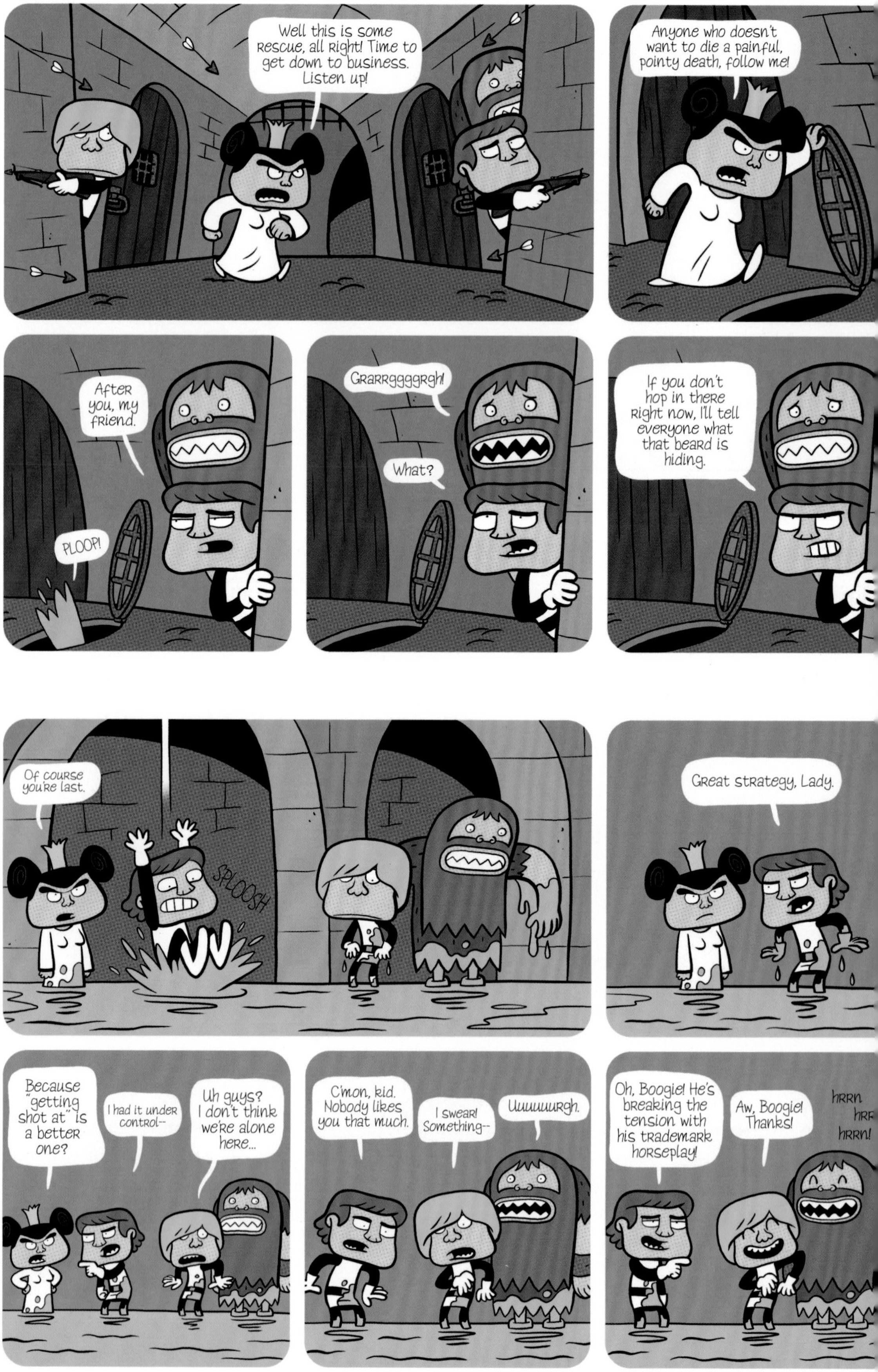

Well this is some rescue, all right! Time to get down to business. Listen up!
Anyone who doesn't want to die a painful, pointy death, follow me!
After you, my friend.
PLOOP!
Grarrgggggrgh!
What?
If you don't hop in there right now, I'll tell everyone what that beard is hiding.
Of course you're last.
SPLOOSH
Great strategy, Lady.
Because "getting shot at" is a better one?
I had it under control--
Uh guys? I don't think we're alone here...
C'mon, kid. Nobody likes you that much.
I swear! Something--
Uuuuuurgh.
Oh, Boogie! He's breaking the tension with his trademark horseplay!
Aw, Boogie! Thanks!
hrrn
hrr
hrrn!

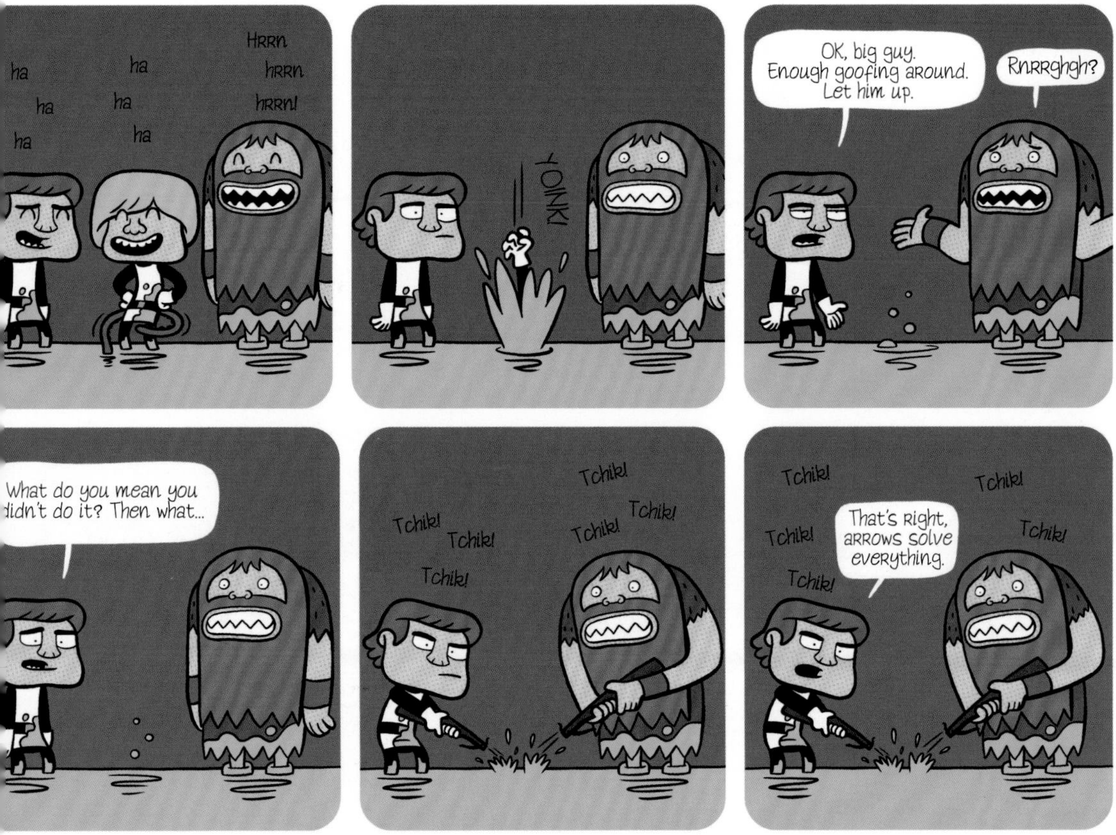
ha
ha
ha
ha
ha
ha
Hrrn
hrrn
hrrn!
YOINK!
OK, big guy. Enough goofing around. Let him up.
Rnrrghgh?
What do you mean you
idn't do it? Then what...
Tchik!
Tchik!
Tchik!
Tchik!
Tchik!
Tchik!
Tchik!
Tchik!
Tchik!
Tchik!
That's right, arrows solve everything.
Tchik!

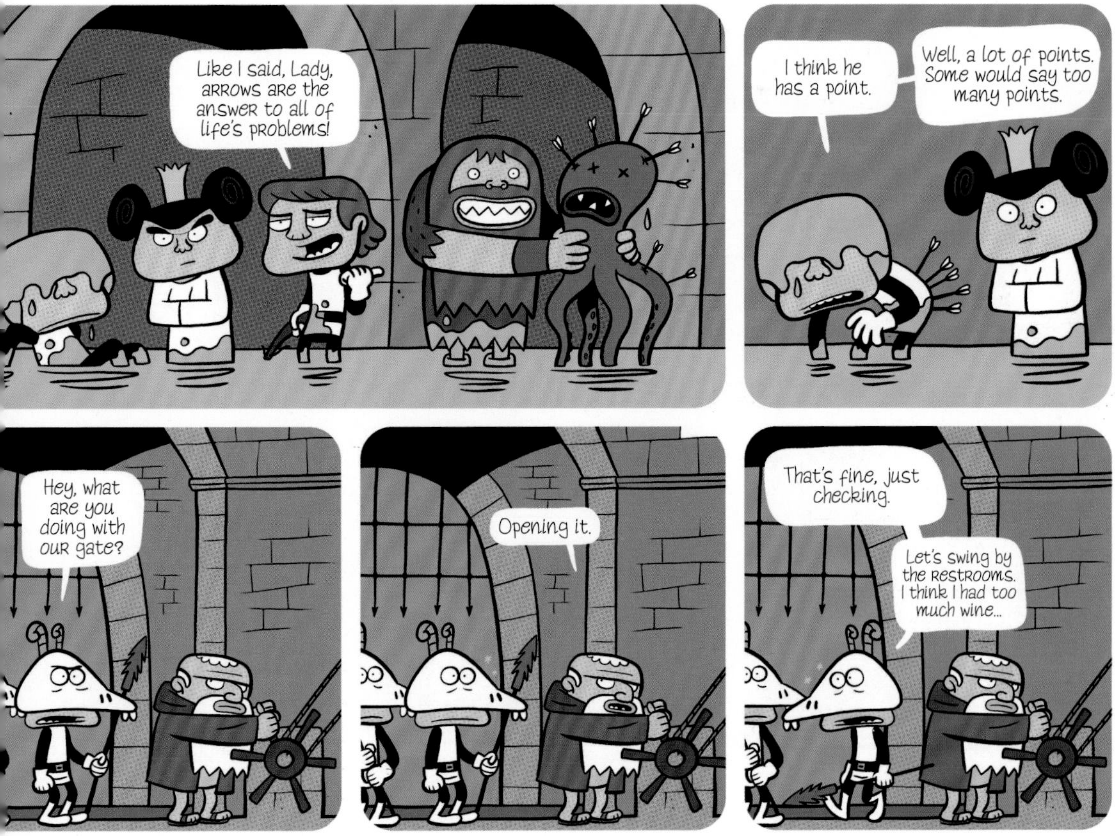
Like I said, Lady, arrows are the answer to all of life's problems!
I think he has a point.
Well, a lot of points. Some would say too many points.
Hey, what are you doing with our gate?
Opening it.
That's fine, just checking.
Let's swing by the restrooms. I think I had too much wine...

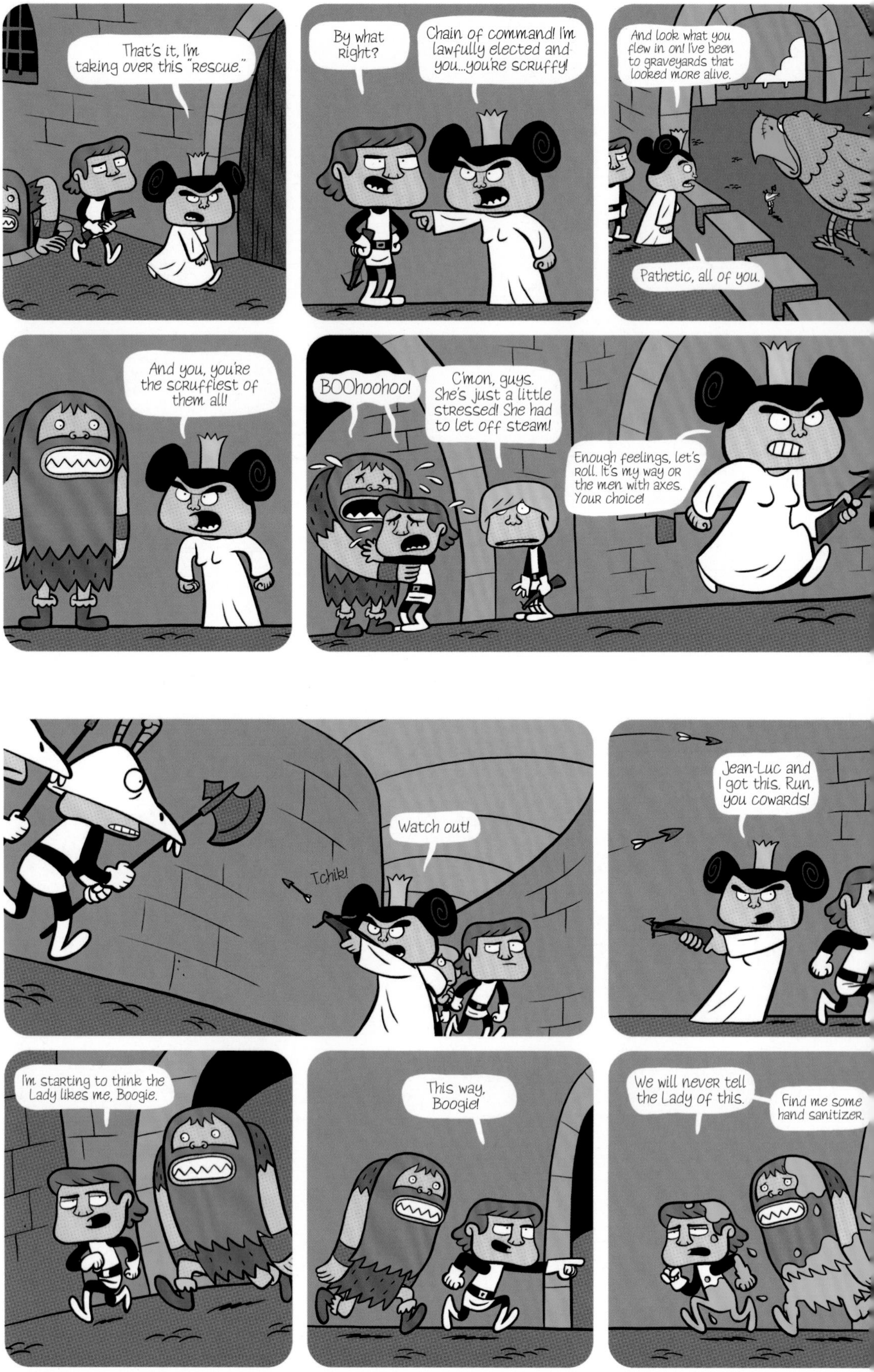
That's it, I'm taking over this "rescue."
By what right?
Chain of command! I'm lawfully elected and you...you're scruffy!
And look what you flew in on! I've been to graveyards that looked more alive.
Pathetic, all of you.
And you, you're the scruffiest of them all!
BOOhoohoo!
C'mon, guys. She's just a little stressed! She had to let off steam!
Enough feelings, let's roll. It's my way or the men with axes. Your choice!
Watch out!
Tchik!
Jean-Luc and I got this. Run, you cowards!
I'm starting to think the Lady likes me, Boogie.
This way, Boogie!
We will never tell the Lady of this.
Find me some hand sanitizer.

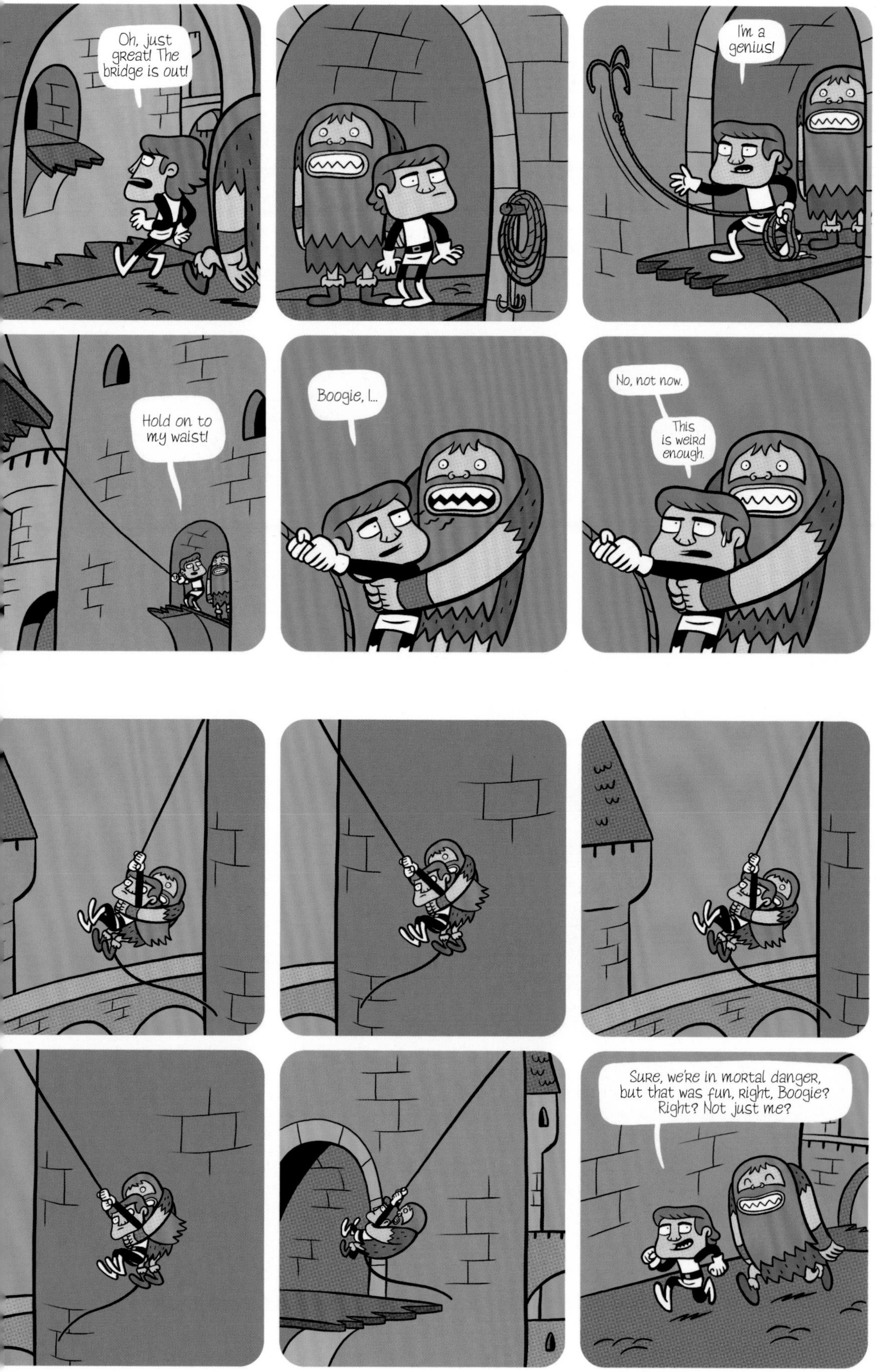

Oh, just great! The bridge is out!
I'm a genius!
Hold on to my waist!
Boogie, I...
No, not now.
This is weird enough.
Sure, we're in mortal danger, but that was fun, right, Boogie? Right? Not just me?

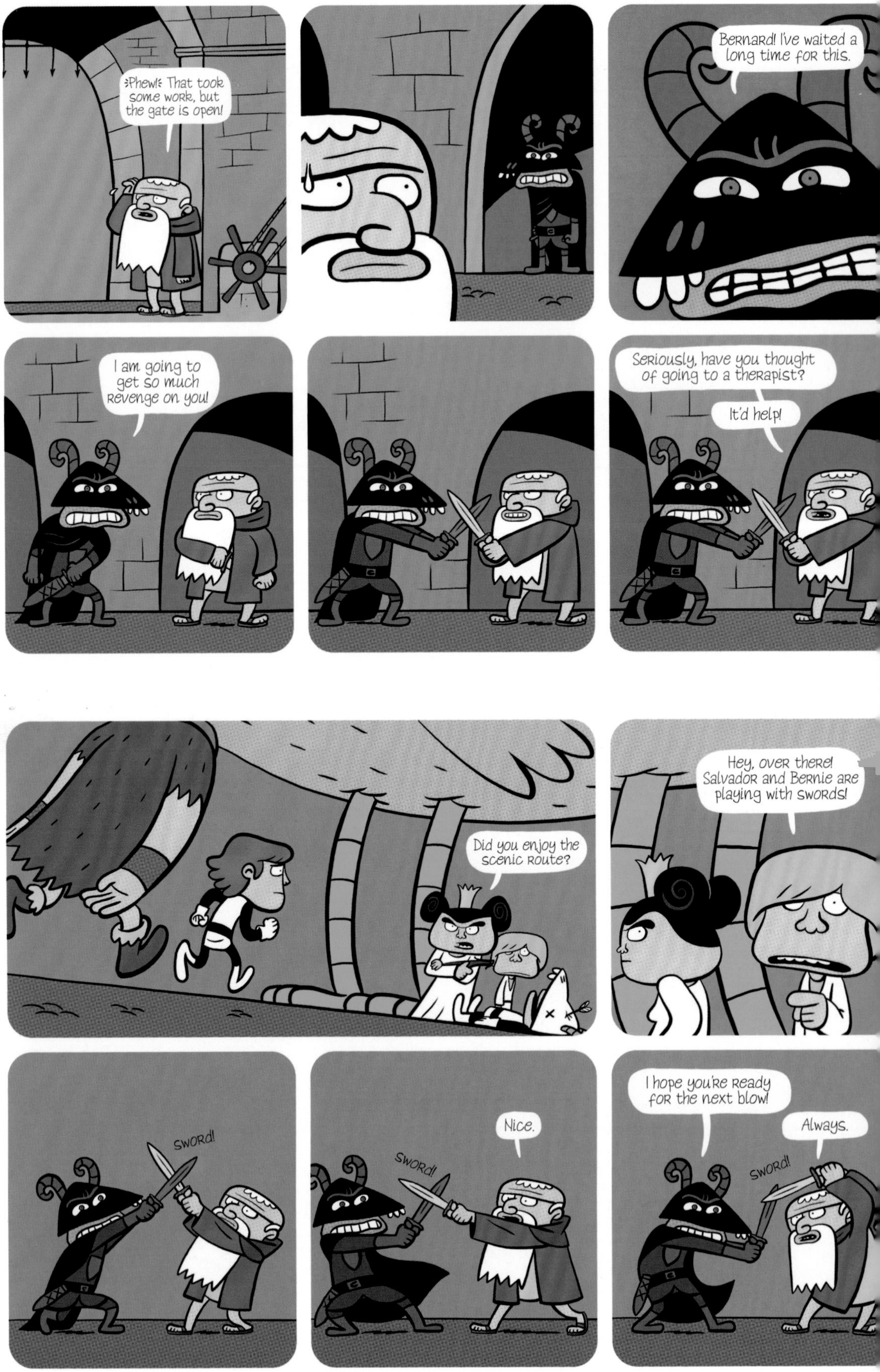

Phew! That took some work, but the gate is open!
Bernard! I've waited a long time for this.
I am going to get so much revenge on you!
Seriously, have you thought of going to a therapist?
It'd help!
Did you enjoy the scenic route?
Hey, over there! Salvador and Bernie are playing with swords!
SWORD!
SWORD!
Nice.
I hope you're ready for the next blow!
SWORD!
Always.

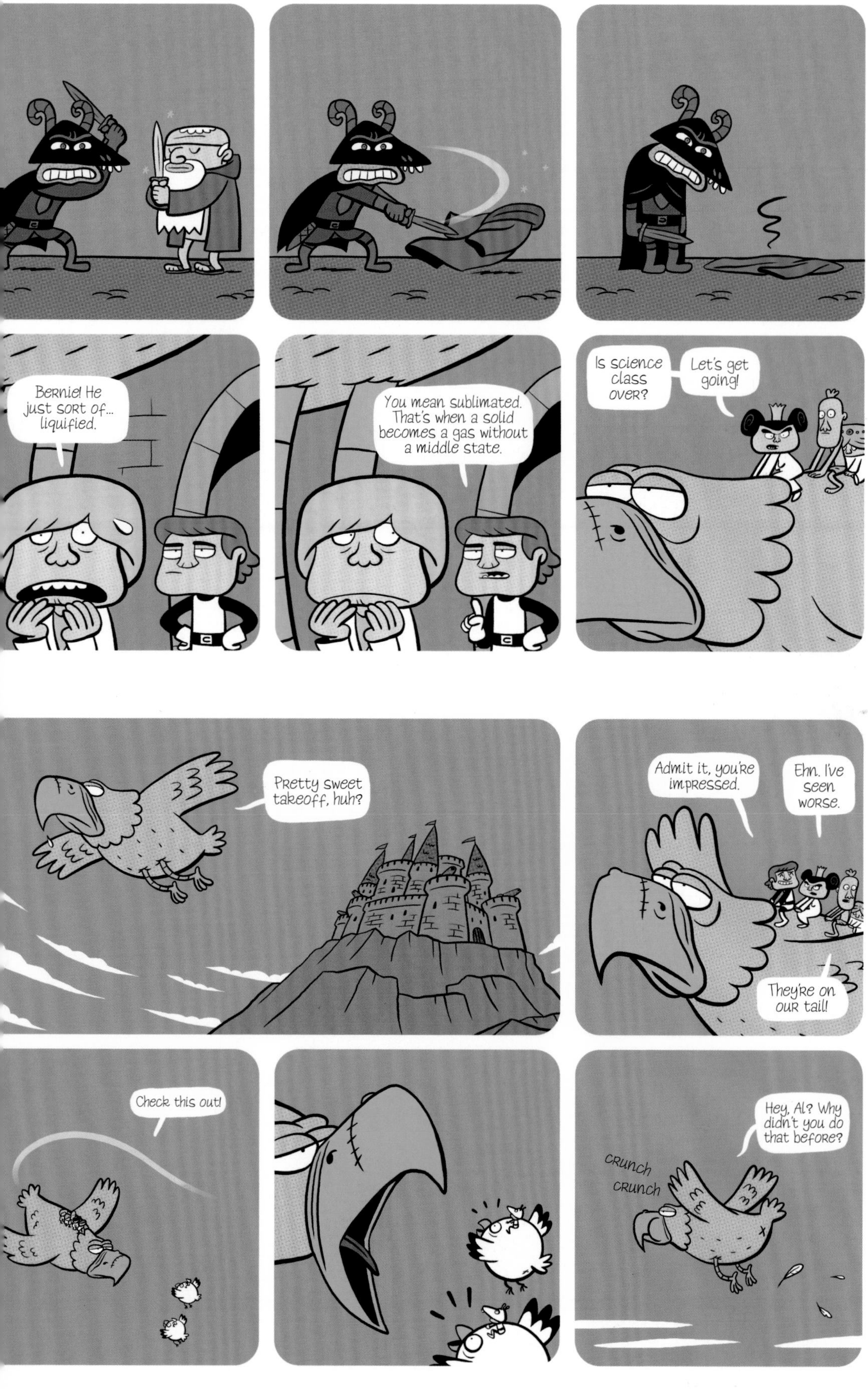
Bernie! He just sort of... liquified.
You mean sublimated. That's when a solid becomes a gas without a middle state.
Is science class over?
Let's get going!
Pretty sweet takeoff, huh?
Admit it, you're impressed.
Ehn. I've seen worse.
They're on our tail!
Check this out!
CRUNCH
CRUNCH
Hey, Al? Why didn't you do that before?

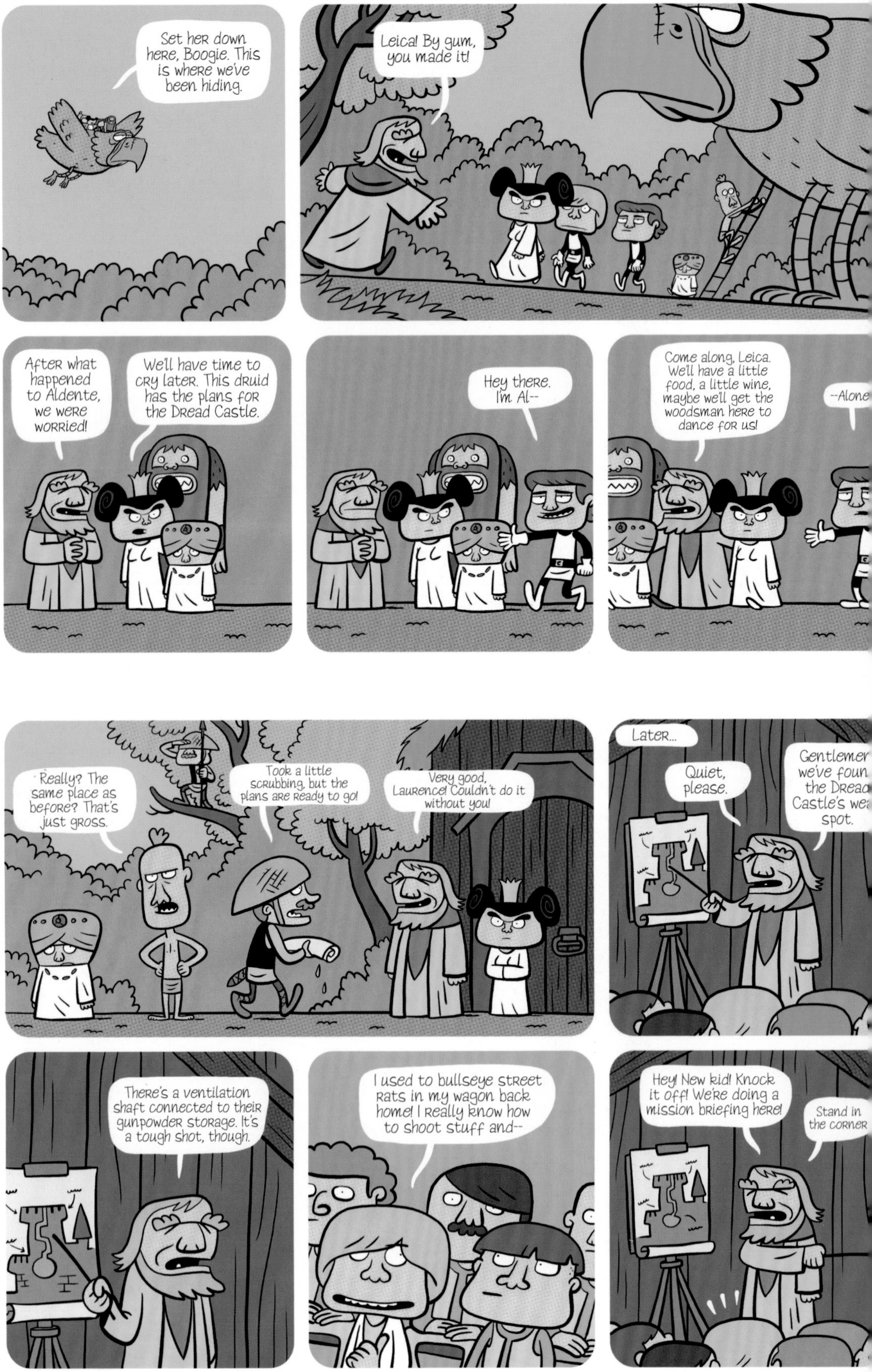

Set her down here, Boogie. This is where we've been hiding.
Leica! By gum, you made it!
After what happened to Aldente, we were worried!
We'll have time to cry later. This druid has the plans for the Dread Castle.
Hey there. I'm Al--
Come along, Leica. We'll have a little food, a little wine, maybe we'll get the woodsman here to dance for us!
--Alone
Really? The same place as before? That's just gross.
Took a little scrubbing, but the plans are ready to go!
Very good, Laurence! Couldn't do it without you!
Later...
Quiet, please.
Gentlemen we've foun the Drea Castle's we spot.
There's a ventilation shaft connected to their gunpowder storage. It's a tough shot, though.
I used to bullseye street rats in my wagon back home! I really know how to shoot stuff and--
Hey! New kid! Knock it off! We're doing a mission briefing here!
Stand in the corner

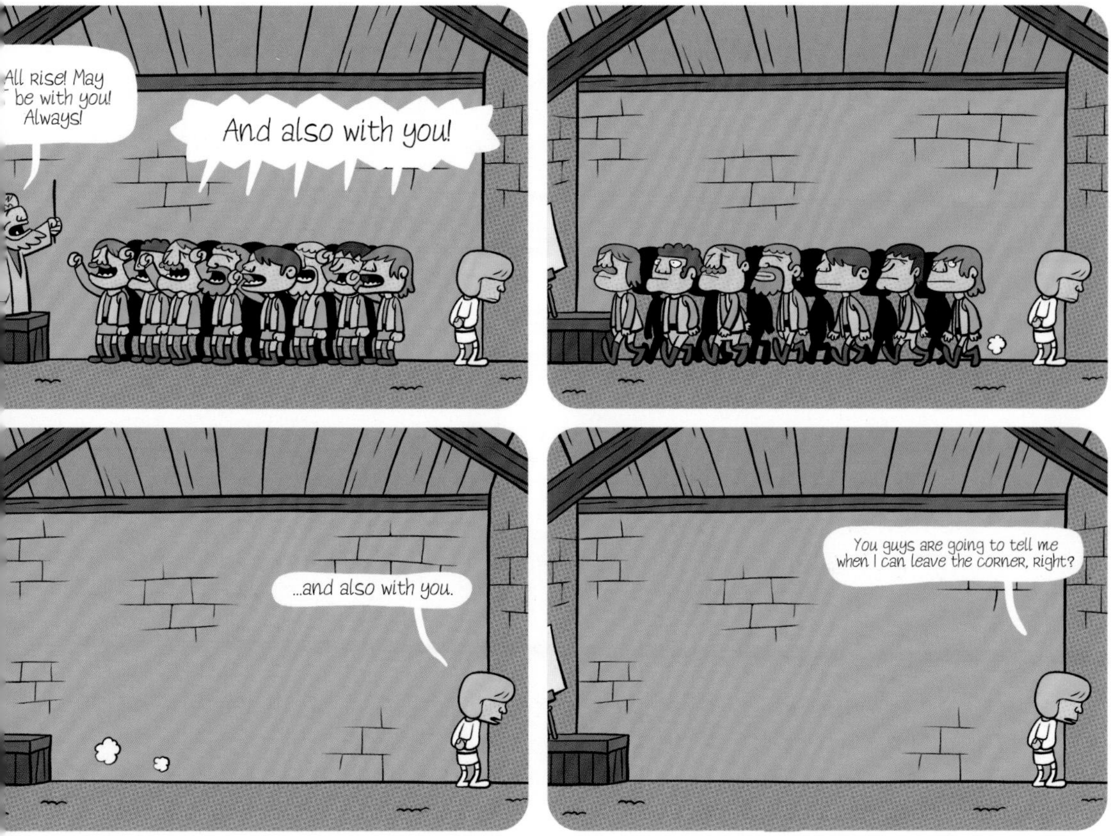
All rise! May be with you! Always!
And also with you!
...and also with you.
You guys are going to tell me when I can leave the corner, right?

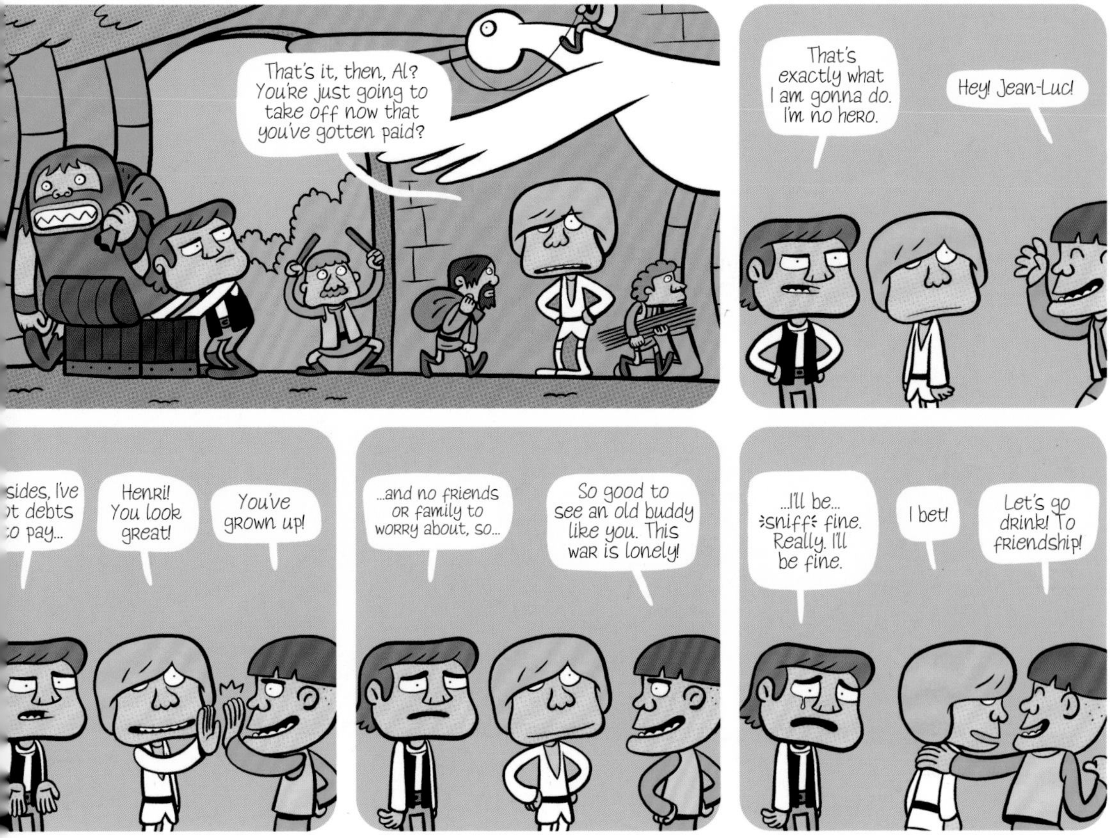
That's it, then, Al? You're just going to take off now that you've gotten paid?
That's exactly what I am gonna do. I'm no hero.
Hey! Jean-Luc!
sides, I've t debts o pay...
Henri! You look great!
You've grown up!
...and no friends or family to worry about, so...
So good to see an old buddy like you. This war is lonely!
...I'll be... sniff fine. Really. I'll be fine.
I bet!
Let's go drink! To friendship!

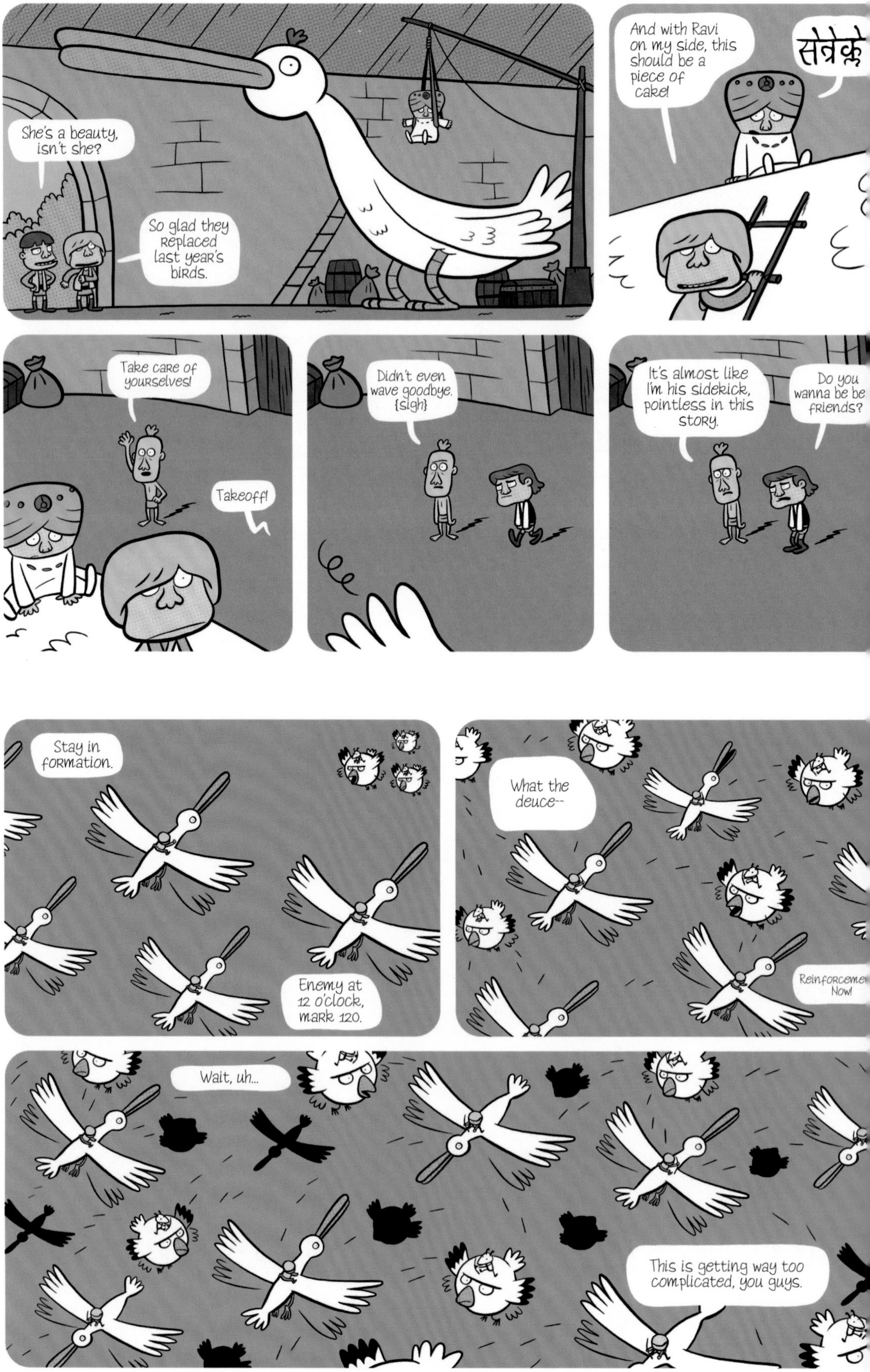
She's a beauty, isn't she?
So glad they replaced last year's birds.
And with Ravi on my side, this should be a piece of cake!
सेत्रेक्के
Take care of yourselves!
Takeoff!
Didn't even wave goodbye. {sigh}
It's almost like I'm his sidekick, pointless in this story.
Do you wanna be be friends?
Stay in formation.
Enemy at 12 o'clock, mark 120.
What the deuce--
Reinforceme Now!
Wait, uh...
This is getting way too complicated, you guys.

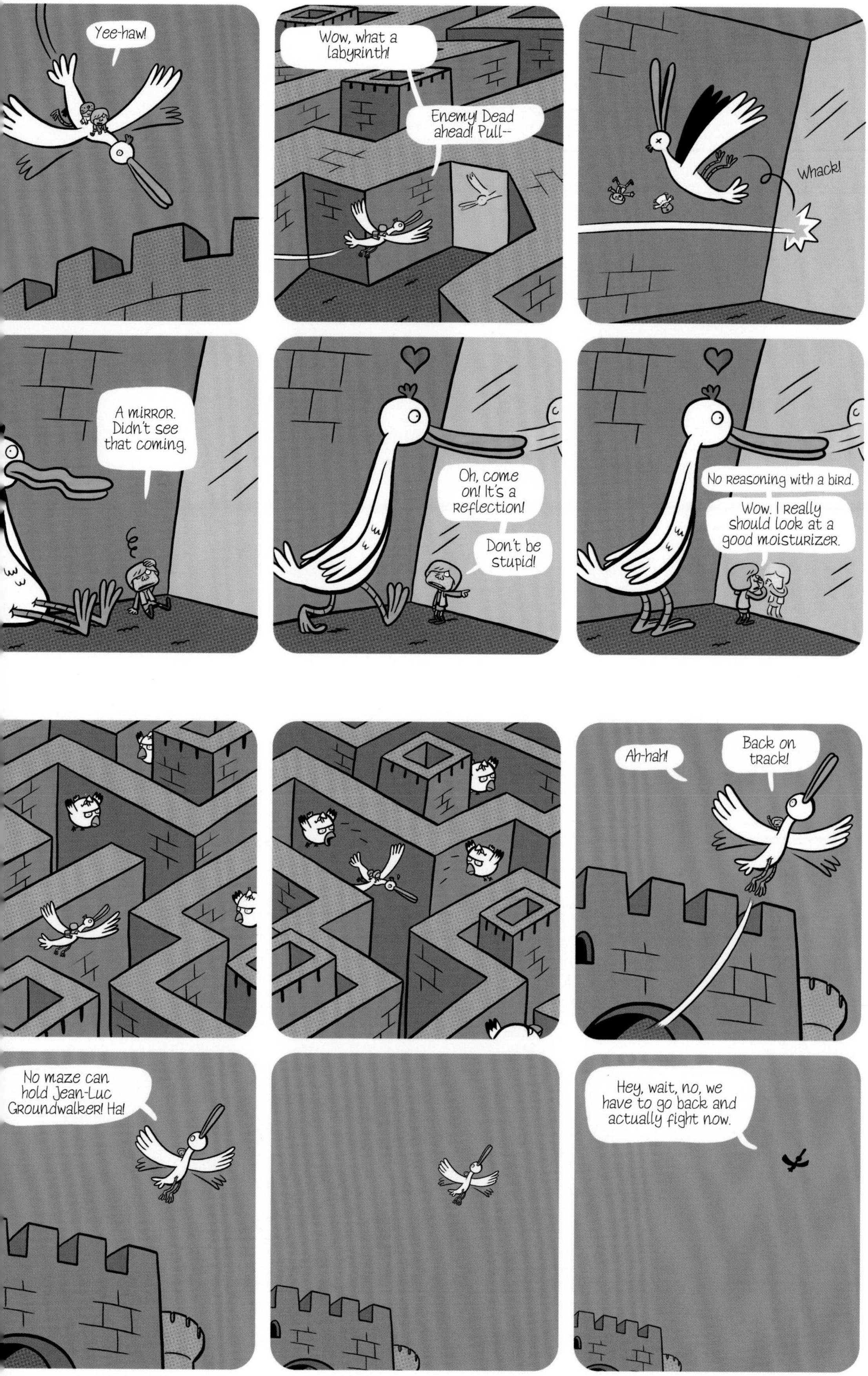
Yee-haw!
Wow, what a labyrinth!
Enemy! Dead ahead! Pull--
Whack!
A mirror. Didn't see that coming.
Oh, come on! It's a reflection!
Don't be stupid!
No reasoning with a bird.
Wow. I really should look at a good moisturizer.
Ah-hah!
Back on track!
No maze can hold Jean-Luc Groundwalker! Ha!
Hey, wait, no, we have to go back and actually fight now.

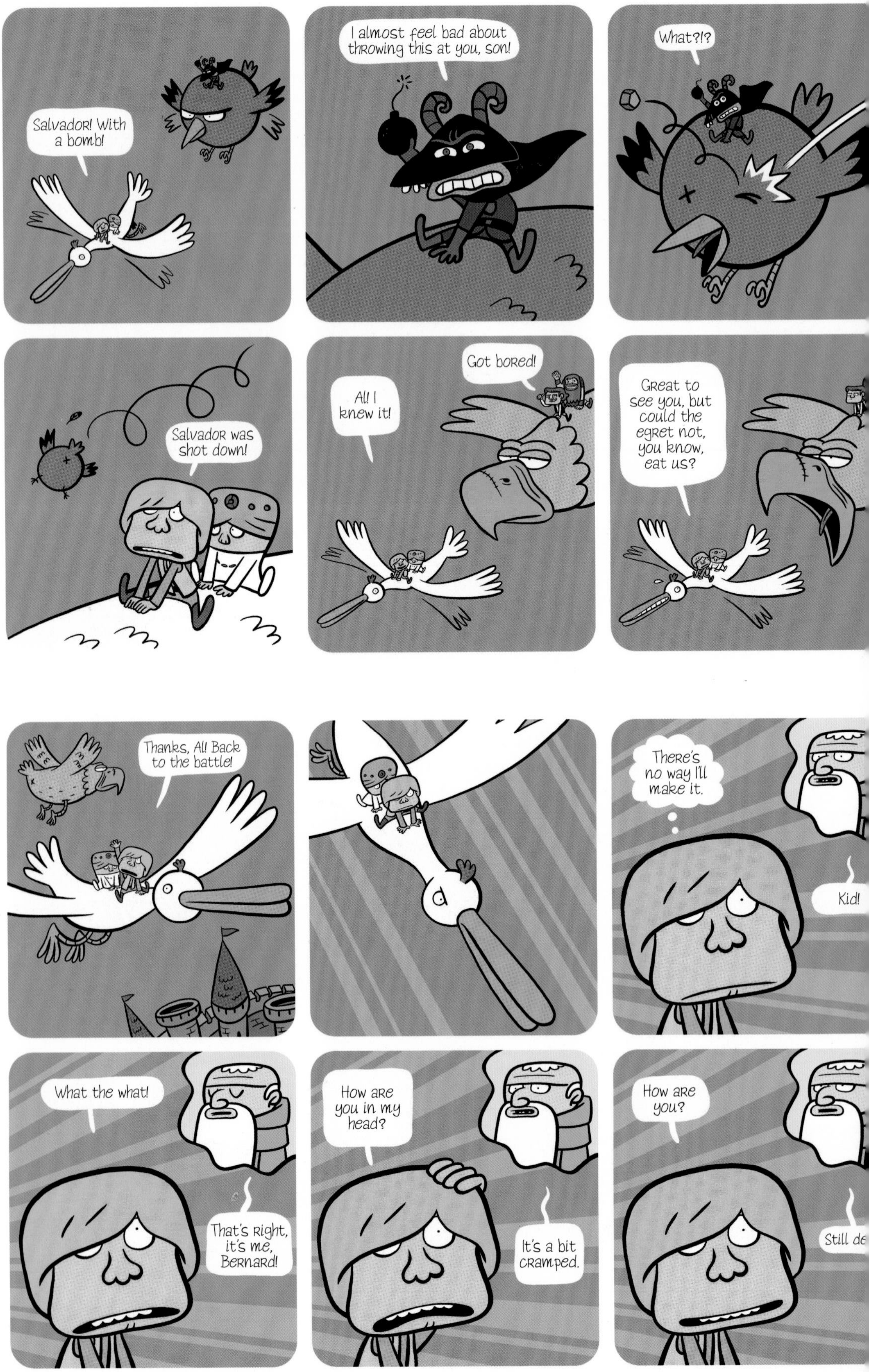

Salvador! With a bomb!
I almost feel bad about throwing this at you, son!
What?!?
Salvador was shot down!
Al! I knew it!
Got bored!
Great to see you, but could the egret not, you know, eat us?
Thanks, Al! Back to the battle!
There's no way I'll make it.
Kid!
What the what!
That's right, it's me, Bernard!
How are you in my head?
It's a bit cramped.
How are you?

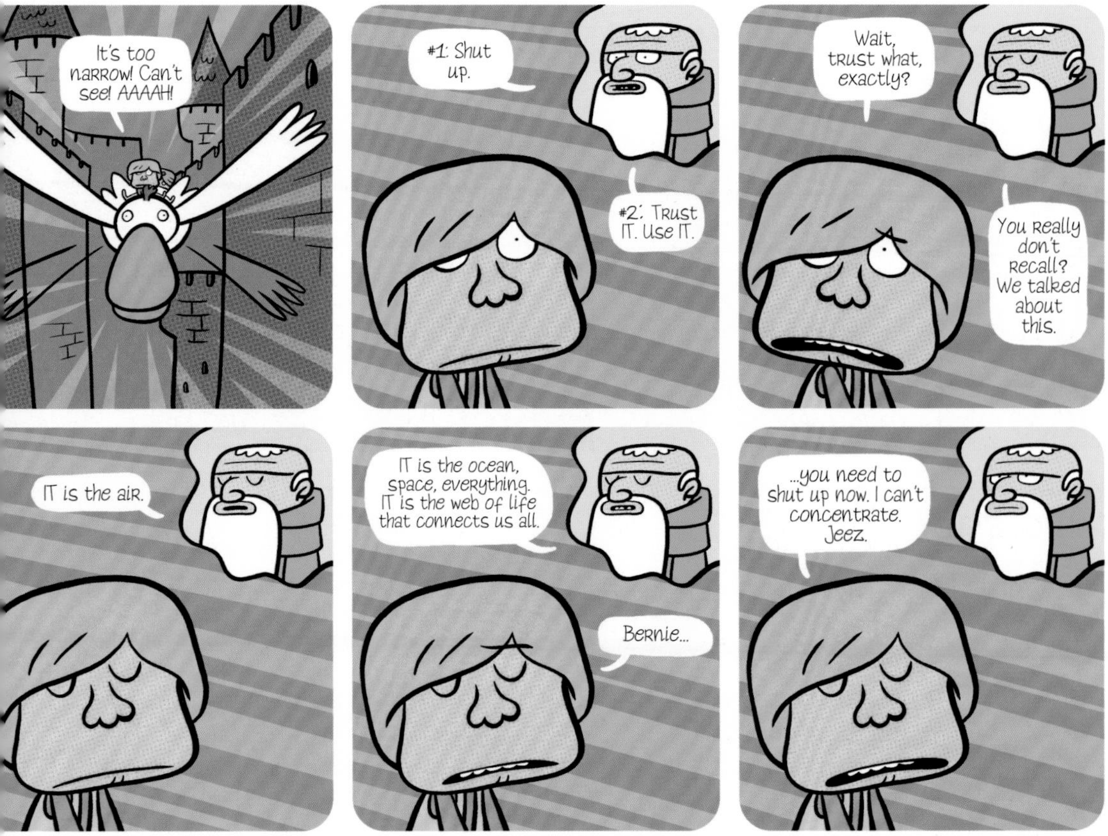
It's too narrow! Can't see! AAAAH!
#1: Shut up.
#2: Trust IT. Use IT.
Wait, trust what, exactly?
You really don't recall? We talked about this.
IT is the air.
IT is the ocean, space, everything. IT is the web of life that connects us all.
Bernie...
...you need to shut up now. I can't concentrate. Jeez.

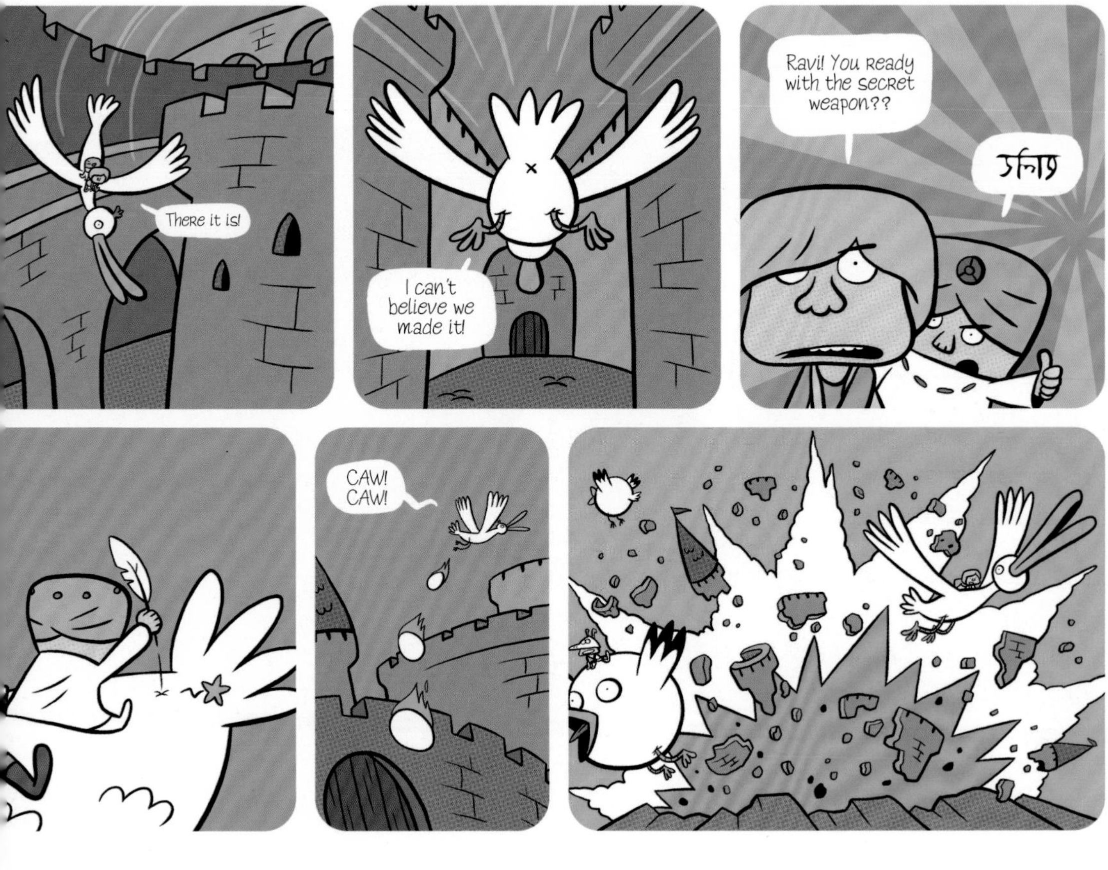
There it is!
I can't believe we made it!
Ravi! You ready with the secret weapon??
CAW! CAW!

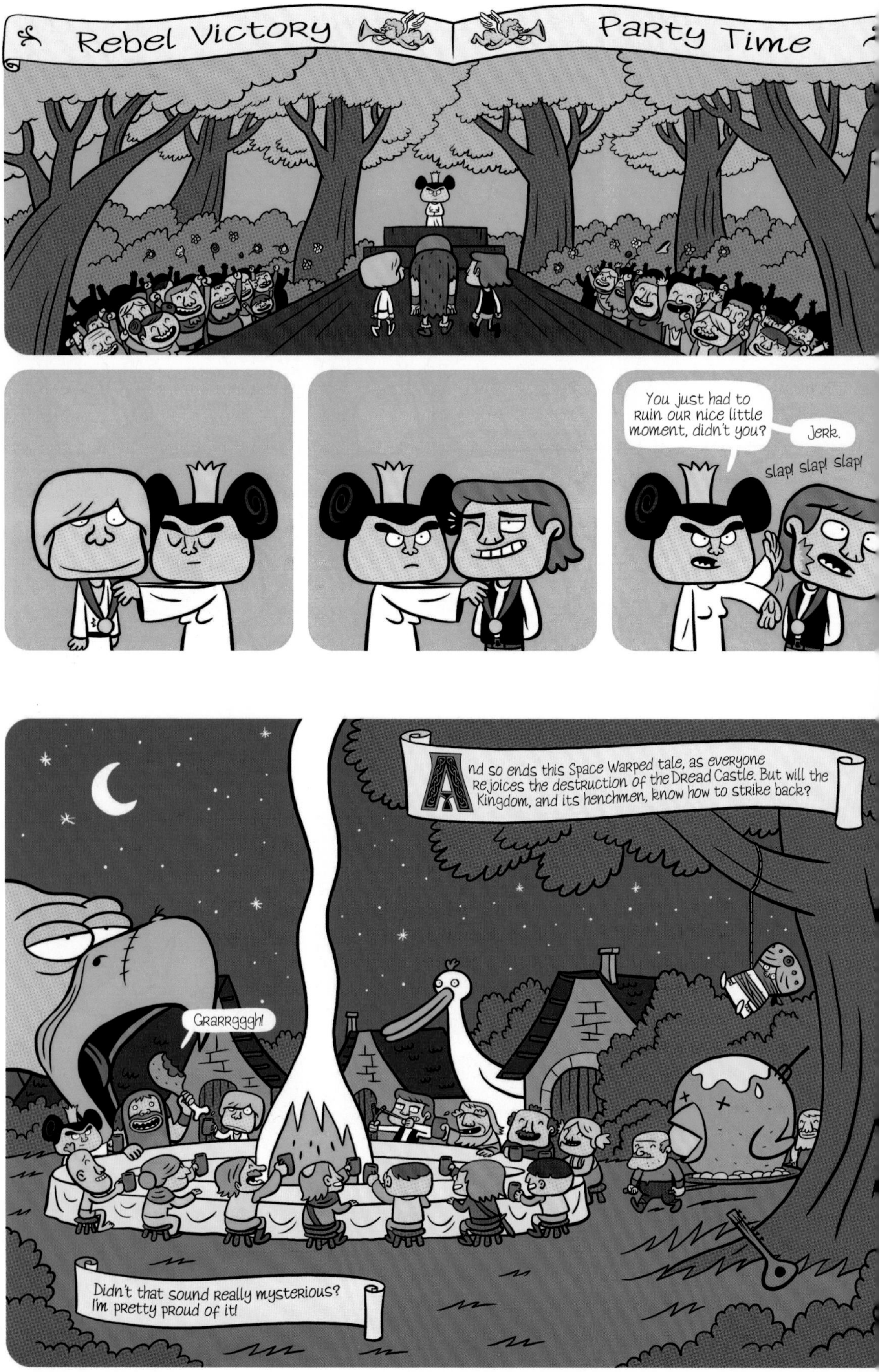
Rebel Victory
Party Time
You just had to Ruin our nice little moment, didn't you?
Jerk.
slap! slap! slap!
And so ends this Space Warped tale, as everyone Rejoices the destruction of the Dread Castle. But will the Kingdom, and its henchmen, know how to strike back?
GRARRgggh!
Didn't that sound Really mysterious? I'm pretty proud of it!

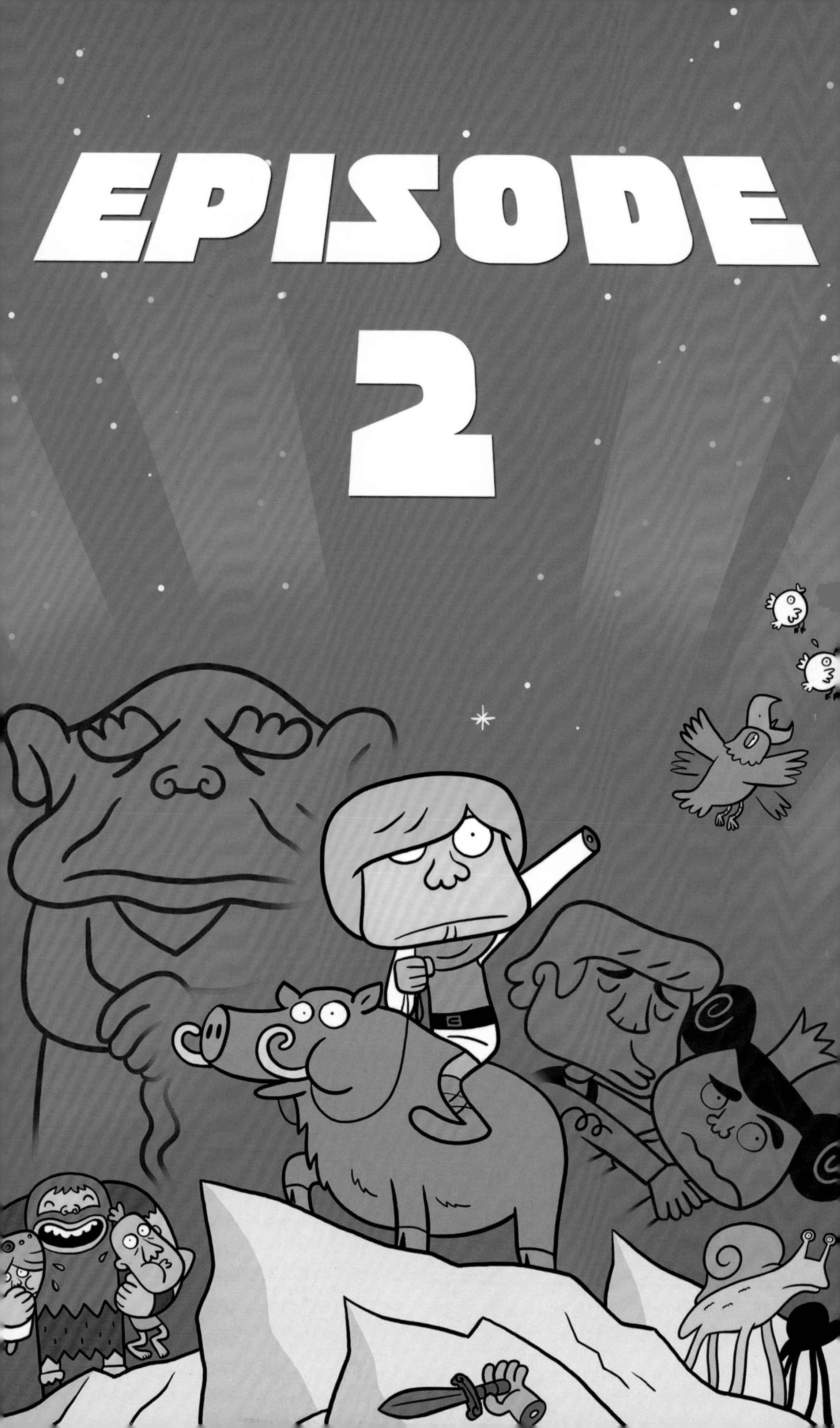
EPISODE
2

It is a dark time for the Kingdom. After the destruction of the Dread Castle, Lord Salvador has gone on the attack.

Thousands of reconnaissance parrots have been catapulted to the far reaches of the realm. Salvador has not said why.

Nevertheless, one of them has touched down in the icy wastes of Hött, an ironically named place.

Yes, we should probably put some more jokes in the opening bit and it's likely that you're disappointed. It gets funnier. We promise.

I mean, it does depend on how you're feeling and if you have a sense of humor.

Who knows? It's all personal. One man's banana peel is another man's paralysis, after all! But the science of silly aside, let's get down to business.

Steady, boy.

Grarr.

Shouldn't have gone for the discount owl.

Can't even see three feet with this thing.

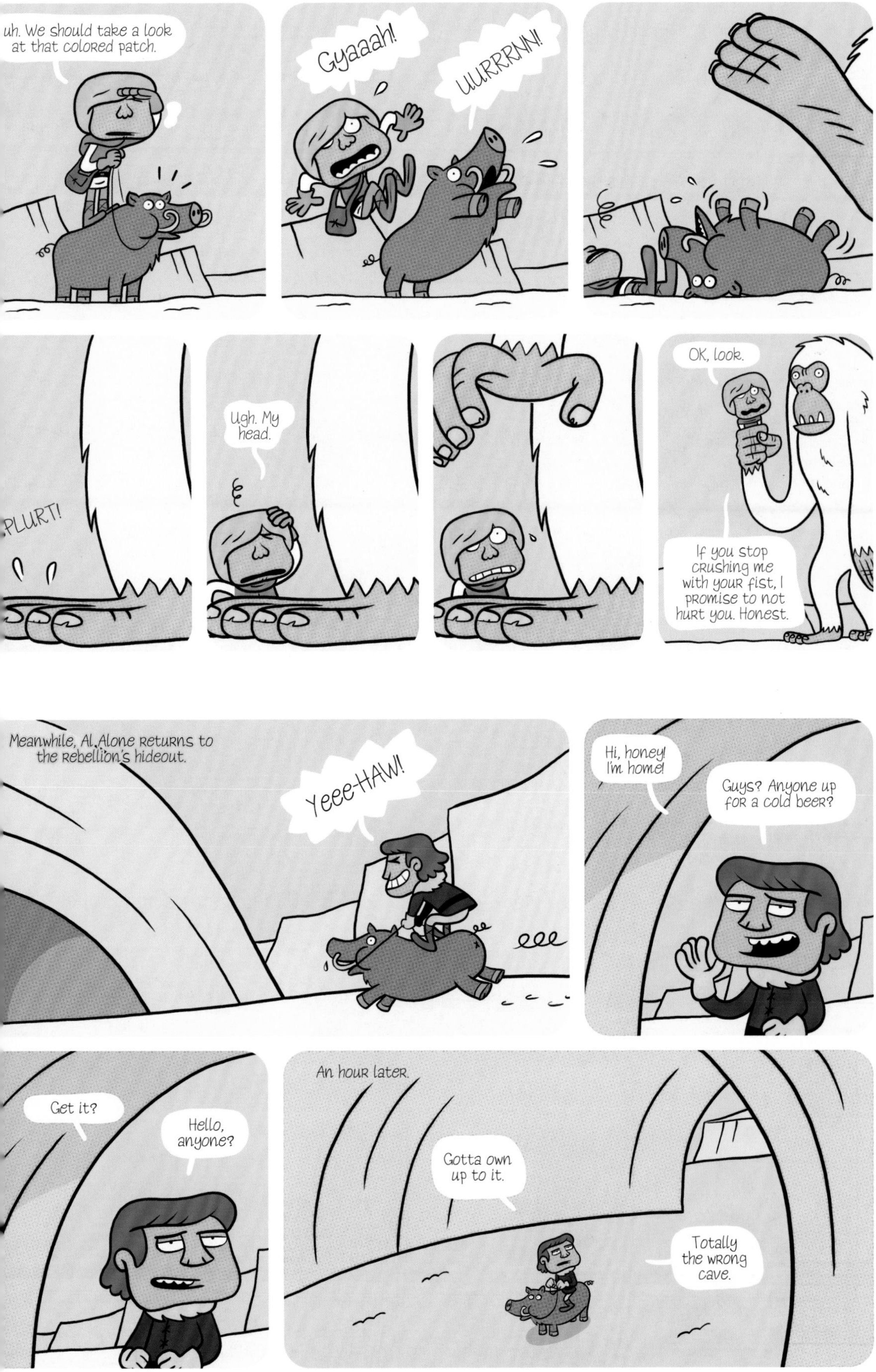
uh. We should take a look at that colored patch.
Gyaaah!
UURRRNN!
PLURT!
Ugh. My head.
OK, look.
If you stop crushing me with your fist, I promise to not hurt you. Honest.
Meanwhile, Al Alone returns to the Rebellion's hideout.
Yeee-HAW!
Hi, honey! I'm home!
Guys? Anyone up for a cold beer?
Get it?
Hello, anyone?
An hour later.
Gotta own up to it.
Totally the wrong cave.

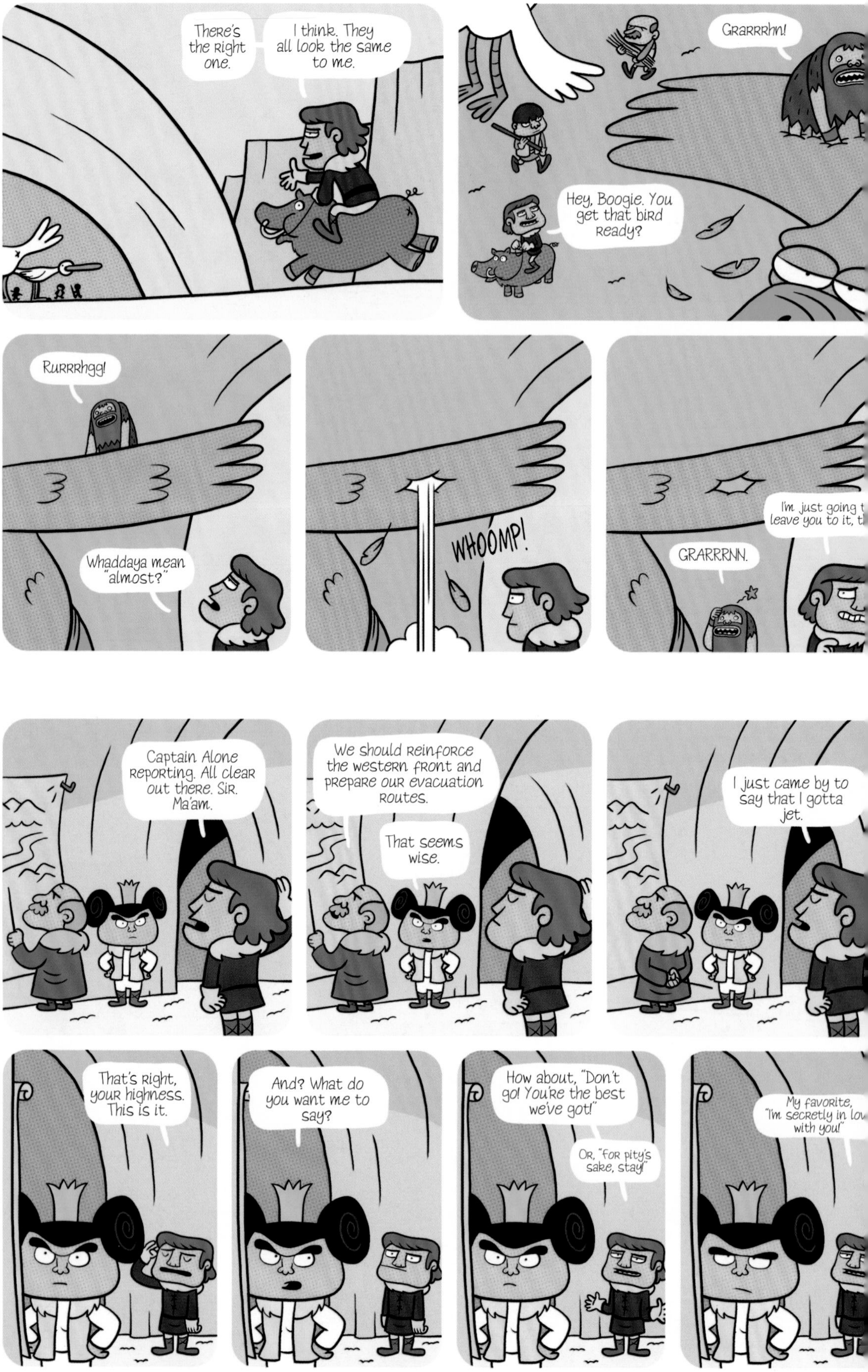

There's the right one.
I think. They all look the same to me.
Grarrrhn!
Hey, Boogie. You get that bird ready?
Rurrrhgg!
Whaddaya mean "almost?"
WHOOMP!
GRARRRNN.
I'm just going t
leave you to it, t
Captain Alone reporting. All clear out there. Sir. Ma'am.
We should reinforce the western front and prepare our evacuation routes.
That seems wise.
I just came by to say that I gotta jet.
That's right, your highness. This is it.
And? What do you want me to say?
How about, "Don't go! You're the best we've got!"
Or, "For pity's sake, stay!"
My favorite,
"I'm secretly in lov
with you!"

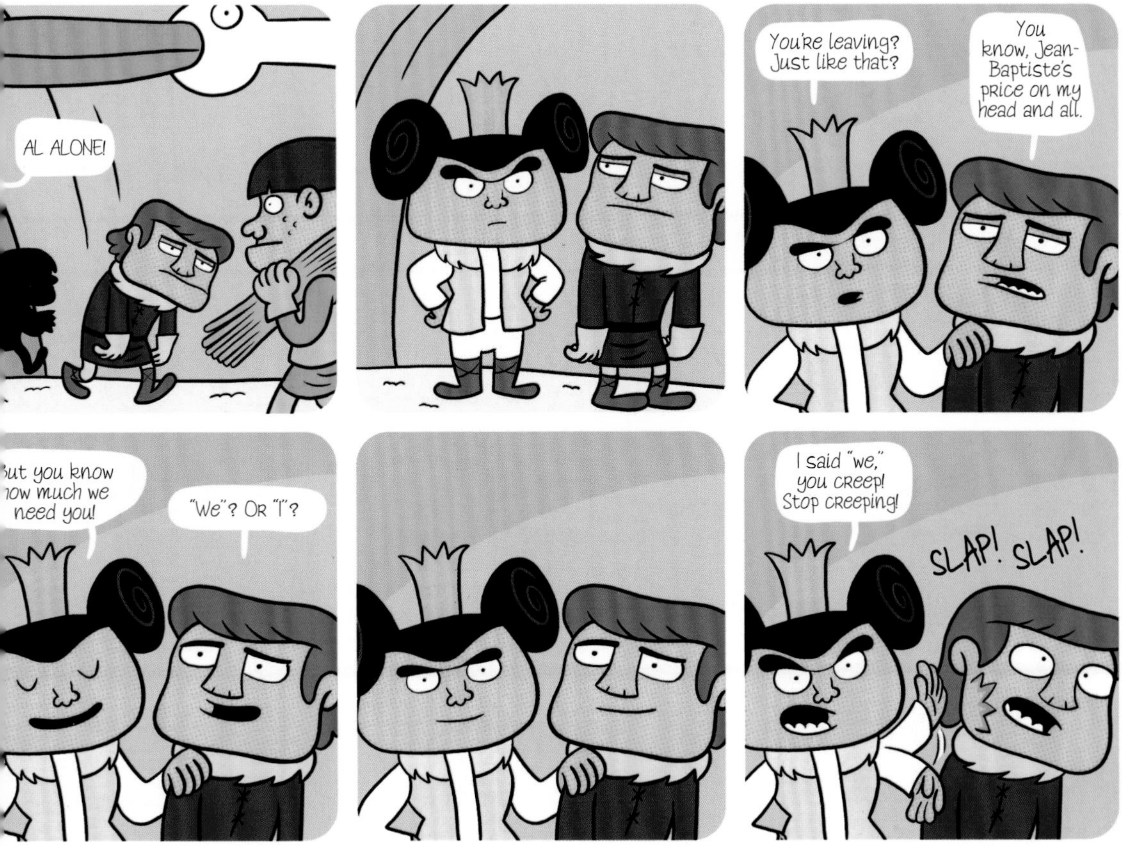
AL ALONE!
You're leaving? Just like that?
You know, Jean-Baptiste's price on my head and all.
ut you know ow much we need you!
"We"? Or "I"?
I said "we," you creep! Stop creeping!
SLAP! SLAP!

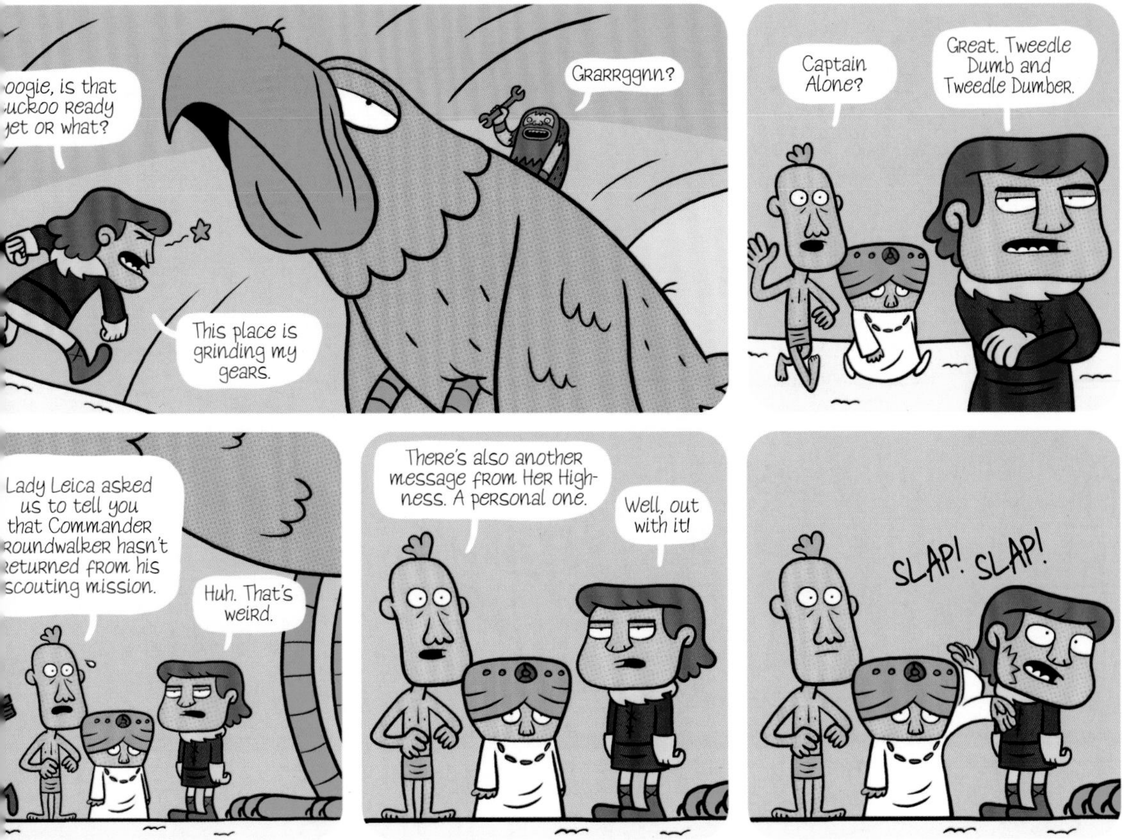
oogie, is that uckoo ready yet or what?
This place is grinding my gears.
Grarrggnn?
Captain Alone?
Great. Tweedle Dumb and Tweedle Dumber.
Lady Leica asked us to tell you that Commander roundwalker hasn't returned from his scouting mission.
Huh. That's weird.
There's also another message from Her High-ness. A personal one.
Well, out with it!
SLAP! SLAP!

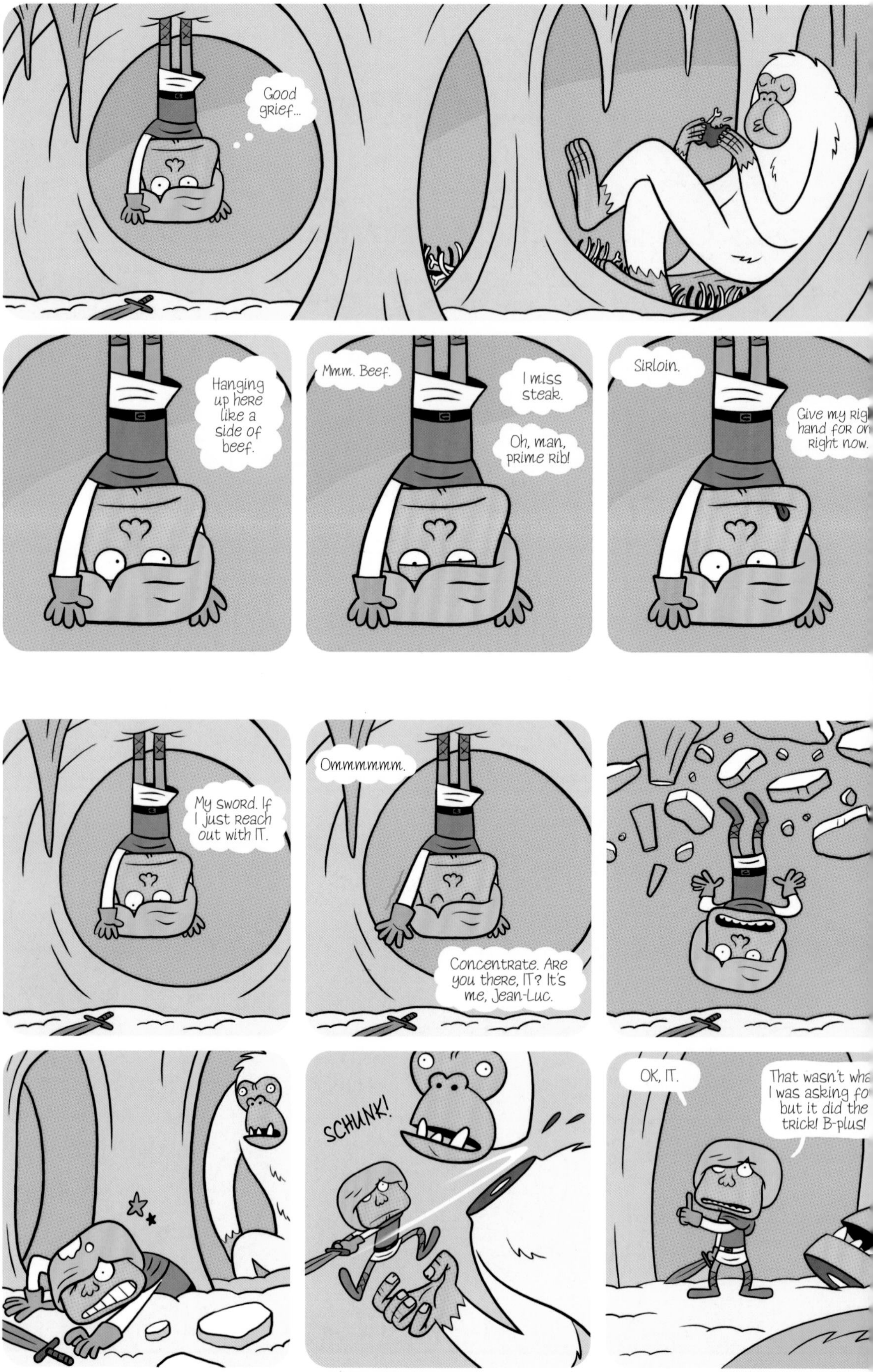

Good grief...
Hanging up here like a side of beef.
Mmm. Beef.
I miss steak.
Oh, man, prime rib!
Sirloin.
Give my rig
hand for on
right now.
My sword. If I just reach out with IT.
Ommmmmm.
Concentrate. Are you there, IT? It's me, Jean-Luc.
SCHUNK!
OK, IT.
That wasn't wha
I was asking fo
but it did the
trick! B-plus!

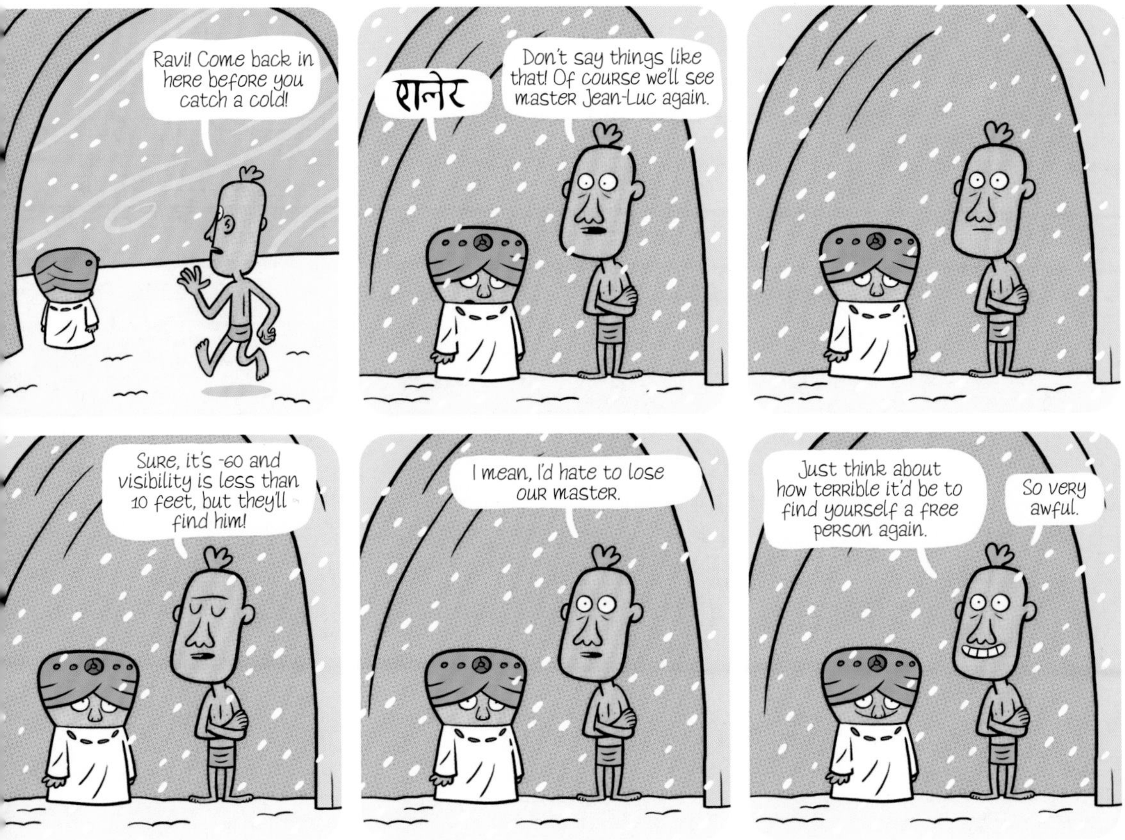
Ravi! Come back in here before you catch a cold!
शनेर
Don't say things like that! Of course we'll see master Jean-Luc again.
Sure, it's -60 and visibility is less than 10 feet, but they'll find him!
I mean, I'd hate to lose our master.
Just think about how terrible it'd be to find yourself a free person again.
So very awful.

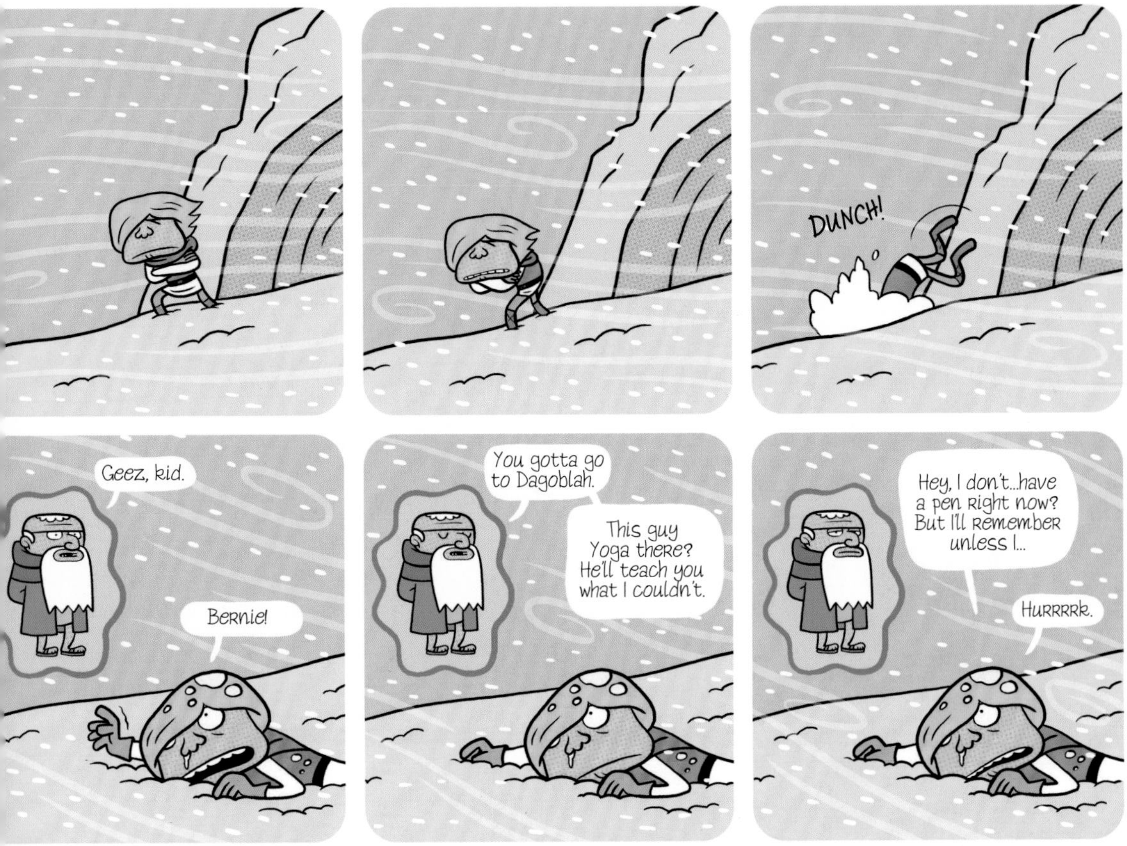
DUNCH!
Geez, kid.
Bernie!
You gotta go to Dagoblah.
This guy Yoga there? He'll teach you what I couldn't.
Hey, I don't...have a pen right now? But I'll remember unless I...
Hurrrrk.

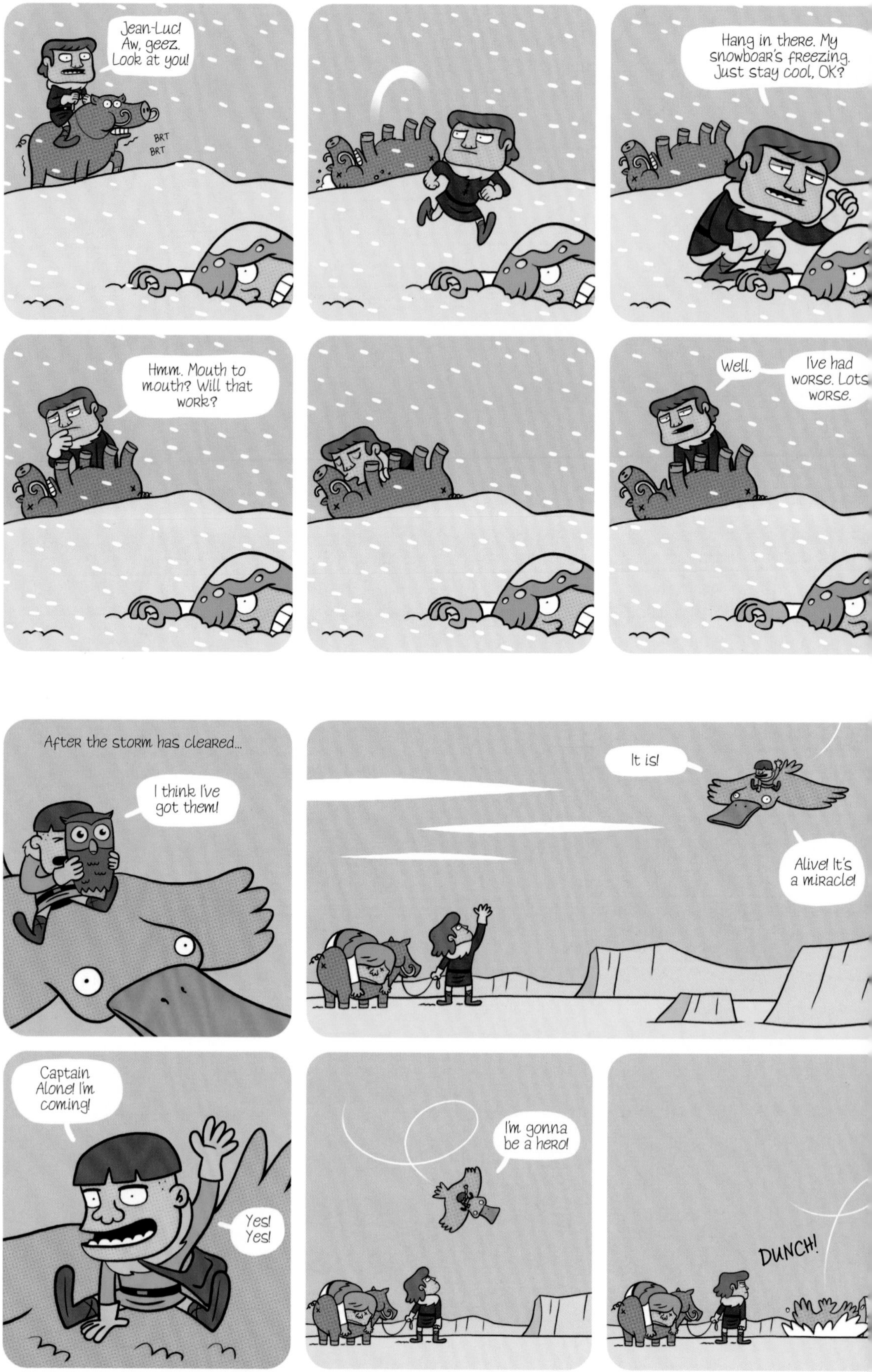
Jean-Luc! Aw, geez. Look at you!
BRT BRT
Hang in there. My snowboar's freezing. Just stay cool, OK?
Hmm. Mouth to mouth? Will that work?
Well.
I've had worse. Lots worse.
After the storm has cleared...
I think I've got them!
It is!
Alive! It's a miracle!
Captain Alone! I'm coming!
Yes! Yes!
I'm gonna be a hero!
DUNCH!

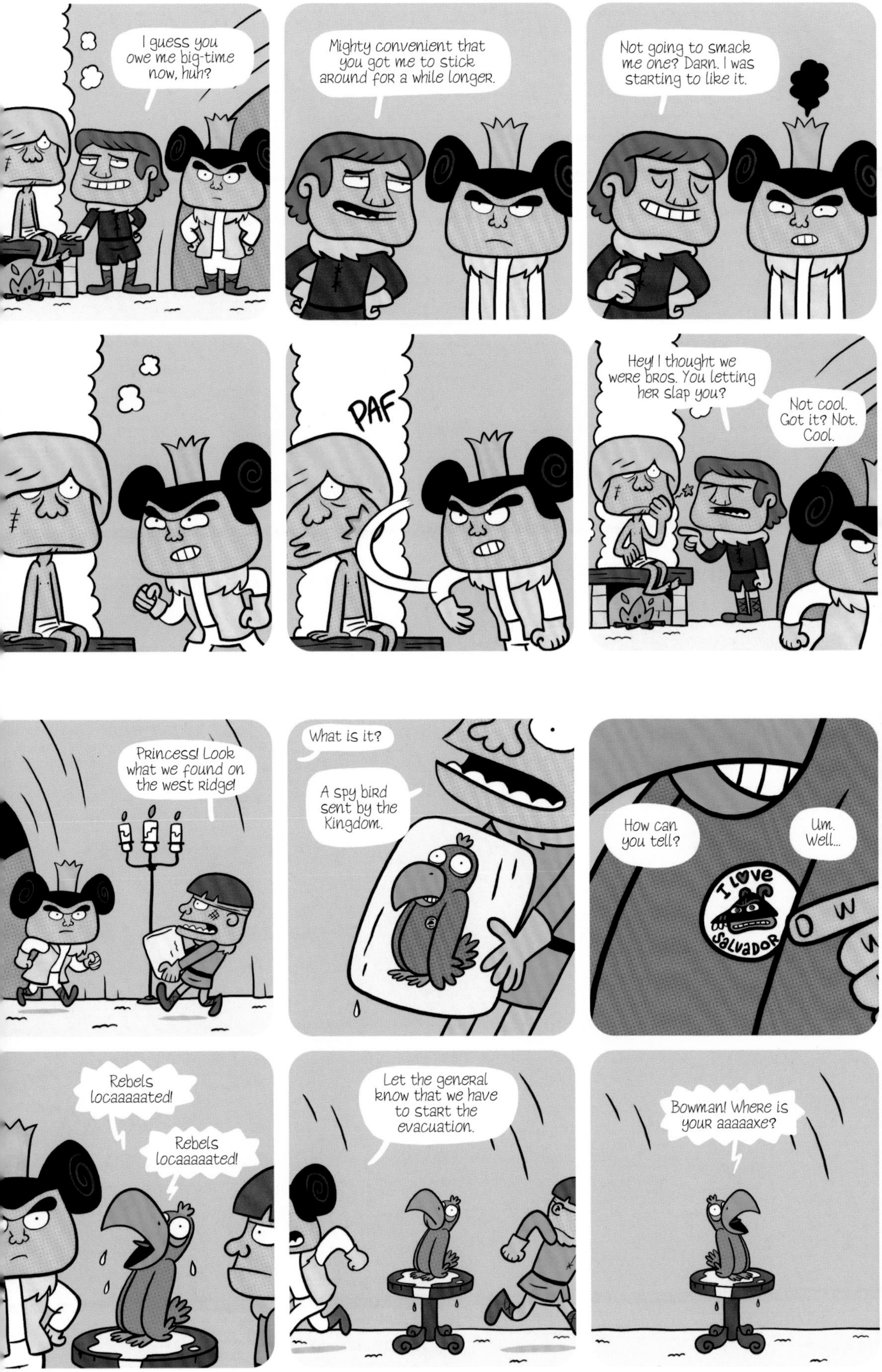
I guess you owe me big-time now, huh?
Mighty convenient that you got me to stick around for a while longer.
Not going to smack me one? Darn. I was starting to like it.
PAF
Hey! I thought we were bros. You letting her slap you?
Not cool. Got it? Not. Cool.
Princess! Look what we found on the west ridge!
What is it?
A spy bird sent by the Kingdom.
How can you tell?
Um. Well...
I love Salvador
Rebels locaaaaated!
Rebels locaaaaated!
Let the general know that we have to start the evacuation.
Bowman! Where is your aaaaaxe?

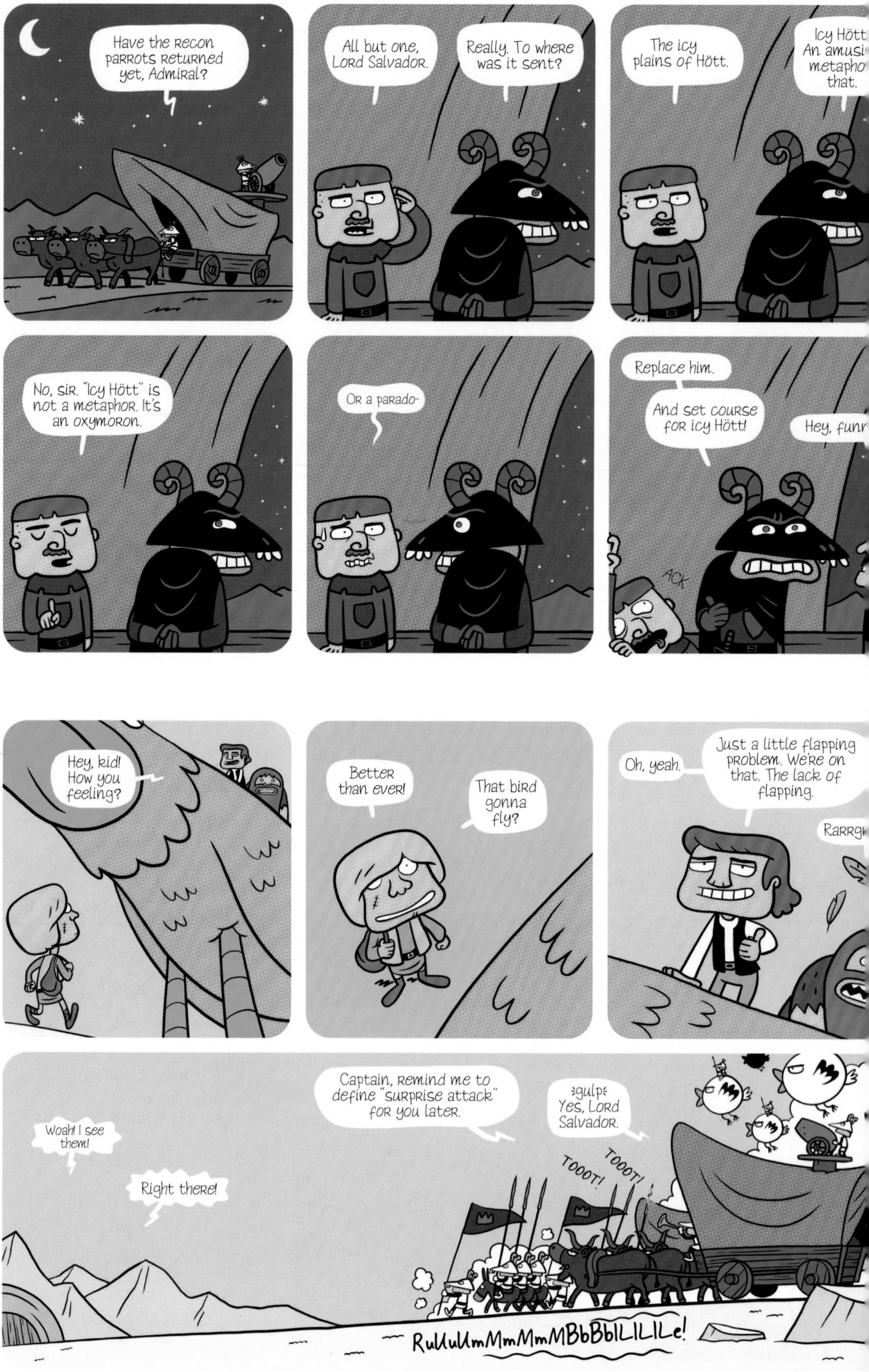
Have the recon parrots returned yet, Admiral?
All but one, Lord Salvador.
Really. To where was it sent?
The icy plains of Hött.
Icy Hött An amusi metapho that.
No, sir. "Icy Hött" is not a metaphor. It's an oxymoron.
Or a parado-
Replace him.
And set course for icy Hött!
Hey, funr
ACK
Hey, kid! How you feeling?
Better than ever!
That bird gonna fly?
Oh, yeah.
Just a little flapping problem. We're on that. The lack of flapping.
Rarrg
Woah! I see them!
Right there!
Captain, remind me to define "surprise attack" for you later.
gulp
Yes, Lord Salvador.
TOOOT!
TOOOT!
RuUuUmMmMmMBbBbILILILe!

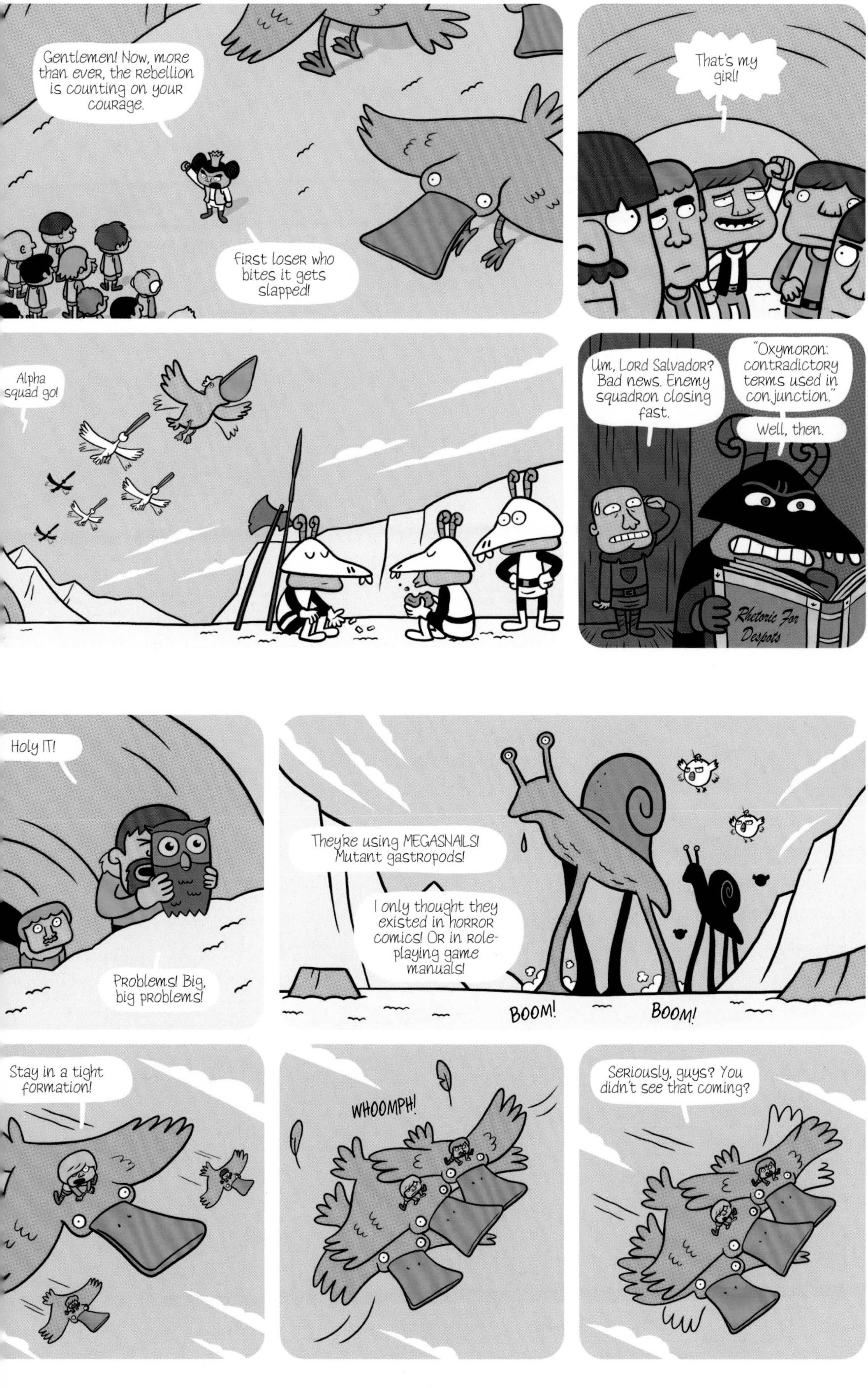
Gentlemen! Now, more than ever, the Rebellion is counting on your courage.
First loser who bites it gets slapped!
That's my girl!
Alpha squad go!
Um, Lord Salvador? Bad news. Enemy squadron closing fast.
"Oxymoron: contradictory terms used in conjunction."
Well, then.
Rhetoric For Despots
Holy IT!
Problems! Big, big problems!
They're using MEGASNAILS! Mutant gastropods!
I only thought they existed in horror comics! Or in role-playing game manuals!
BOOM!
BOOM!
Stay in a tight formation!
WHOOMPH!
Seriously, guys? You didn't see that coming?

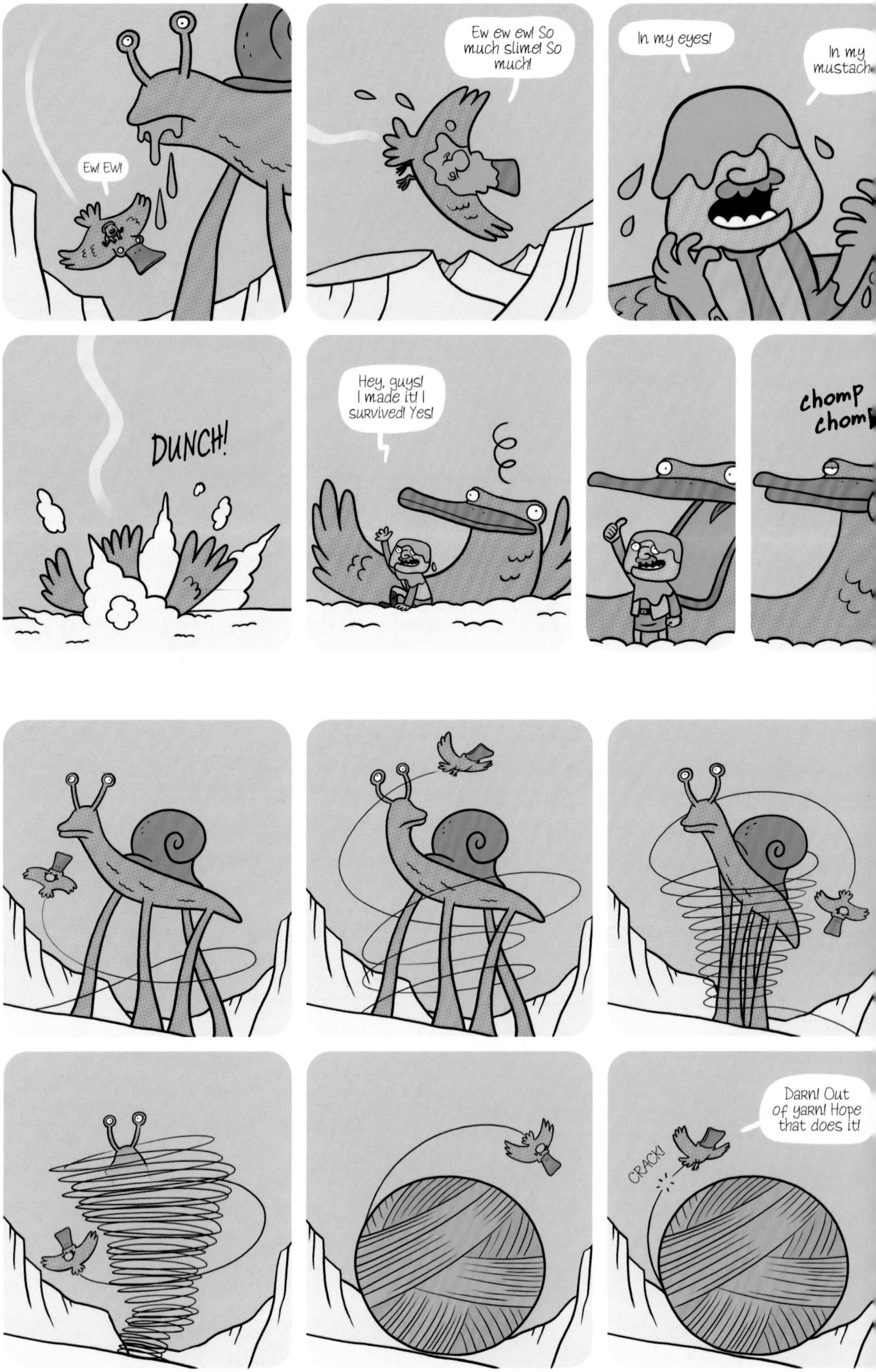
Ew! EW!
Ew ew ew! So much slime! So much!
In my eyes!
In my mustach
DUNCH!
Hey, guys! I made it! I survived! Yes!
chomp chomp
CRACK!
Darn! Out of yarn! Hope that does it!

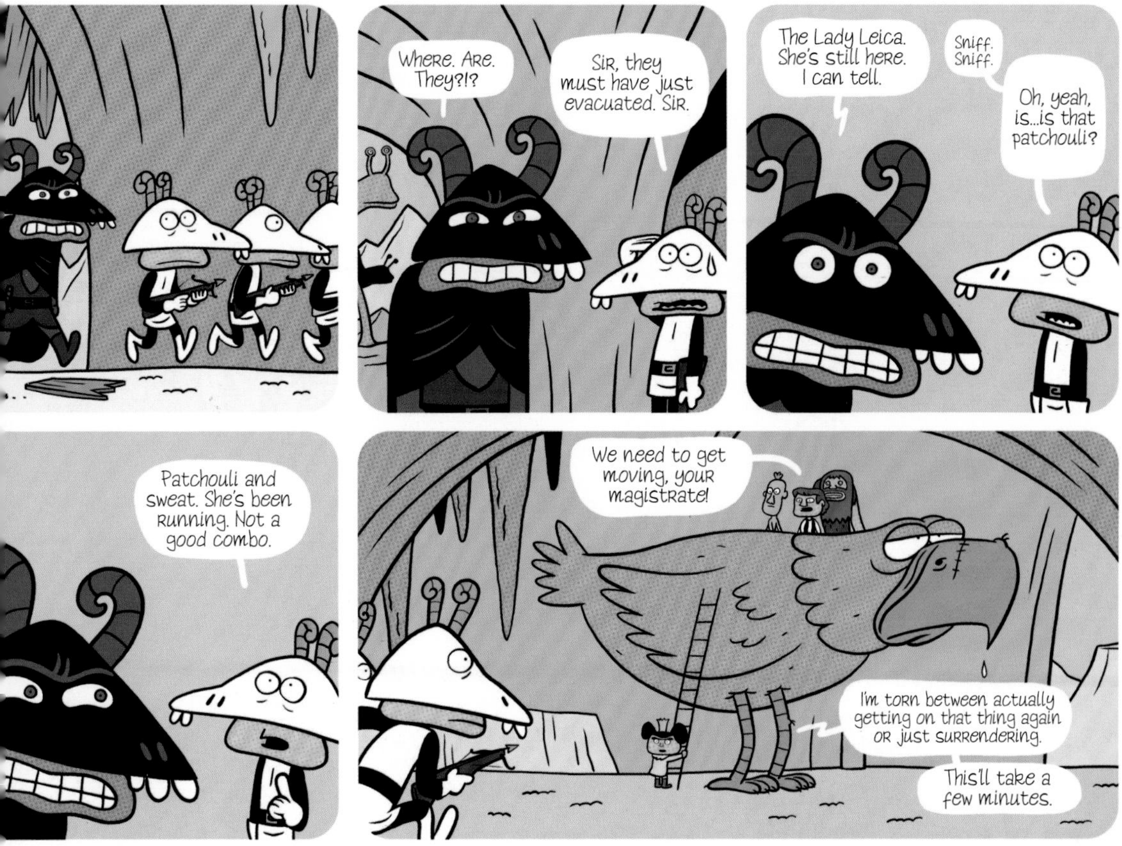
Where. Are. They?!?
Sir, they must have just evacuated. Sir.
The Lady Leica. She's still here. I can tell.
Sniff. Sniff.
Oh, yeah, is...is that patchouli?
Patchouli and sweat. She's been running. Not a good combo.
We need to get moving, your magistrate!
I'm torn between actually getting on that thing again or just surrendering.
This'll take a few minutes.

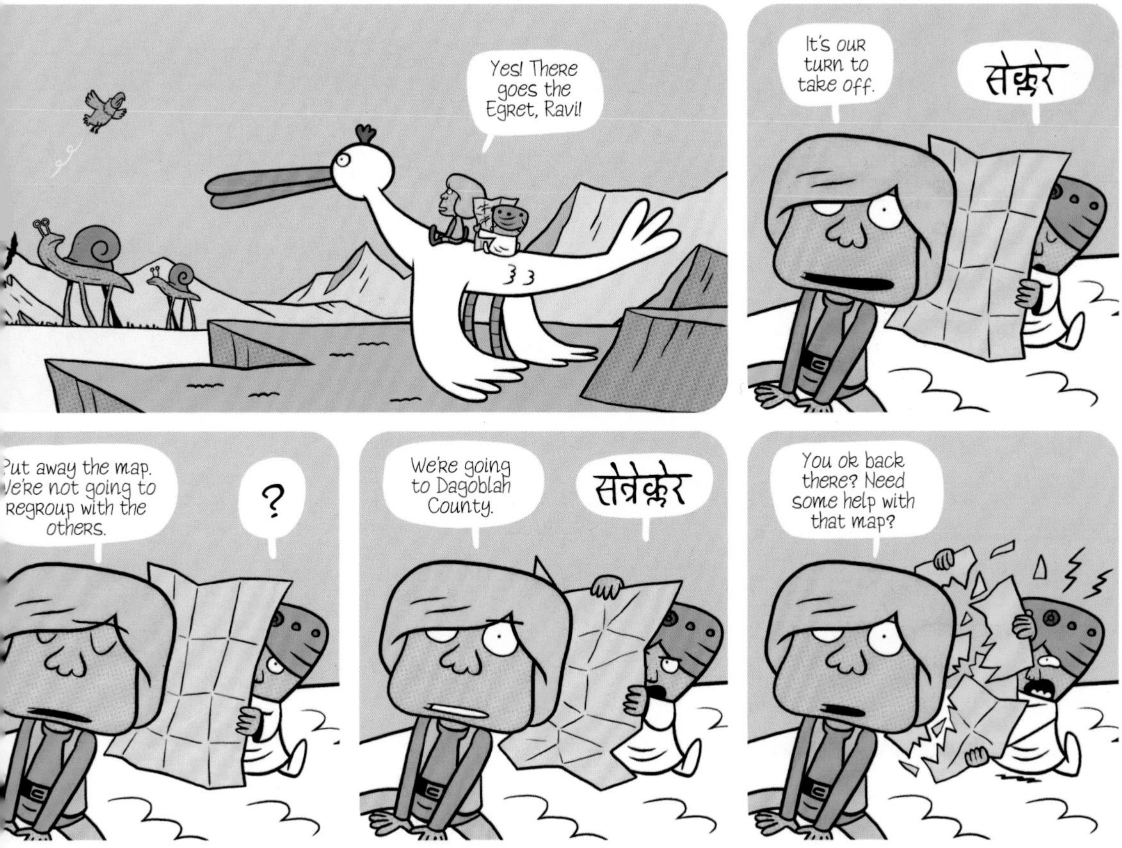
Yes! There goes the Egret, Ravi!
It's our turn to take off.
सेक्रेर
ut away the map. e're not going to regroup with the others.
?
We're going to Dagoblah County.
सेत्रेक्रेर
You ok back there? Need some help with that map?

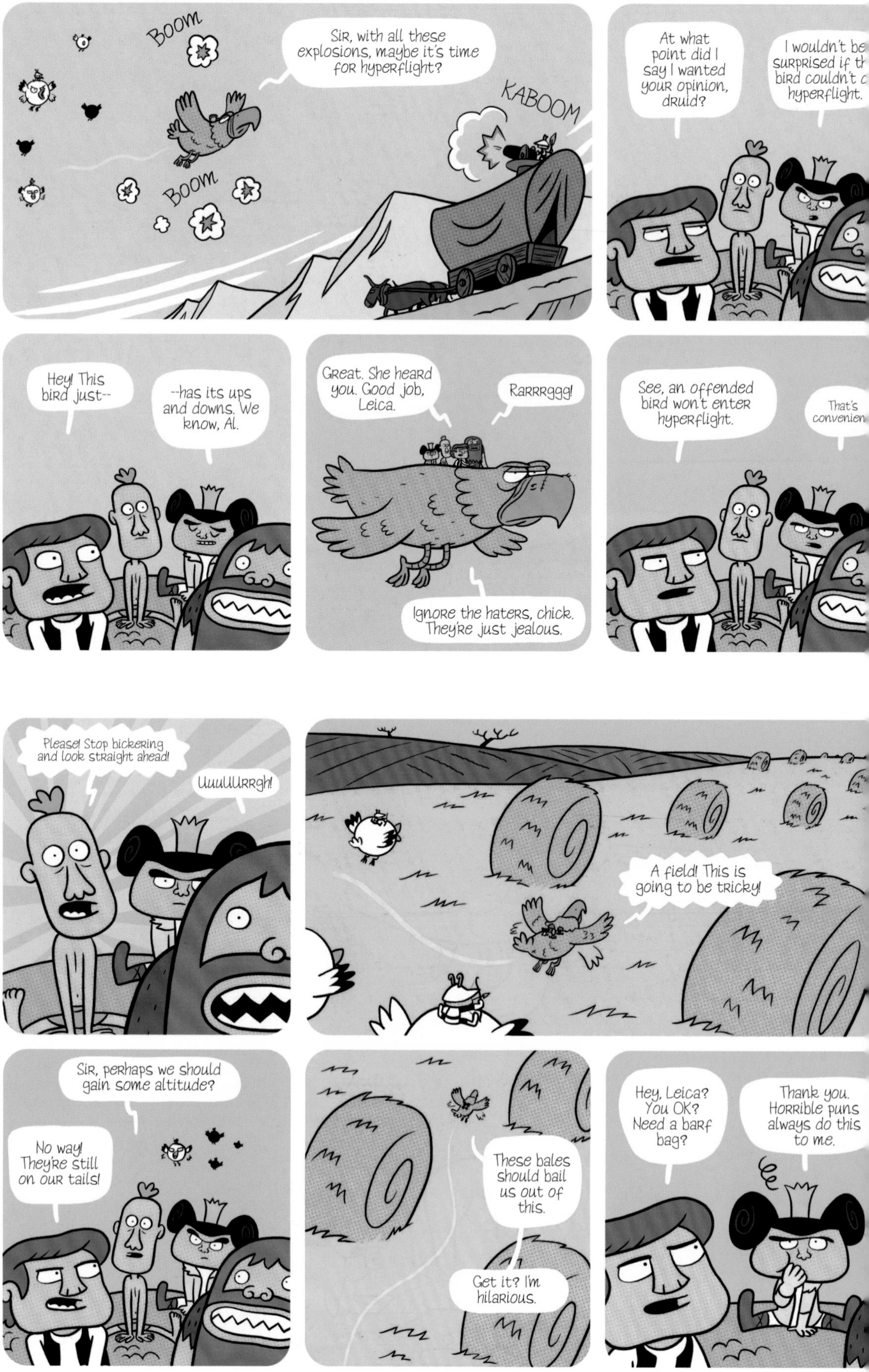
BOOM
Sir, with all these explosions, maybe it's time for hyperflight?
KABOOM
BOOM
At what point did I say I wanted your opinion, druid?
I wouldn't be surprised if th bird couldn't c hyperflight.
Hey! This bird just--
--has its ups and downs. We know, Al.
Great. She heard you. Good job, Leica.
Rarrrggg!
Ignore the haters, chick. They're just jealous.
See, an offended bird won't enter hyperflight.
That's convenien
Please! Stop bickering and look straight ahead!
UuuUUrrgh!
A field! This is going to be tricky!
Sir, perhaps we should gain some altitude?
No way! They're still on our tails!
These bales should bail us out of this.
Get it? I'm hilarious.
Hey, Leica? You OK? Need a barf bag?
Thank you. Horrible puns always do this to me.

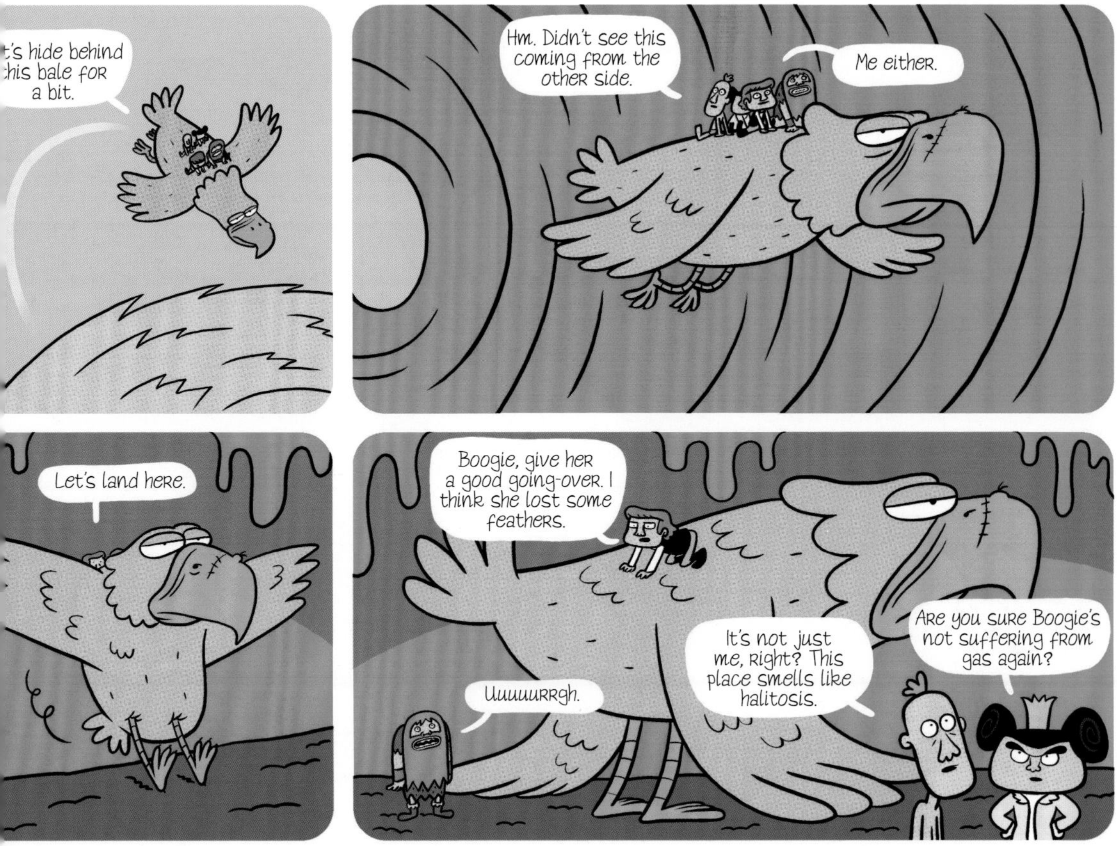
t's hide behind
this bale for
a bit.
Hm. Didn't see this
coming from the
other side.
Me either.
Let's land here.
Boogie, give her
a good going-over. I
think she lost some
feathers.
Uuuuurrgh.
It's not just
me, right? This
place smells like
halitosis.
Are you sure Boogie's
not suffering from
gas again?

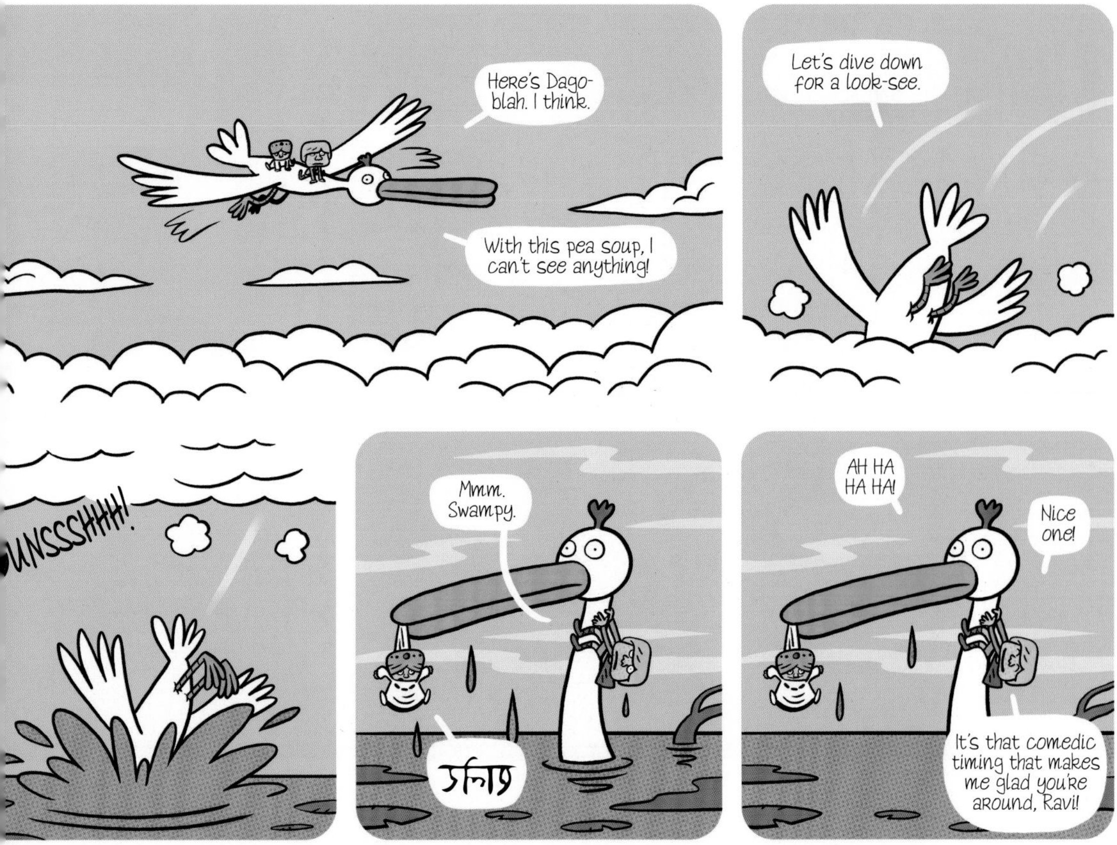
Here's Dago-
blah. I think.
With this pea soup, I
can't see anything!
Let's dive down
for a look-see.
UNSSSHHH!
Mmm.
Swampy.
AH HA
HA HA!
Nice
one!
It's that comedic
timing that makes
me glad you're
around, Ravi!

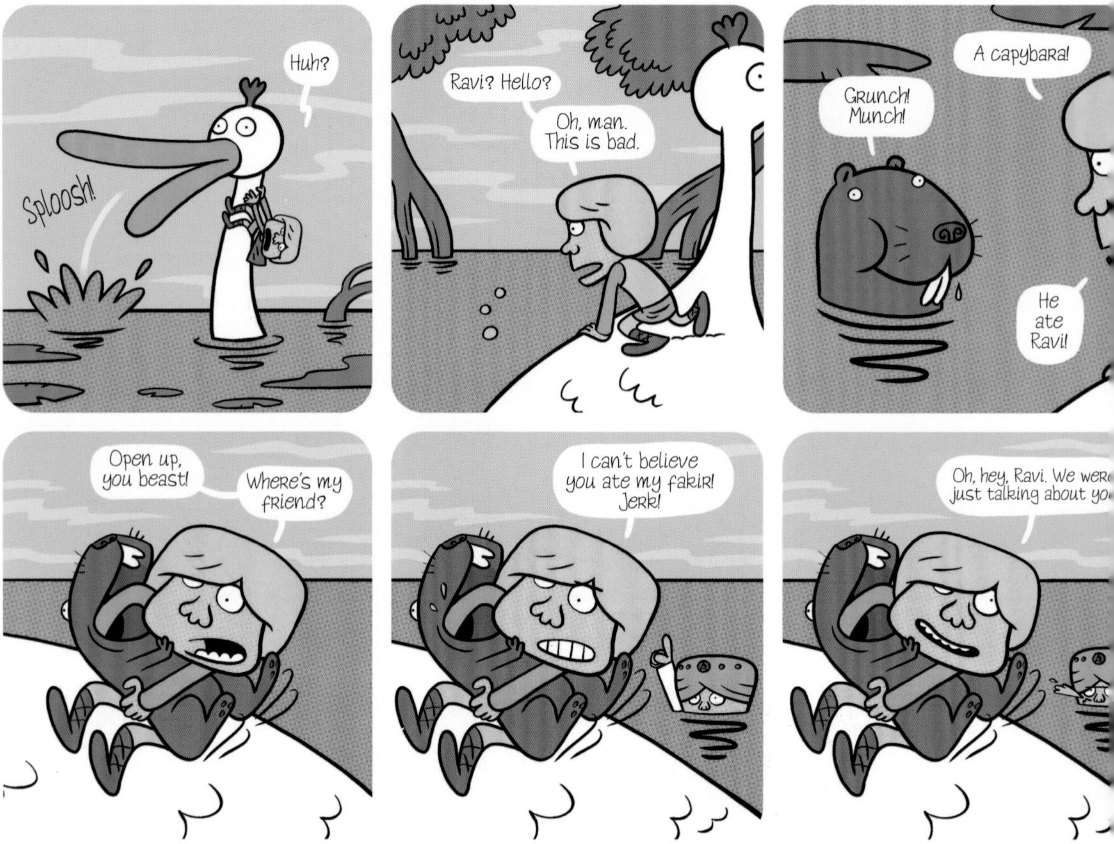
Huh?
Sploosh!
Ravi? Hello?
Oh, man. This is bad.
Grunch! Munch!
A capybara!
He ate Ravi!
Open up, you beast!
Where's my friend?
I can't believe you ate my fakir! Jerk!
Oh, hey, Ravi. We wer
just talking about yo

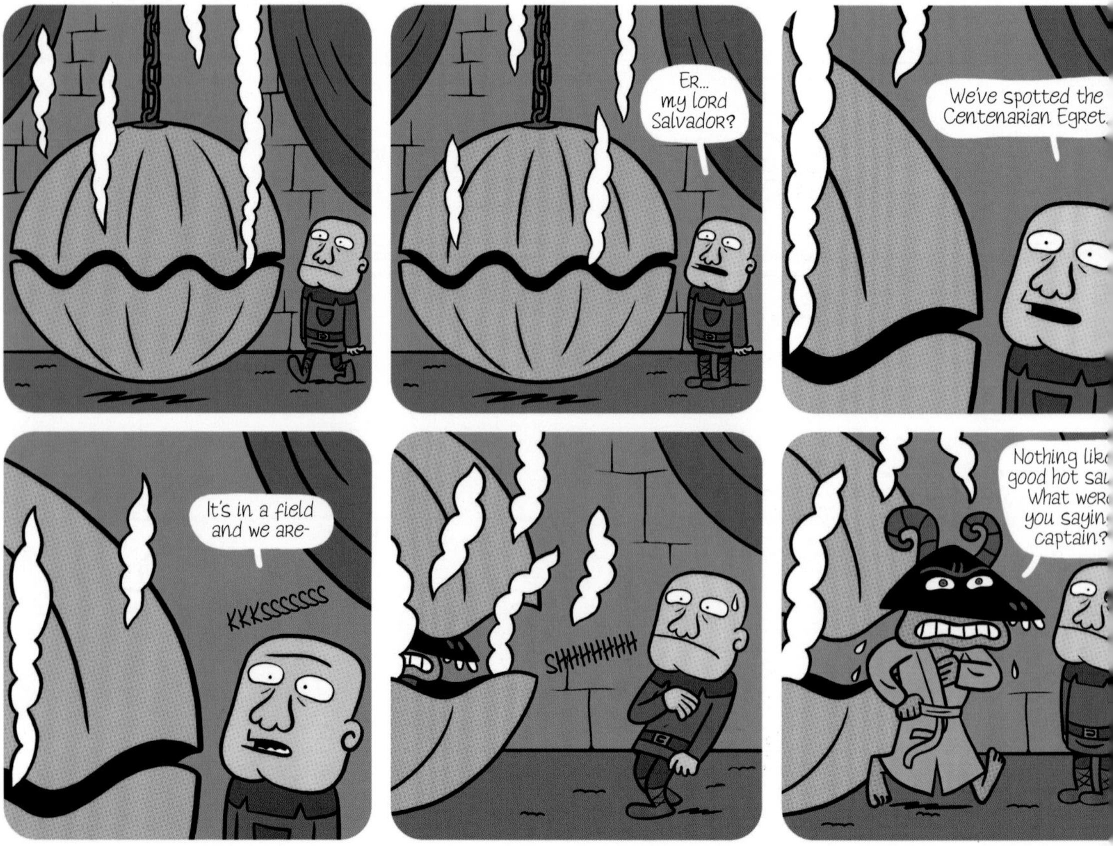
Er... my lord Salvador?
We've spotted the Centenarian Egret.
It's in a field and we are-
KKKSSSSSSS
SHHHHHHHH
Nothing lik
good hot sau
What wer
you sayin
captain?

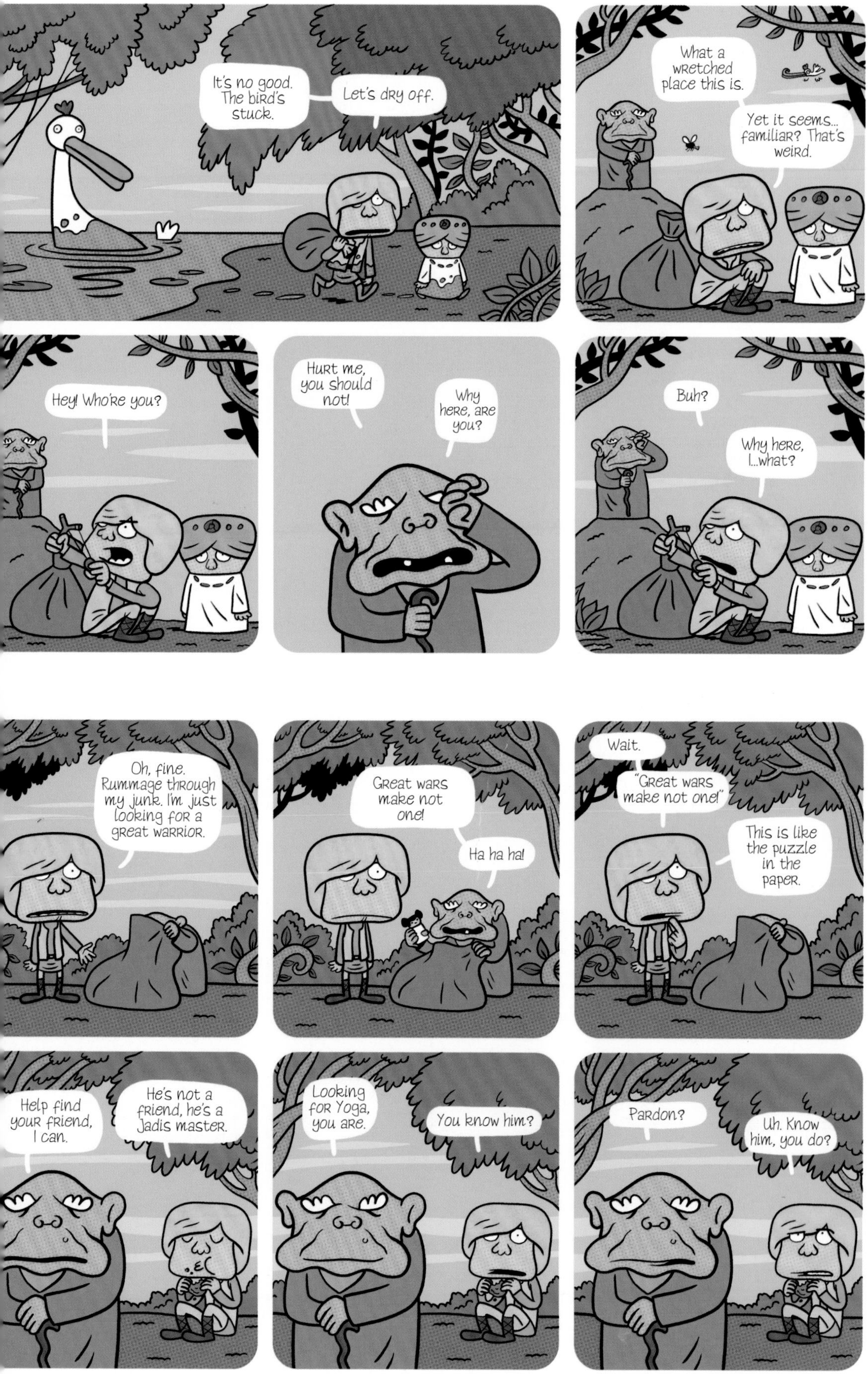

It's no good. The bird's stuck.
Let's dry off.
What a wretched place this is.
Yet it seems... familiar? That's weird.
Hey! Who're you?
Hurt me, you should not!
Why here, are you?
Buh?
Why here, I...what?
Oh, fine. Rummage through my junk. I'm just looking for a great warrior.
Great wars make not one!
Ha ha ha!
Wait.
"Great wars make not one!"
This is like the puzzle in the paper.
Help find your friend, I can.
He's not a friend, he's a Jadis master.
Looking for Yoga, you are.
You know him?
Pardon?
Uh. Know him, you do?

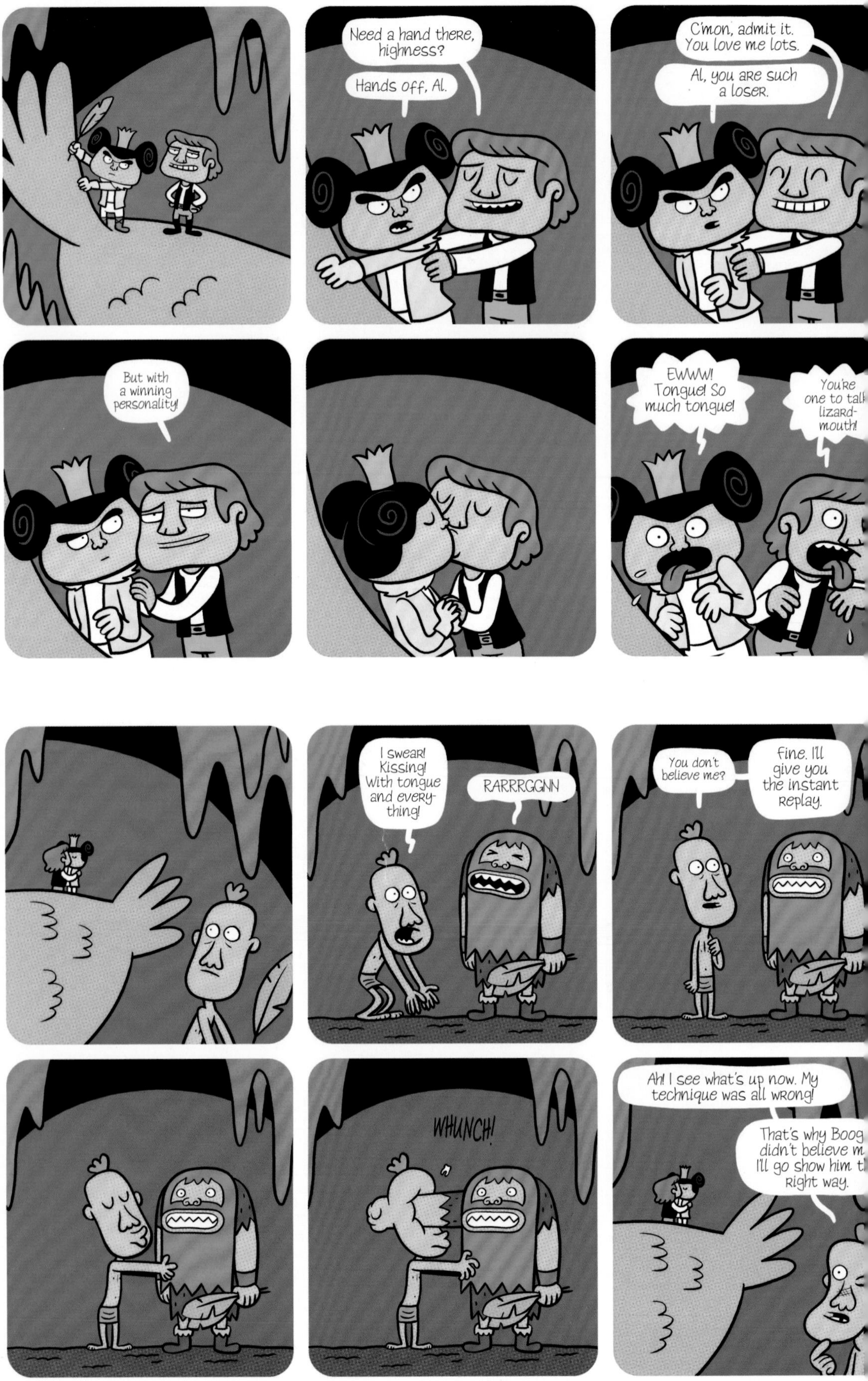
Need a hand there, highness?
Hands off, Al.
C'mon, admit it. You love me lots.
Al, you are such a loser.
But with a winning personality!
EWWW! Tongue! So much tongue!
You're one to tal lizard-mouth!
I swear! Kissing! With tongue and every-thing!
RARRRGGNN
You don't believe me?
Fine. I'll give you the instant Replay.
WHUNCH!
Ah! I see what's up now. My technique was all wrong!
That's why Boog didn't believe m I'll go show him t Right way.

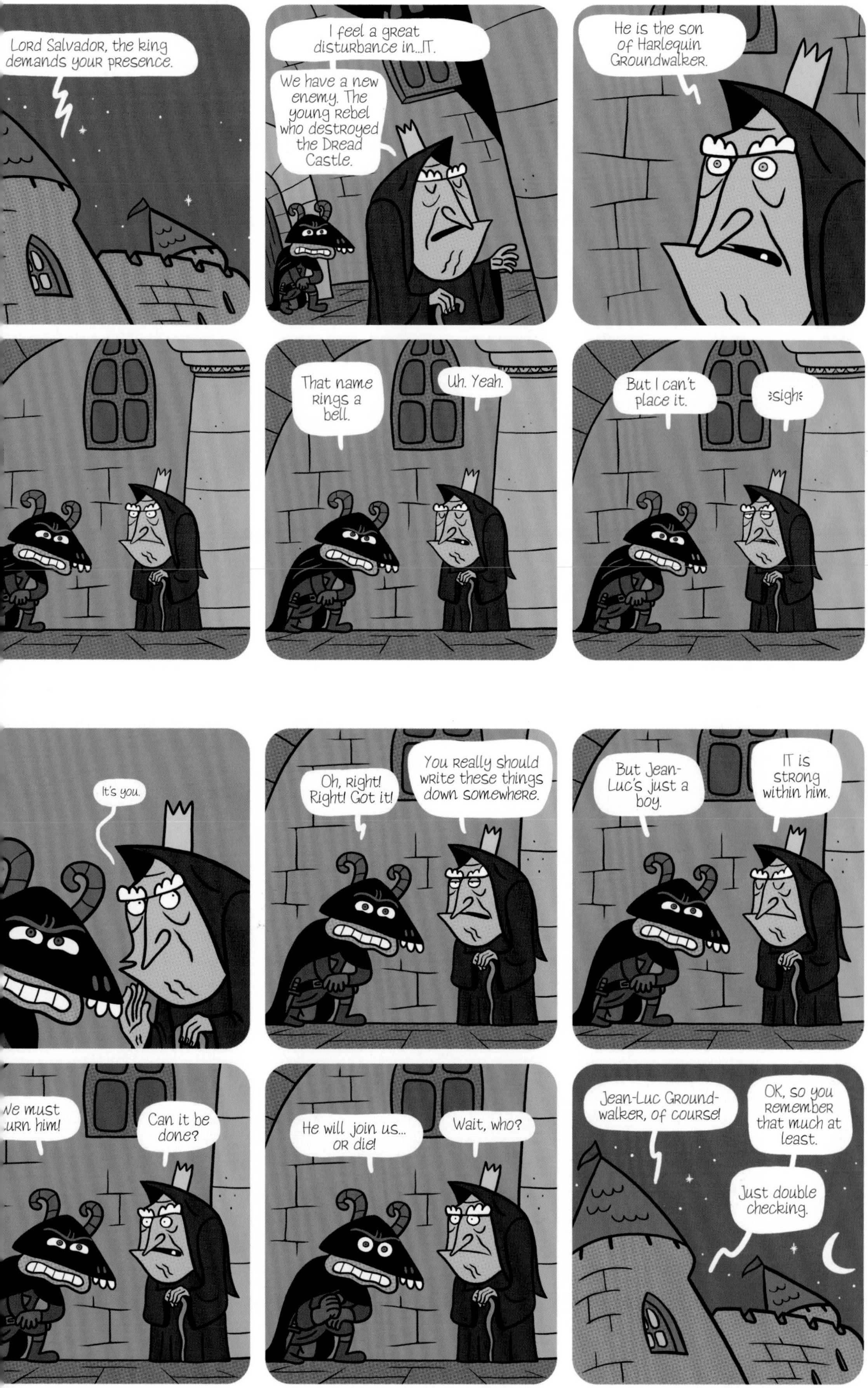
Lord Salvador, the king demands your presence.
I feel a great disturbance in...IT.
We have a new enemy. The young rebel who destroyed the Dread Castle.
He is the son of Harlequin Groundwalker.
That name rings a bell.
Uh. Yeah.
But I can't place it.
sigh
It's you.
Oh, right! Right! Got it!
You really should write these things down somewhere.
But Jean-Luc's just a boy.
IT is strong within him.
We must turn him!
Can it be done?
He will join us... or die!
Wait, who?
Jean-Luc Groundwalker, of course!
OK, so you remember that much at least.
Just double checking.

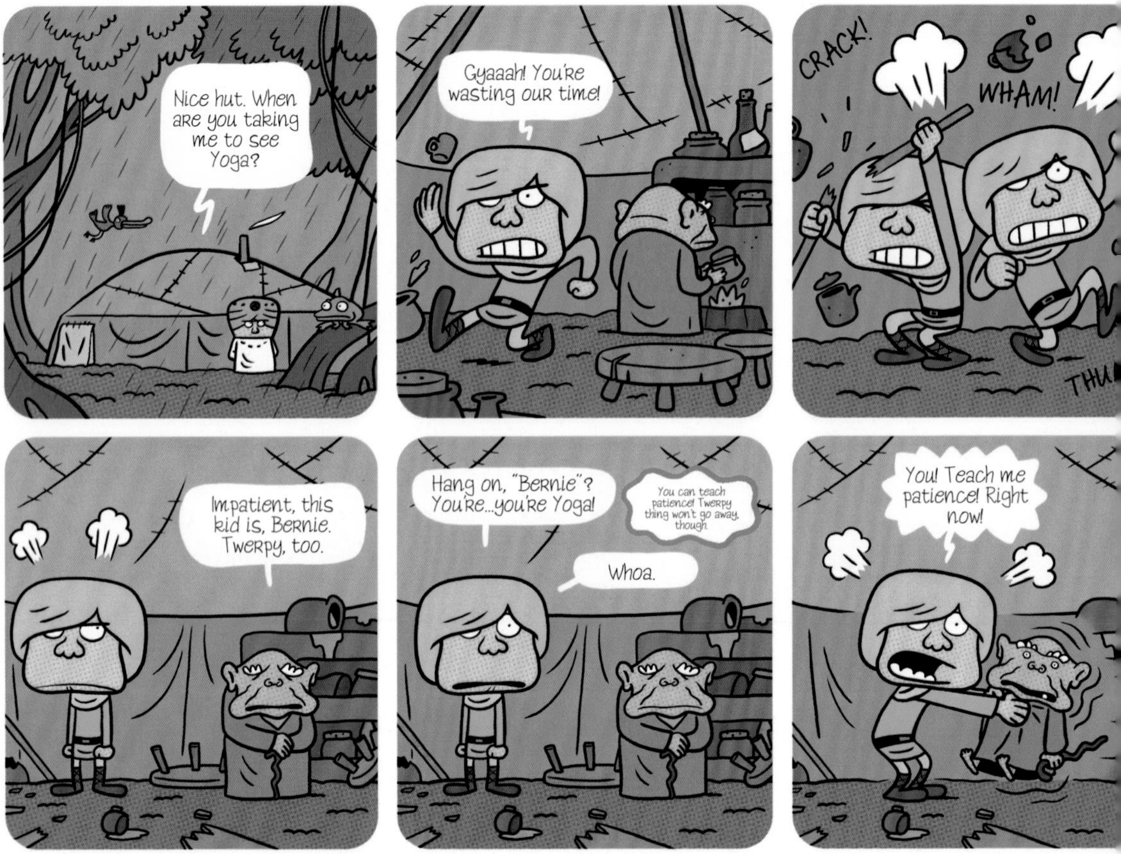
Nice hut. When are you taking me to see Yoga?
Gyaaah! You're wasting our time!
CRACK!
WHAM!
Impatient, this kid is, Bernie. Twerpy, too.
Hang on, "Bernie"? You're...you're Yoga!
You can teach patience! Twerpy thing won't go away, though.
Whoa.
You! Teach me patience! Right now!

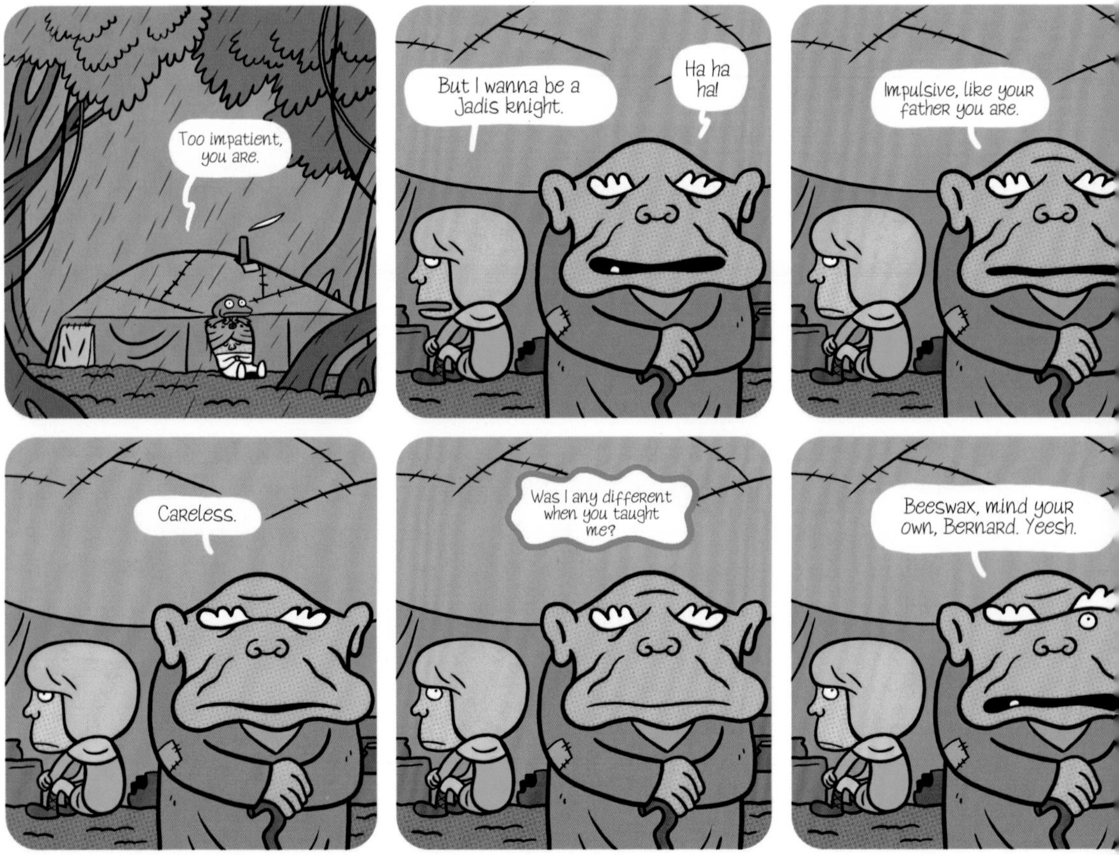
Too impatient, you are.
But I wanna be a Jadis knight.
Ha ha ha!
Impulsive, like your father you are.
Careless.
Was I any different when you taught me?
Beeswax, mind your own, Bernard. Yeesh.

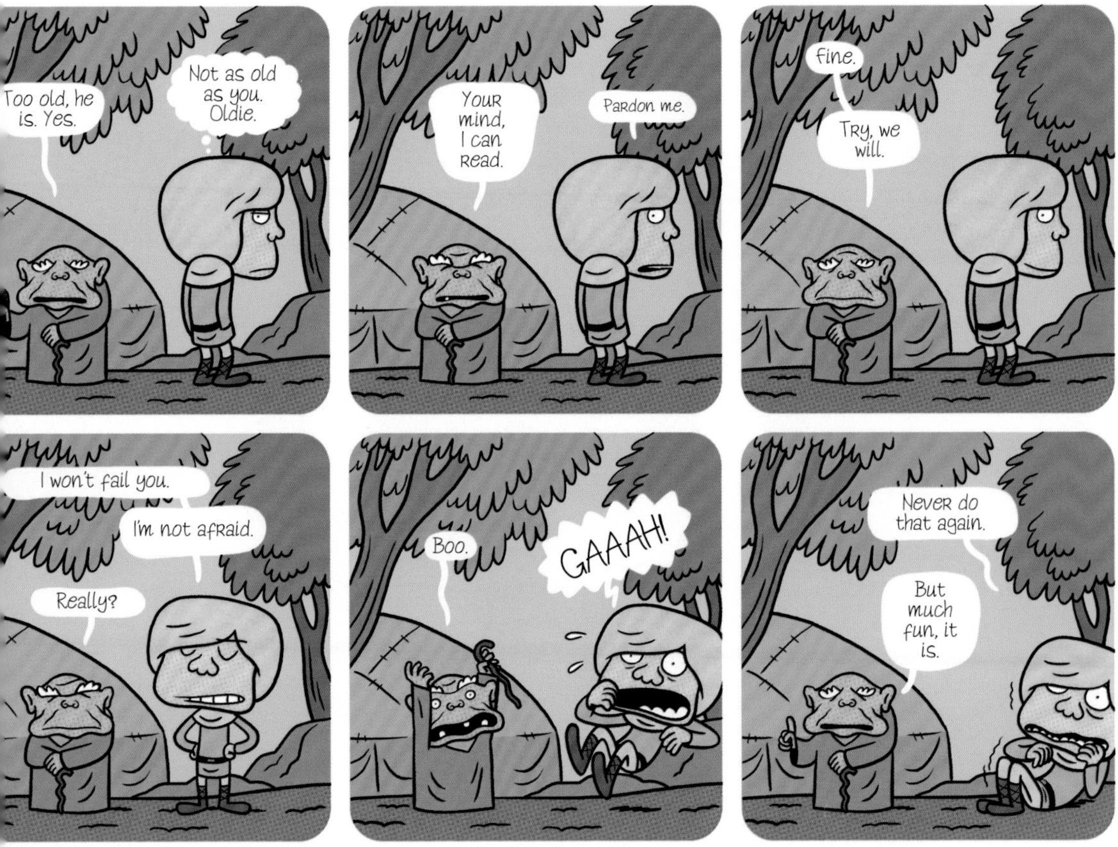
Too old, he is. Yes.
Not as old as you. Oldie.
Your mind, I can read.
Pardon me.
Fine.
Try, we will.
I won't fail you.
I'm not afraid.
Really?
Boo.
GAAAH!
Never do that again.
But much fun, it is.

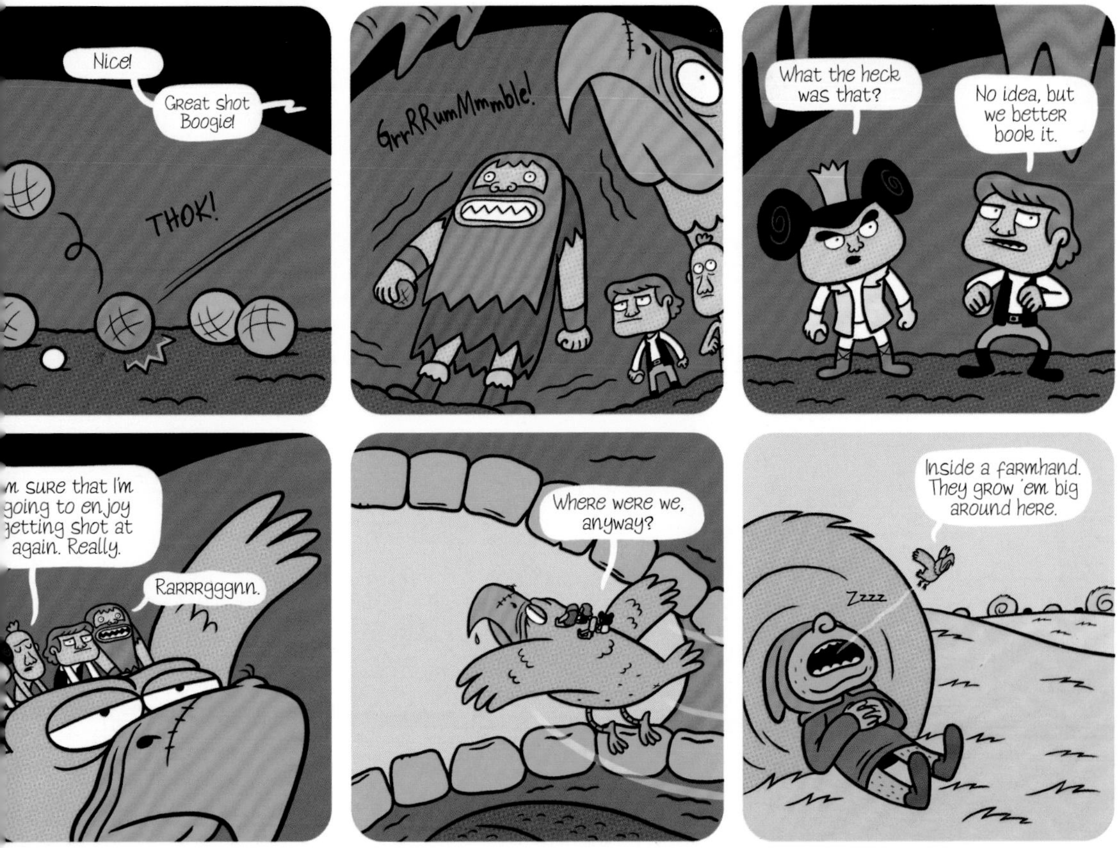
Nice!
Great shot Boogie!
THOK!
GrrRRumMmmble!
What the heck was that?
No idea, but we better book it.
m sure that I'm going to enjoy getting shot at again. Really.
Rarrrgggnn.
Where were we, anyway?
Zzzz
Inside a farmhand. They grow 'em big around here.

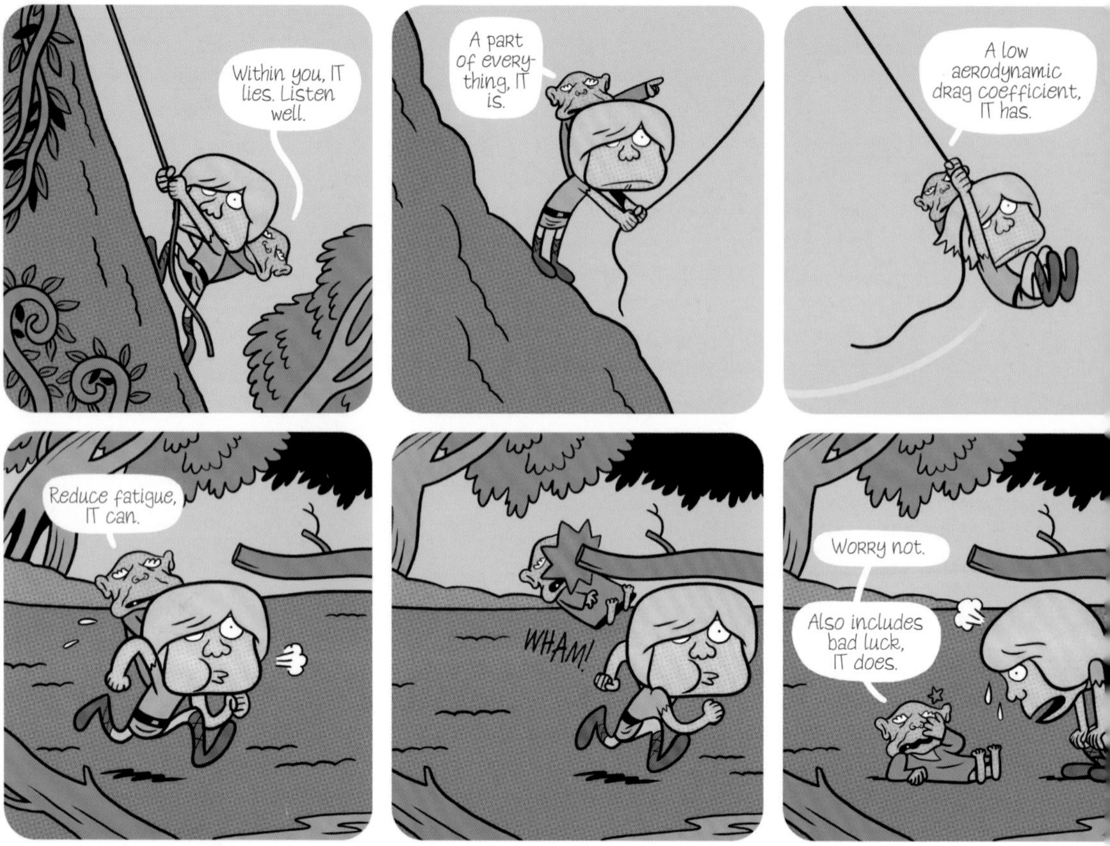
Within you, IT lies. Listen well.
A part of every-thing, IT is.
A low aerodynamic drag coefficient, IT has.
Reduce fatigue, IT can.
WHAM!
Worry not.
Also includes bad luck, IT does.

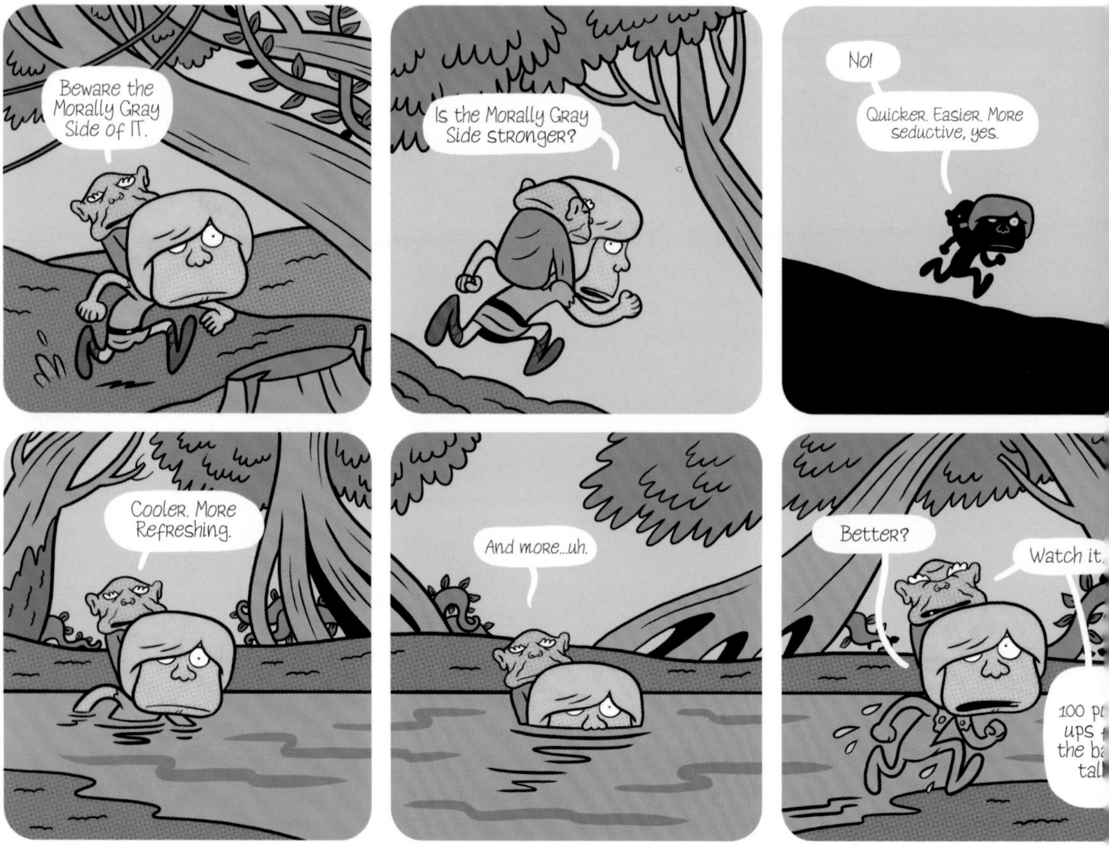
Beware the Morally Gray Side of IT.
Is the Morally Gray Side stronger?
No!
Quicker. Easier. More seductive, yes.
Cooler. More Refreshing.
And more...uh.
Better?
Watch it.

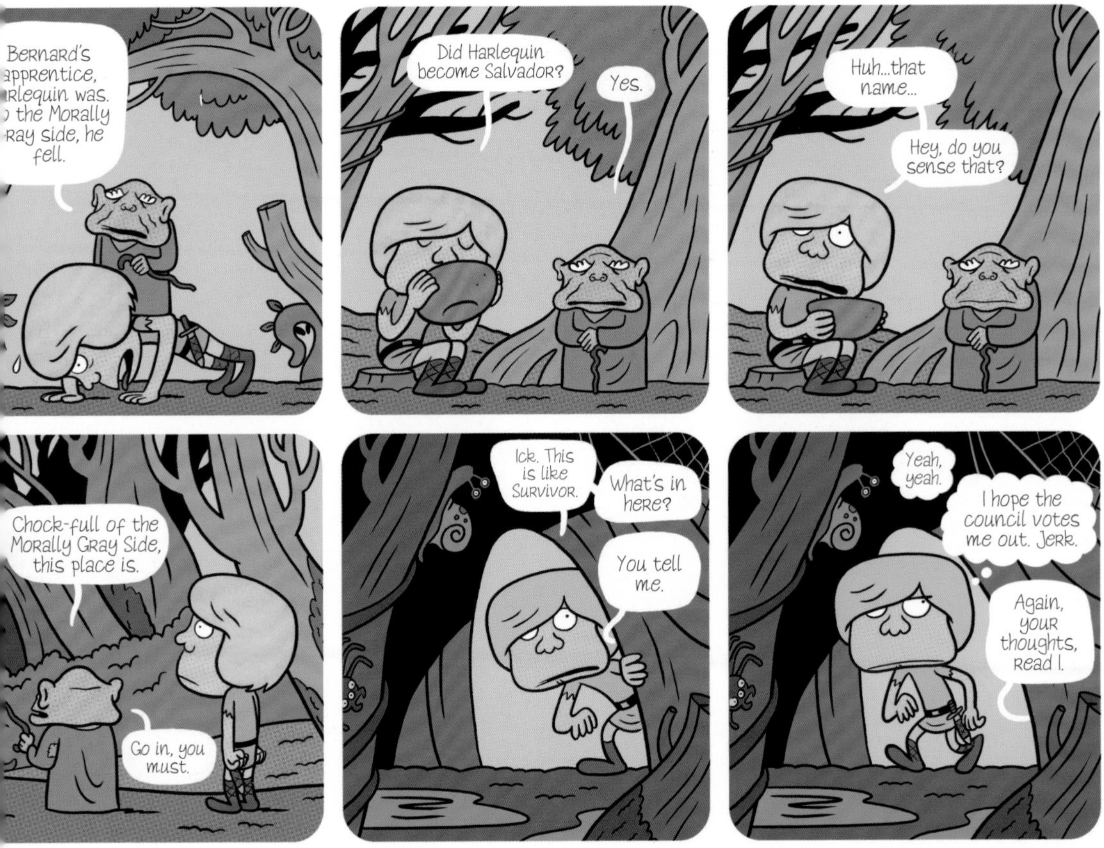
Bernard's
apprentice,
rlequin was.
the Morally
ray side, he
fell.
Did Harlequin
become Salvador?
Yes.
Huh...that
name...
Hey, do you
sense that?
Chock-full of the
Morally Gray Side,
this place is.
Go in, you
must.
Ick. This
is like
Survivor.
What's in
here?
You tell
me.
Yeah,
yeah.
I hope the
council votes
me out. Jerk.
Again,
your
thoughts,
Read I.

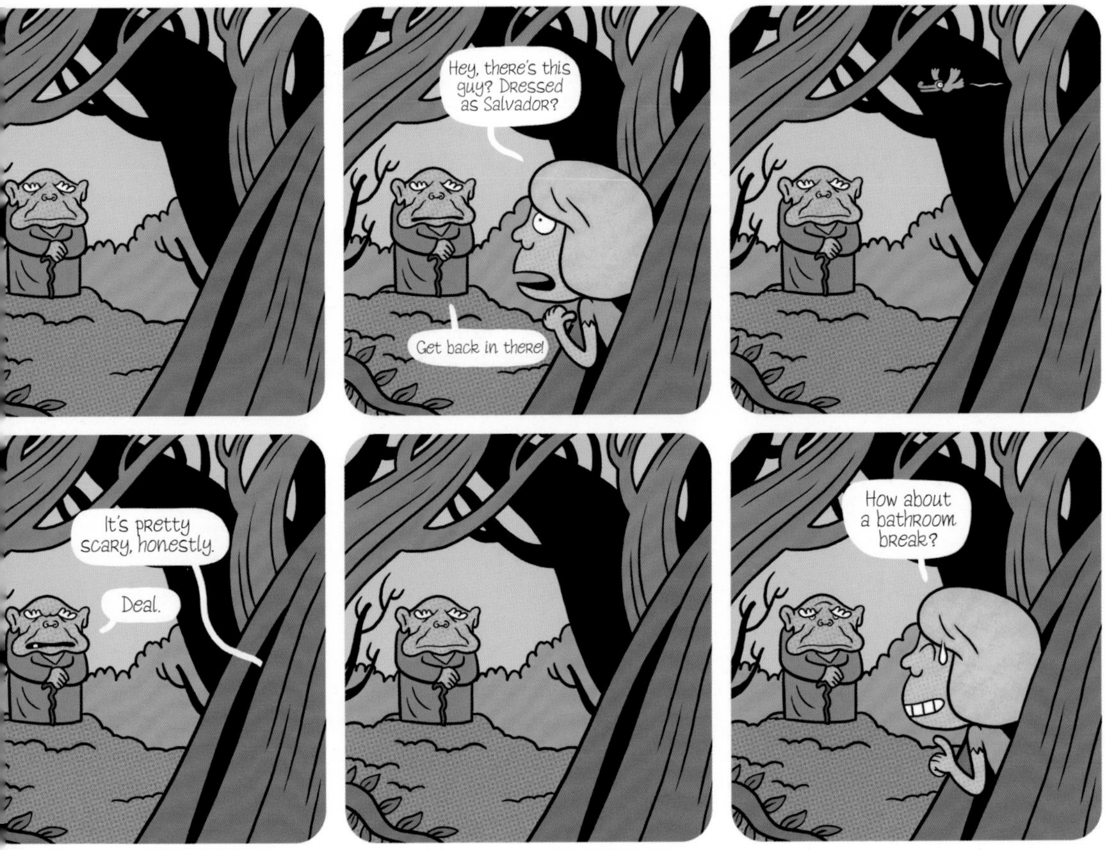
Hey, there's this
guy? Dressed
as Salvador?
Get back in there!
It's pretty
scary, honestly.
Deal.
How about
a bathroom
break?

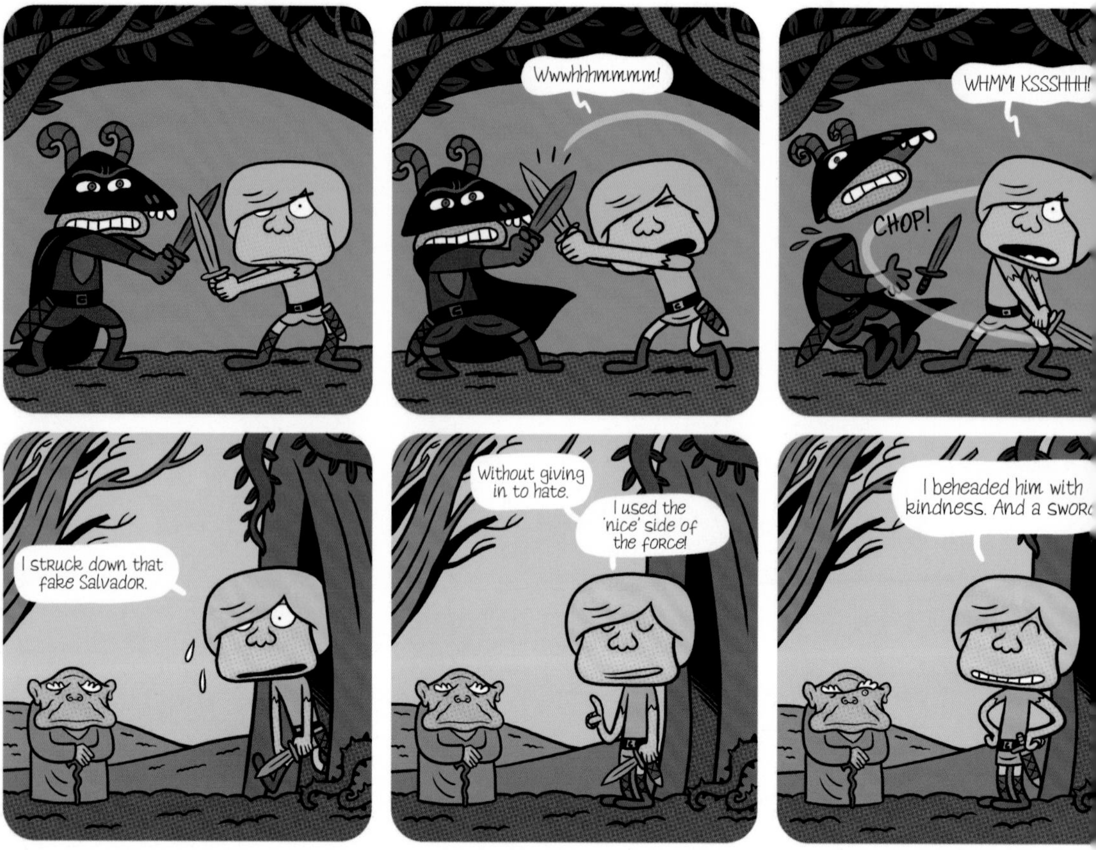
Wwwhhhmmmm!
WHMM! KSSSHHH!
CHOP!
I struck down that fake Salvador.
Without giving in to hate.
I used the 'nice' side of the force!
I beheaded him with kindness. And a SWOR

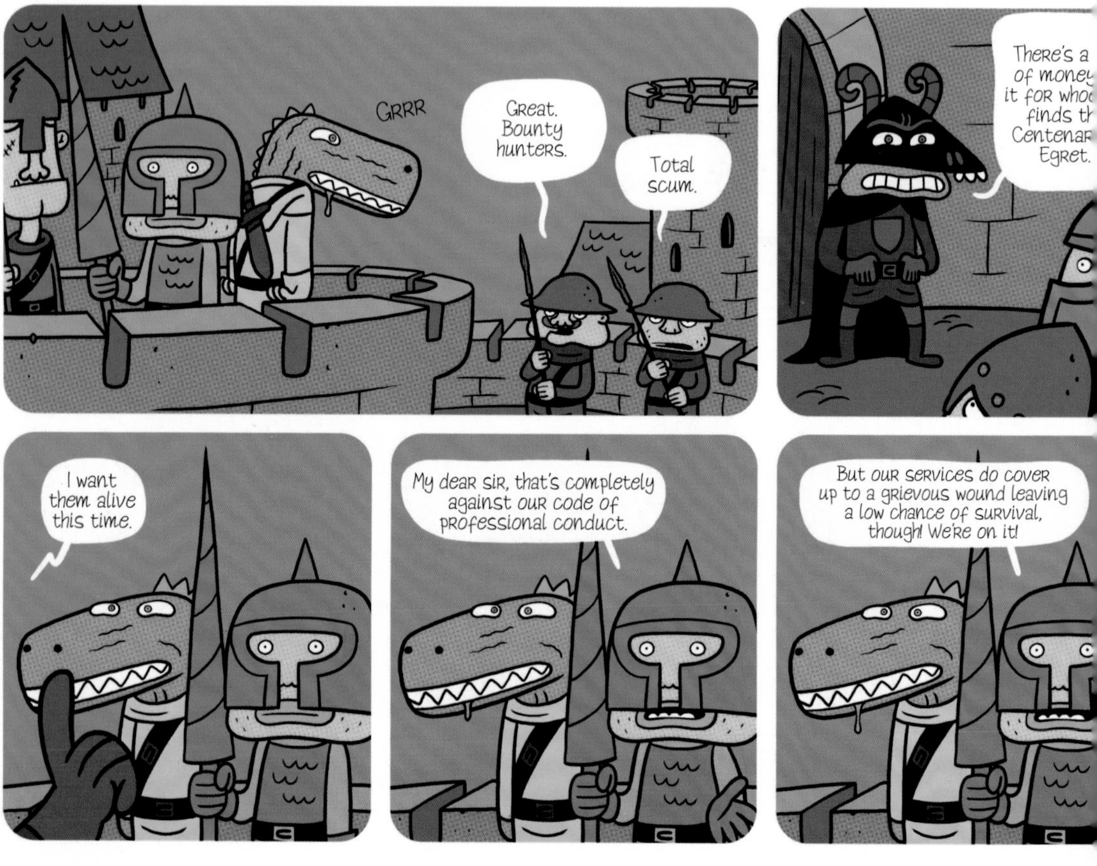
GRRR
Great. Bounty hunters.
Total scum.
There's a
of mone
it for wh
finds t
Centena
Egret.
I want them alive this time.
My dear sir, that's completely against our code of professional conduct.
But our services do cover up to a grievous wound leaving a low chance of survival, though! We're on it!

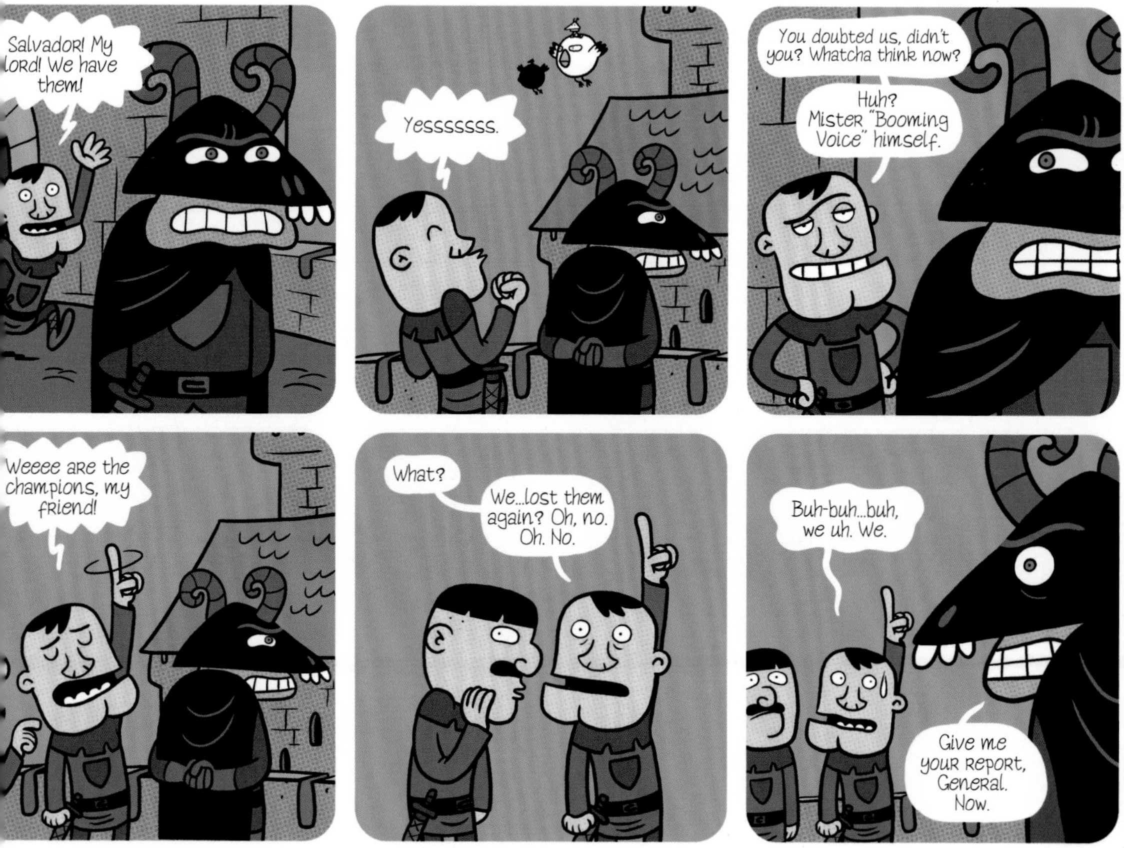
Salvador! My lord! We have them!
Yessssssss.
You doubted us, didn't you? Whatcha think now?
Huh? Mister "Booming Voice" himself.
Weeee are the champions, my friend!
What?
We...lost them again? Oh, no. Oh. No.
Buh-buh...buh, we uh. We.
Give me your report, General. Now.

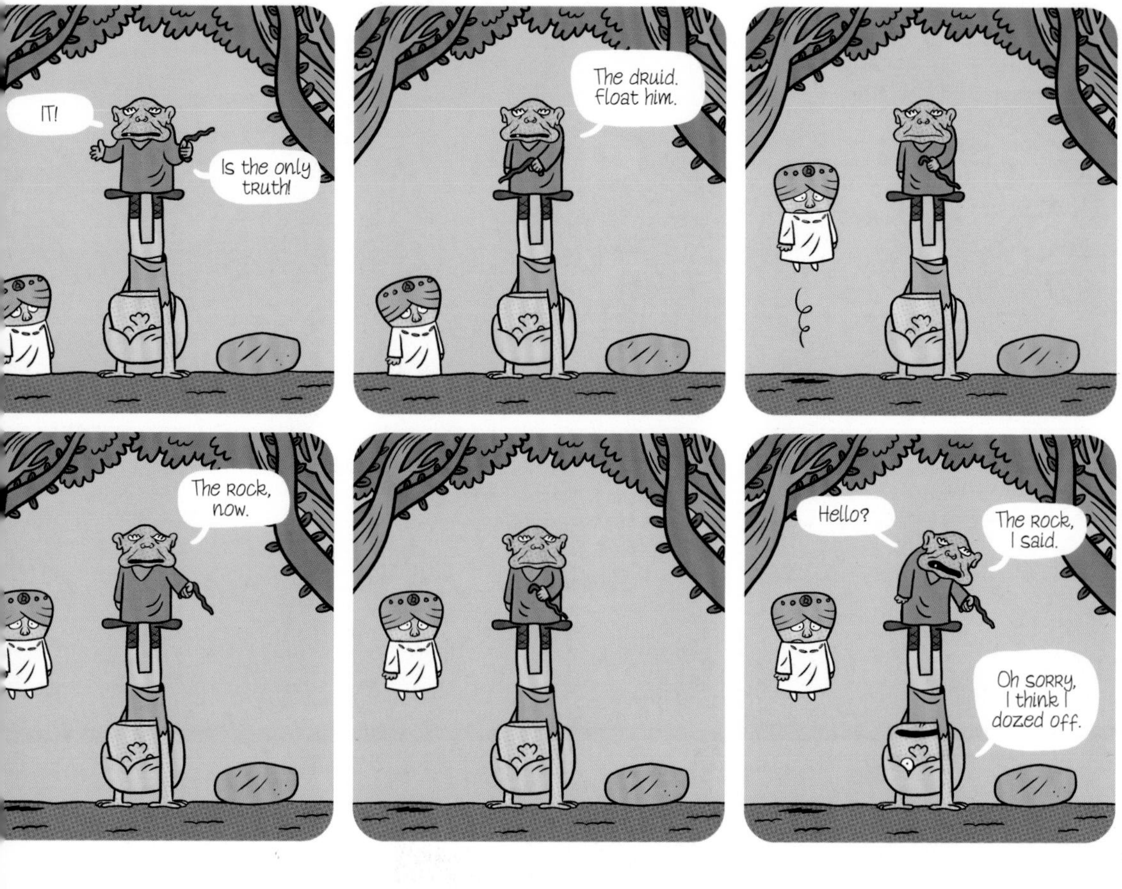
IT!
Is the only truth!
The druid. Float him.
The rock, now.
Hello?
The rock, I said.
Oh sorry, I think I dozed off.

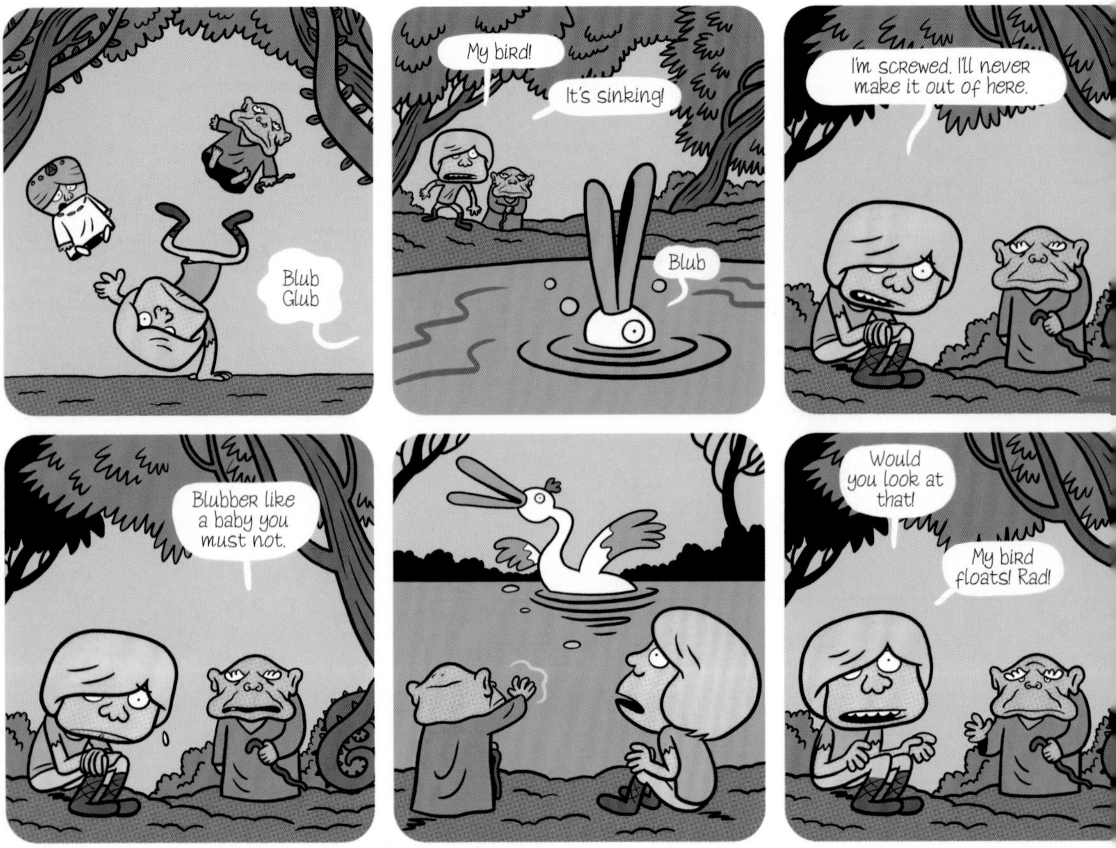
Blub
Glub
My bird!
It's sinking!
Blub
I'm screwed. I'll never make it out of here.
Blubber like a baby you must not.
Would you look at that!
My bird floats! Rad!

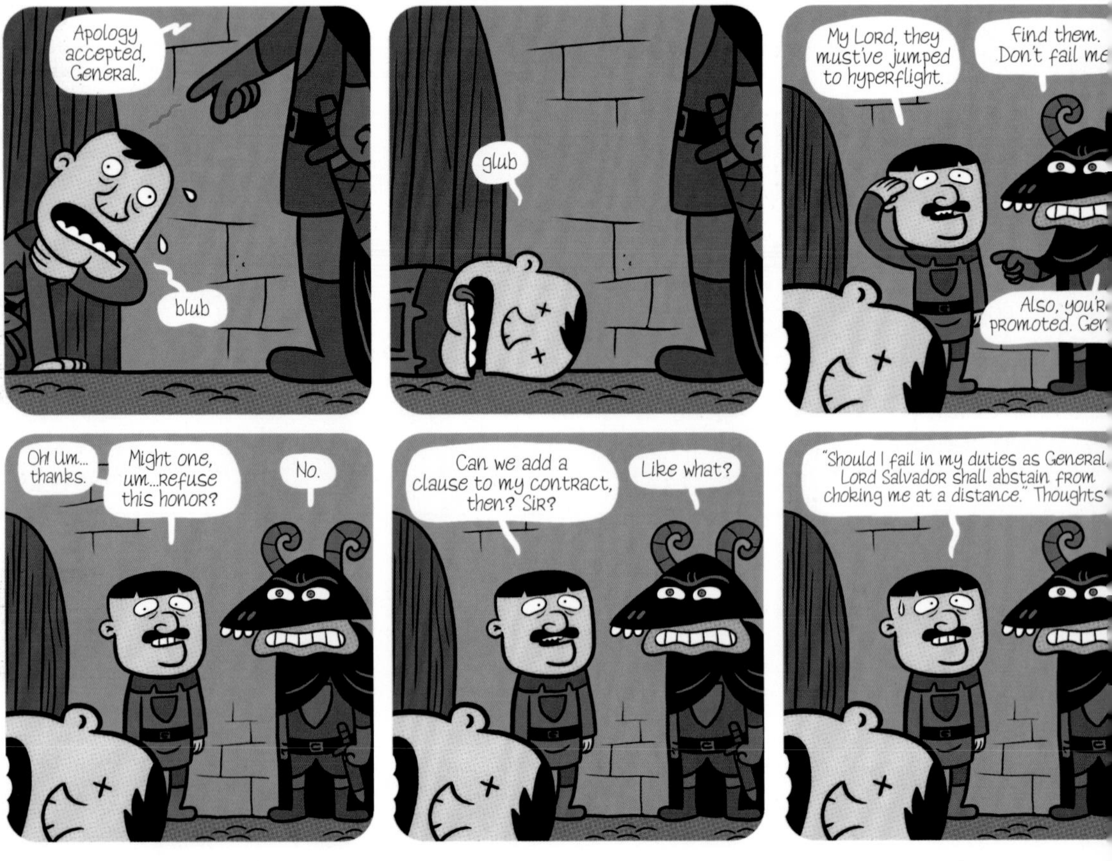
Apology accepted, General.
blub
glub
My Lord, they must've jumped to hyperflight.
Find them. Don't fail me
Also, you'r
promoted. Ge
Oh! Um... thanks.
Might one, um...refuse this honor?
No.
Can we add a clause to my contract, then? Sir?
Like what?
"Should I fail in my duties as General, Lord Salvador shall abstain from choking me at a distance." Thoughts

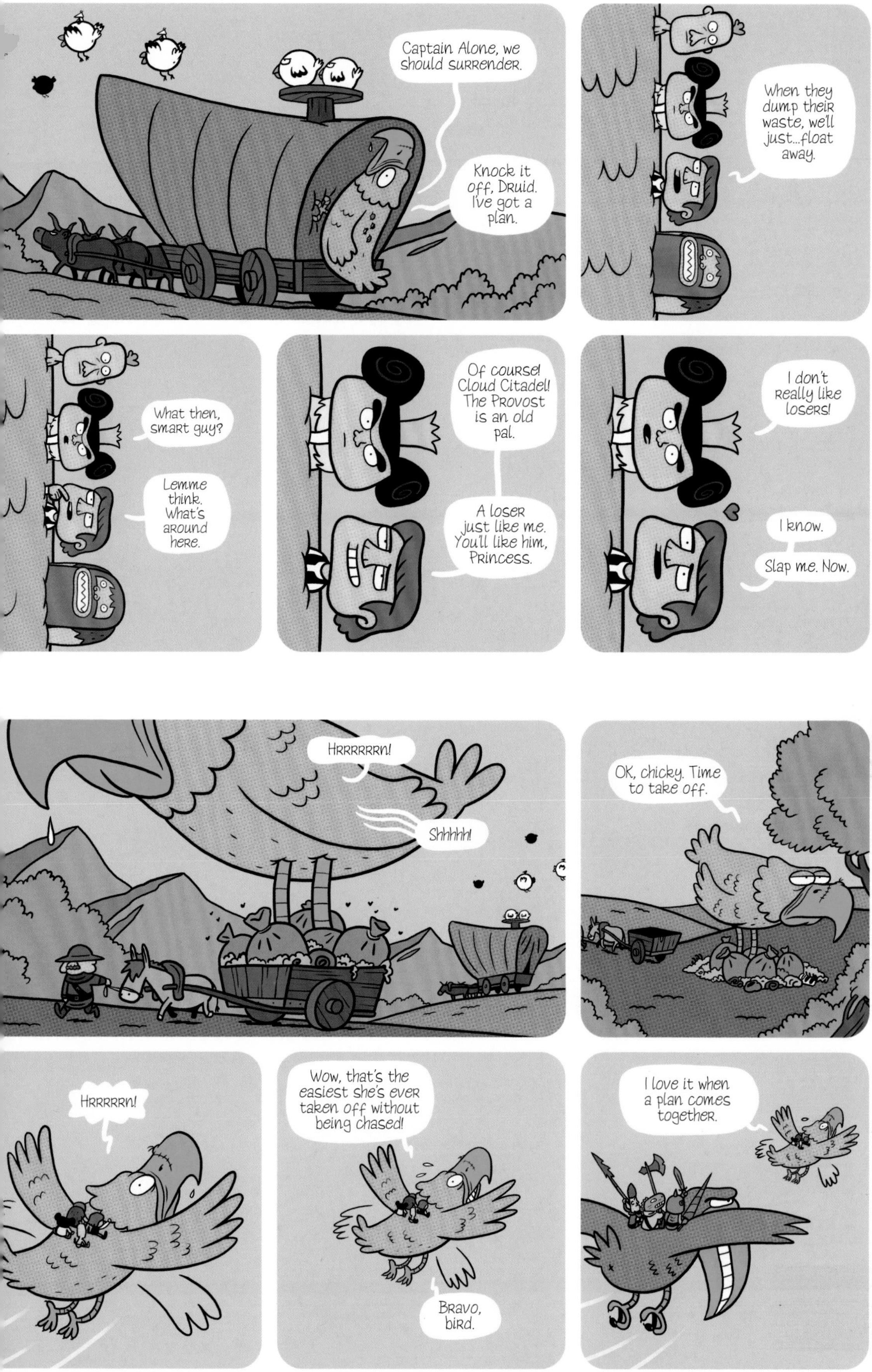
Captain Alone, we should surrender.
Knock it off, Druid. I've got a plan.
When they dump their waste, we'll just...float away.
What then, smart guy?
Lemme think. What's around here.
Of course! Cloud Citadel! The Provost is an old pal.
A loser just like me. You'll like him, Princess.
I don't really like losers!
I know.
Slap me. Now.
HRRRRRRN!
Shhhh!
OK, chicky. Time to take off.
HRRRRRN!
Wow, that's the easiest she's ever taken off without being chased!
Bravo, bird.
I love it when a plan comes together.

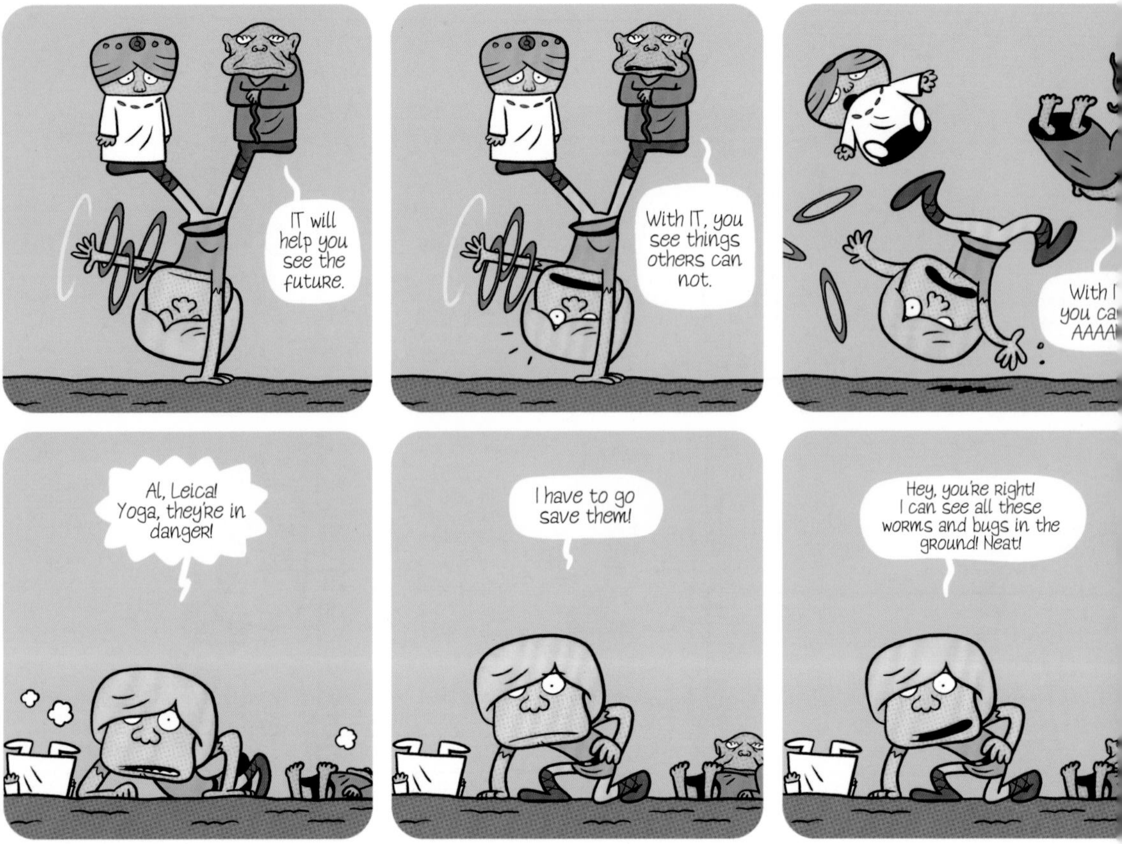
IT will help you see the future.
With IT, you see things others can not.
Al, Leica! Yoga, they're in danger!
I have to go save them!
Hey, you're right! I can see all these worms and bugs in the ground! Neat!

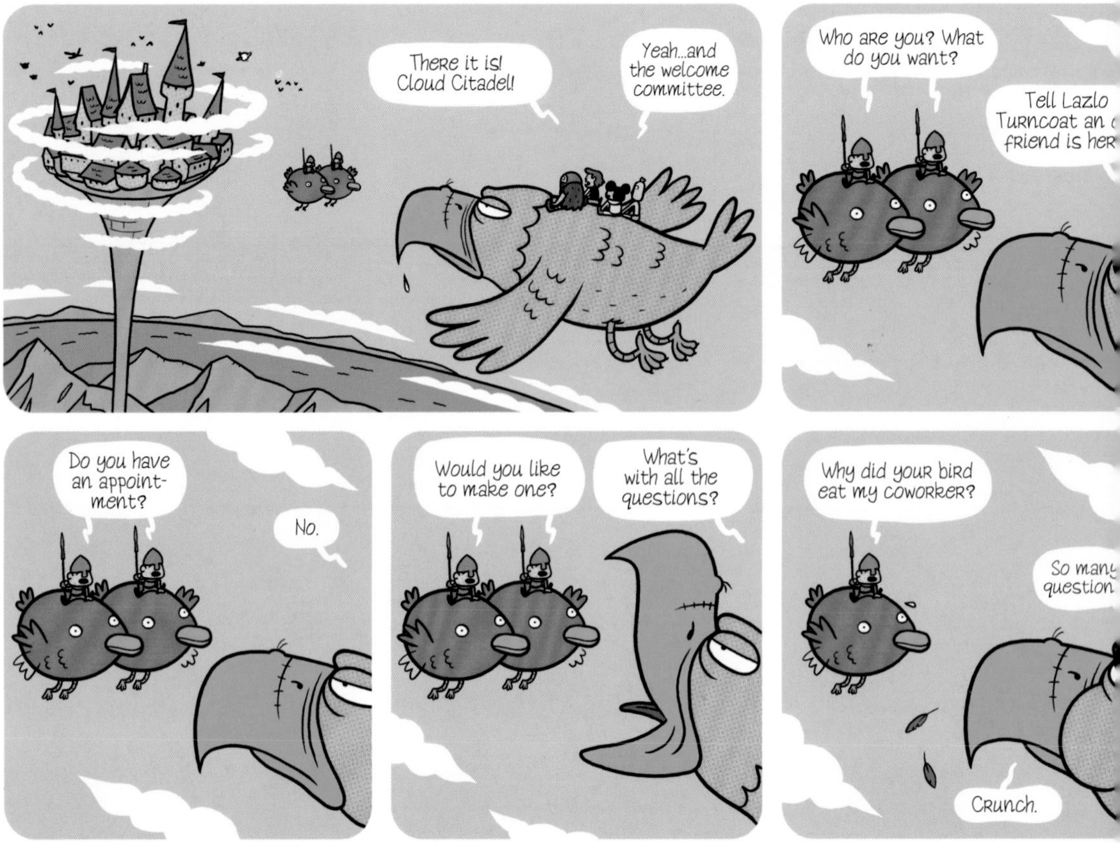
There it is! Cloud Citadel!
Yeah...and the welcome committee.
Who are you? What do you want?
Tell Lazlo
Do you have an appoint-ment?
No.
Would you like to make one?
What's with all the questions?
Why did your bird eat my coworker?
Crunch.

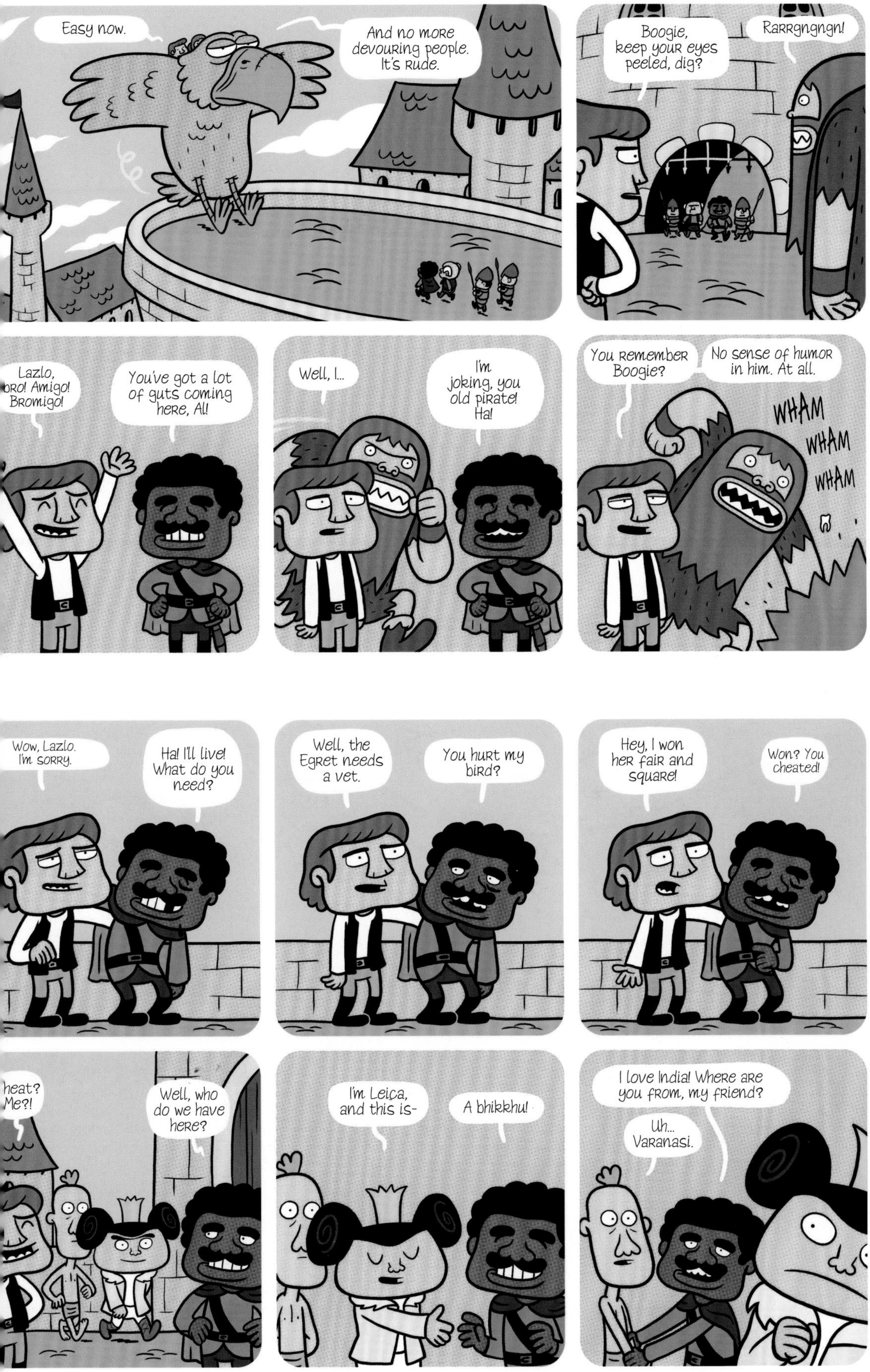
Easy now.
And no more devouring people. It's rude.
Boogie, keep your eyes peeled, dig?
Rarrgngngn!
Lazlo, ...ro! Amigo! Bromigo!
You've got a lot of guts coming here, Al!
Well, I...
I'm joking, you old pirate! Ha!
You remember Boogie?
No sense of humor in him. At all.
WHAM
WHAM
WHAM
Wow, Lazlo. I'm sorry.
Ha! I'll live! What do you need?
Well, the Egret needs a vet.
You hurt my bird?
Hey, I won her fair and square!
Won? You cheated!
...heat? Me?!
Well, who do we have here?
I'm Leica, and this is-
A bhikkhu!
I love India! Where are you from, my friend?
Uh... Varanasi.

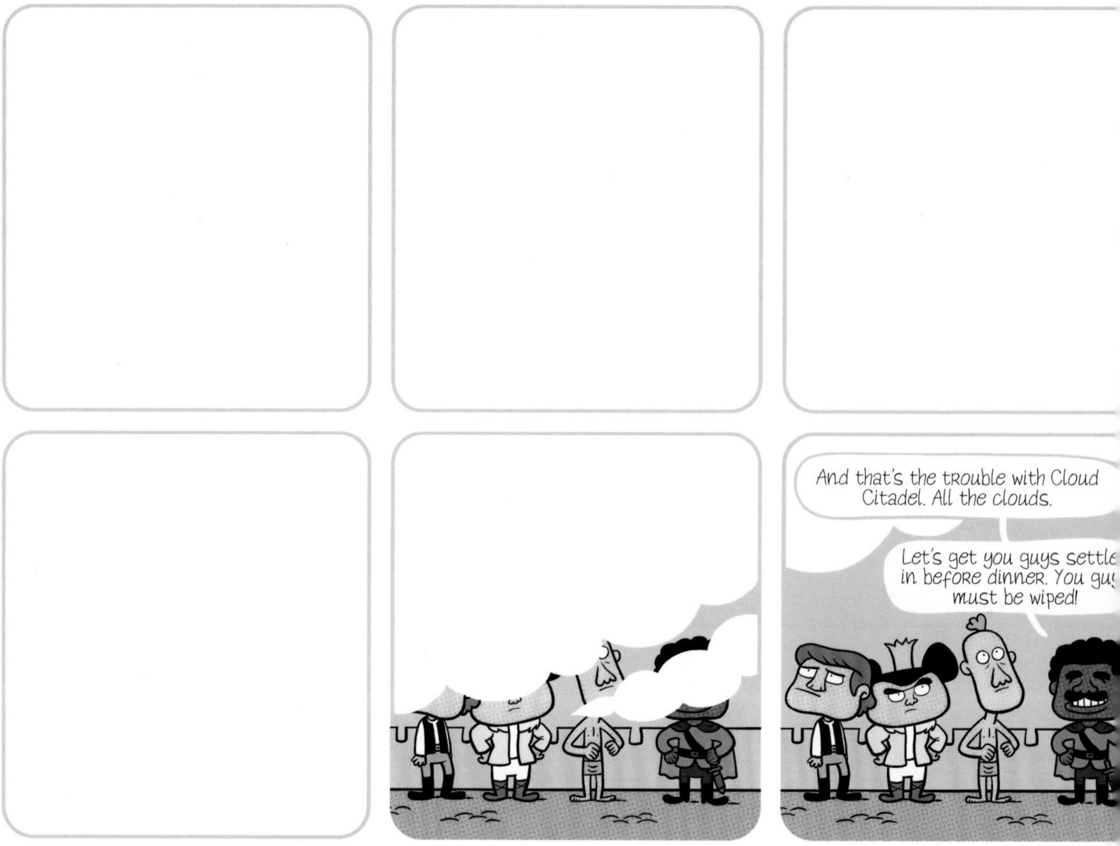
And that's the trouble with Cloud Citadel. All the clouds.
Let's get you guys settle in before dinner. You gu must be wiped!

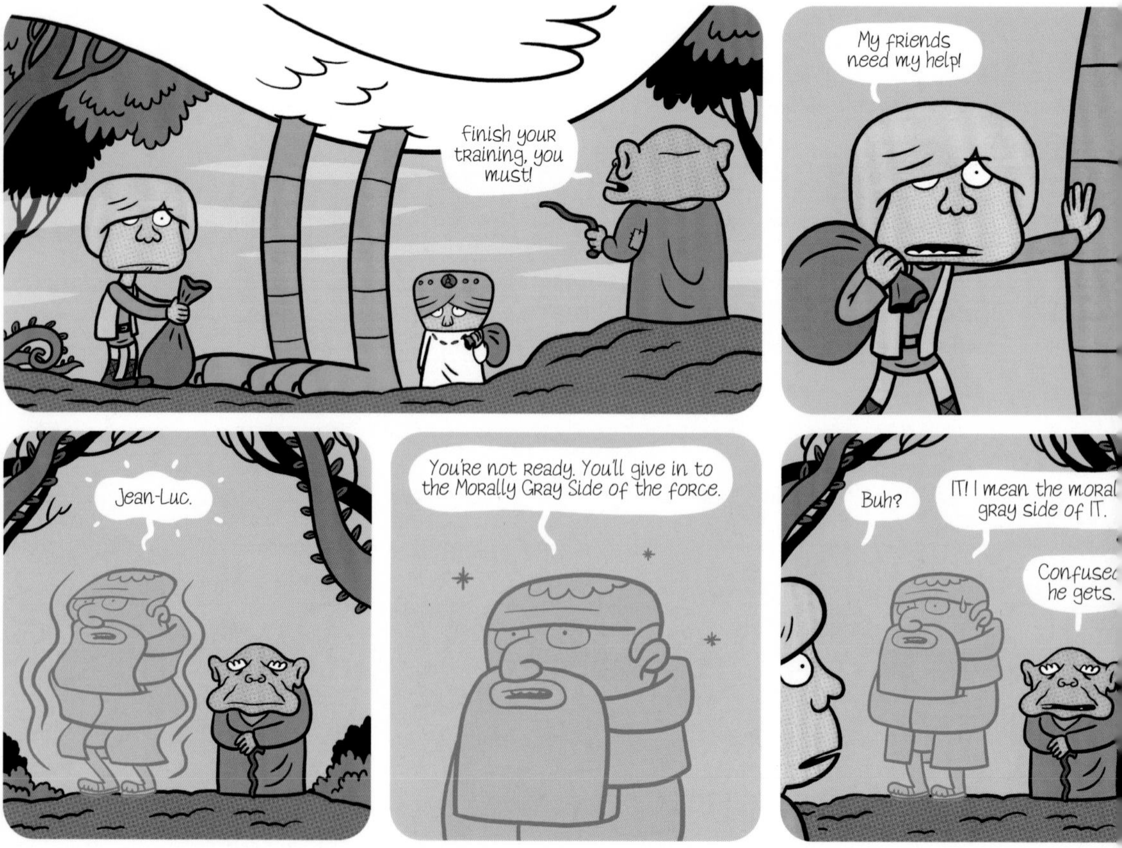
Finish your training, you must!
My friends need my help!
Jean-Luc.
You're not ready. You'll give in to the Morally Gray Side of the force.
Buh?
IT! I mean the moral gray side of IT.
Confusec he gets.

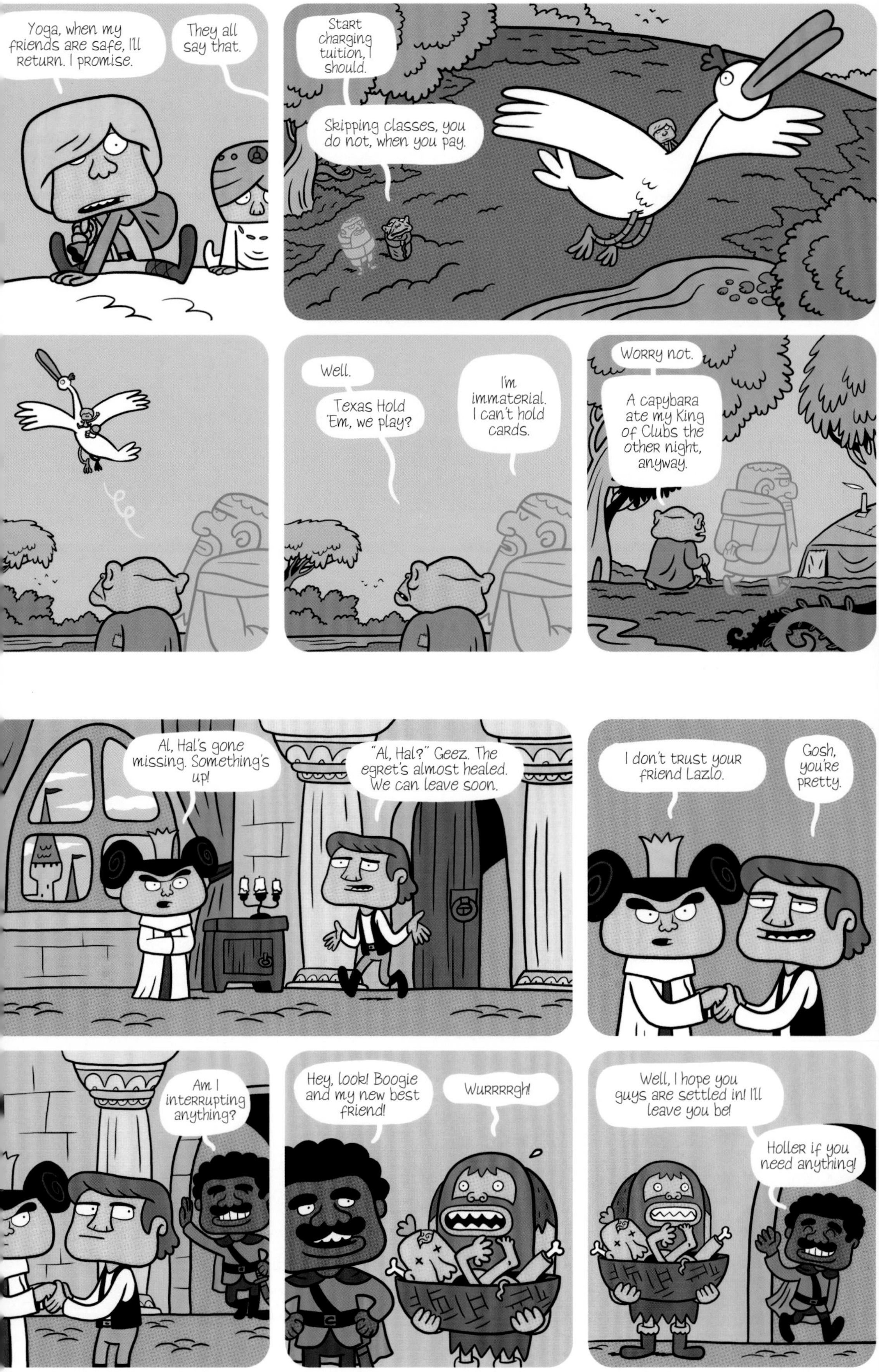
Yoga, when my friends are safe, I'll return. I promise.
They all say that.
Start charging tuition, I should.
Skipping classes, you do not, when you pay.
Well.
Texas Hold 'Em, we play?
I'm immaterial. I can't hold cards.
Worry not.
A capybara ate my King of Clubs the other night, anyway.
Al, Hal's gone missing. Something's up!
"Al, Hal?" Geez. The egret's almost healed. We can leave soon.
I don't trust your friend Lazlo.
Gosh, you're pretty.
Am I interrupting anything?
Hey, look! Boogie and my new best friend!
Wurrrrgh!
Well, I hope you guys are settled in! I'll leave you be!
Holler if you need anything!

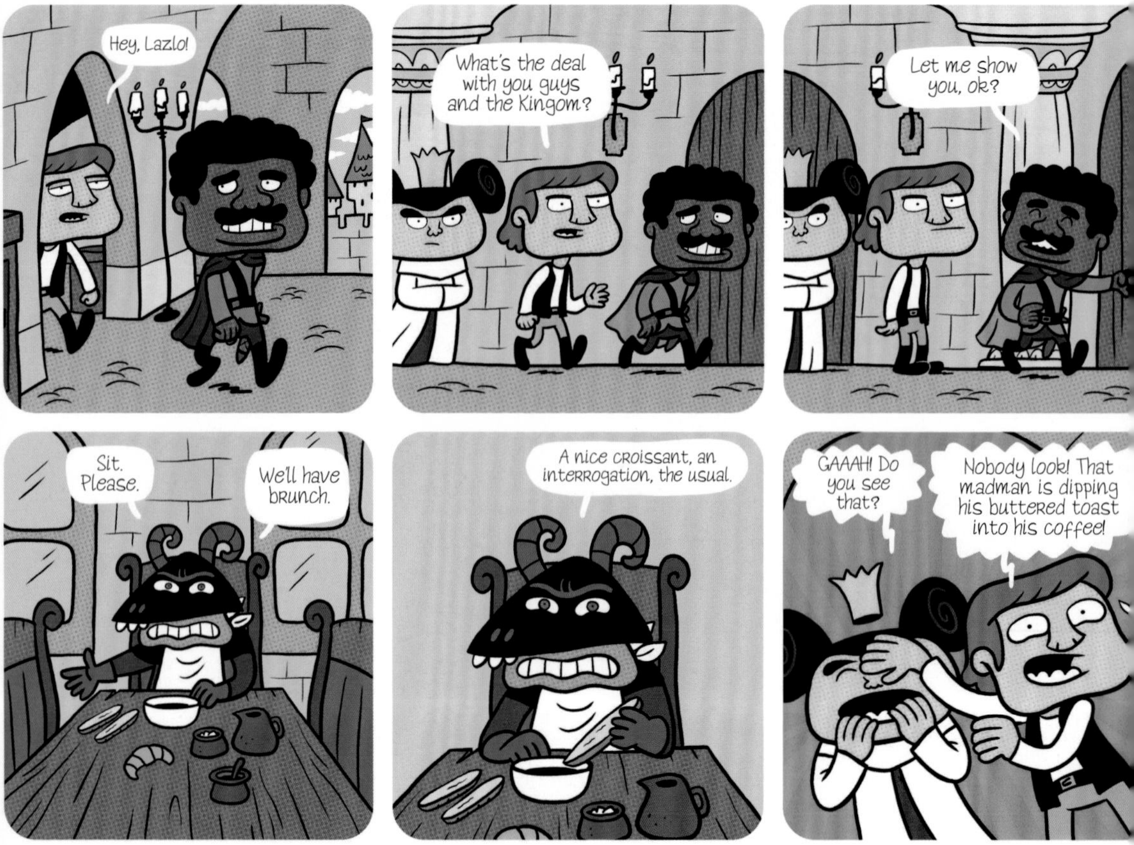
Hey, Lazlo!
What's the deal with you guys and the Kingom?
Let me show you, ok?
Sit. Please.
We'll have brunch.
A nice croissant, an interrogation, the usual.
GAAAH! Do you see that?
Nobody look! That madman is dipping his buttered toast into his coffee!

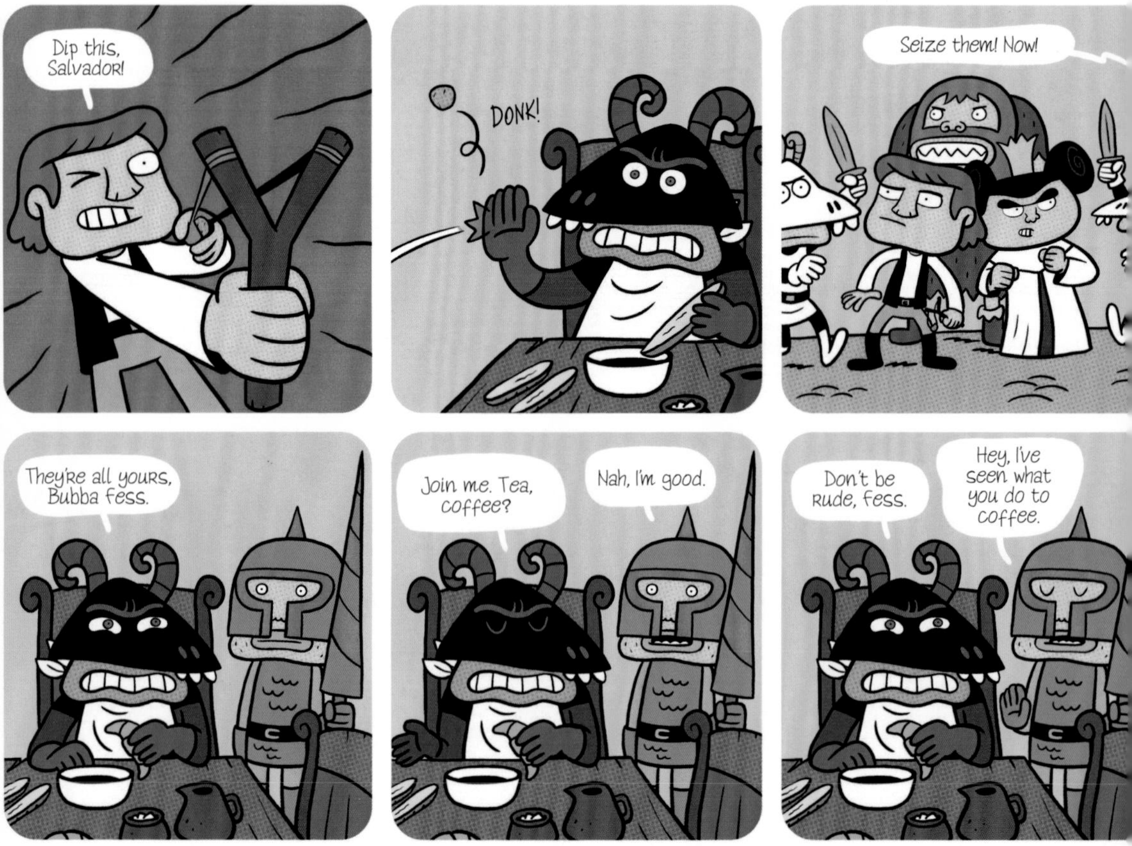
Dip this, Salvador!
DONK!
Seize them! Now!
They're all yours, Bubba Fess.
Join me. Tea, coffee?
Nah, I'm good.
Don't be rude, Fess.
Hey, I've seen what you do to coffee.

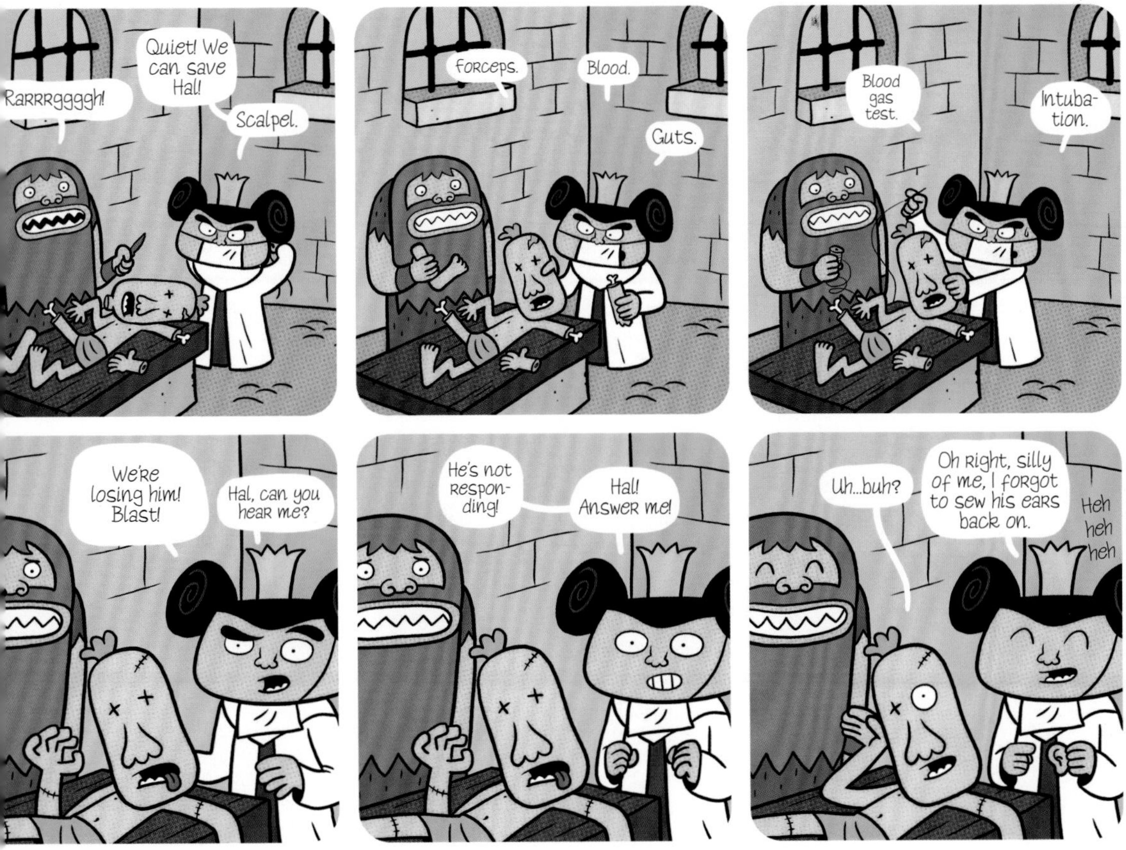
Rarrrggggh!
Quiet! We can save Hal!
Scalpel.
Forceps.
Blood.
Guts.
Blood gas test.
Intuba-tion.
We're losing him! Blast!
Hal, can you hear me?
He's not respon-ding!
Hal! Answer me!
Uh...buh?
Oh right, silly of me, I forgot to sew his ears back on.
Heh heh heh

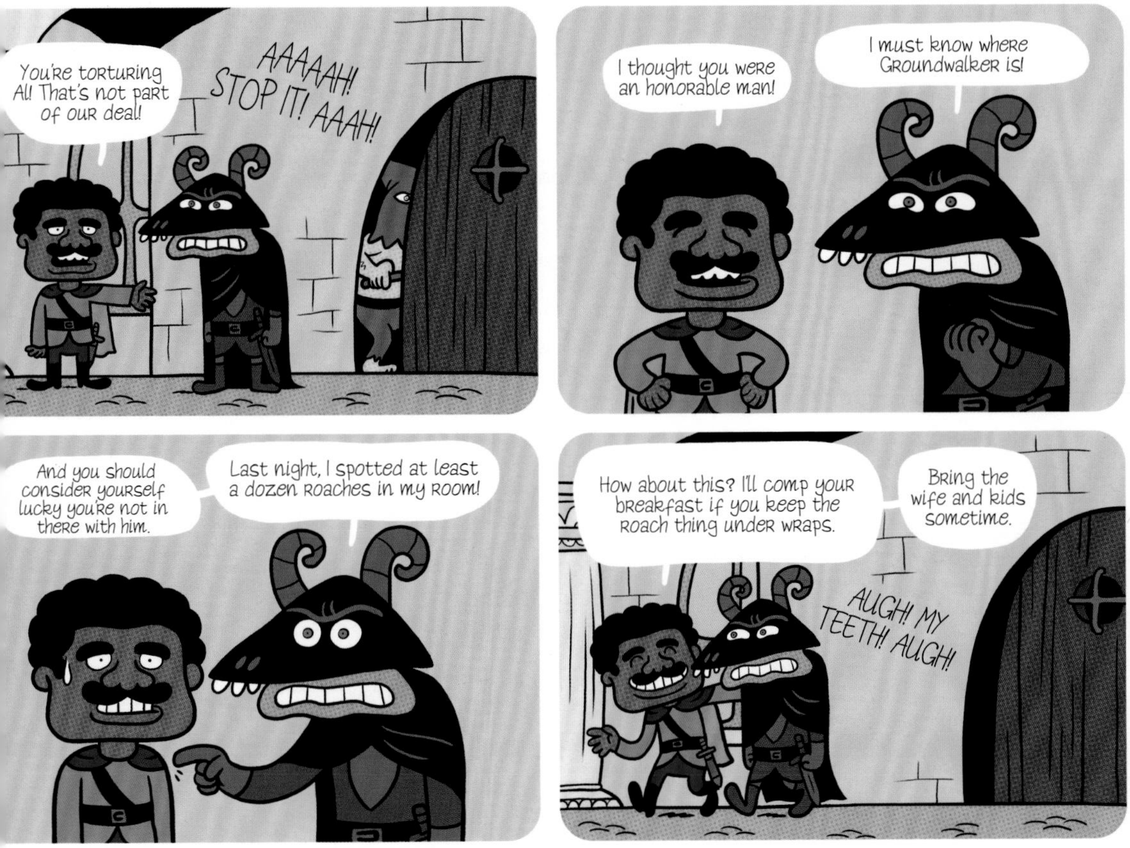
You're torturing Al! That's not part of our deal!
AAAAAH! STOP IT! AAAH!
I thought you were an honorable man!
I must know where Groundwalker is!
And you should consider yourself lucky you're not in there with him.
Last night, I spotted at least a dozen roaches in my room!
How about this? I'll comp your breakfast if you keep the roach thing under wraps.
Bring the wife and kids sometime.
AUGH! MY TEETH! AUGH!

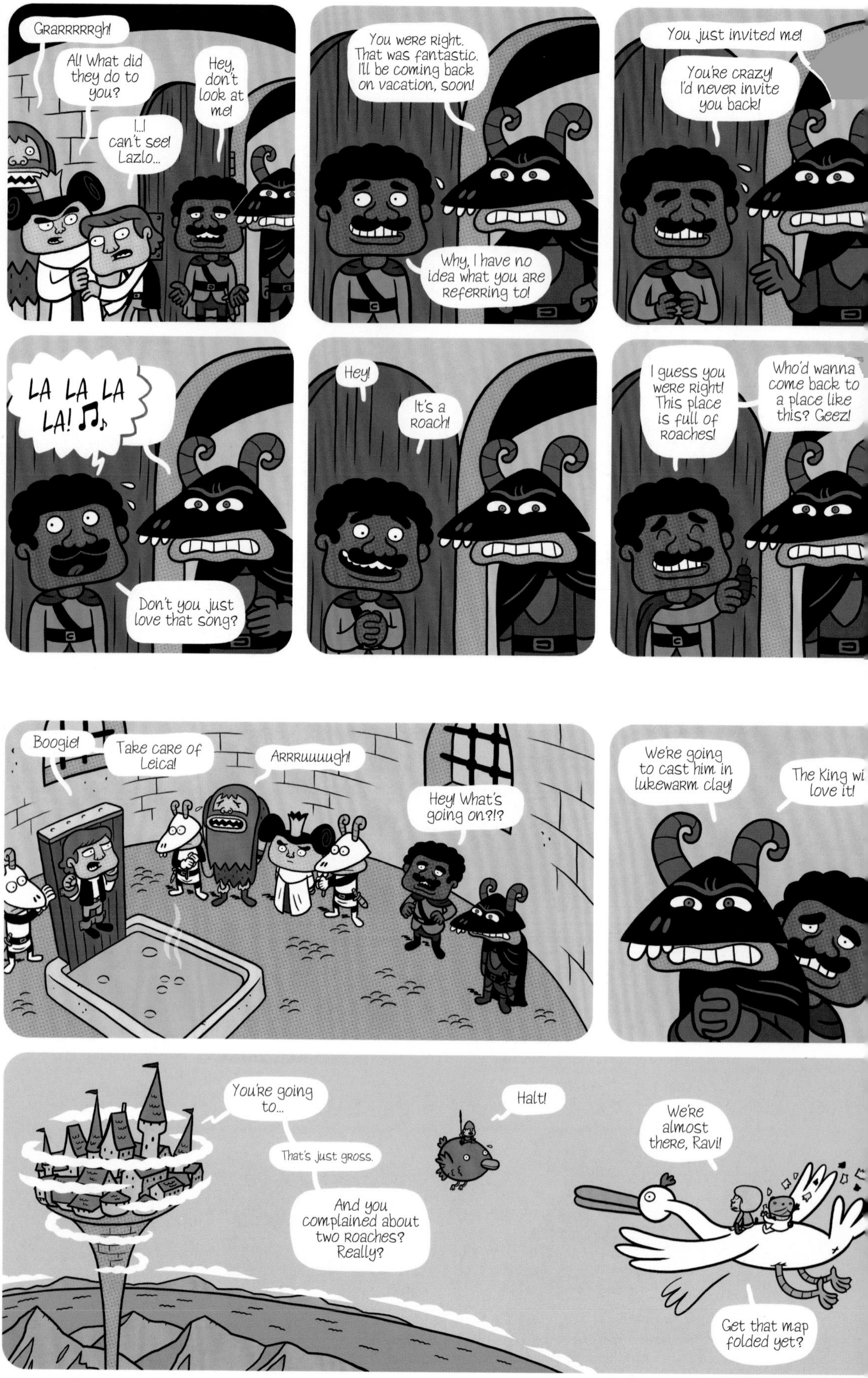
GRARRRRRgh!
Al! What did they do to you?
I...I can't see! Lazlo...
Hey, don't look at me!
You were right. That was fantastic. I'll be coming back on vacation, soon!
Why, I have no idea what you are referring to!
You just invited me!
You're crazy! I'd never invite you back!
LA LA LA LA!
Don't you just love that song?
Hey!
It's a Roach!
I guess you were right! This place is full of Roaches!
Who'd wanna come back to a place like this? Geez!
Boogie!
Take care of Leica!
ARRRuuuugh!
Hey! What's going on?!?
We're going to cast him in lukewarm clay!
The King wi love it!
You're going to...
That's just gross.
And you complained about two Roaches? Really?
Halt!
We're almost there, Ravi!
Get that map folded yet?

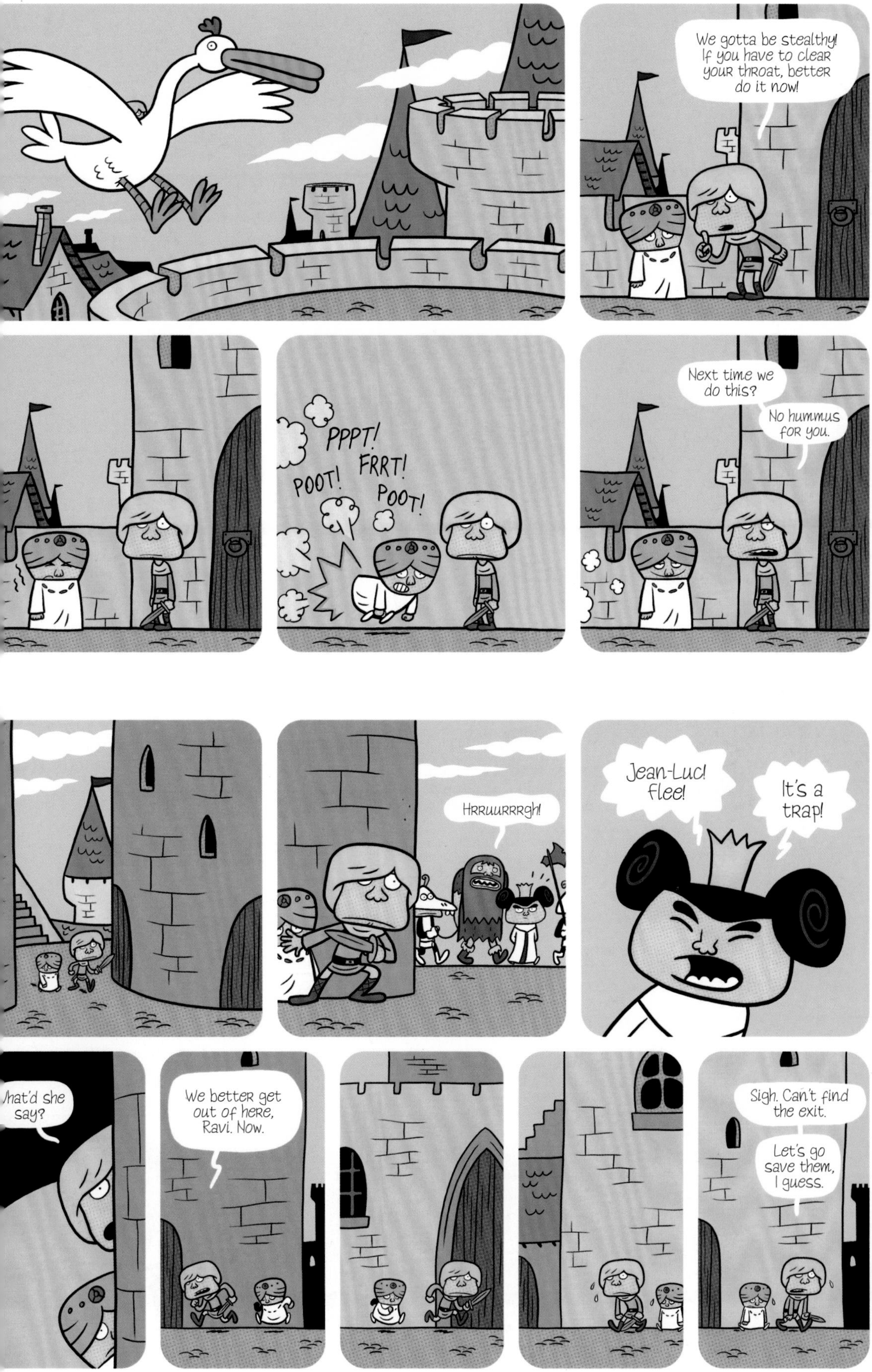
We gotta be stealthy! If you have to clear your throat, better do it now!
PPPT!
FRRT!
POOT!
POOT!
Next time we do this?
No hummus for you.
Hrruurrrgh!
Jean-Luc! Flee!
It's a trap!
hat'd she say?
We better get out of here, Ravi. Now.
Sigh. Can't find the exit.
Let's go save them, I guess.

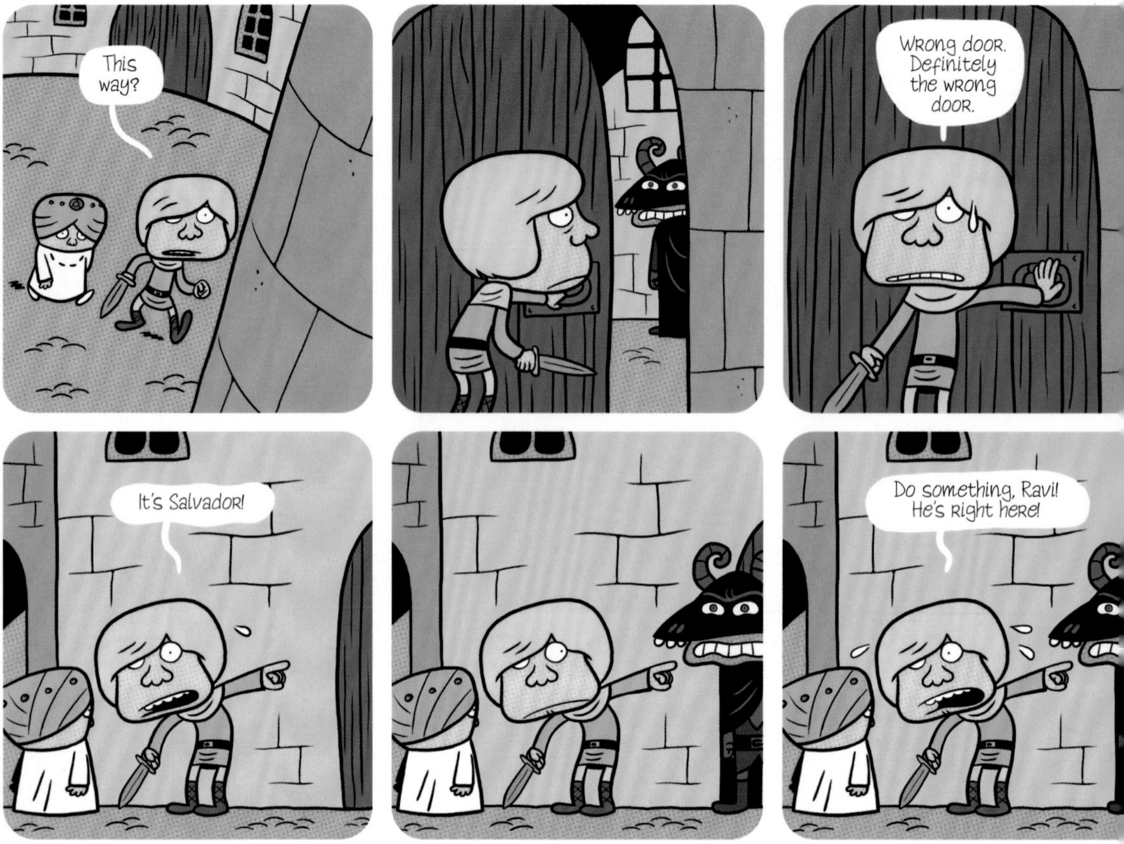
This way?
Wrong door. Definitely the wrong door.
It's Salvador!
Do something, Ravi! He's right here!

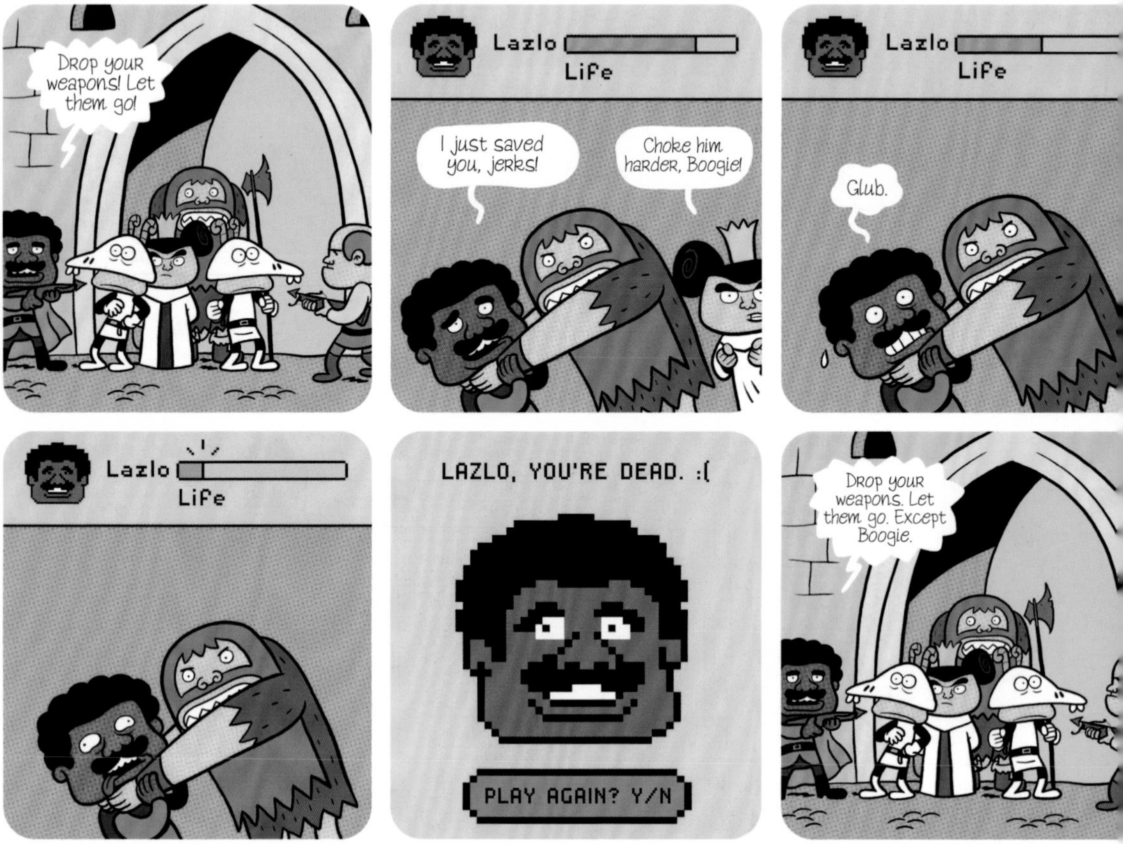
Drop your weapons! Let them go!
Lazlo
Life
I just saved you, jerks!
Choke him harder, Boogie!
Lazlo
Life
Glub.
Lazlo
Life
LAZLO, YOU'RE DEAD. :(
PLAY AGAIN? Y/N
Drop your weapons. Let them go. Except Boogie.

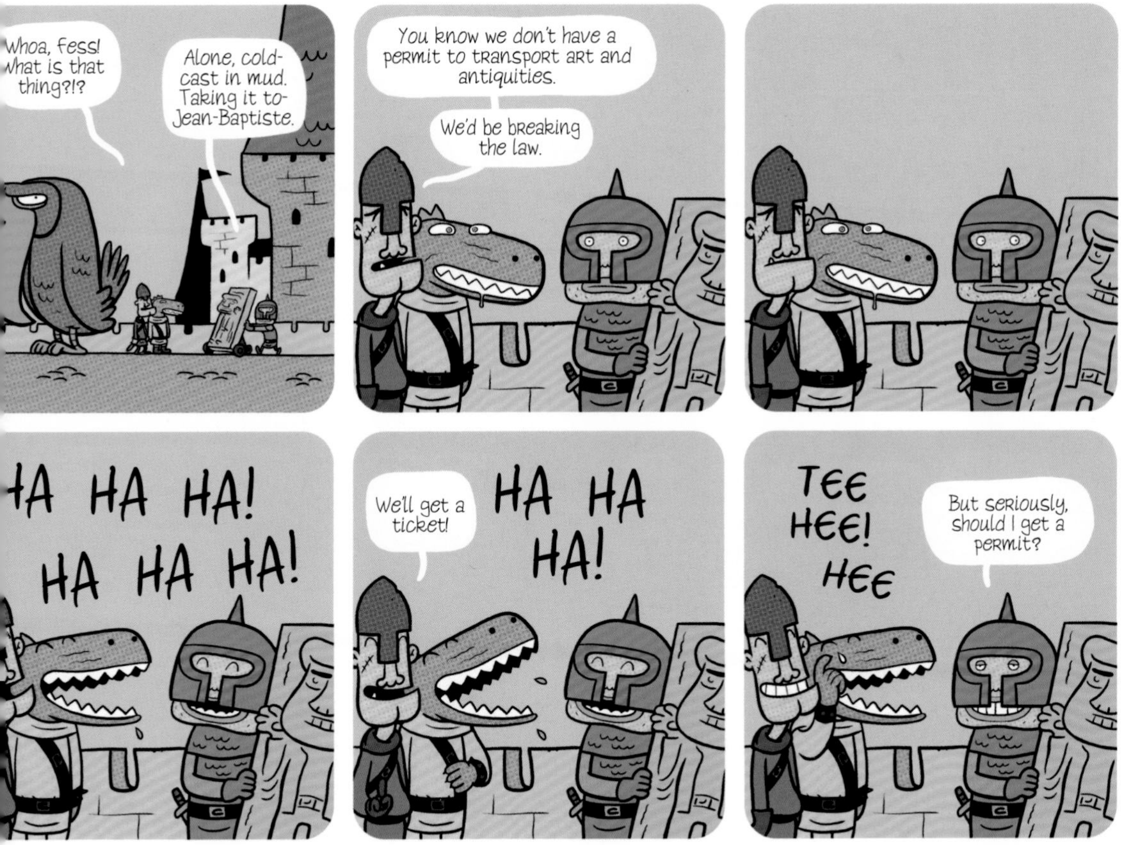
Whoa, Fess! What is that thing?!?
Alone, cold-cast in mud. Taking it to Jean-Baptiste.
You know we don't have a permit to transport art and antiquities.
We'd be breaking the law.
HA HA HA! HA HA HA!
We'll get a ticket!
HA HA HA!
TEE HEE! HEE
But seriously, should I get a permit?

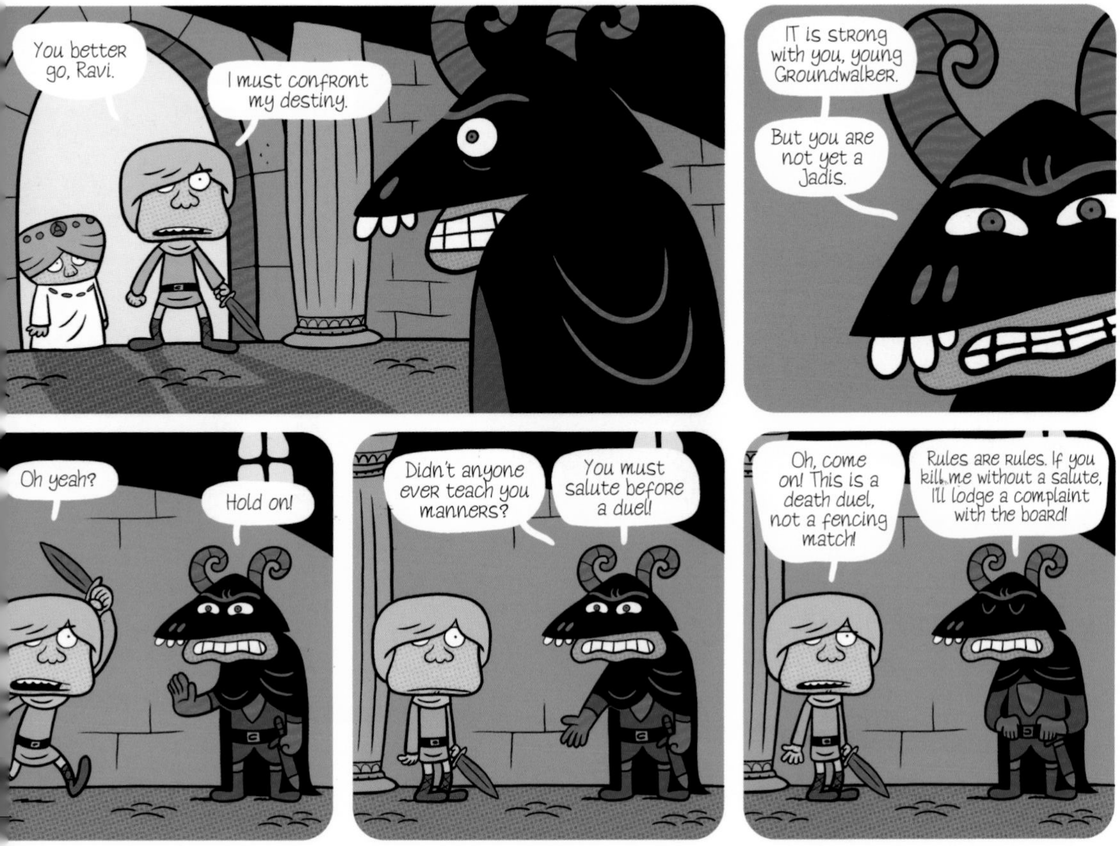
You better go, Ravi.
I must confront my destiny.
IT is strong with you, young Groundwalker.
But you are not yet a Jadis.
Oh yeah?
Hold on!
Didn't anyone ever teach you manners?
You must salute before a duel!
Oh, come on! This is a death duel, not a fencing match!
Rules are rules. If you kill me without a salute, I'll lodge a complaint with the board!

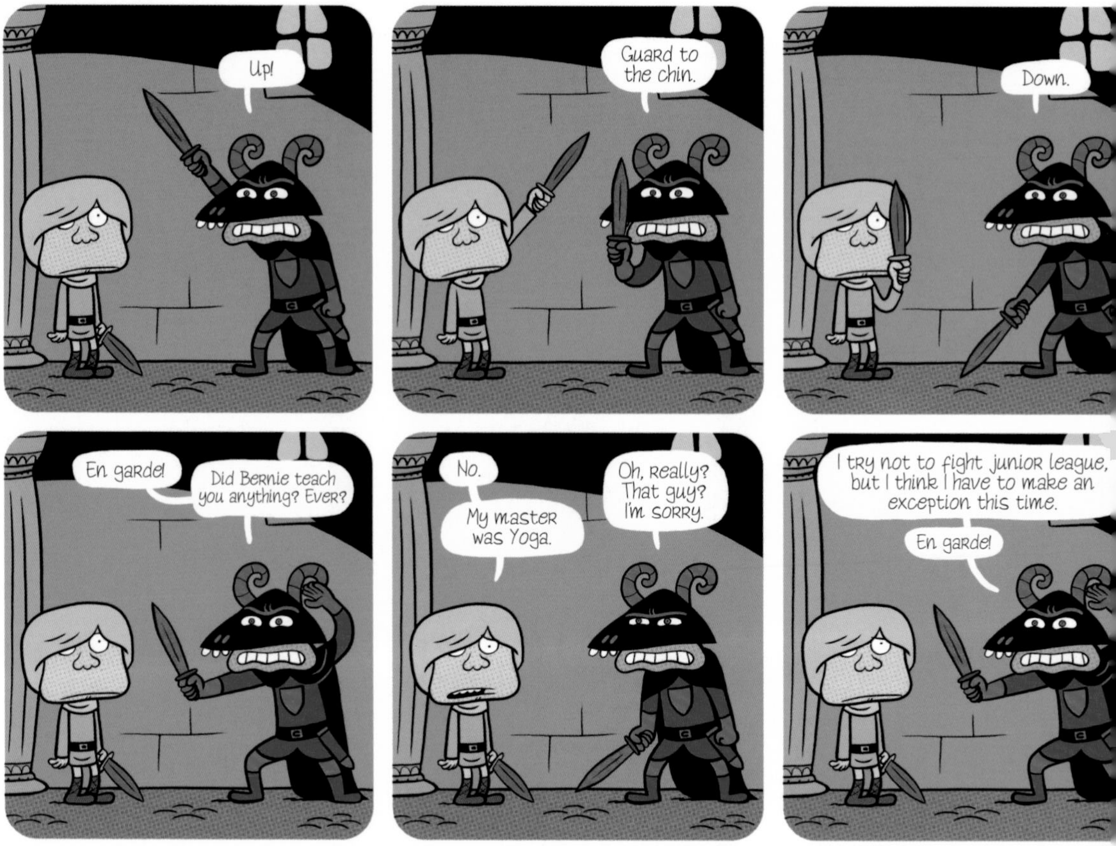
Up!
Guard to the chin.
Down.
En garde!
Did Bernie teach you anything? Ever?
No.
My master was Yoga.
Oh, really? That guy? I'm sorry.
I try not to fight junior league, but I think I have to make an exception this time.
En garde!

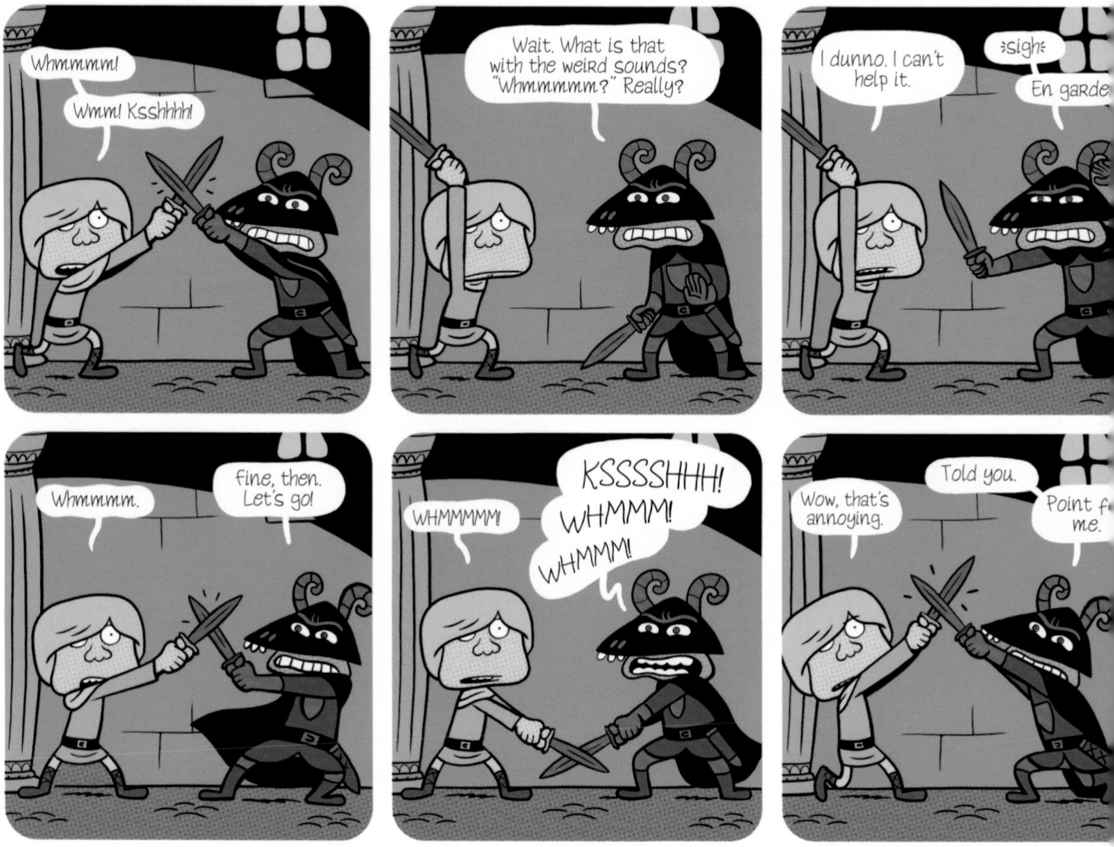
Whmmmm!
Wmm! Ksshhhh!
Wait. What is that with the weird sounds? "Whmmmmm?" Really?
I dunno. I can't help it.
:sigh:
En garde
Whmmmm.
Fine, then. Let's go!
WHMMMMM!
KSSSSHHH!
WHMMM!
WHMMM!
Wow, that's annoying.
Told you.
Point f
me.

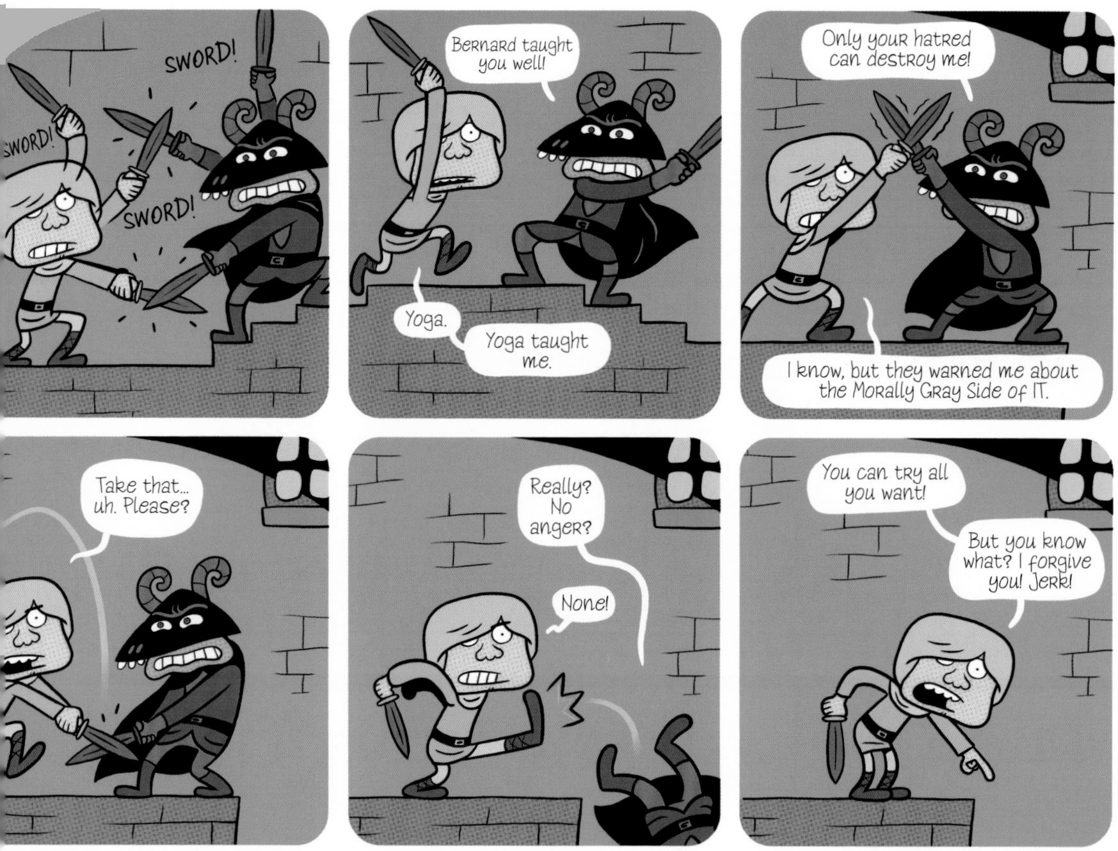
SWORD!
SWORD!
SWORD!
Bernard taught you well!
Yoga.
Yoga taught me.
Only your hatred can destroy me!
I know, but they warned me about the Morally Gray Side of IT.
Take that... uh. Please?
Really? No anger?
None!
You can try all you want!
But you know what? I forgive you! Jerk!

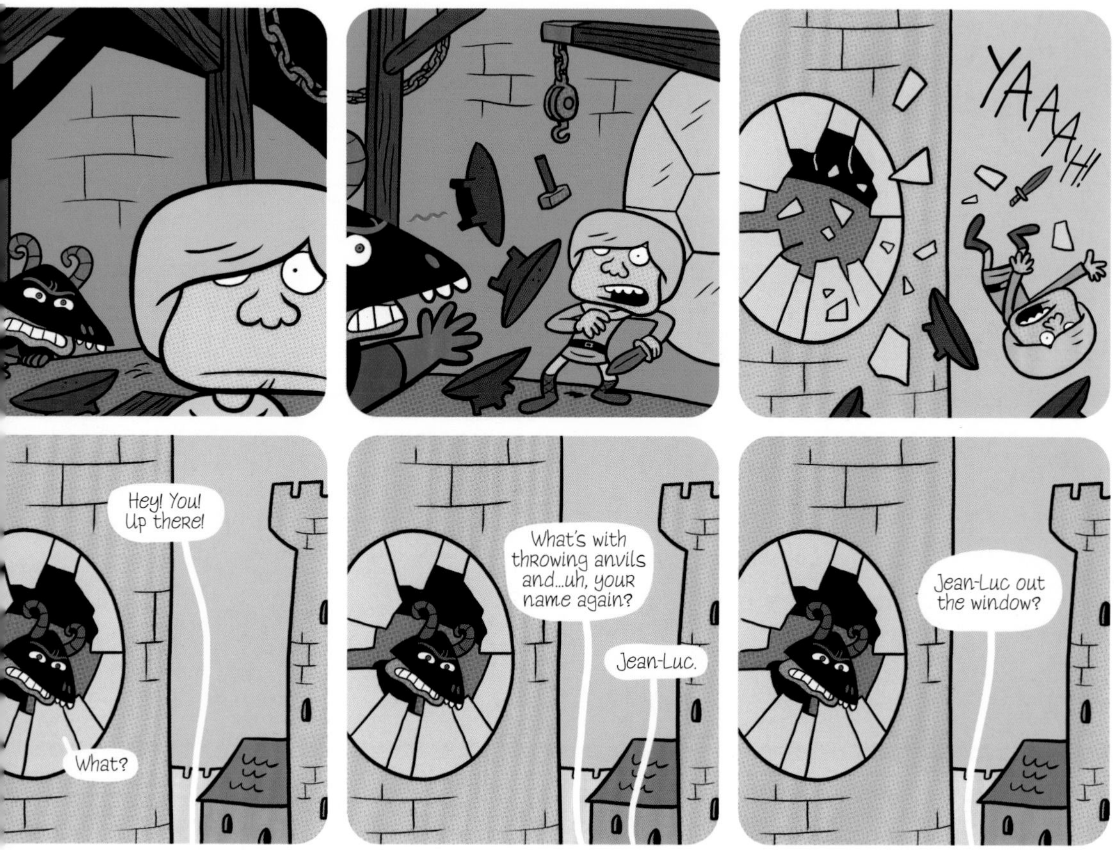
YAAAH!
Hey! You! Up there!
What?
What's with throwing anvils and...uh, your name again?
Jean-Luc.
Jean-Luc out the window?

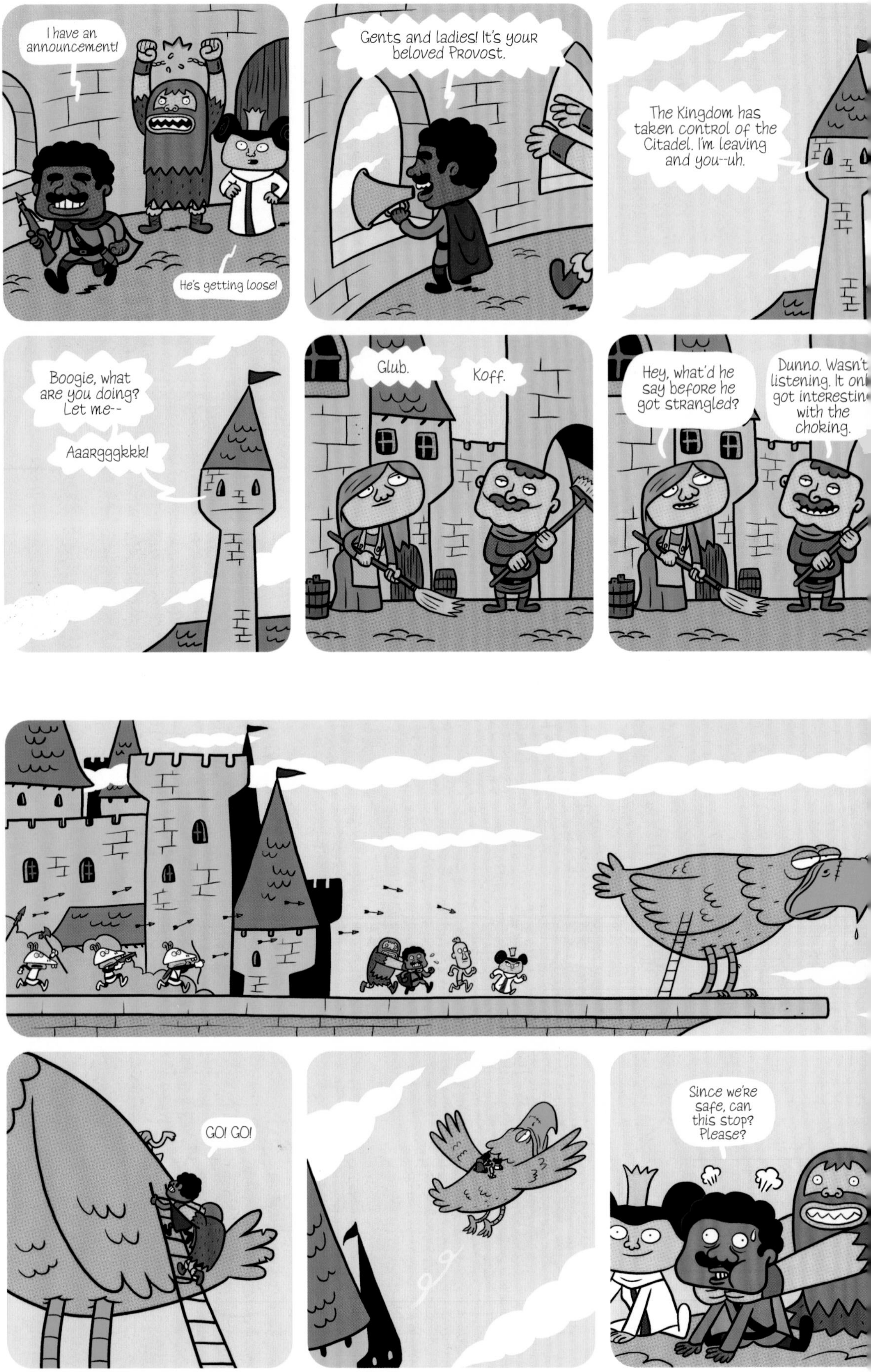
I have an announcement!
He's getting loose!
Gents and ladies! It's your beloved Provost.
The Kingdom has taken control of the Citadel. I'm leaving and you--uh.
Boogie, what are you doing? Let me--
Aaargggkkk!
Glub.
Koff.
Hey, what'd he say before he got strangled?
Dunno. Wasn't listening. It onl got interestin with the choking.
GO! GO!
Since we're safe, can this stop? Please?

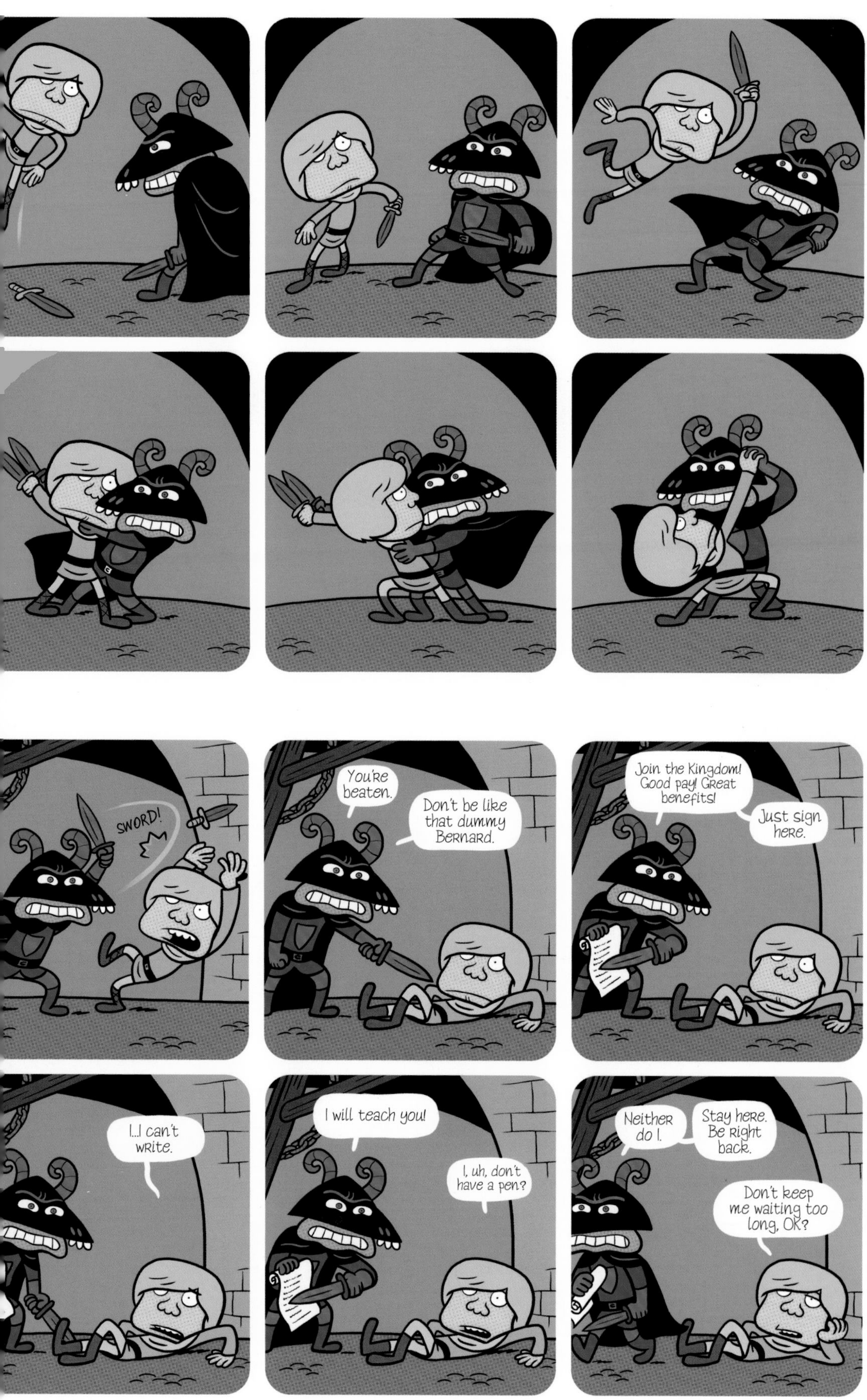

SWORD!
You're beaten.
Don't be like that dummy Bernard.
Join the Kingdom! Good pay! Great benefits!
Just sign here.
I...I can't write.
I will teach you!
I, uh, don't have a pen?
Neither do I.
Stay here. Be right back.
Don't keep me waiting too long, OK?

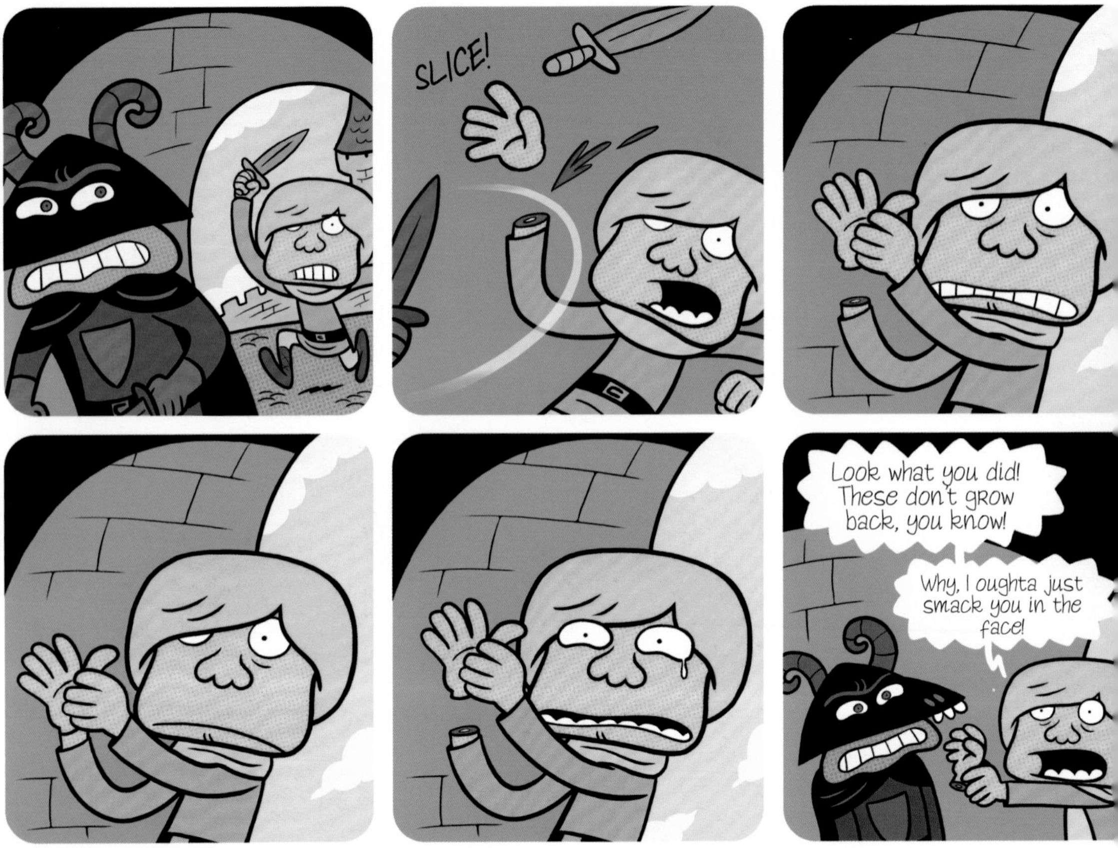
SLICE!
Look what you did! These don't grow back, you know!
Why, I oughta just smack you in the face!

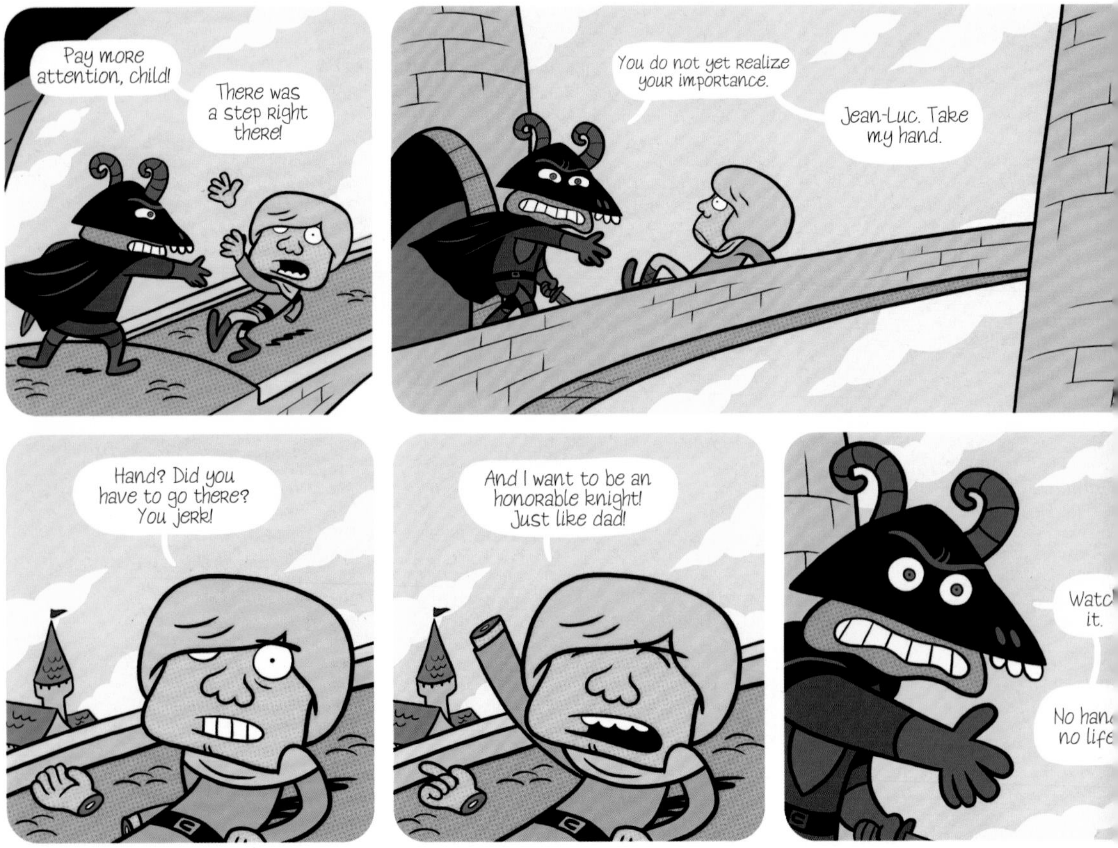
Pay more attention, child!
There was a step right there!
You do not yet realize your importance.
Jean-Luc. Take my hand.
Hand? Did you have to go there? You jerk!
And I want to be an honorable knight! Just like dad!
Watc it.
No han no life

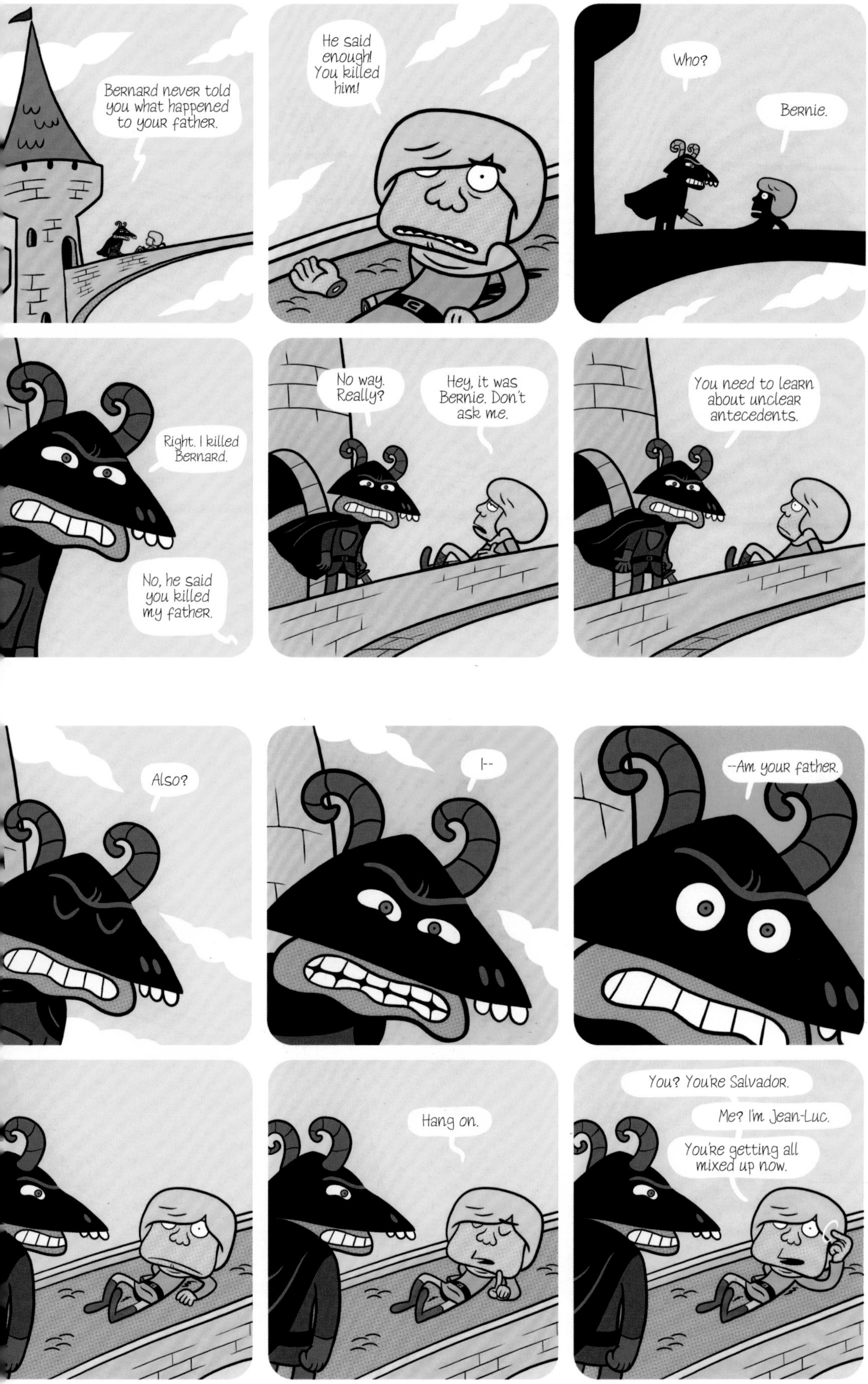
Bernard never told you what happened to your father.
He said enough! You killed him!
Who?
Bernie.
Right. I killed Bernard.
No, he said you killed my father.
No way. Really?
Hey, it was Bernie. Don't ask me.
You need to learn about unclear antecedents.
Also?
I--
--Am your father.
Hang on.
You? You're Salvador.
Me? I'm Jean-Luc.
You're getting all mixed up now.

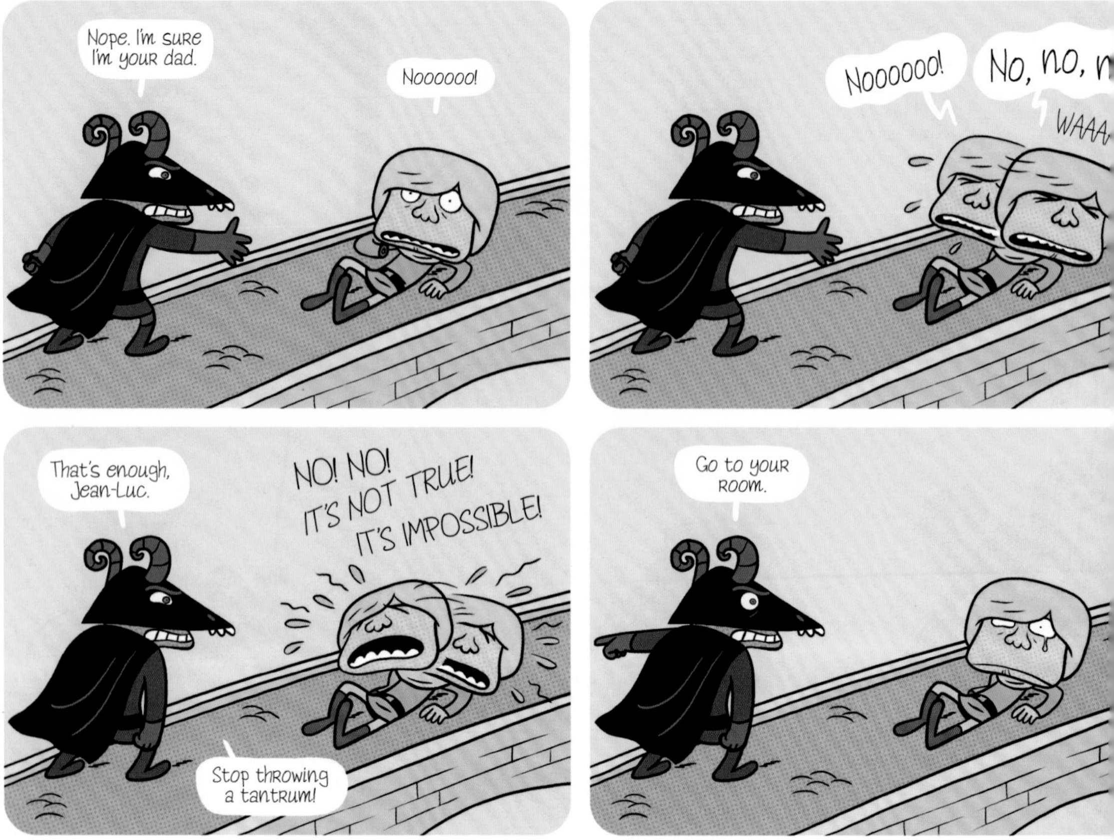
Nope. I'm sure I'm your dad.
Noooooo!
Noooooo!
No, no,
WAAA
That's enough, Jean-Luc.
NO! NO! IT'S NOT TRUE! IT'S IMPOSSIBLE!
Stop throwing a tantrum!
Go to your room.

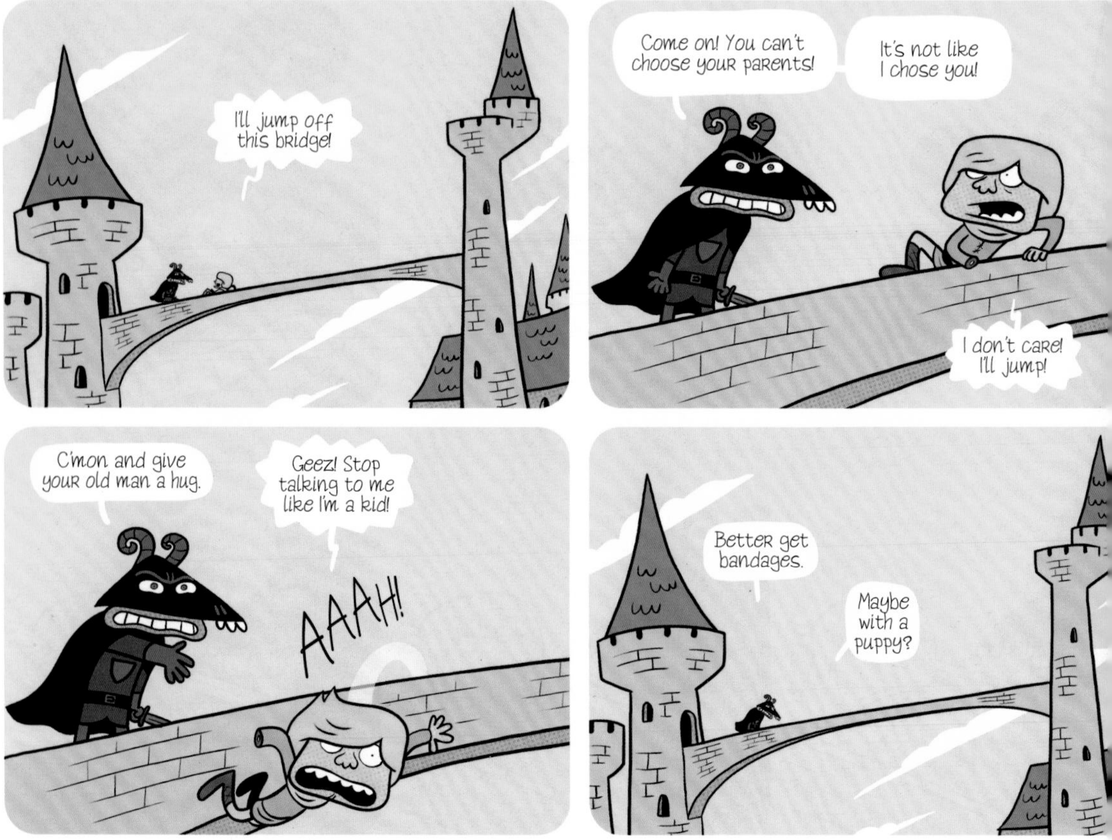
I'll jump off this bridge!
Come on! You can't choose your parents!
It's not like I chose you!
I don't care! I'll jump!
C'mon and give your old man a hug.
Geez! Stop talking to me like I'm a kid!
AAAH!
Better get bandages.
Maybe with a puppy?

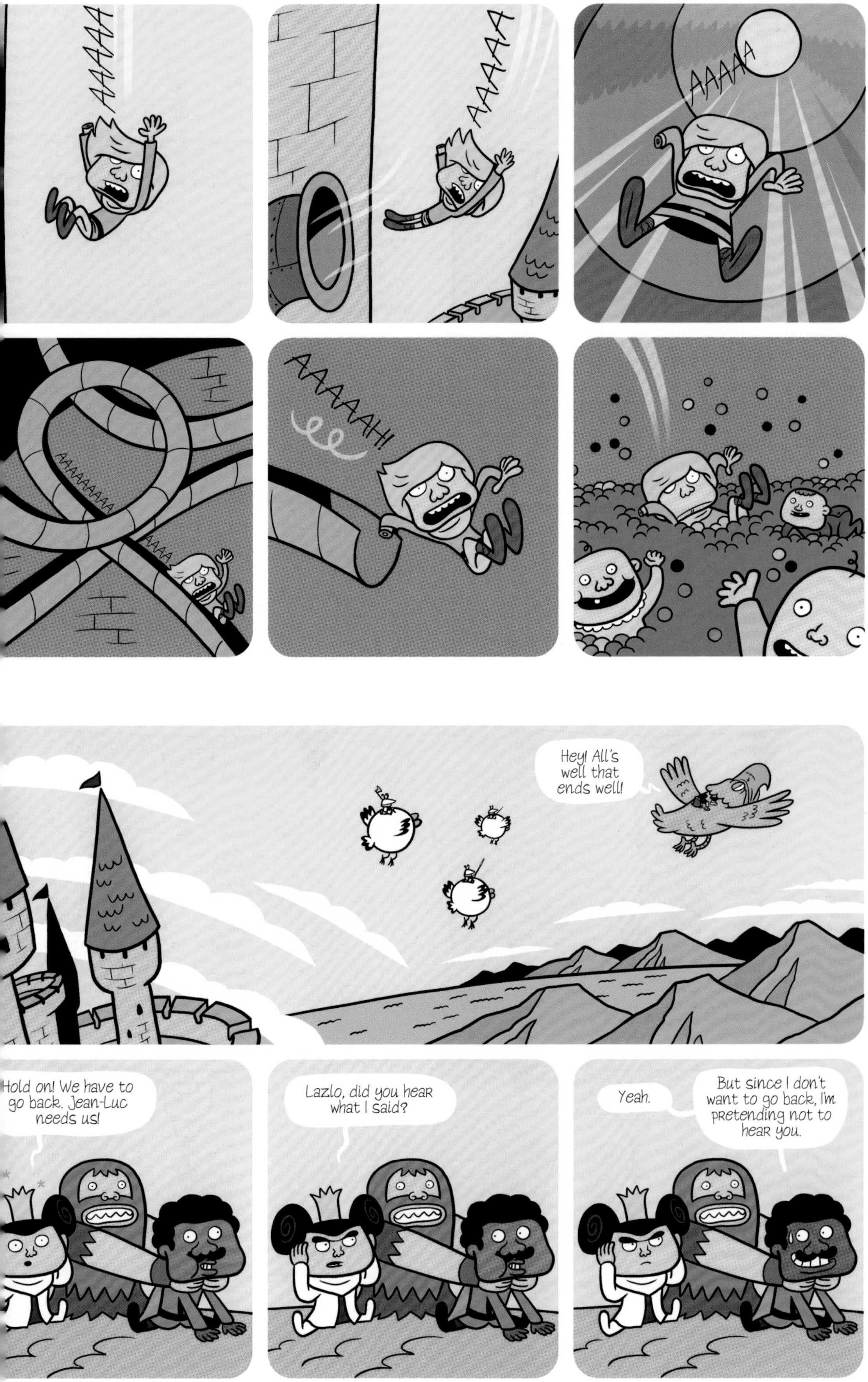
AAAAA
AAAAA
AAAAA
AAAAAAAAA
AAAA
AAAAAAAH!
Hey! All's well that ends well!
Hold on! We have to go back. Jean-Luc needs us!
Lazlo, did you hear what I said?
Yeah.
But since I don't want to go back, I'm pretending not to hear you.

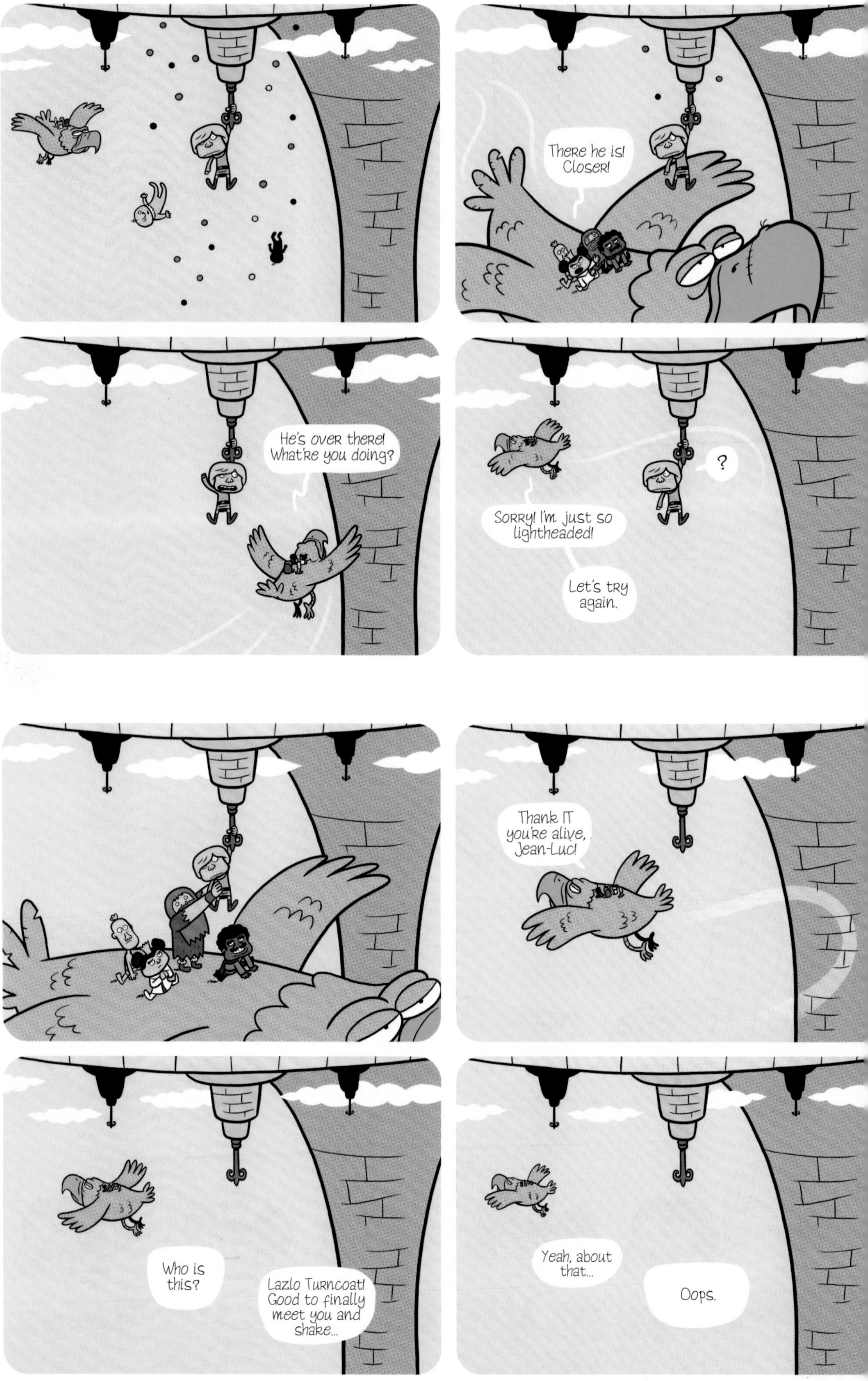
There he is! Closer!
He's over there! What're you doing?
?
Sorry! I'm just so lightheaded!
Let's try again.
Thank IT you're alive, Jean-Luc!
Who is this?
Lazlo Turncoat! Good to finally meet you and shake...
Yeah, about that...
Oops.

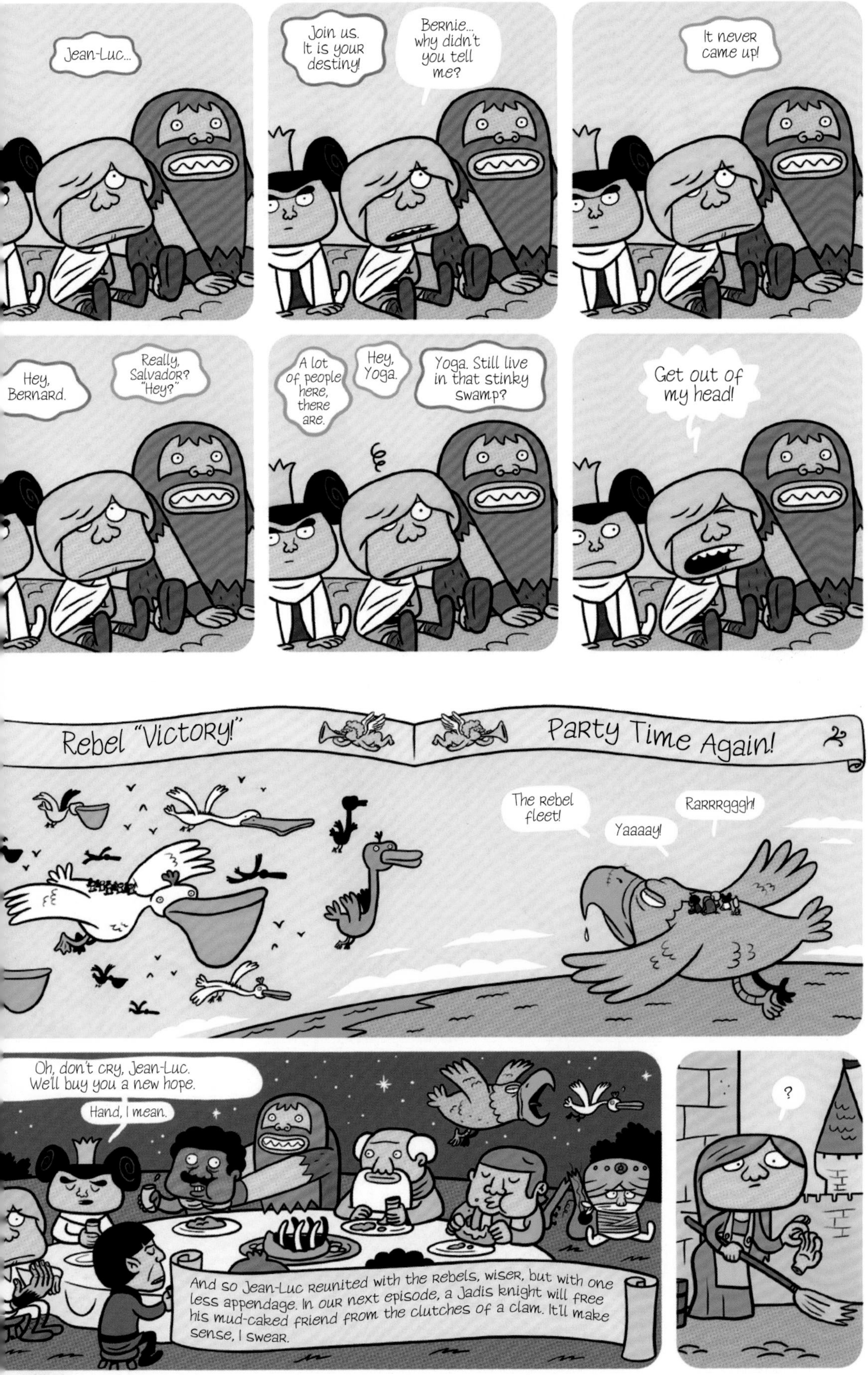
Jean-Luc...
Join us. It is your destiny!
Bernie... why didn't you tell me?
It never came up!
Hey, Bernard.
Really, Salvador? "Hey?"
A lot of people here, there are.
Hey, Yoga.
Yoga. Still live in that stinky swamp?
Get out of my head!
Rebel "Victory!"
Party Time Again!
The rebel fleet!
Yaaaay!
Rarrrgggh!
Oh, don't cry, Jean-Luc. We'll buy you a new hope.
Hand, I mean.
And so Jean-Luc reunited with the Rebels, wiser, but with one less appendage. In our next episode, a Jadis knight will free his mud-caked friend from the clutches of a clam. It'll make sense, I swear.
?

EPISODE 3

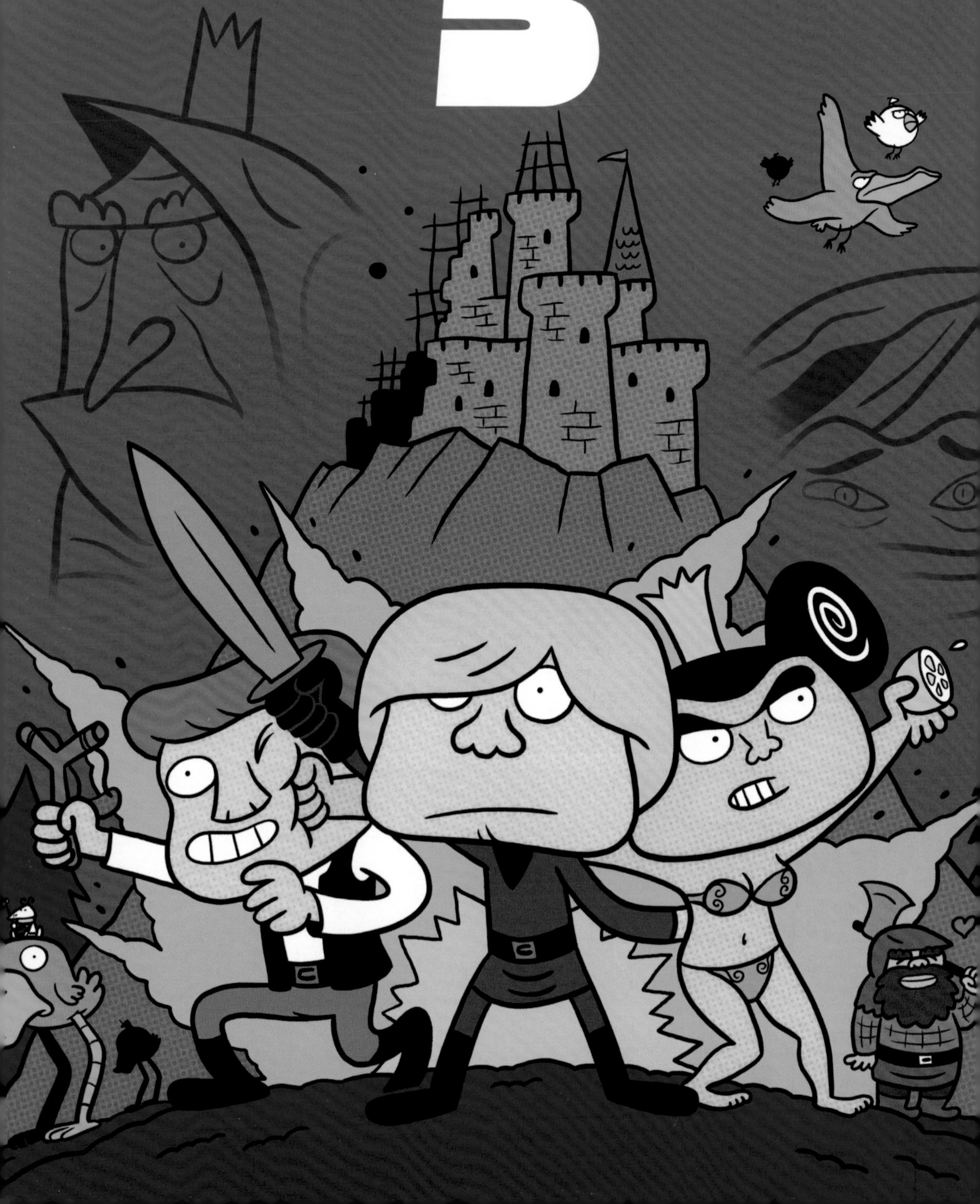

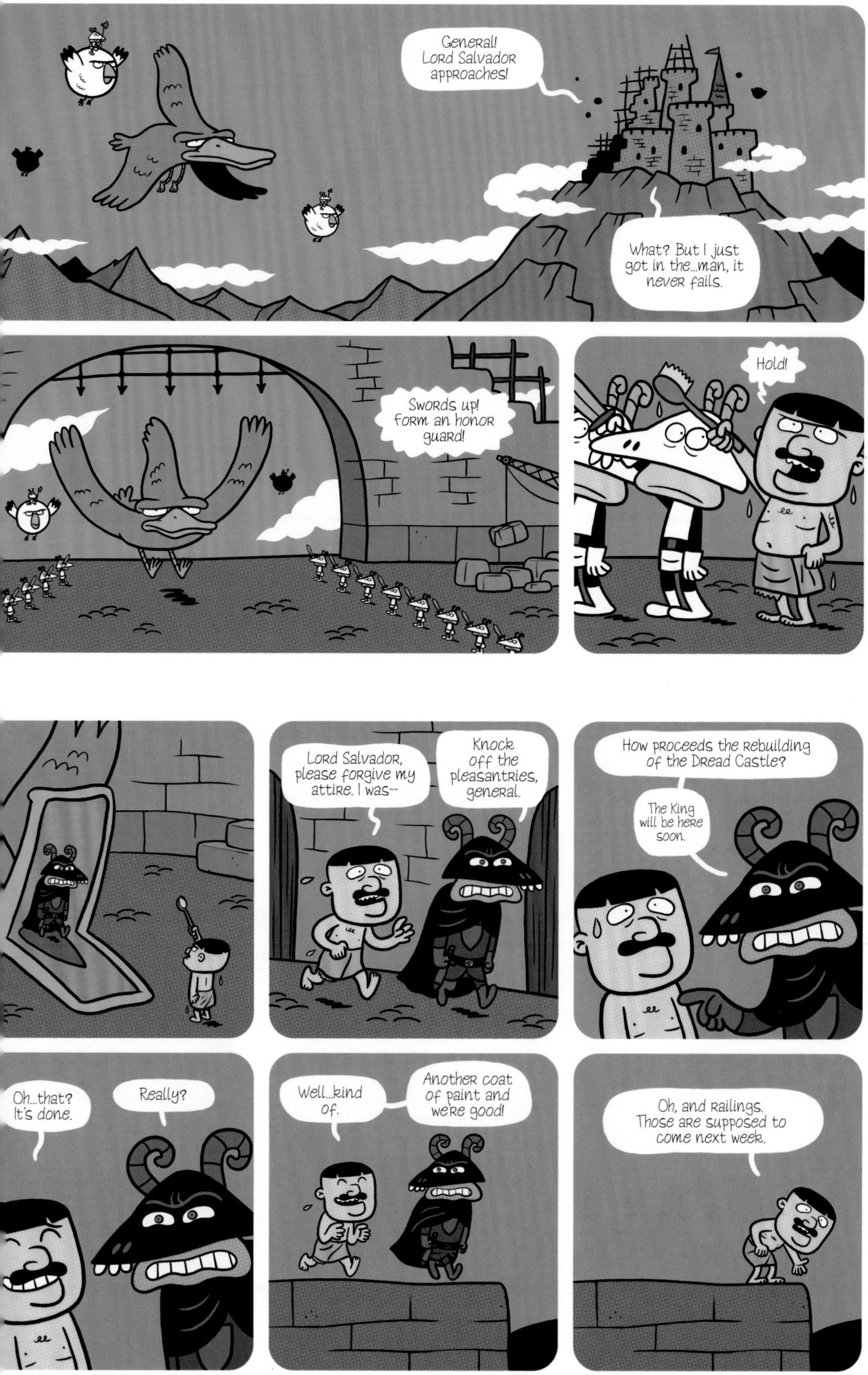
General! Lord Salvador approaches!
What? But I just got in the...man, it never fails.
Swords up! Form an honor guard!
Hold!
Lord Salvador, please forgive my attire. I was--
Knock off the pleasantries, general.
How proceeds the rebuilding of the Dread Castle?
The King will be here soon.
Oh...that? It's done.
Really?
Well...kind of.
Another coat of paint and we're good!
Oh, and railings. Those are supposed to come next week.

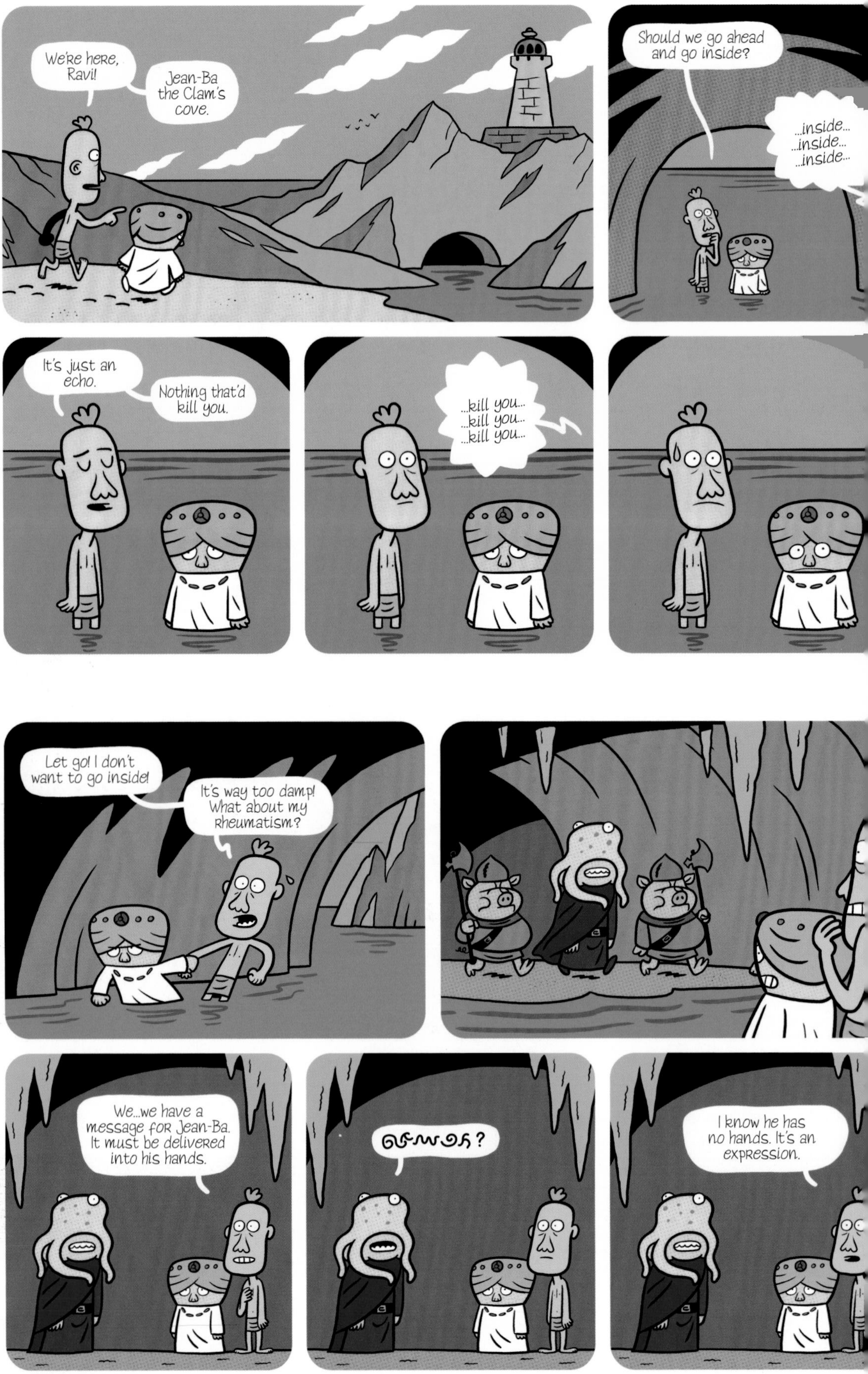
We're here, Ravi!
Jean-Ba the Clam's cove.
Should we go ahead and go inside?
...inside... ...inside... ...inside...
It's just an echo.
Nothing that'd kill you.
...kill you... ...kill you... ...kill you...
Let go! I don't want to go inside!
It's way too damp! What about my Rheumatism?
We...we have a message for Jean-Ba. It must be delivered into his hands.
I know he has no hands. It's an expression.

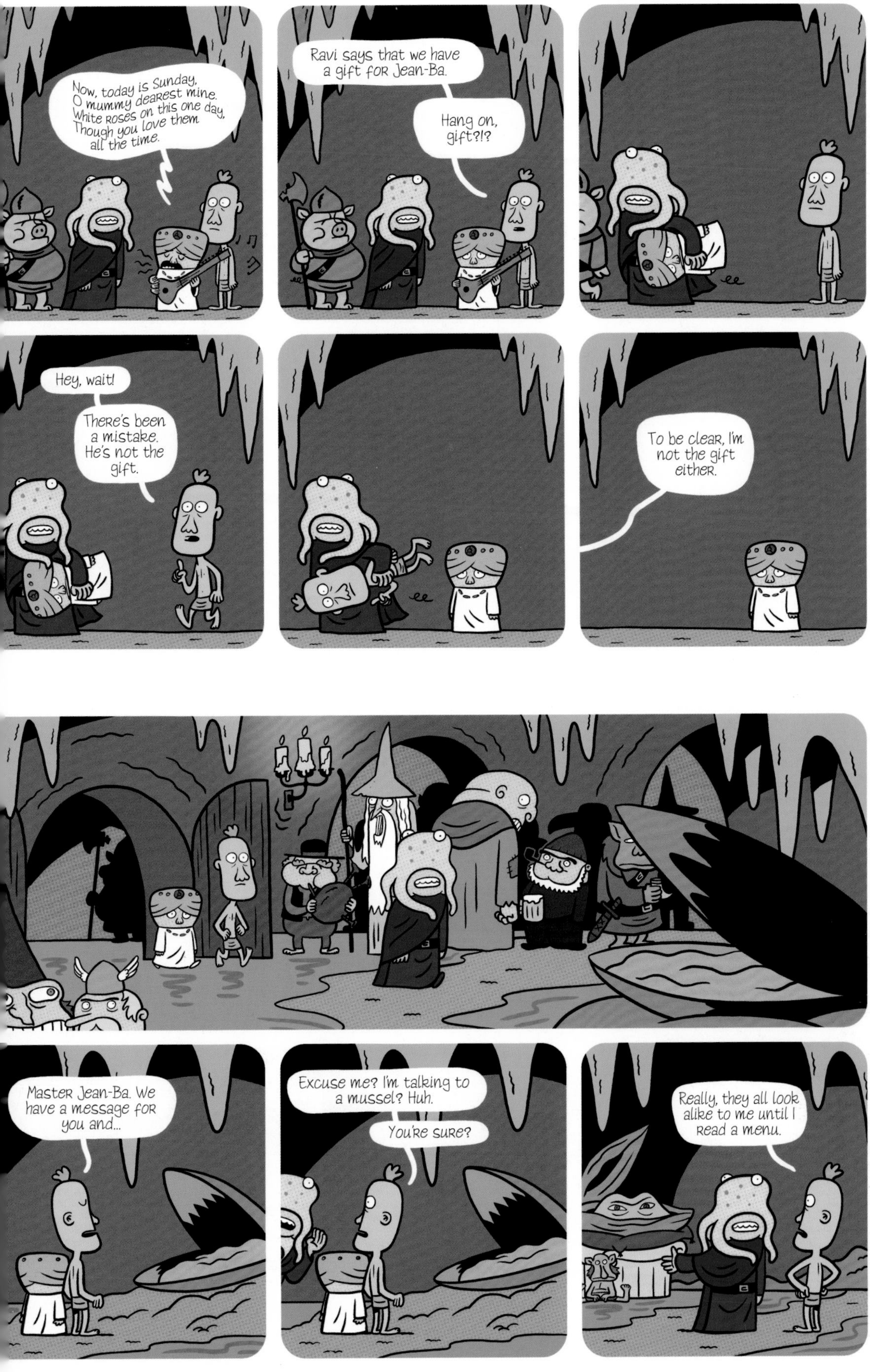
Now, today is Sunday,
O mummy dearest mine.
White roses on this one day,
Though you love them
all the time.
Ravi says that we have
a gift for Jean-Ba.
Hang on,
gift?!?
Hey, wait!
There's been
a mistake.
He's not the
gift.
To be clear, I'm
not the gift
either.
Master Jean-Ba. We
have a message for
you and...
Excuse me? I'm talking to
a mussel? Huh.
You're sure?
Really, they all look
alike to me until I
read a menu.

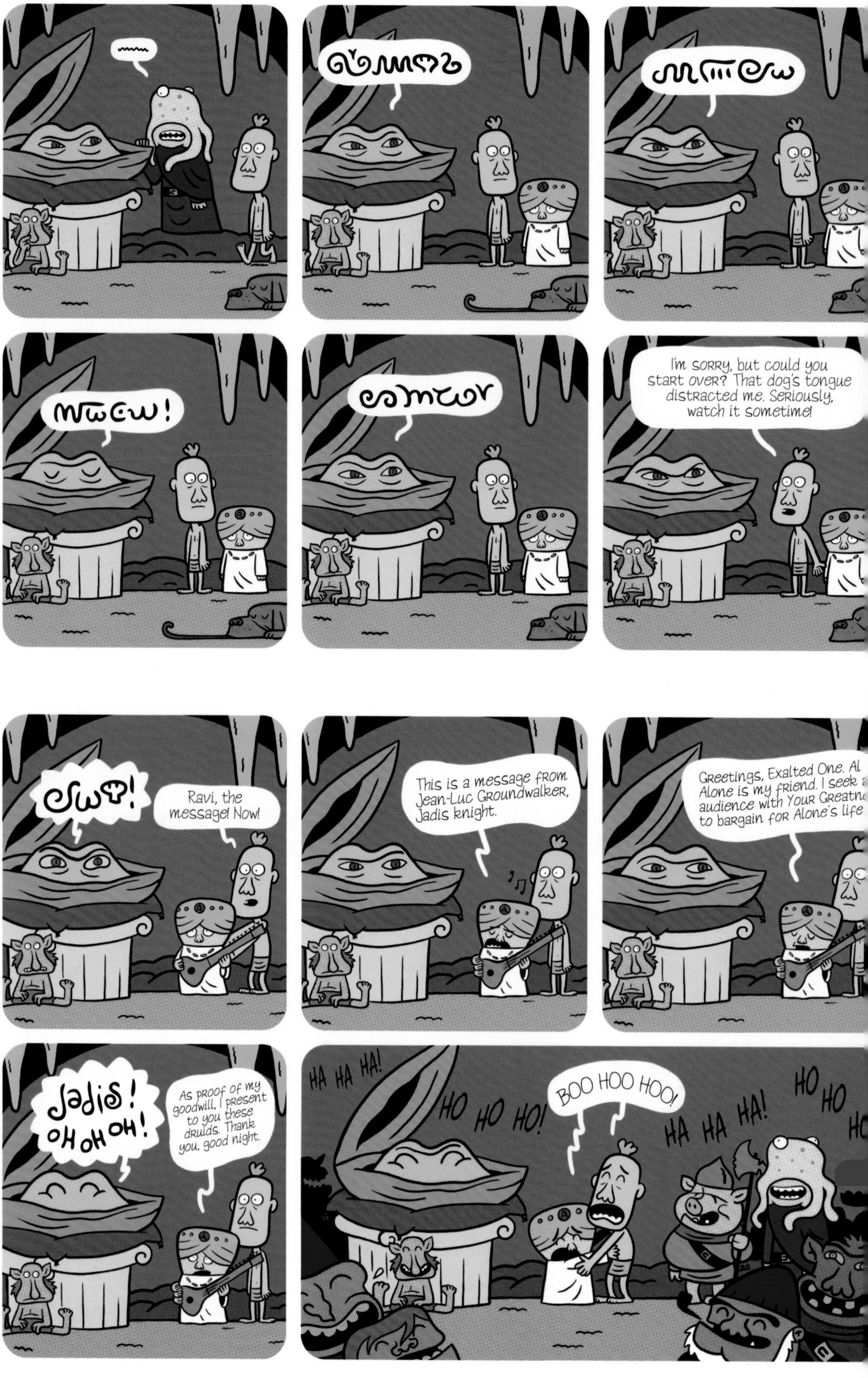
I'm sorry, but could you start over? That dog's tongue distracted me. Seriously, watch it sometime!
Ravi, the message! Now!
This is a message from Jean-Luc Groundwalker, Jadis knight.
Greetings, Exalted One.
Alone is my friend. I seek
audience with Your
to bargain for Alone's life
Jadis! OH OH OH!
As proof of my goodwill, I present to you these druids. Thank you, good night.
HA HA HA!
HO HO HO!
BOO HOO HOO!
HA HA HA!
HO HO

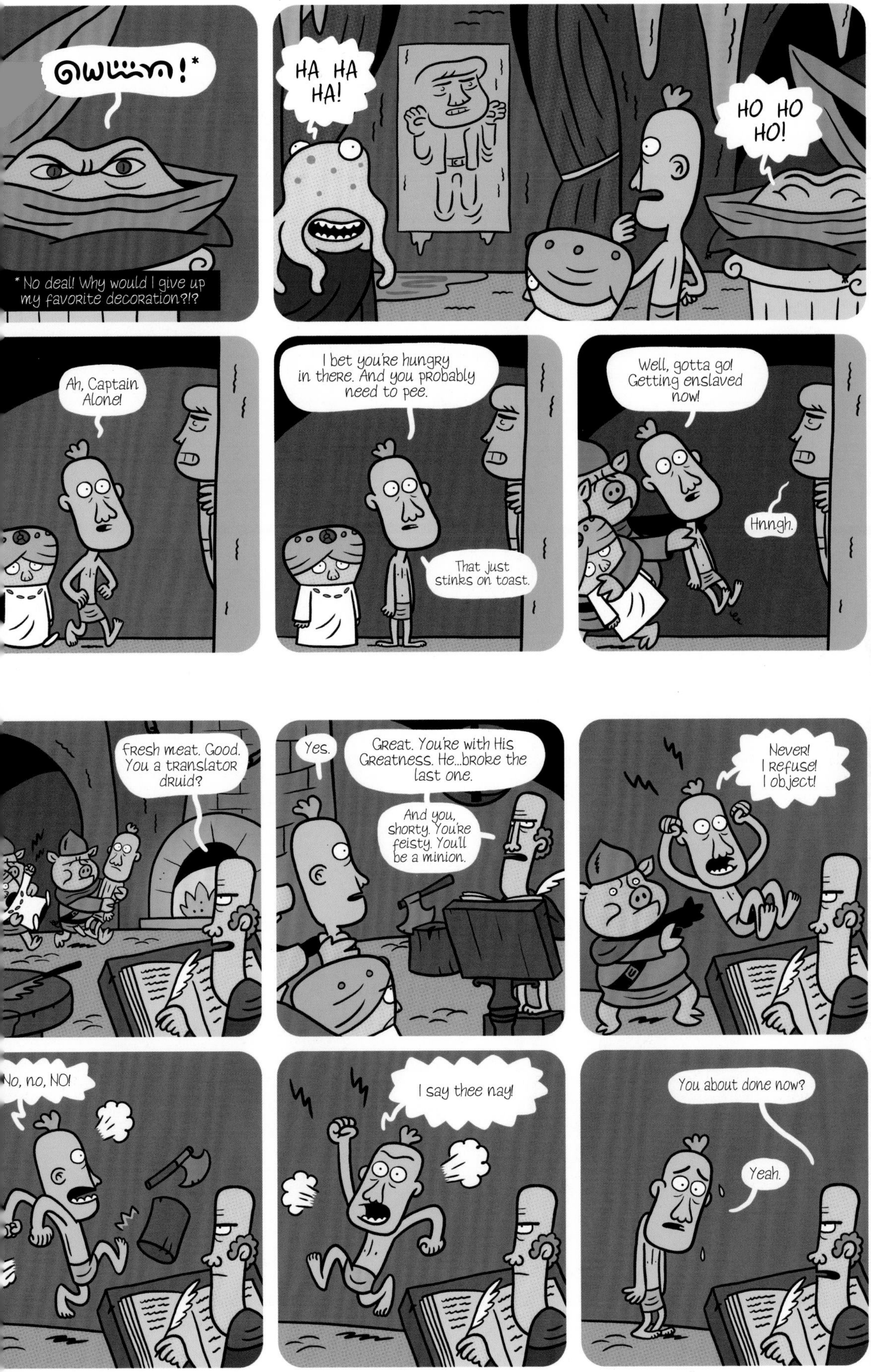
ɑwʟ̈ɴ! *
* No deal! Why would I give up my favorite decoration?!?
HA HA HA!
HO HO HO!
Ah, Captain Alone!
I bet you're hungry in there. And you probably need to pee.
That just stinks on toast.
Well, gotta go! Getting enslaved now!
Hnngh.
Fresh meat. Good. You a translator druid?
Yes.
Great. You're with His Greatness. He...broke the last one.
And you, shorty. You're feisty. You'll be a minion.
Never! I refuse! I object!
No, no, NO!
I say thee nay!
You about done now?
Yeah.

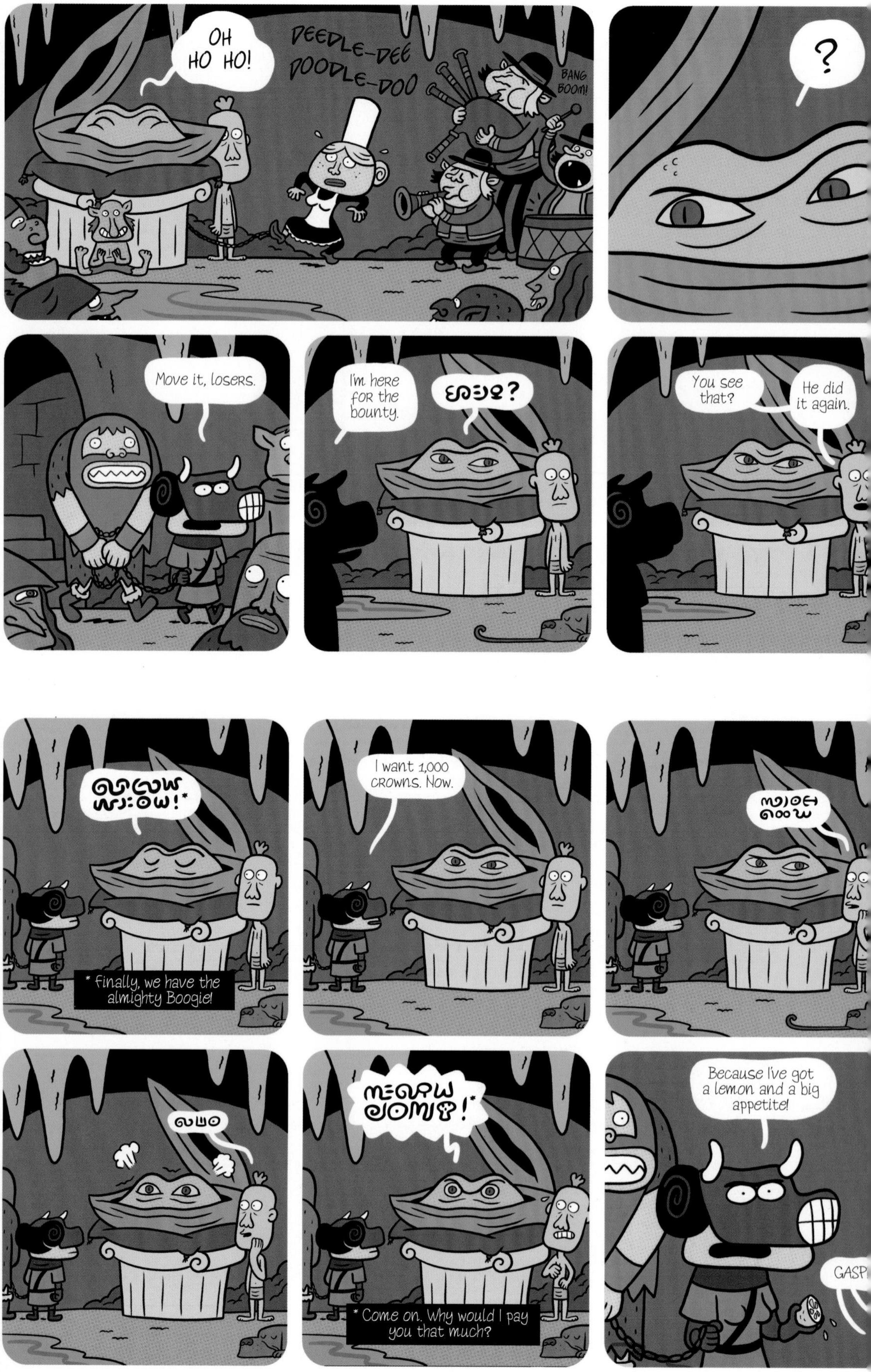
OH HO HO!
DEEDLE-DEE DOODLE-DOO
BANG BOOM!
?
Move it, losers.
I'm here for the bounty.
You see that?
He did it again.
* Finally, we have the almighty Boogie!
I want 1,000 crowns. Now.
* Come on. Why would I pay you that much?
Because I've got a lemon and a big appetite!
GASP

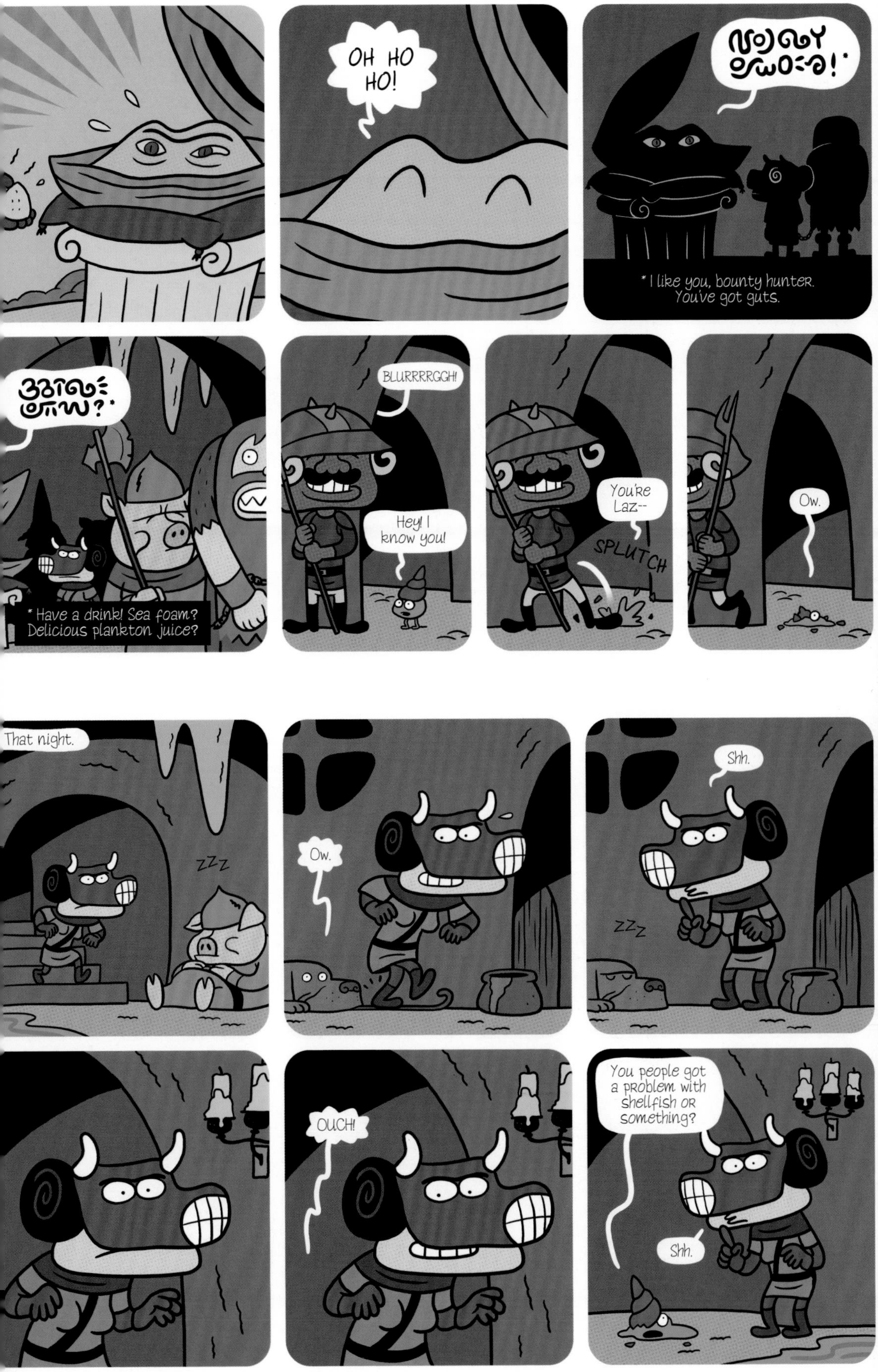
OH HO HO!
* I like you, bounty hunter. You've got guts.
* Have a drink! Sea foam? Delicious plankton juice?
BLURRRRGGH!
Hey! I know you!
You're Laz--
SPLUTCH
Ow.
That night.
ZZZ
Ow.
Shh.
ZZZ
OUCH!
You people got a problem with shellfish or something?
Shh.

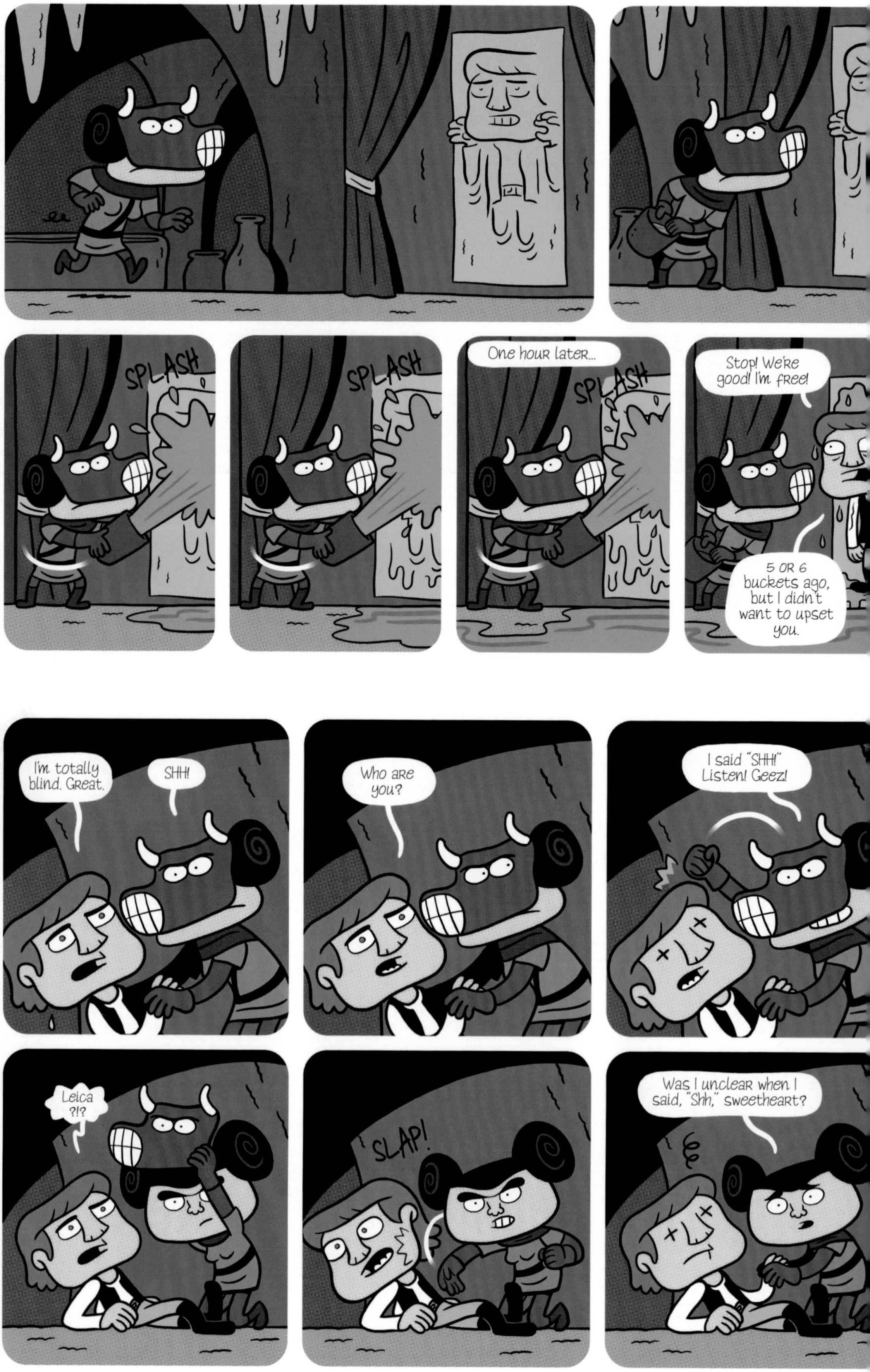

SPLASH
SPLASH
One hour later...
SPLASH
Stop! We're good! I'm free!
5 OR 6 buckets ago, but I didn't want to upset you.
I'm totally blind. Great.
SHH!
Who are you?
I said "SHH!" Listen! Geez!
Leica ?!?
SLAP!
Was I unclear when I said, "Shh," sweetheart?

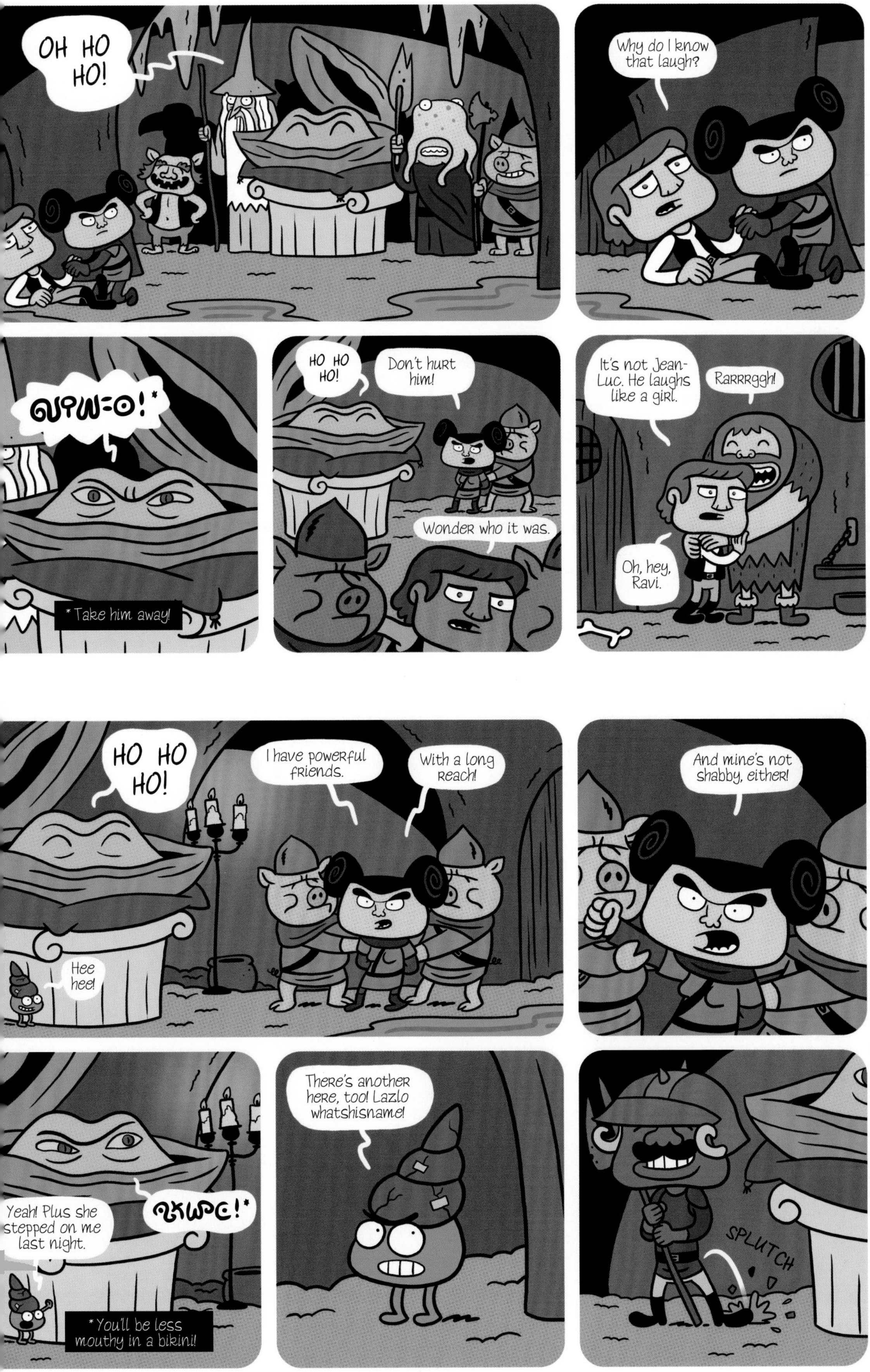
OH HO HO!
Why do I know that laugh?
*Take him away!
HO HO HO!
Don't hurt him!
Wonder who it was.
It's not Jean-Luc. He laughs like a girl.
Rarrrggh!
Oh, hey, Ravi.
HO HO HO!
I have powerful friends.
With a long reach!
Hee hee!
And mine's not shabby, either!
Yeah! Plus she stepped on me last night.
*You'll be less mouthy in a bikini!
There's another here, too! Lazlo whatshisname!
SPLUTCH

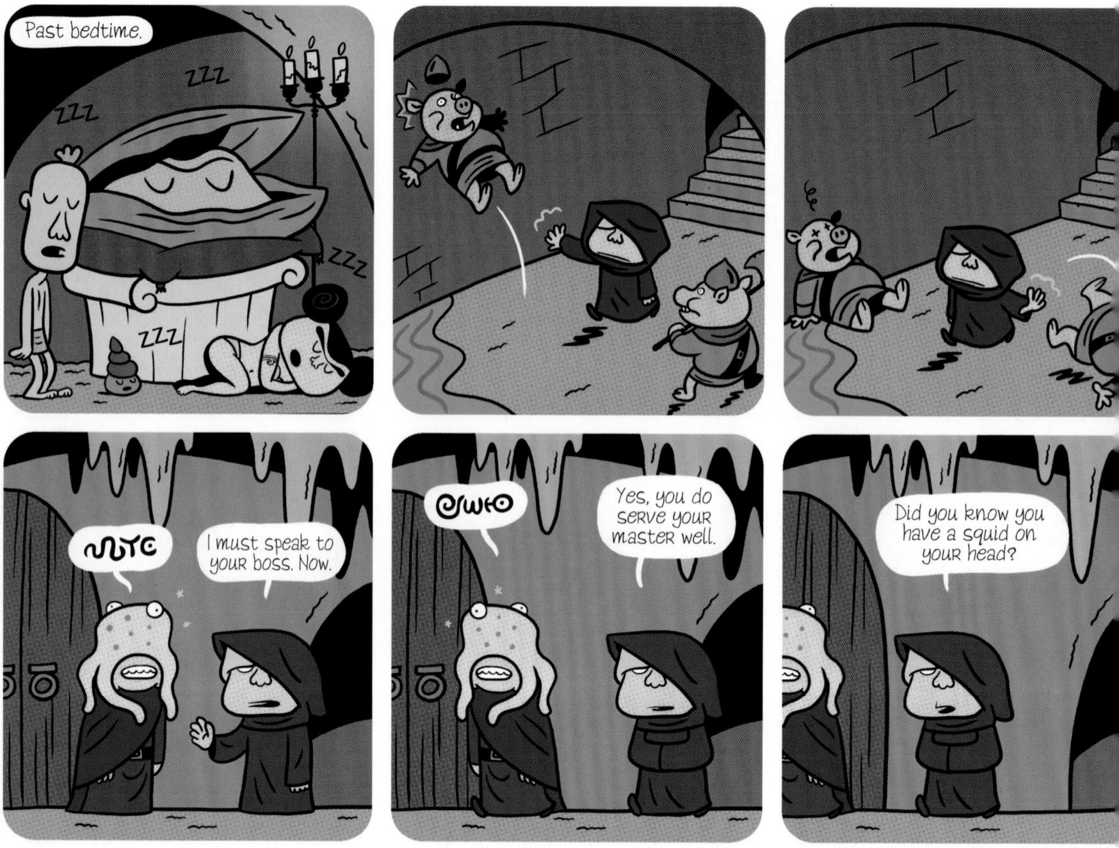
Past bedtime.
I must speak to your boss. Now.
Yes, you do serve your master well.
Did you know you have a squid on your head?

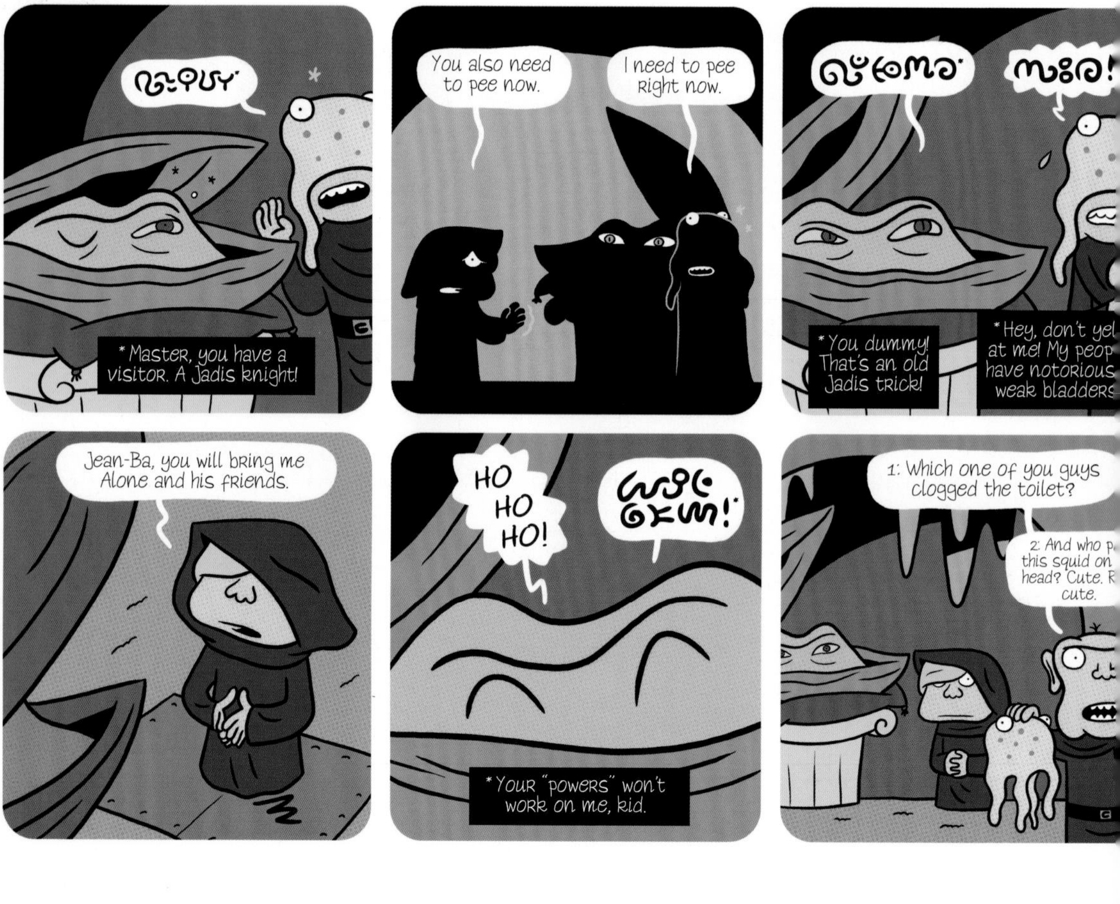
*Master, you have a visitor. A Jadis knight!
You also need to pee now.
I need to pee right now.
*You dummy! That's an old Jadis trick!
*Hey, don't yel at me! My peop have notorious weak bladders
Jean-Ba, you will bring me Alone and his friends.
HO HO HO!
*Your "powers" won't work on me, kid.
1: Which one of you guys clogged the toilet?
2: And who p this squid on head? Cute. R cute.

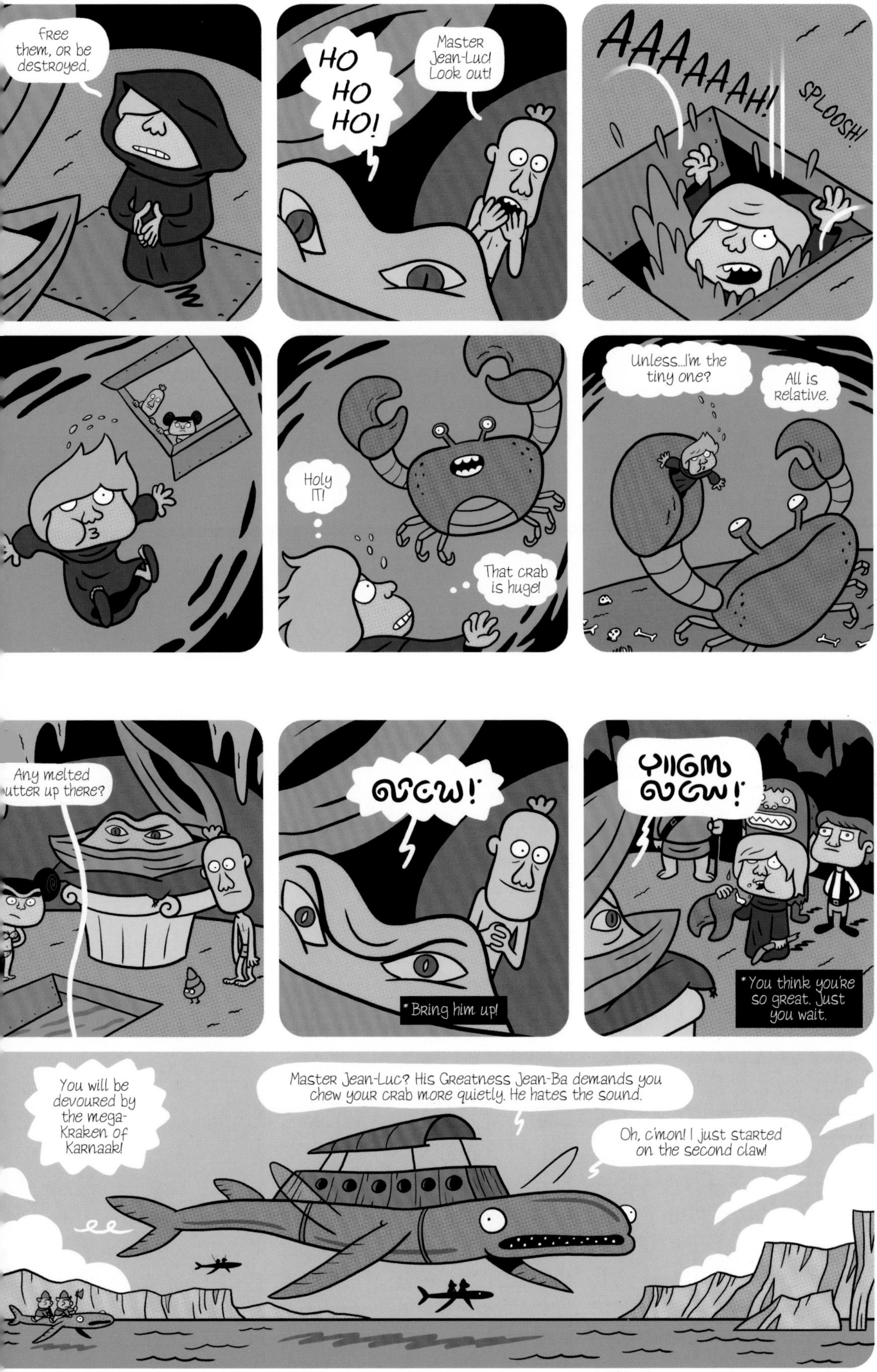
Free them, or be destroyed.
HO HO HO!
Master Jean-Luc! Look out!
AAAAAAAH!
SPLOOSH!
Holy IT!
That crab is huge!
Unless...I'm the tiny one?
All is relative.
Any melted butter up there?
*Bring him up!
*You think you're so great. Just you wait.
You will be devoured by the mega-Kraken of Karnaak!
Master Jean-Luc? His Greatness Jean-Ba demands you chew your crab more quietly. He hates the sound.
Oh, c'mon! I just started on the second claw!

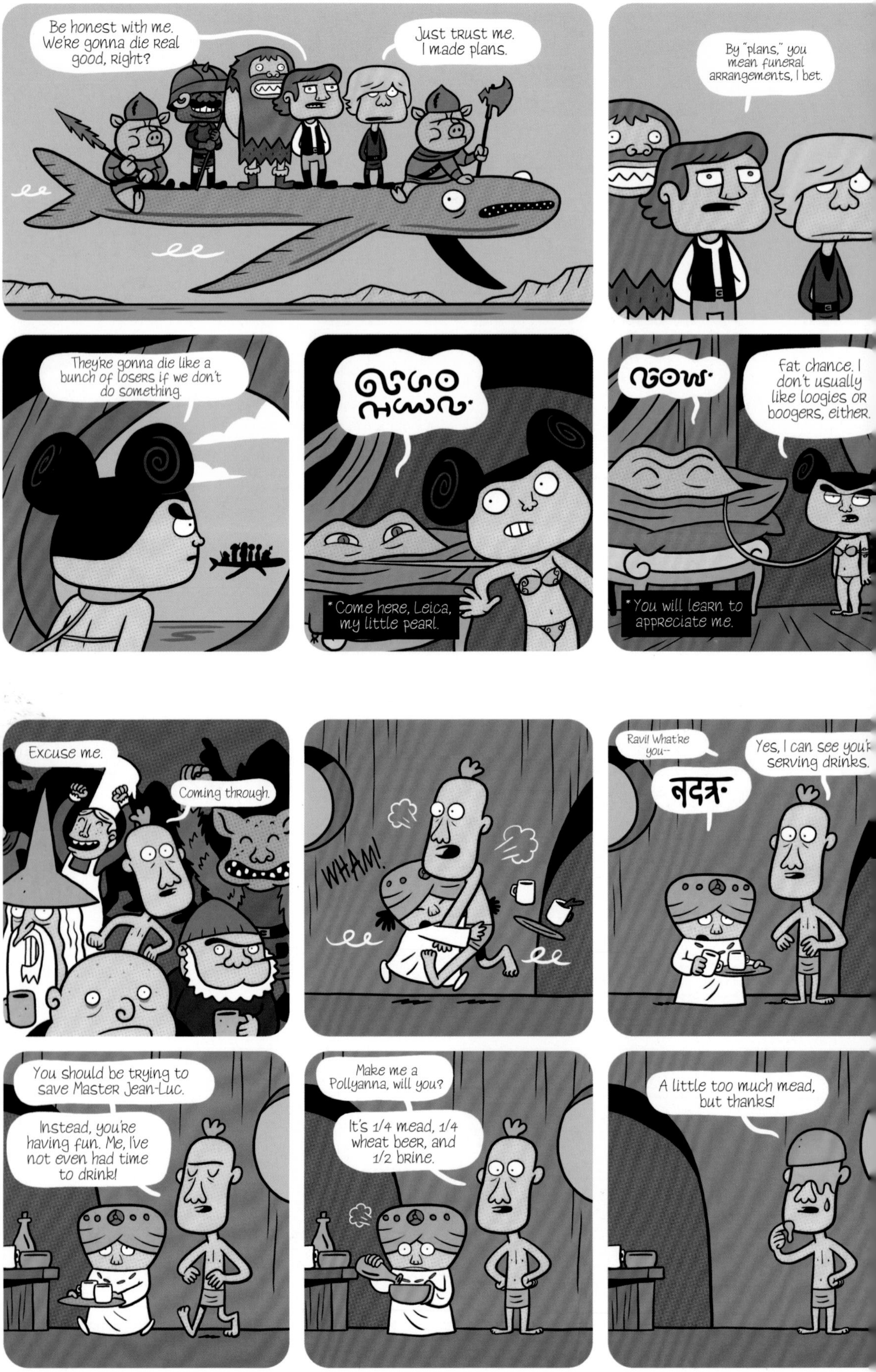

Be honest with me. We're gonna die real good, right?
Just trust me. I made plans.
By "plans," you mean funeral arrangements, I bet.
They're gonna die like a bunch of losers if we don't do something.
*Come here, Leica, my little pearl.
*You will learn to appreciate me.
Fat chance. I don't usually like loogies or boogers, either.
Excuse me.
Coming through.
WHAM!
Ravi! What're you--
Yes, I can see you're serving drinks.
You should be trying to save Master Jean-Luc.
Instead, you're having fun. Me, I've not even had time to drink!
Make me a Pollyanna, will you?
It's 1/4 mead, 1/4 wheat beer, and 1/2 brine.
A little too much mead, but thanks!

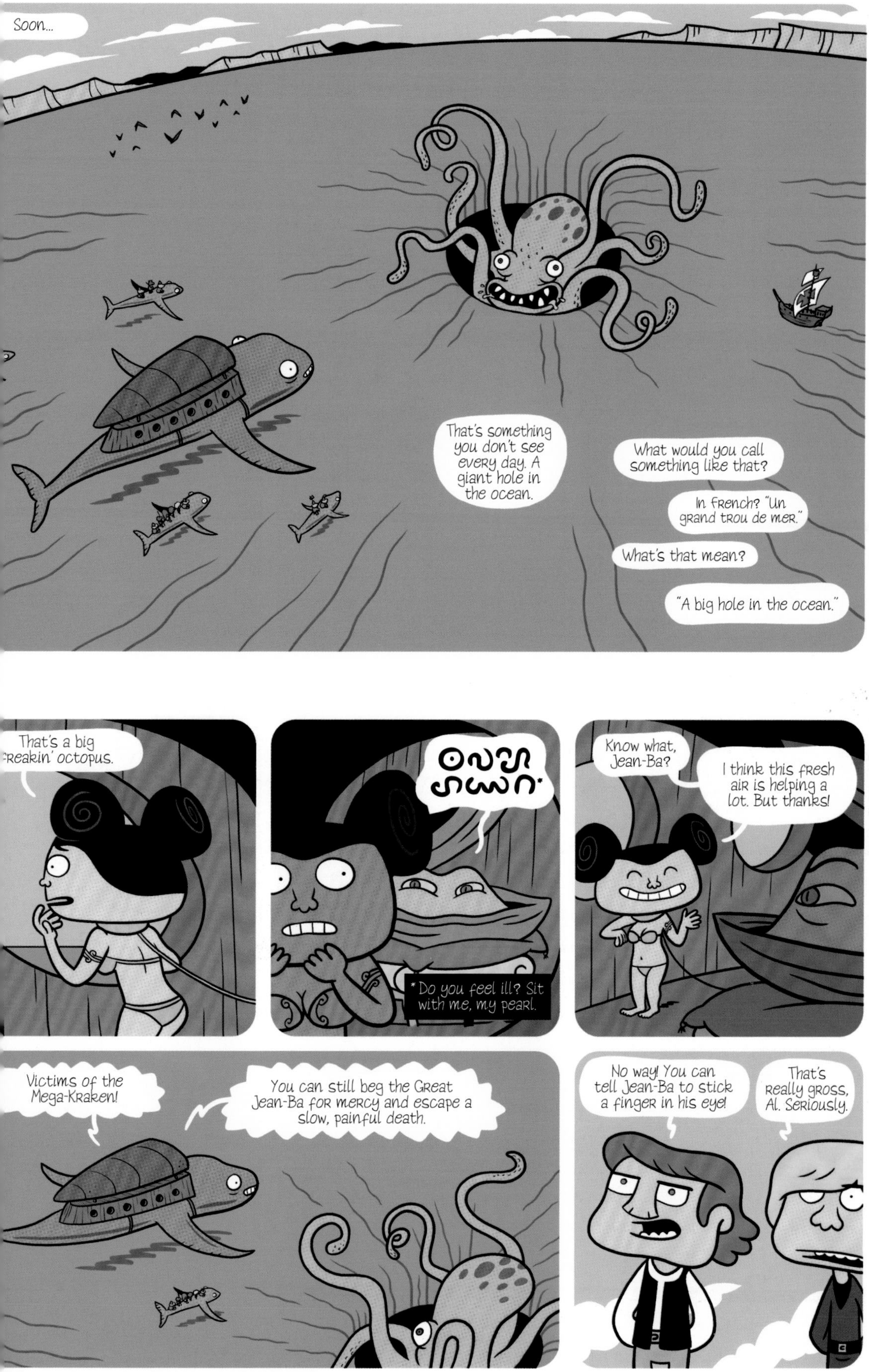
Soon...
That's something you don't see every day. A giant hole in the ocean.
What would you call something like that?
In French? "Un grand trou de mer."
What's that mean?
"A big hole in the ocean."
That's a big freakin' octopus.
*Do you feel ill? Sit with me, my pearl.
Know what, Jean-Ba?
I think this fresh air is helping a lot. But thanks!
Victims of the Mega-Kraken!
You can still beg the Great Jean-Ba for mercy and escape a slow, painful death.
No way! You can tell Jean-Ba to stick a finger in his eye!
That's really gross, Al. Seriously.

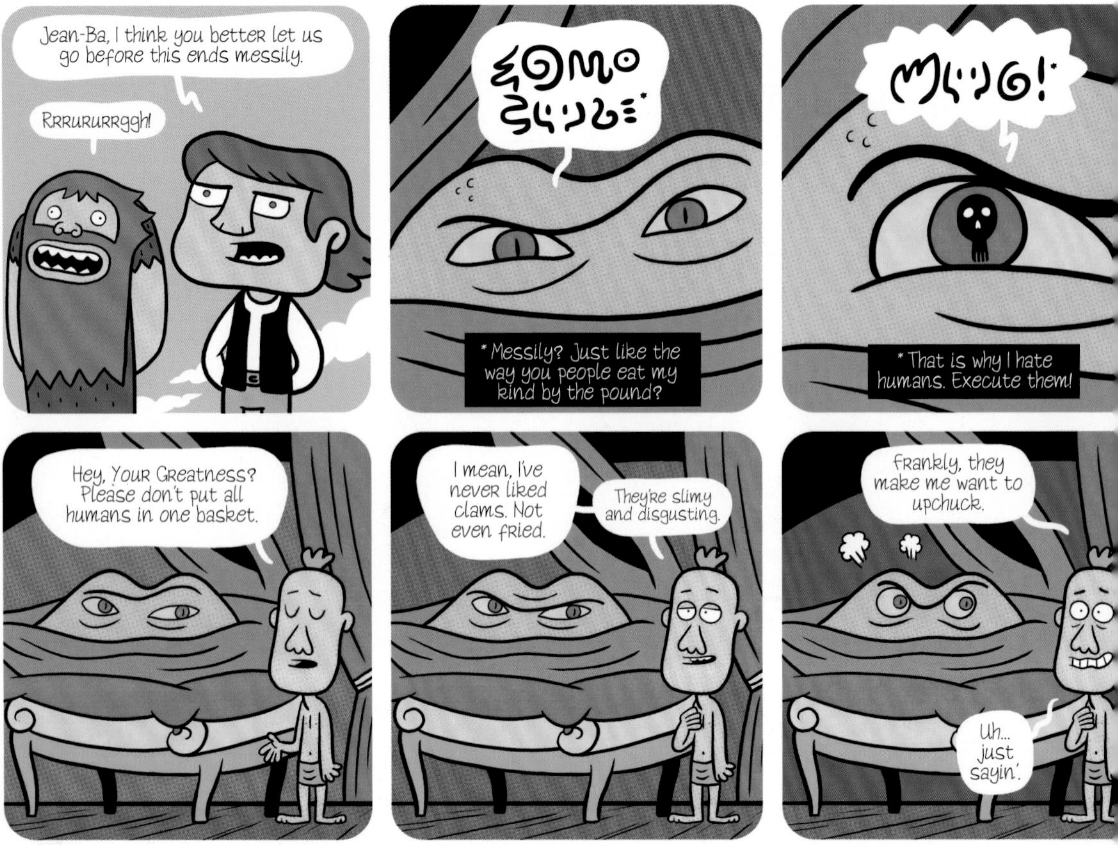
Jean-Ba, I think you better let us go before this ends messily.
Rrrururrrggh!
* Messily? Just like the way you people eat my kind by the pound?
* That is why I hate humans. Execute them!
Hey, Your Greatness? Please don't put all humans in one basket.
I mean, I've never liked clams. Not even fried.
They're slimy and disgusting.
Frankly, they make me want to upchuck.
Uh... just sayin'.

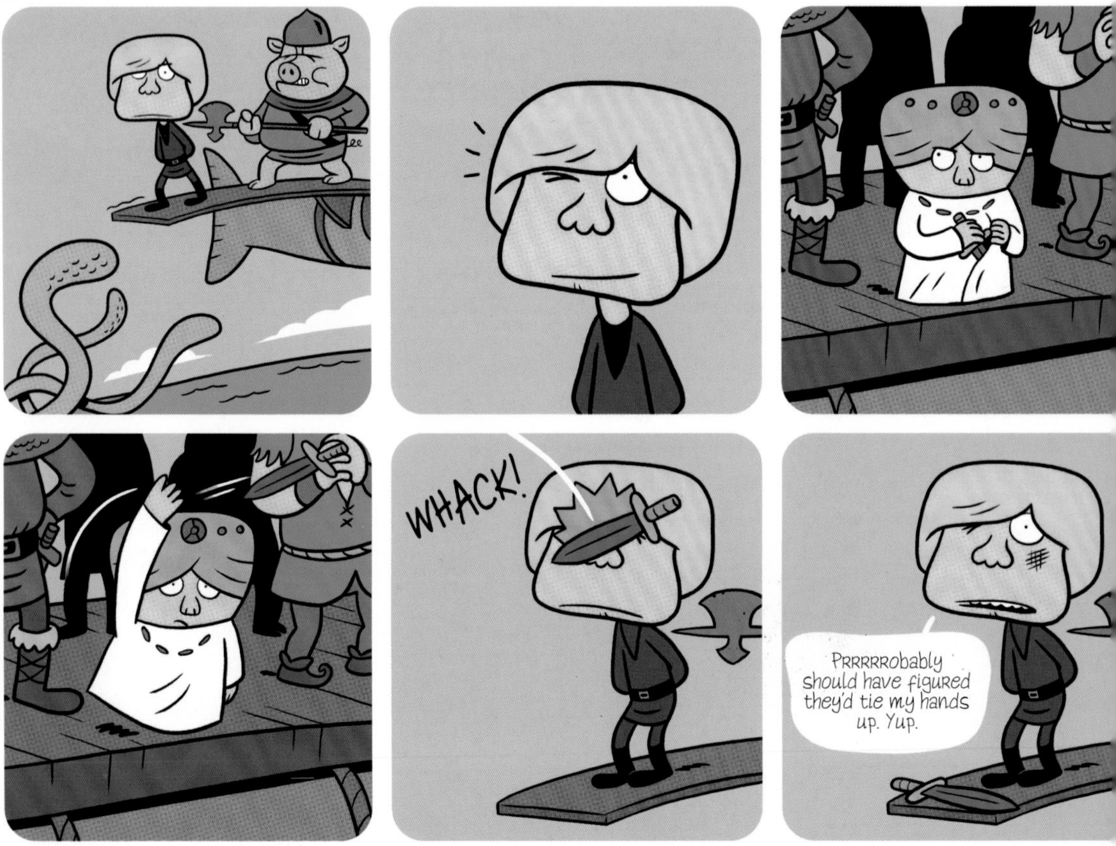
WHACK!
Prrrrrobably should have figured they'd tie my hands up. Yup.

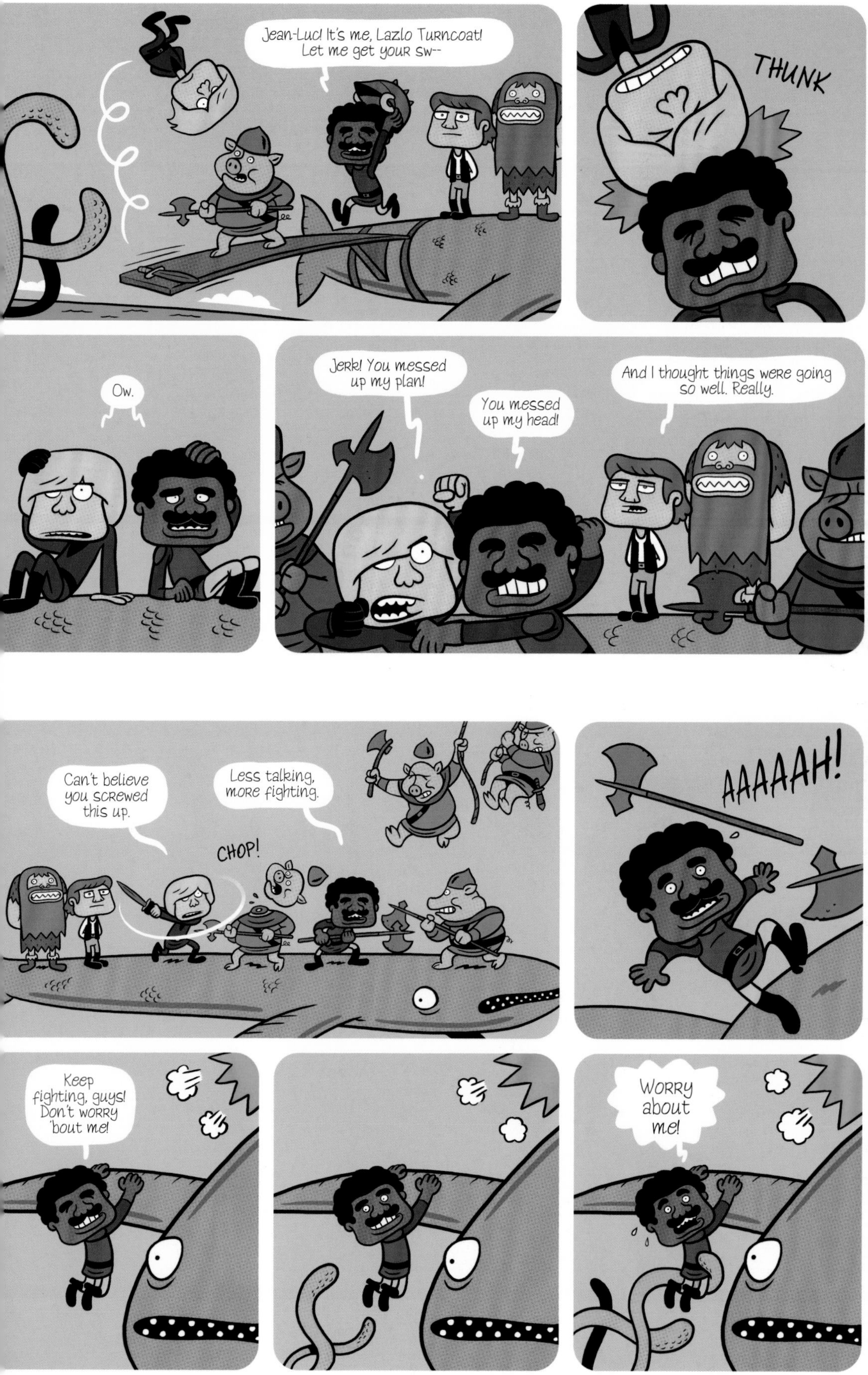

Jean-Luc! It's me, Lazlo Turncoat! Let me get your sw--
THUNK
Ow.
Jerk! You messed up my plan!
You messed up my head!
And I thought things were going so well. Really.
Can't believe you screwed this up.
Less talking, more fighting.
CHOP!
AAAAAH!
Keep fighting, guys! Don't worry 'bout me!
Worry about me!

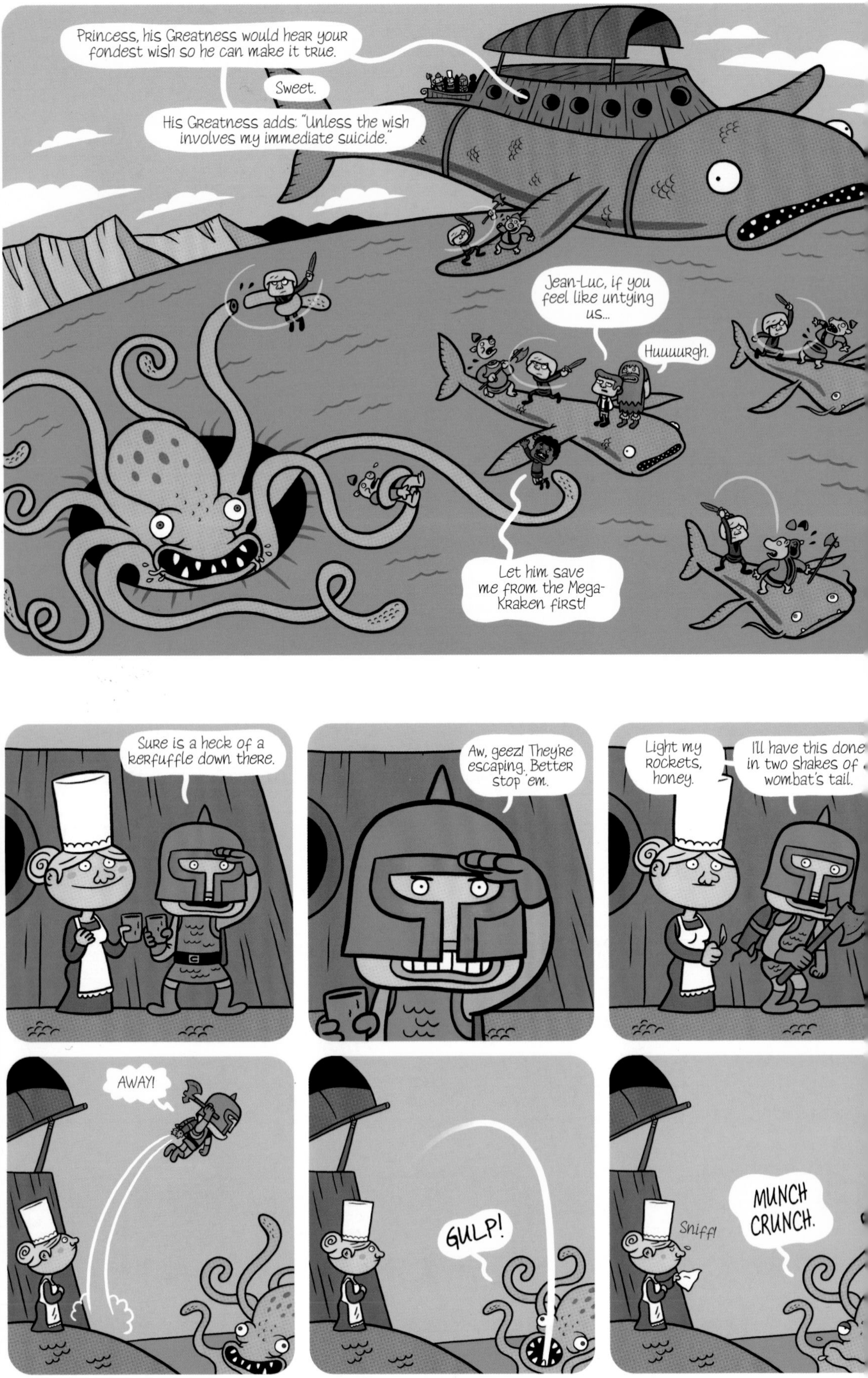
Princess, his Greatness would hear your fondest wish so he can make it true.
Sweet.
His Greatness adds: "Unless the wish involves my immediate suicide."
Jean-Luc, if you feel like untying us...
Huuuurgh.
Let him save me from the Mega-Kraken first!
Sure is a heck of a kerfuffle down there.
Aw, geez! They're escaping. Better stop 'em.
Light my rockets, honey.
I'll have this done in two shakes of a wombat's tail.
AWAY!
GULP!
Sniff!
MUNCH CRUNCH.

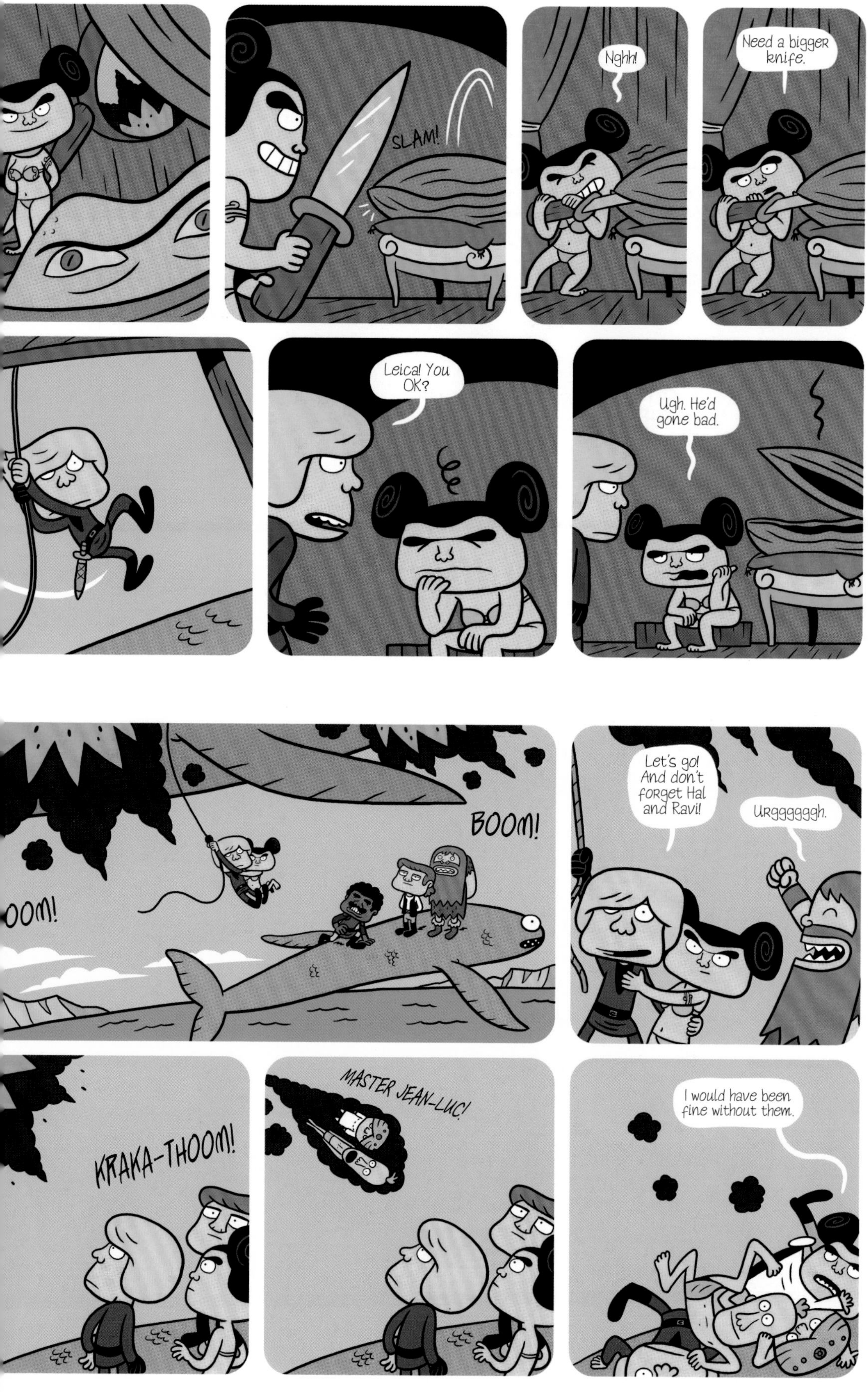
SLAM!
Nghh!
Need a bigger knife.
Leica! You OK?
Ugh. He'd gone bad.
BOOM!
OOM!
Let's go! And don't forget Hal and Ravi!
Urggggggh.
KRAKA-THOOM!
MASTER JEAN-LUC!
I would have been fine without them.

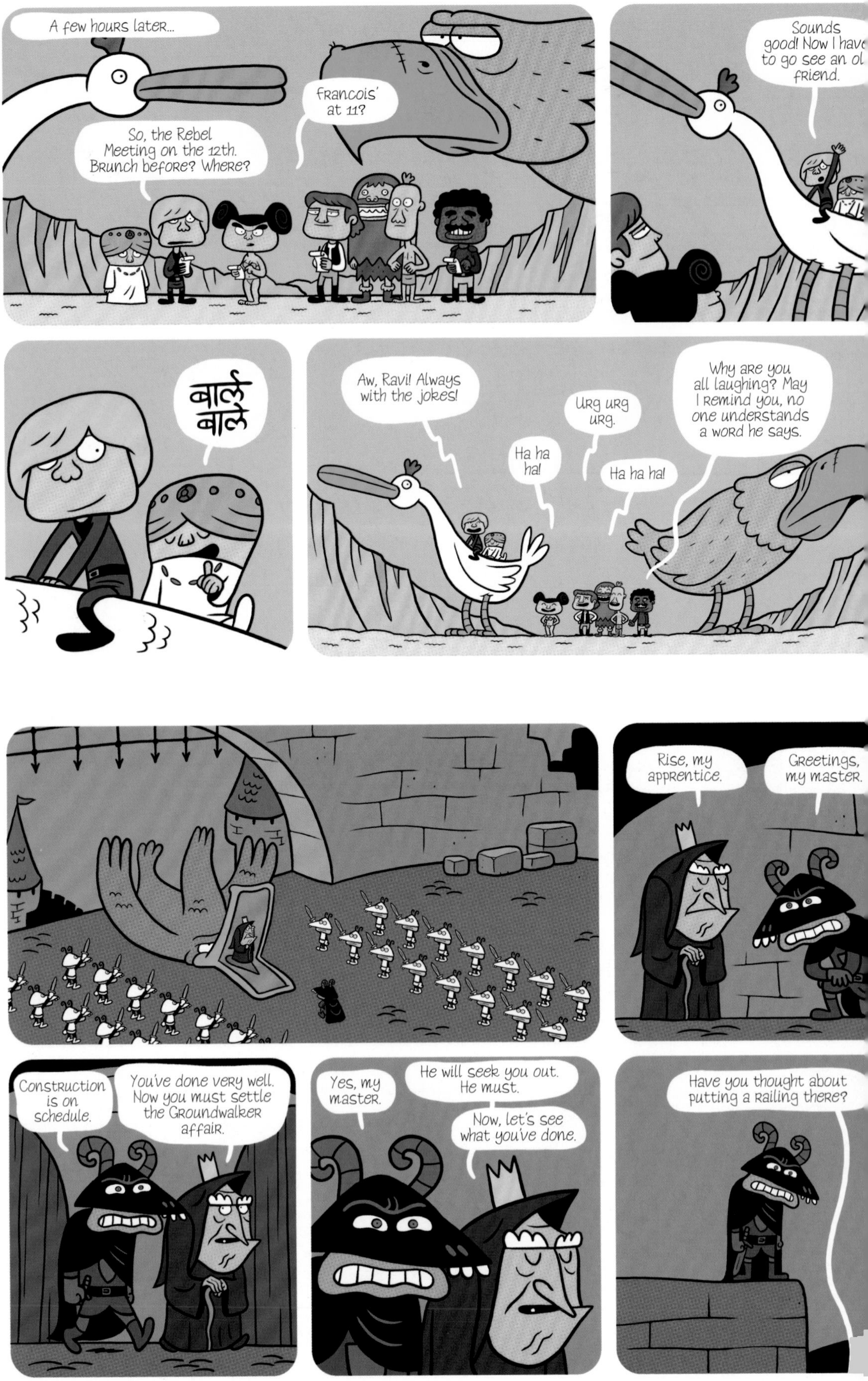
A few hours later...
So, the Rebel Meeting on the 12th. Brunch before? Where?
Francois' at 11?
Sounds good! Now I hav to go see an ol friend.
बाले बाले
Aw, Ravi! Always with the jokes!
Ha ha ha!
Urg urg urg.
Ha ha ha!
Why are you all laughing? May I remind you, no one understands a word he says.
Rise, my apprentice.
Greetings, my master.
Construction is on schedule.
You've done very well. Now you must settle the Groundwalker affair.
Yes, my master.
He will seek you out. He must.
Now, let's see what you've done.
Have you thought about putting a railing there?

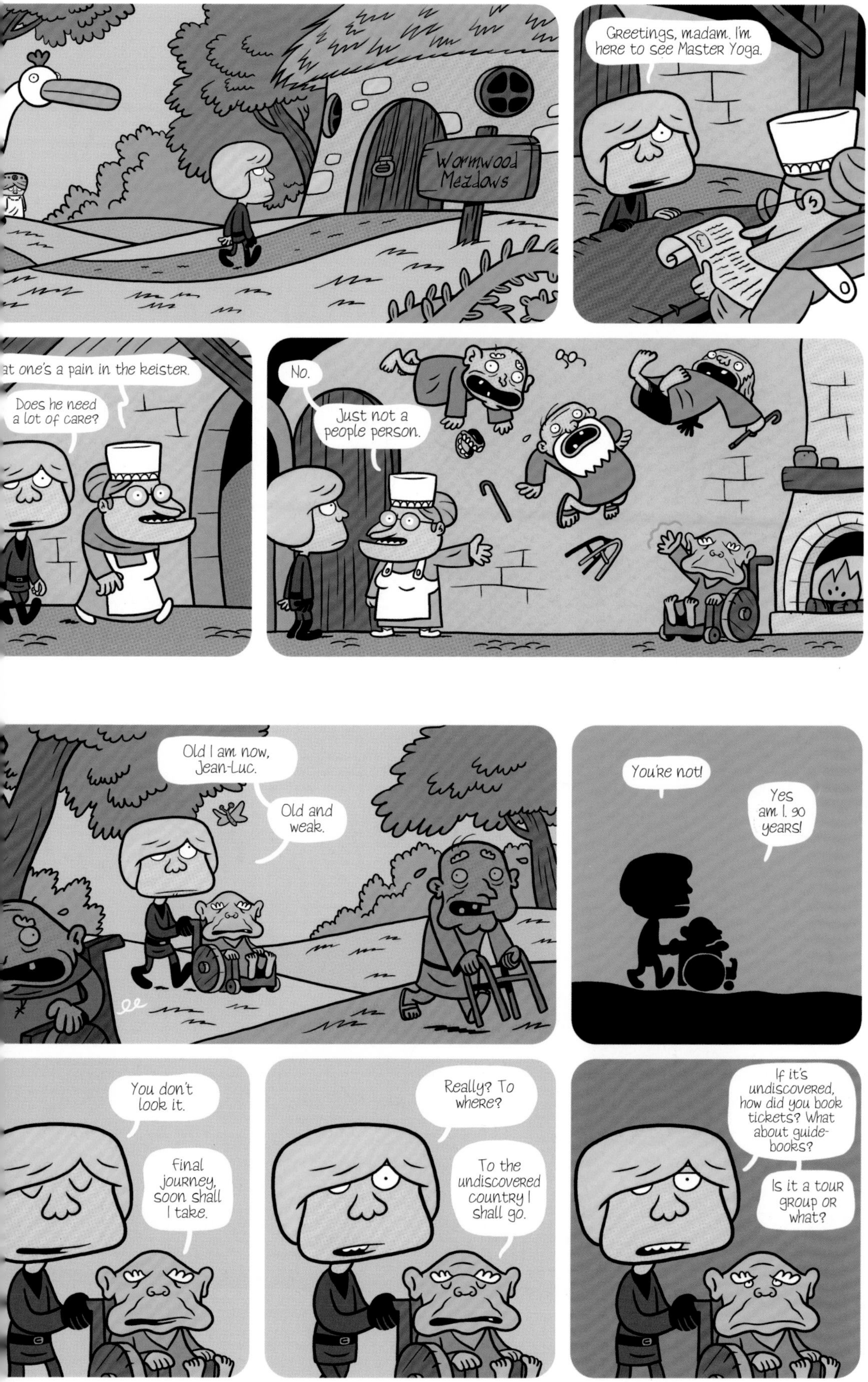
Wormwood Meadows
Greetings, madam. I'm here to see Master Yoga.
at one's a pain in the keister.
Does he need a lot of care?
No.
Just not a people person.
Old I am now, Jean-Luc.
Old and weak.
You're not!
Yes am I. 90 years!
You don't look it.
Final journey, soon shall I take.
Really? To where?
To the undiscovered country I shall go.
If it's undiscovered, how did you book tickets? What about guide-books?
Is it a tour group or what?

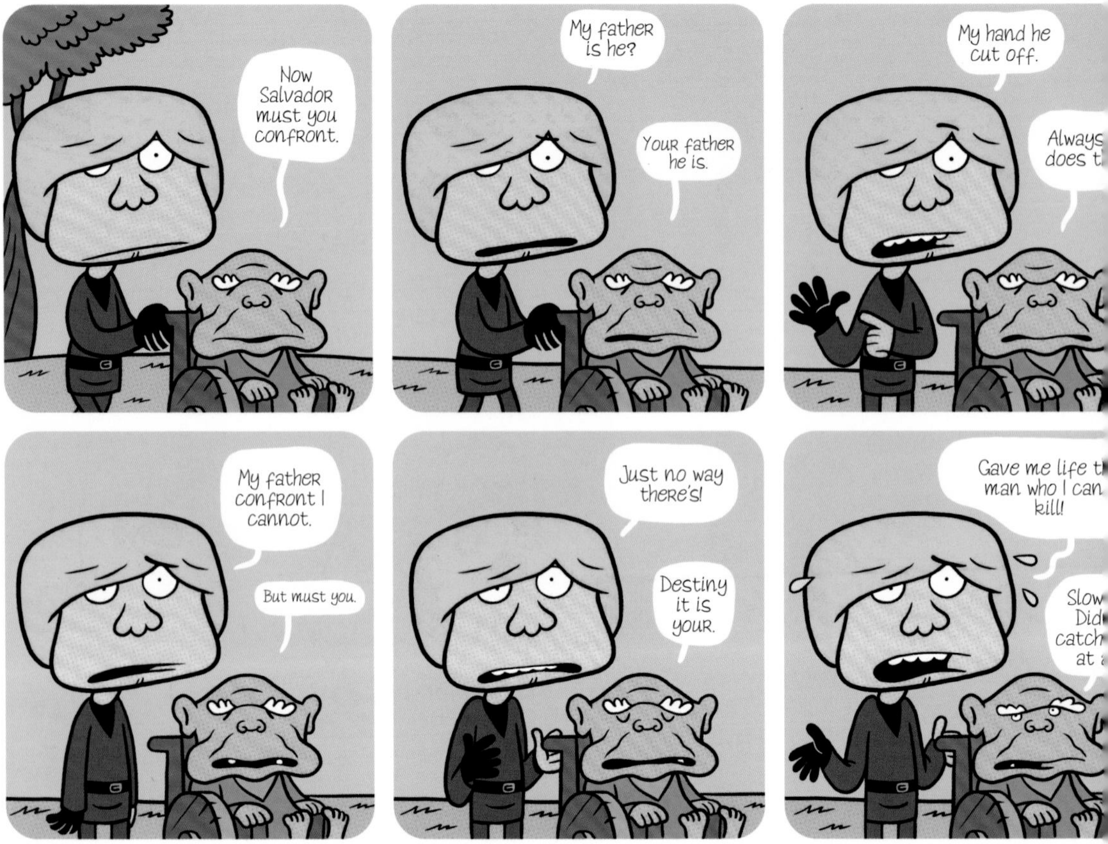
Now Salvador must you confront.
My father is he?
Your father he is.
My hand he cut off.
Always does
My father confront I cannot.
But must you.
Just no way there's!
Destiny it is your.
Gave me life
man who I can
kill!

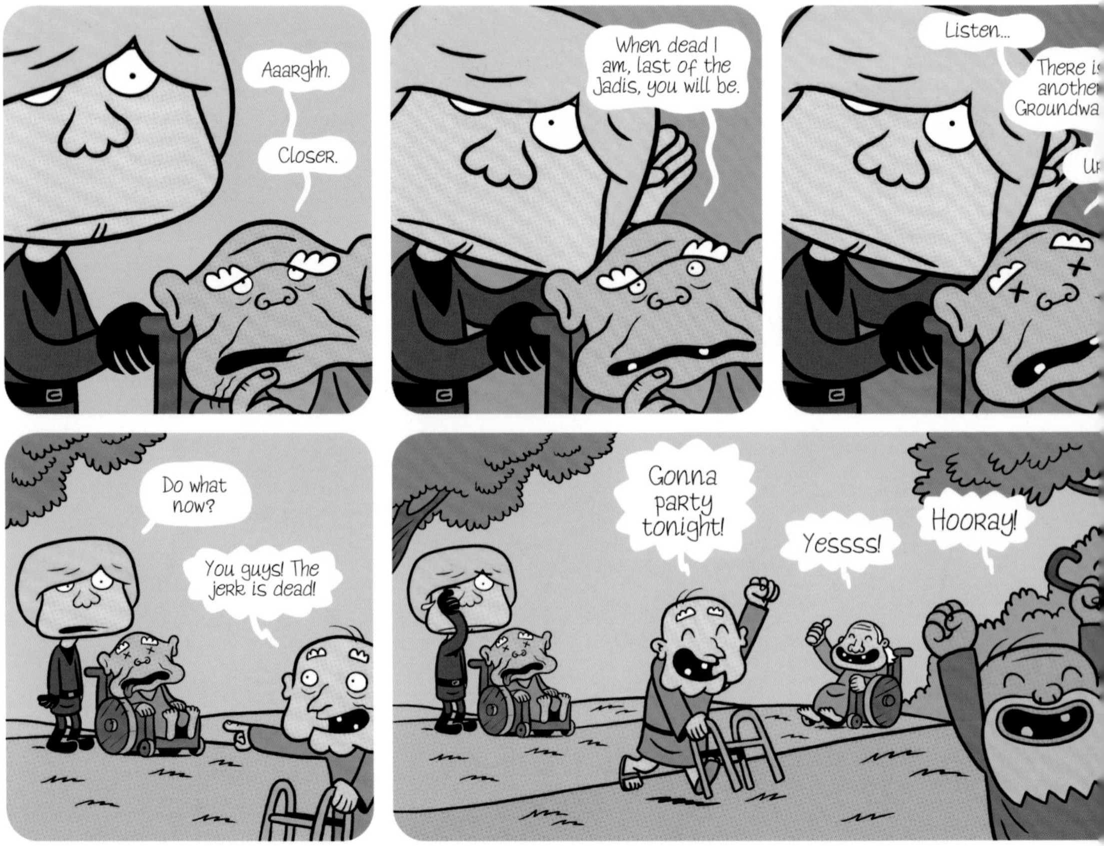
Aaarghh.
Closer.
When dead I am, last of the Jadis, you will be.
Listen...
Do what now?
You guys! The jerk is dead!
Gonna party tonight!
Yessss!
Hooray!

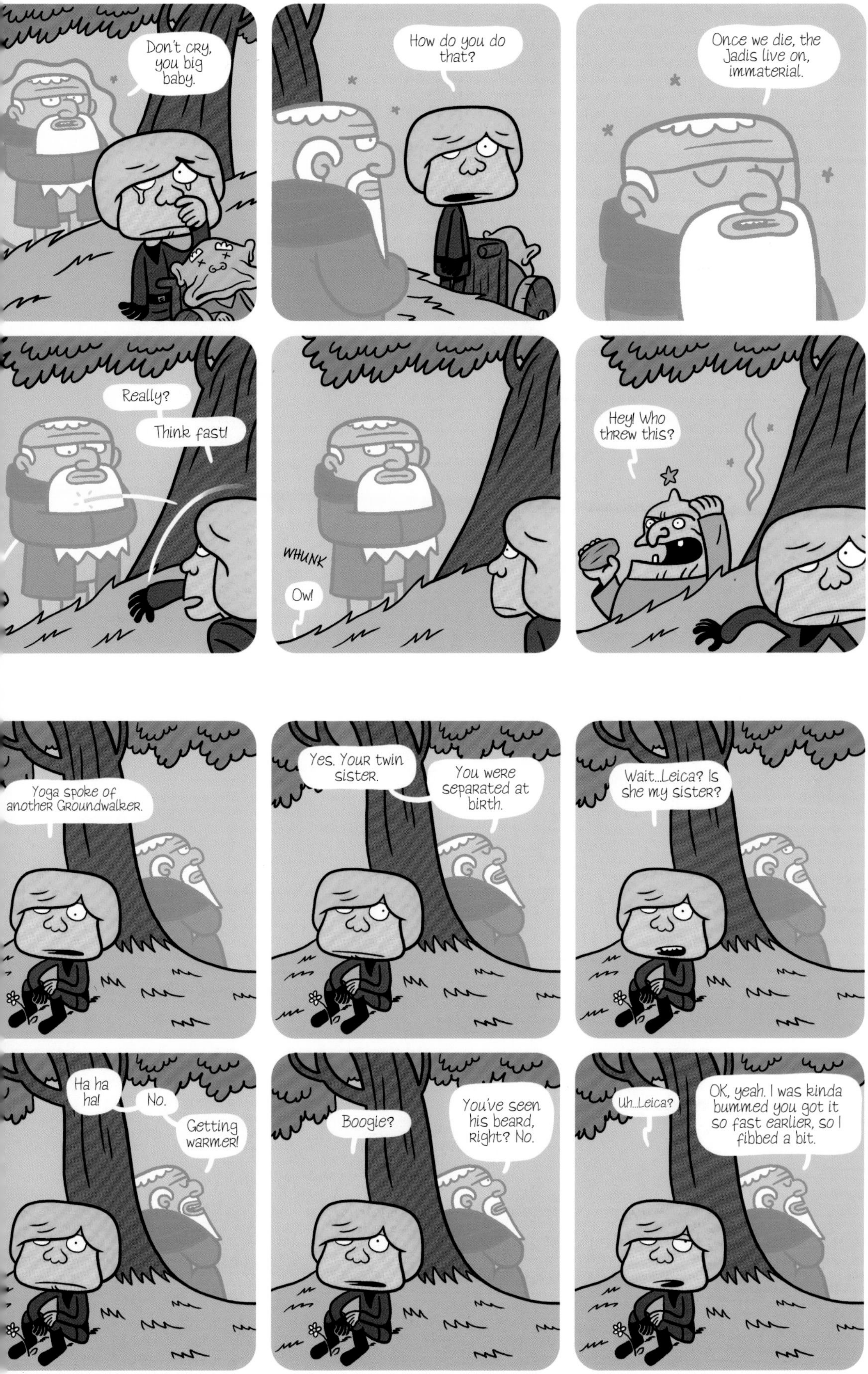
Don't cry, you big baby.
How do you do that?
Once we die, the Jadis live on, immaterial.
Really?
Think fast!
WHUNK
Ow!
Hey! Who threw this?
Yoga spoke of another Groundwalker.
Yes. Your twin sister.
You were separated at birth.
Wait...Leica? Is she my sister?
Ha ha ha!
No.
Getting warmer!
Boogie?
You've seen his beard, right? No.
Uh...Leica?
OK, yeah. I was kinda bummed you got it so fast earlier, so I fibbed a bit.

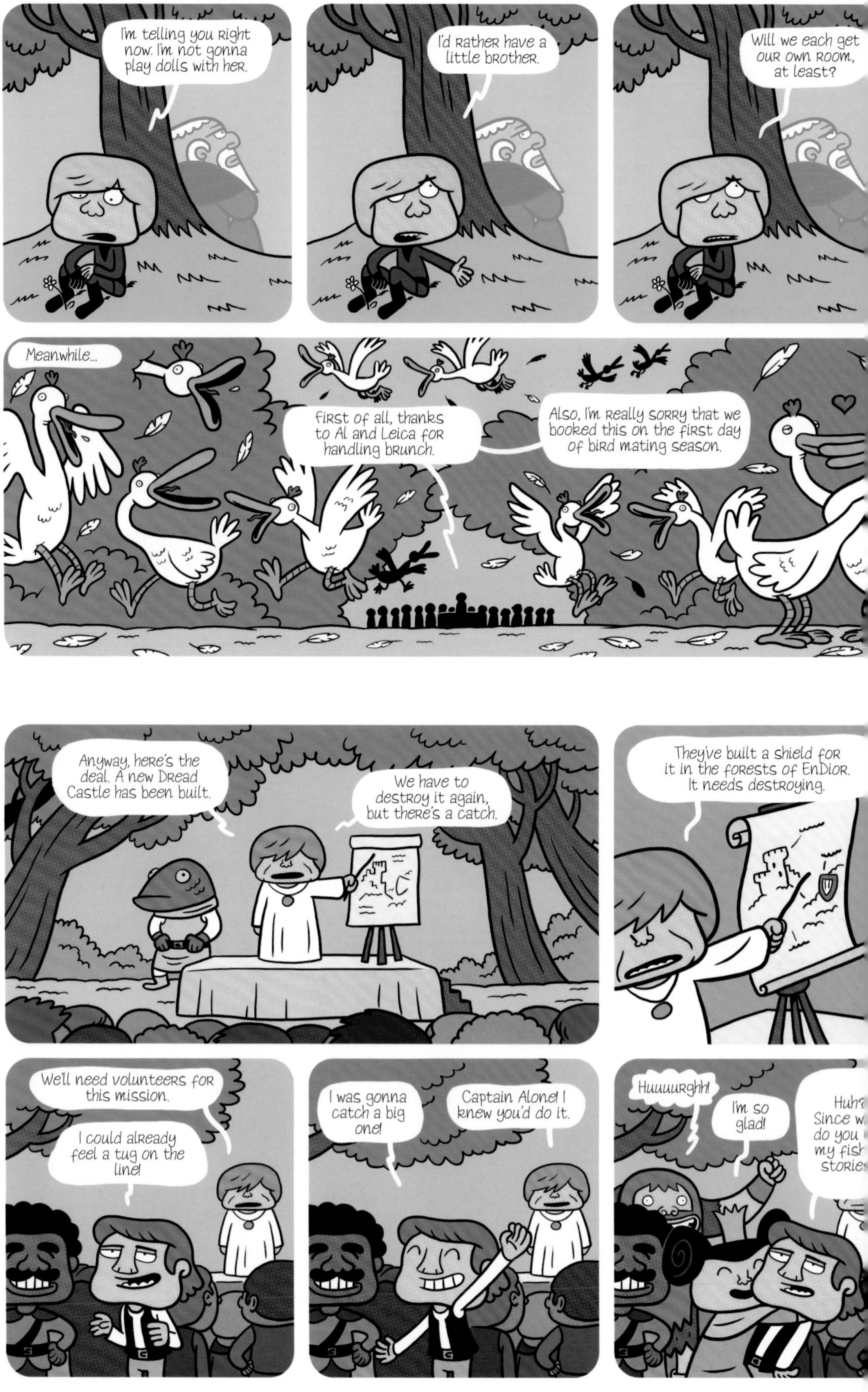

I'm telling you right now: I'm not gonna play dolls with her.
I'd rather have a little brother.
Will we each get our own room, at least?
Meanwhile...
First of all, thanks to Al and Leica for handling brunch.
Also, I'm really sorry that we booked this on the first day of bird mating season.
Anyway, here's the deal. A new Dread Castle has been built.
We have to destroy it again, but there's a catch.
They've built a shield for it in the forests of EnDior. It needs destroying.
We'll need volunteers for this mission.
I could already feel a tug on the line!
I was gonna catch a big one!
Captain Alone! I knew you'd do it.
Huuuurghh!
I'm so glad!
Huh?

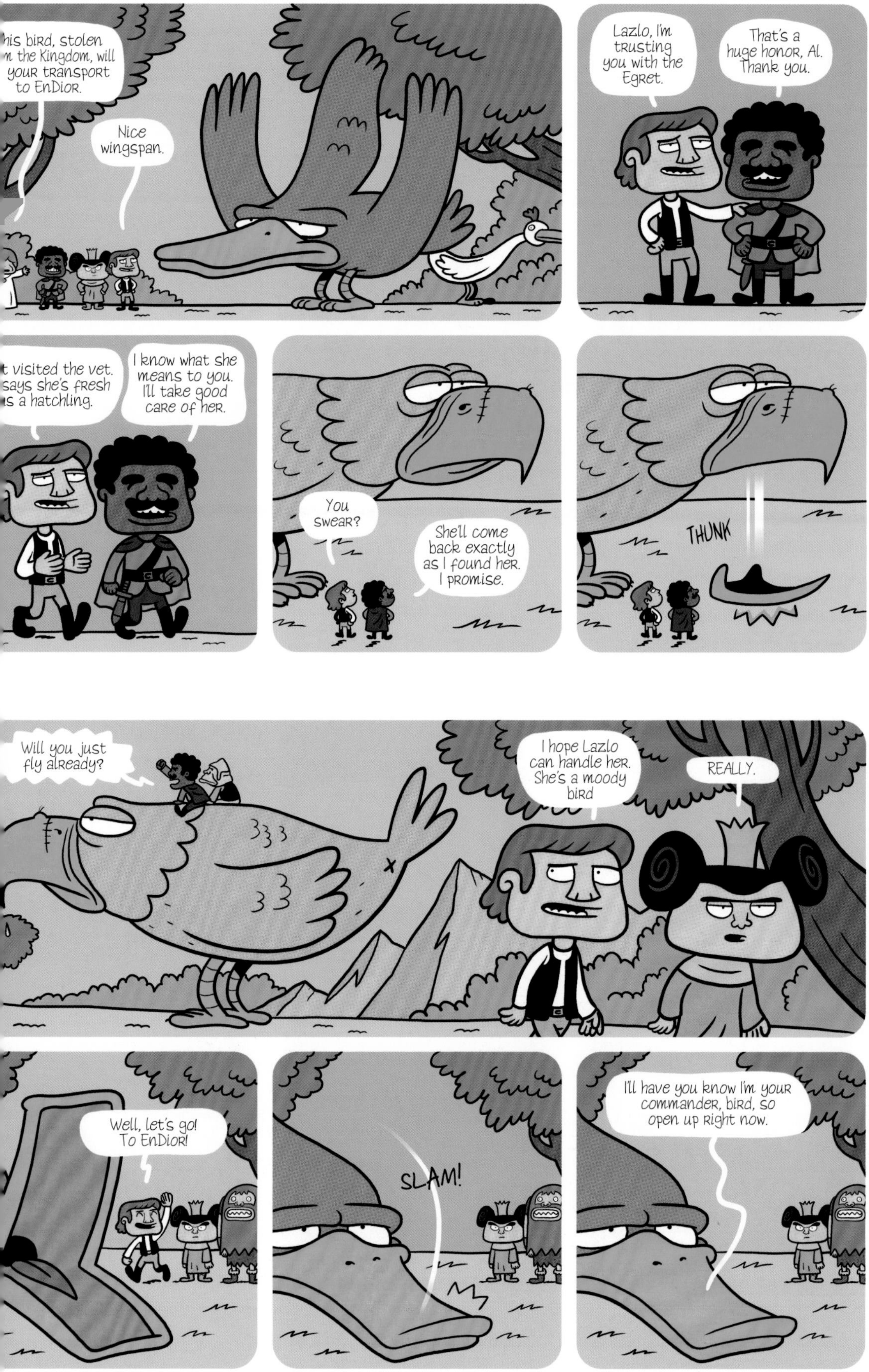
his bird, stolen
m the Kingdom, will
your transport
to EnDior.
Nice wingspan.
Lazlo, I'm trusting you with the Egret.
That's a huge honor, Al. Thank you.
t visited the vet.
says she's fresh
s a hatchling.
I know what she means to you. I'll take good care of her.
You swear?
She'll come back exactly as I found her. I promise.
THUNK
Will you just fly already?
I hope Lazlo can handle her. She's a moody bird
REALLY.
Well, let's go! To EnDior!
SLAM!
I'll have you know I'm your commander, bird, so open up right now.

To be continued...

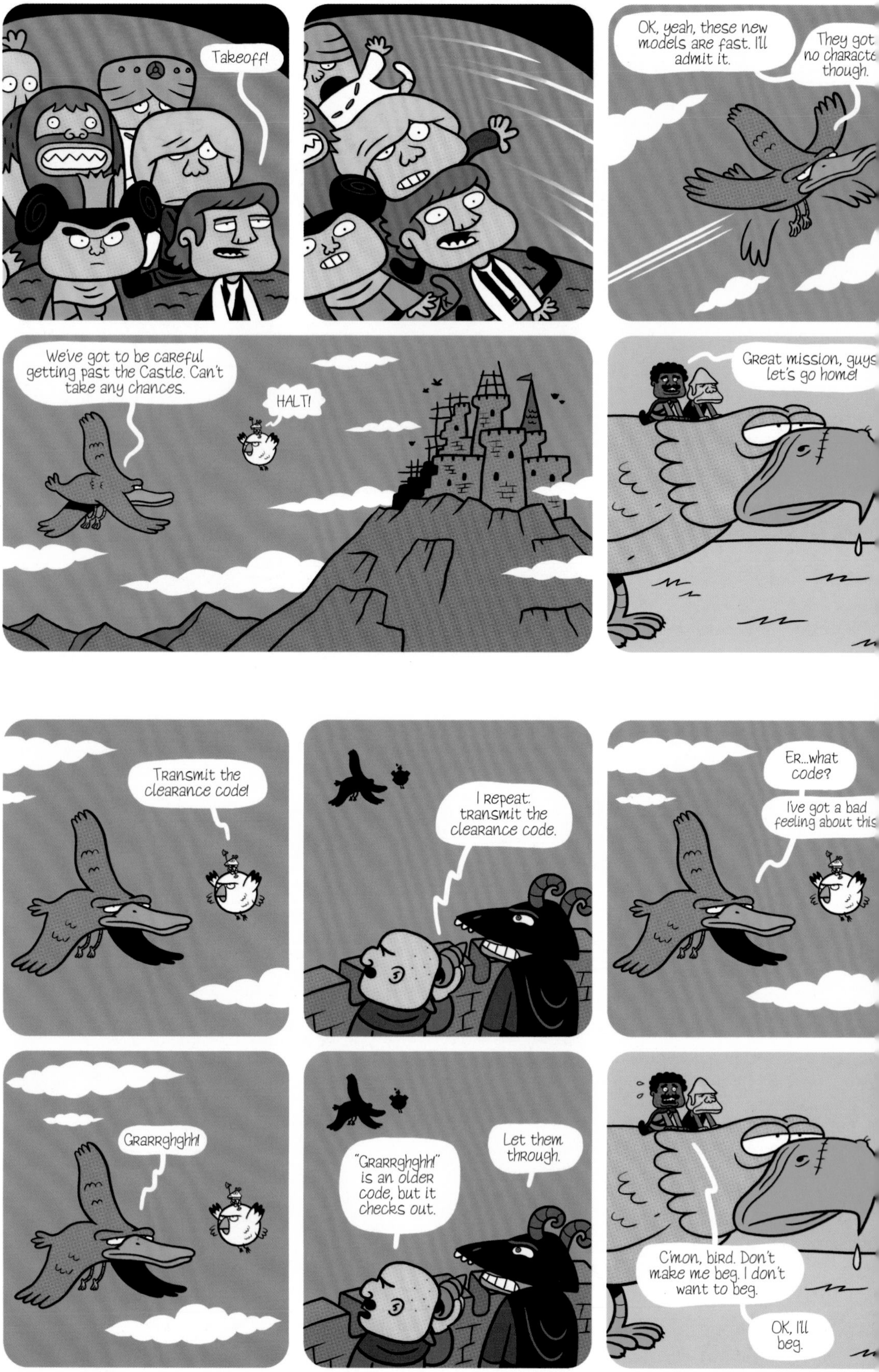
Takeoff!
OK, yeah, these new models are fast. I'll admit it.
They got no characte though.
We've got to be careful getting past the Castle. Can't take any chances.
HALT!
Great mission, guys let's go home!
Transmit the clearance code!
I repeat: transmit the clearance code.
Er...what code?
I've got a bad feeling about thi
Grarrghghh!
"Grarrghghh!" is an older code, but it checks out.
Let them through.
C'mon, bird. Don't make me beg. I don't want to beg.
OK, I'll beg.

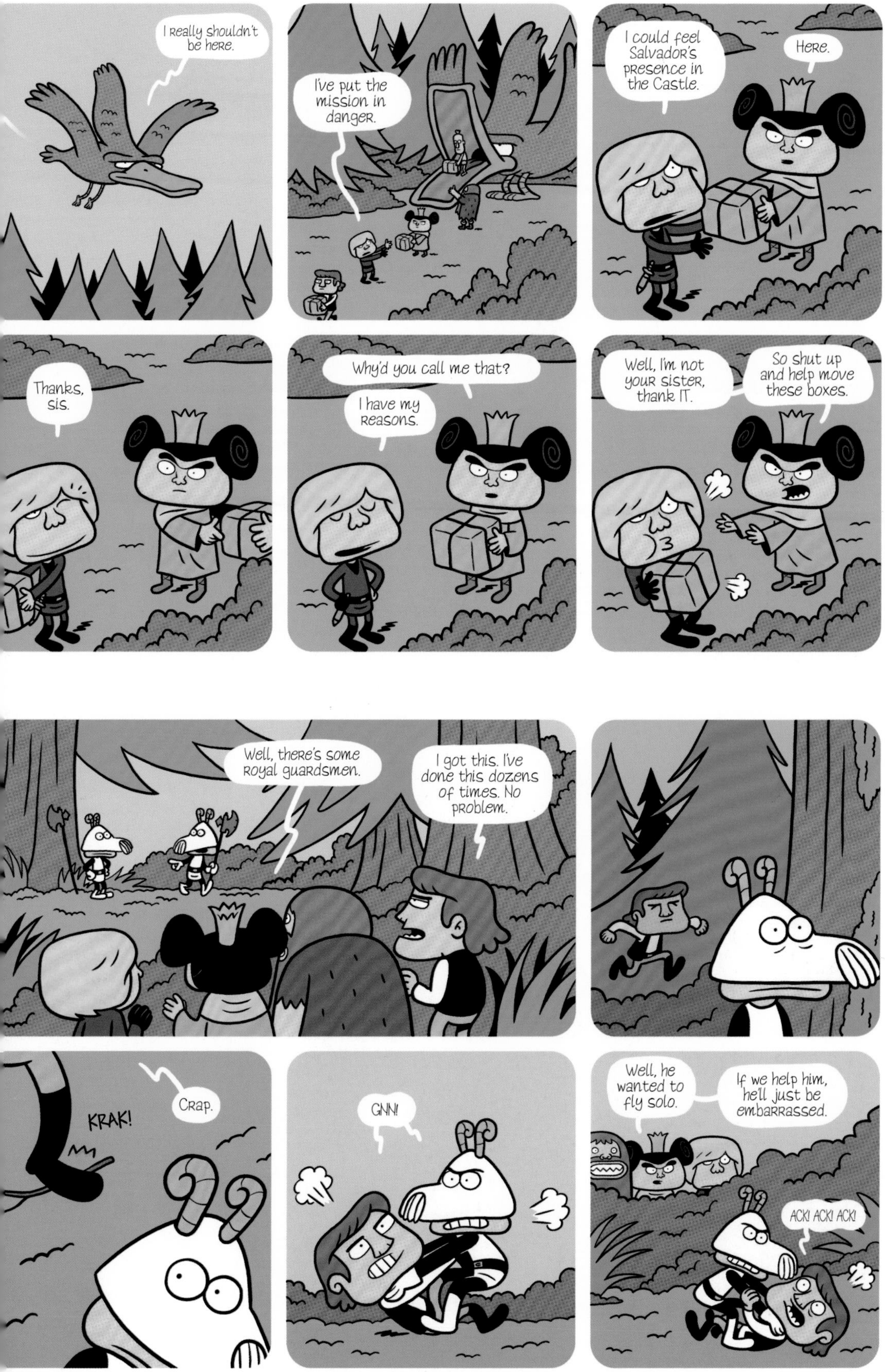
I really shouldn't be here.
I've put the mission in danger.
I could feel Salvador's presence in the Castle.
Here.
Thanks, sis.
Why'd you call me that?
I have my reasons.
Well, I'm not your sister, thank IT.
So shut up and help move these boxes.
Well, there's some royal guardsmen.
I got this. I've done this dozens of times. No problem.
KRAK!
Crap.
GNN!
Well, he wanted to fly solo.
If we help him, he'll just be embarrassed.
ACK! ACK! ACK!

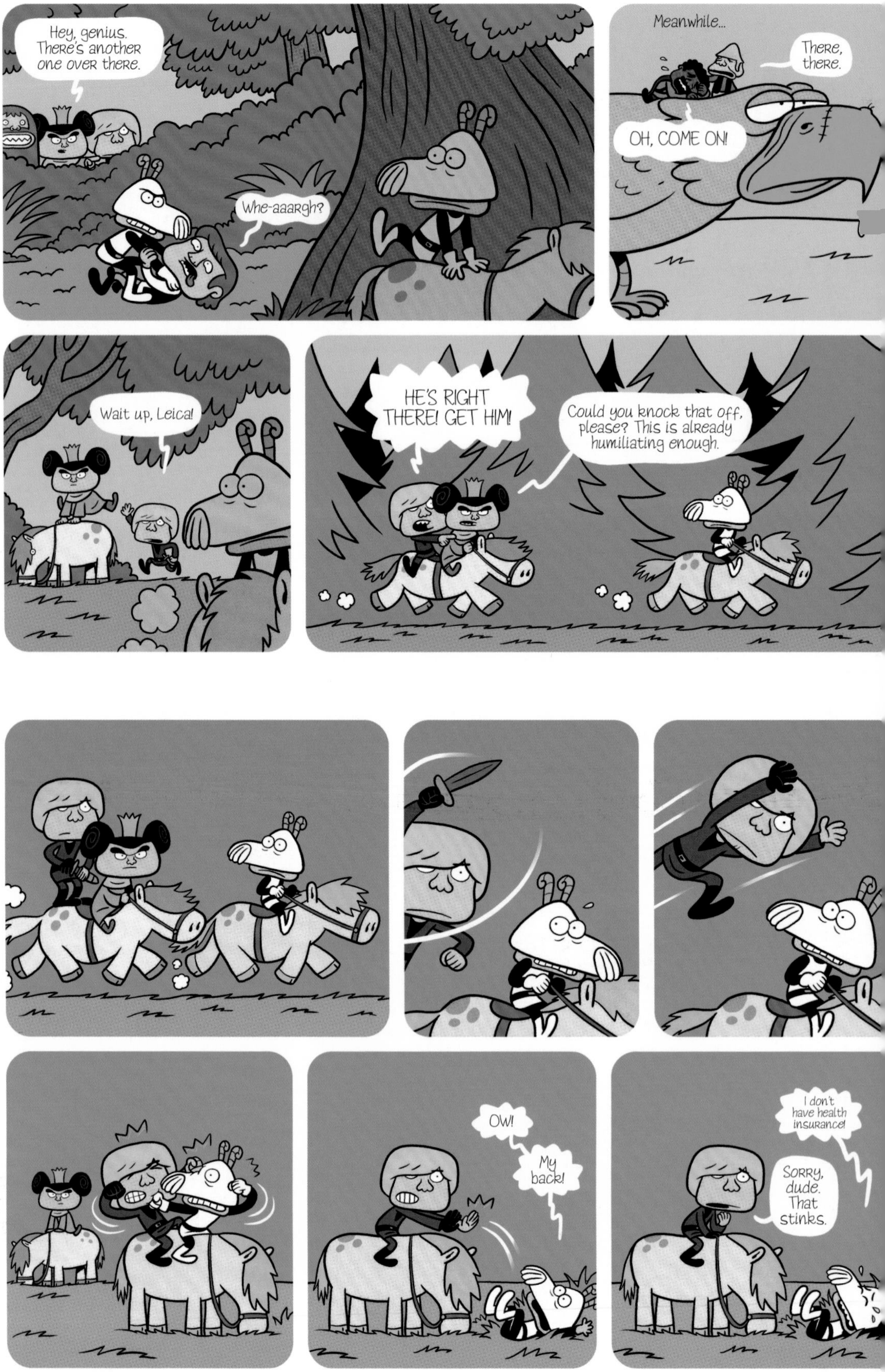

Hey, genius. There's another one over there.
Whe-aaargh?
Meanwhile...
There, there.
OH, COME ON!
Wait up, Leica!
HE'S RIGHT THERE! GET HIM!
Could you knock that off, please? This is already humiliating enough.
OW!
My back!
I don't have health insurance!
Sorry, dude. That stinks.

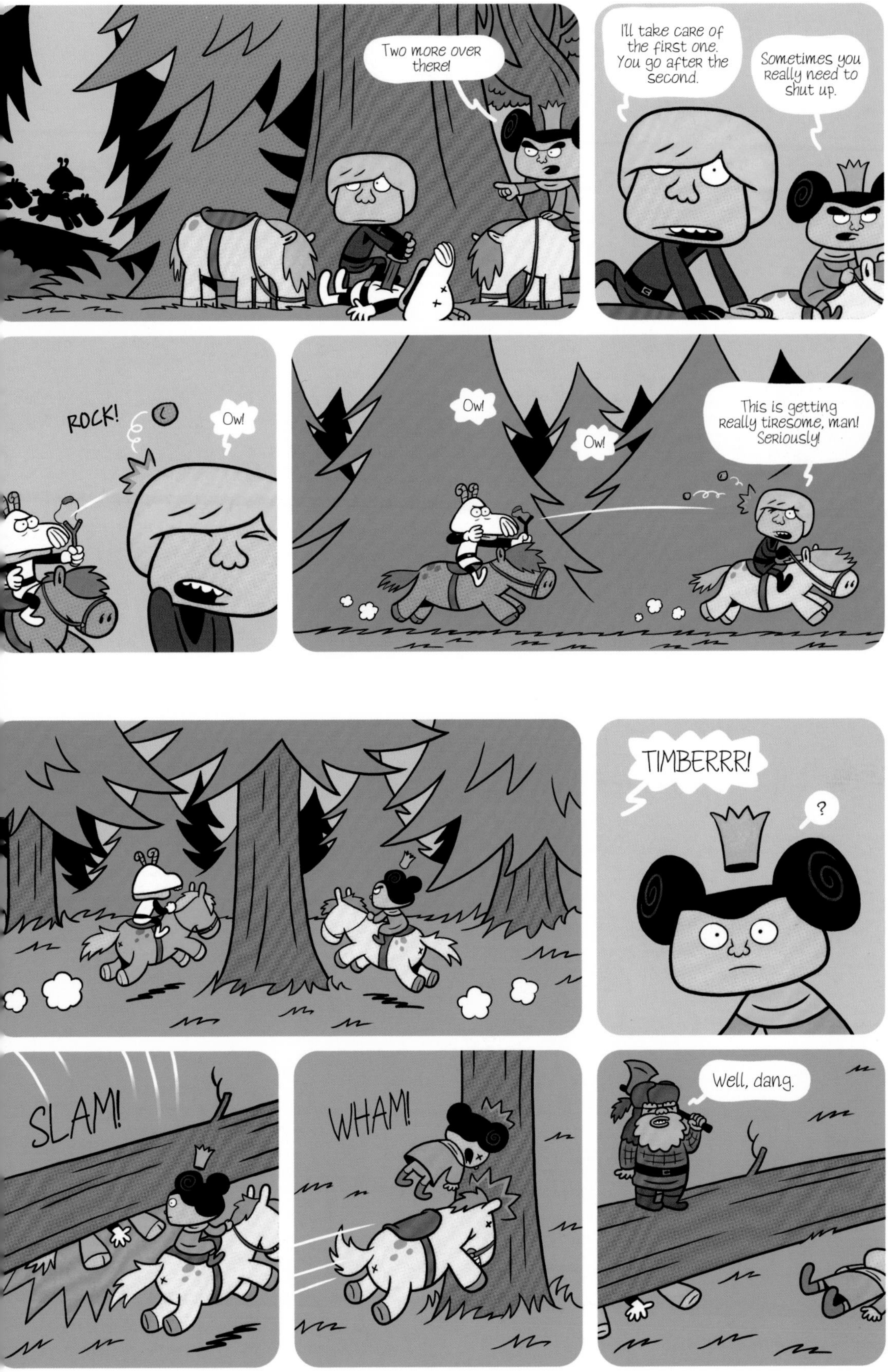
Two more over there!
I'll take care of the first one. You go after the second.
Sometimes you really need to shut up.
ROCK!
Ow!
Ow!
Ow!
This is getting really tiresome, man! Seriously!
TIMBERRR!
?
SLAM!
WHAM!
Well, dang.

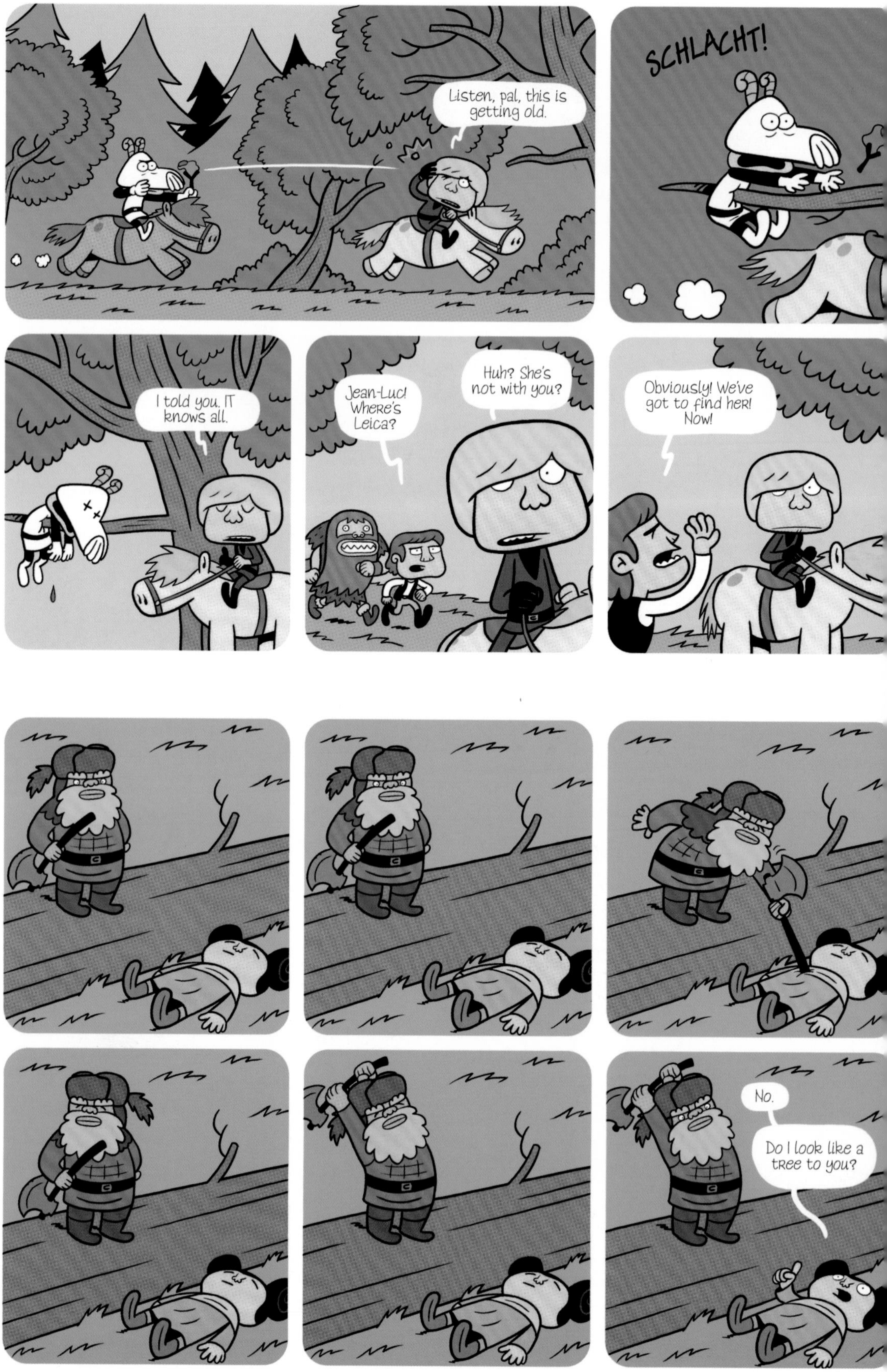
Listen, pal, this is getting old.
SCHLACHT!
I told you. IT knows all.
Jean-Luc! Where's Leica?
Huh? She's not with you?
Obviously! We've got to find her! Now!
No.
Do I look like a tree to you?

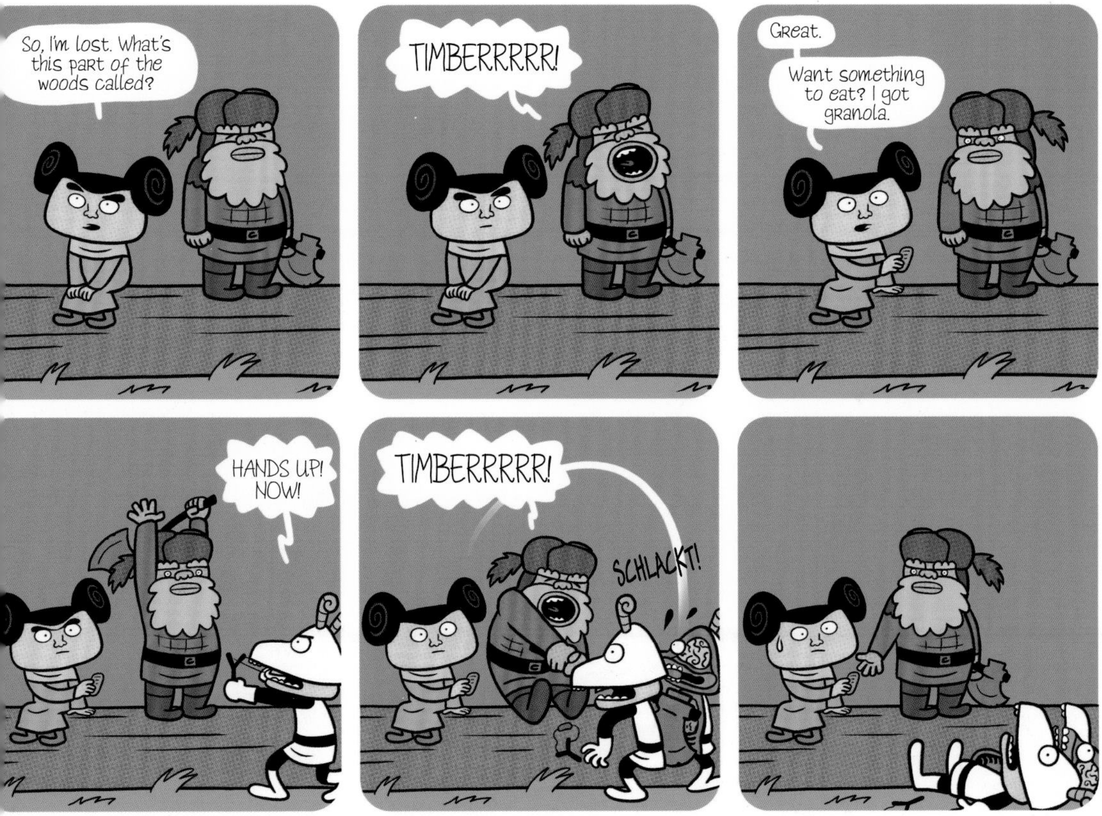
So, I'm lost. What's this part of the woods called?
TIMBERRRRR!
Great.
Want something to eat? I got granola.
HANDS UP! NOW!
TIMBERRRRR!
SCHLACKT!

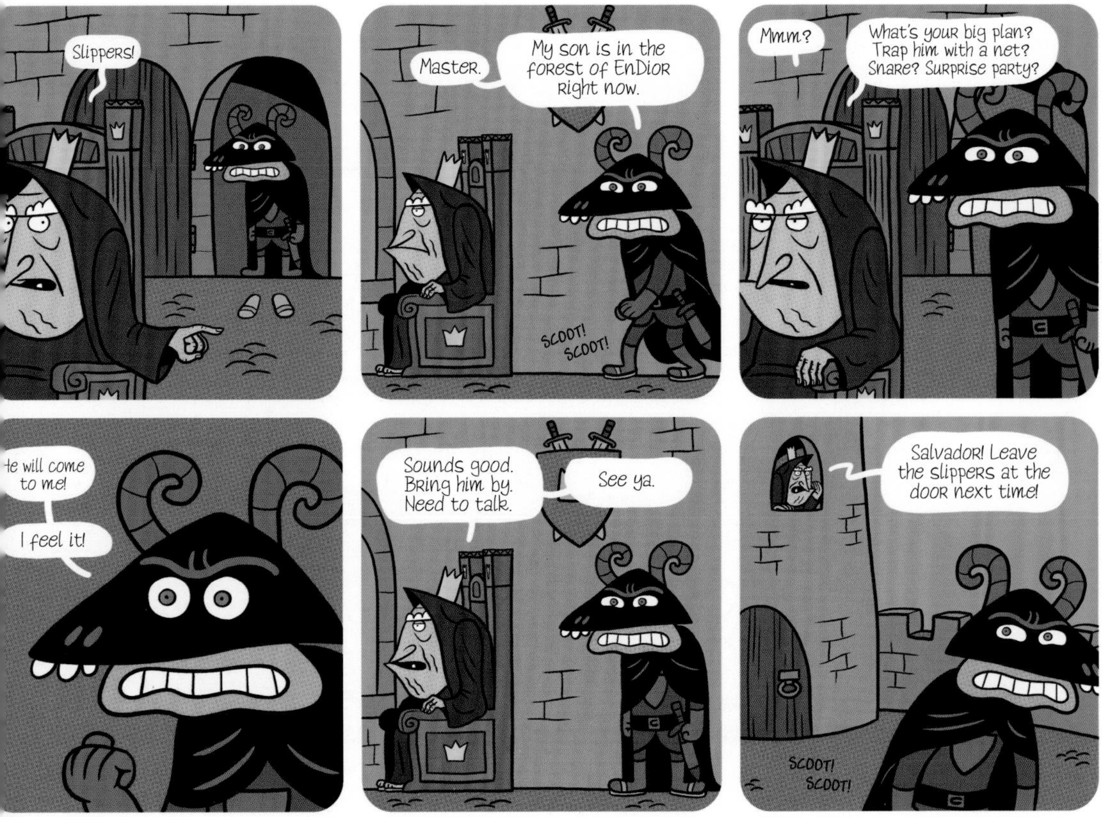
Slippers!
Master.
My son is in the forest of EnDior right now.
SCOOT! SCOOT!
Mmm?
What's your big plan? Trap him with a net? Snare? Surprise party?
He will come to me!
I feel it!
Sounds good. Bring him by. Need to talk.
See ya.
Salvador! Leave the slippers at the door next time!
SCOOT! SCOOT!

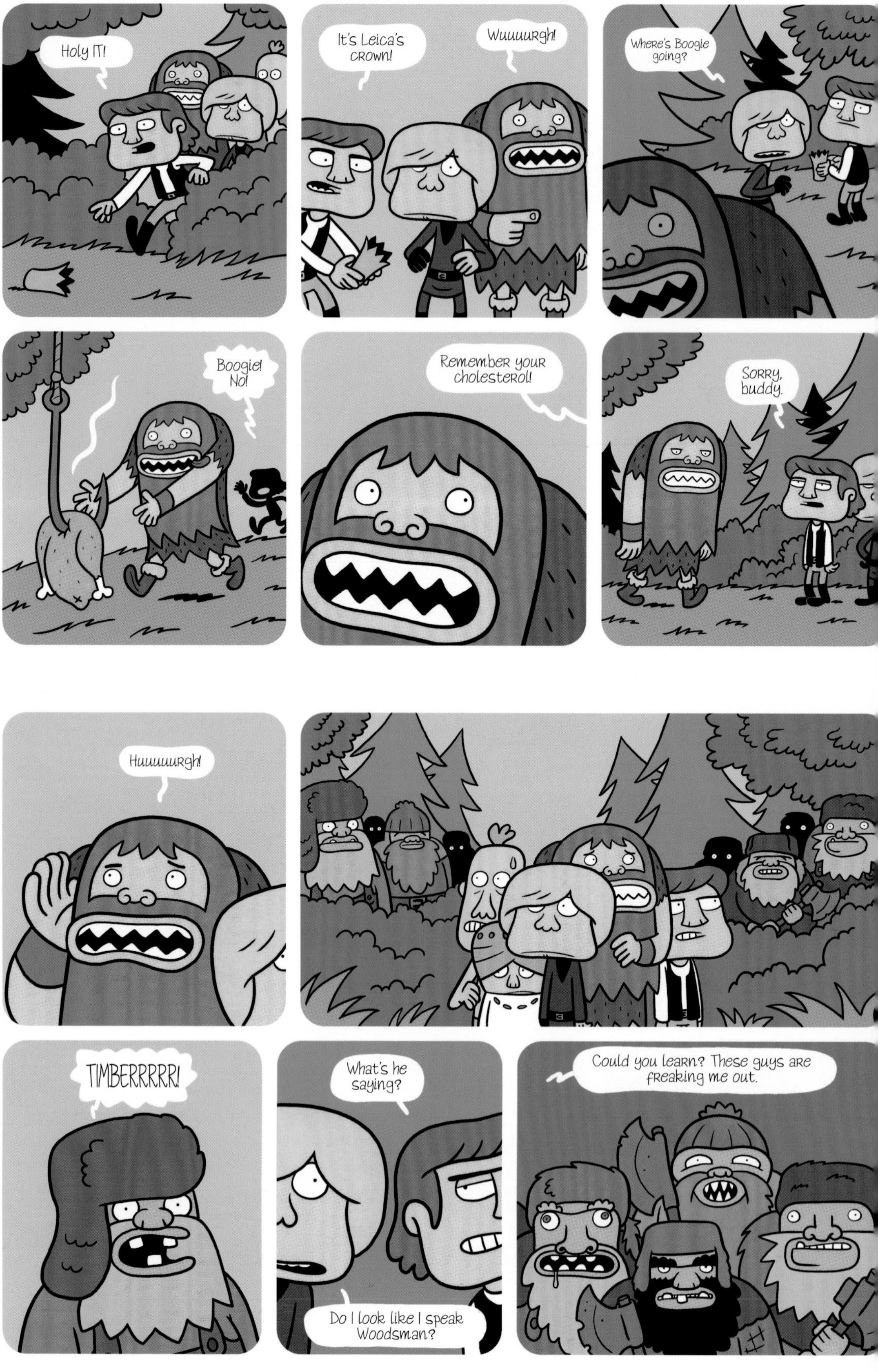

Holy IT!
It's Leica's CROWN!
Wuuuurgh!
Where's Boogie going?
Boogie! No!
Remember your cholesterol!
SORRY, buddy.
Huuuuurgh!
TIMBERRRRR!
What's he saying?
Do I look like I speak Woodsman?
Could you learn? These guys are freaking me out.

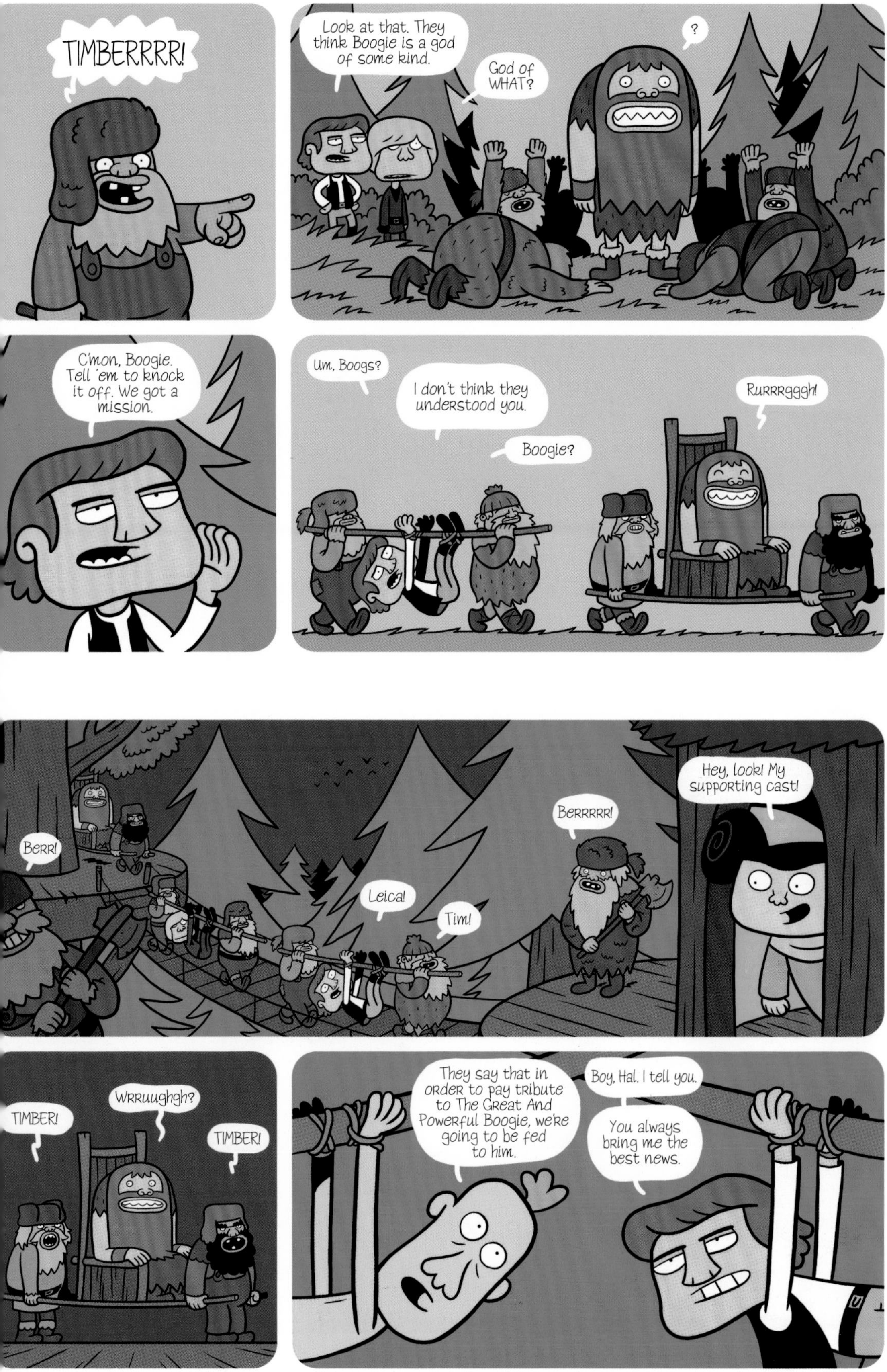
TIMBERRRR!
Look at that. They think Boogie is a god of some kind.
God of WHAT?
?
C'mon, Boogie. Tell 'em to knock it off. We got a mission.
Um, Boogs?
I don't think they understood you.
Boogie?
Rurrrgggh!
Berr!
Leica!
Tim!
Berrrrr!
Hey, look! My supporting cast!
TIMBER!
Wrruughgh?
TIMBER!
They say that in order to pay tribute to The Great And Powerful Boogie, we're going to be fed to him.
Boy, Hal. I tell you.
You always bring me the best news.

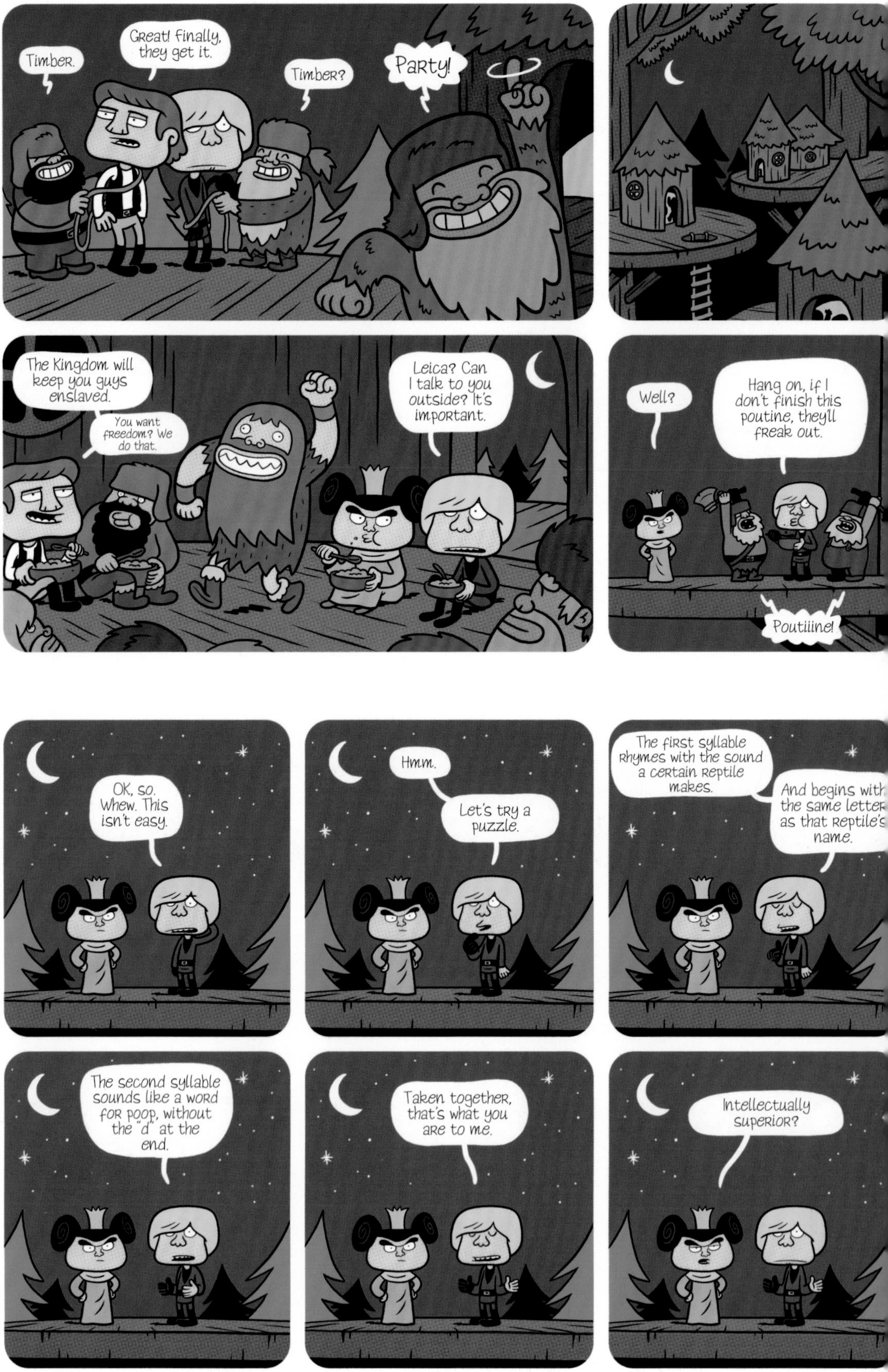
Timber.
Great! finally, they get it.
Timber?
Party!
The Kingdom will keep you guys enslaved.
You want freedom? We do that.
Leica? Can I talk to you outside? It's important.
Well?
Hang on, if I don't finish this poutine, they'll freak out.
Poutiiine!
OK, so. Whew. This isn't easy.
Hmm.
Let's try a puzzle.
The first syllable rhymes with the sound a certain reptile makes.
And begins with the same letter as that reptile's name.
The second syllable sounds like a word for poop, without the "d" at the end.
Taken together, that's what you are to me.
Intellectually superior?

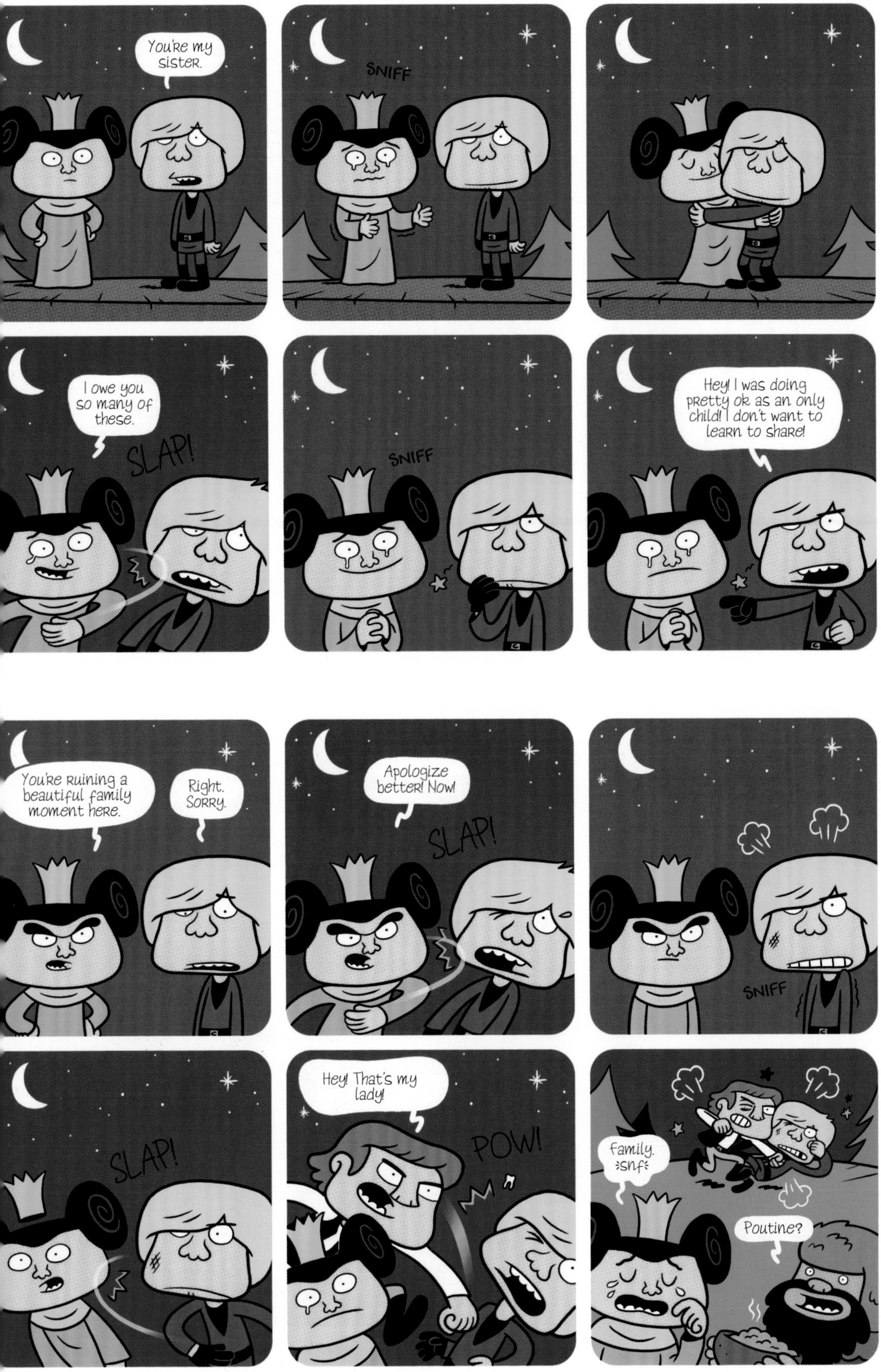

You're my sister.
SNIFF
I owe you so many of these.
SLAP!
SNIFF
Hey! I was doing pretty ok as an only child! I don't want to learn to share!
You're ruining a beautiful family moment here.
Right. Sorry.
Apologize better! Now!
SLAP!
SNIFF
SLAP!
Hey! That's my lady!
POW!
Family. snf
Poutine?

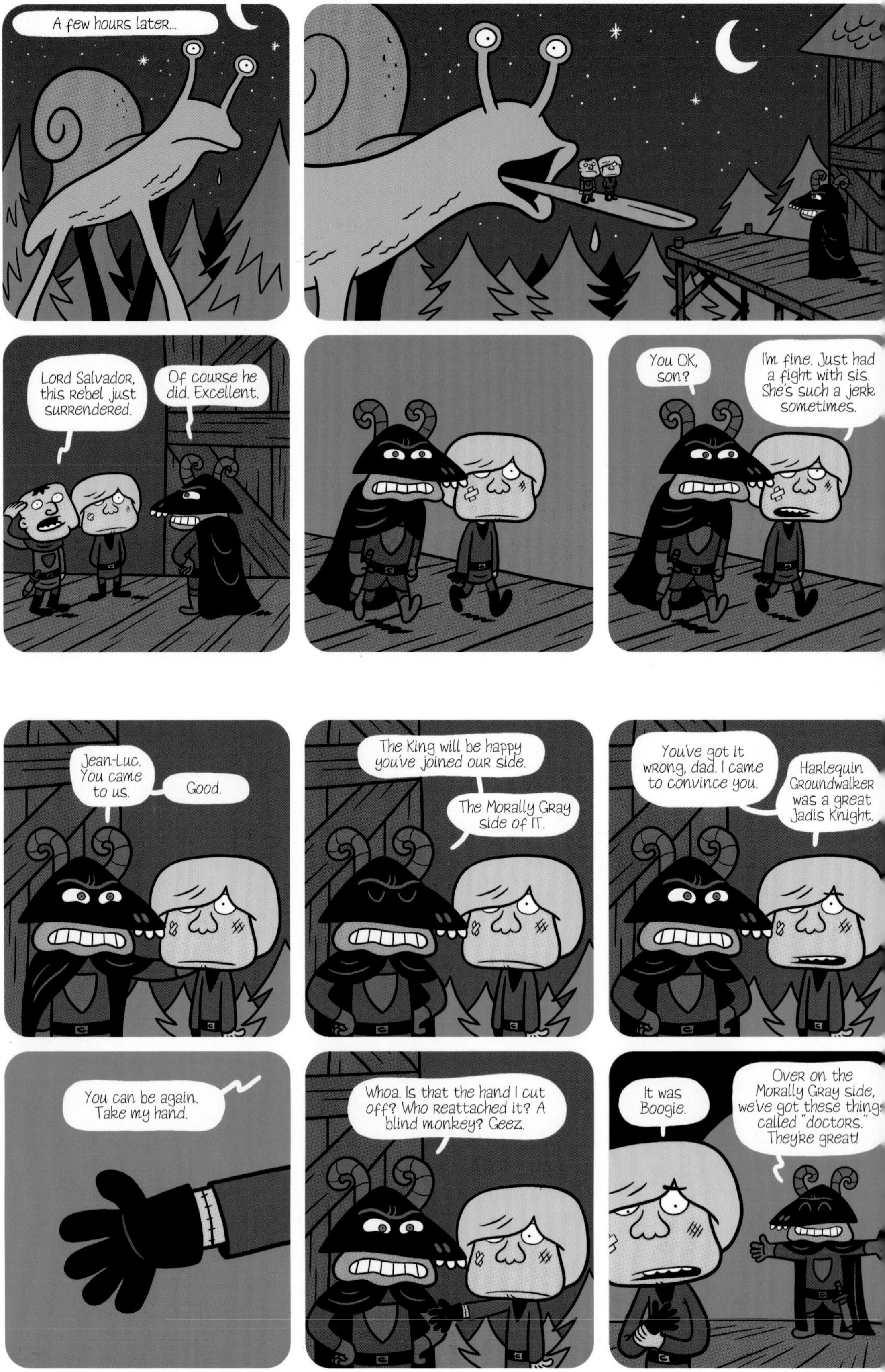
A few hours later...
Lord Salvador, this rebel just surrendered.
Of course he did. Excellent.
You OK, son?
I'm fine. Just had a fight with sis. She's such a jerk sometimes.
Jean-Luc. You came to us.
Good.
The King will be happy you've joined our side.
The Morally Gray side of IT.
You've got it wrong, dad. I came to convince you.
Harlequin Groundwalker was a great Jadis Knight.
You can be again. Take my hand.
Whoa. Is that the hand I cut off? Who reattached it? A blind monkey? Geez.
It was Boogie.
Over on the Morally Gray side, we've got these things called "doctors." They're great!

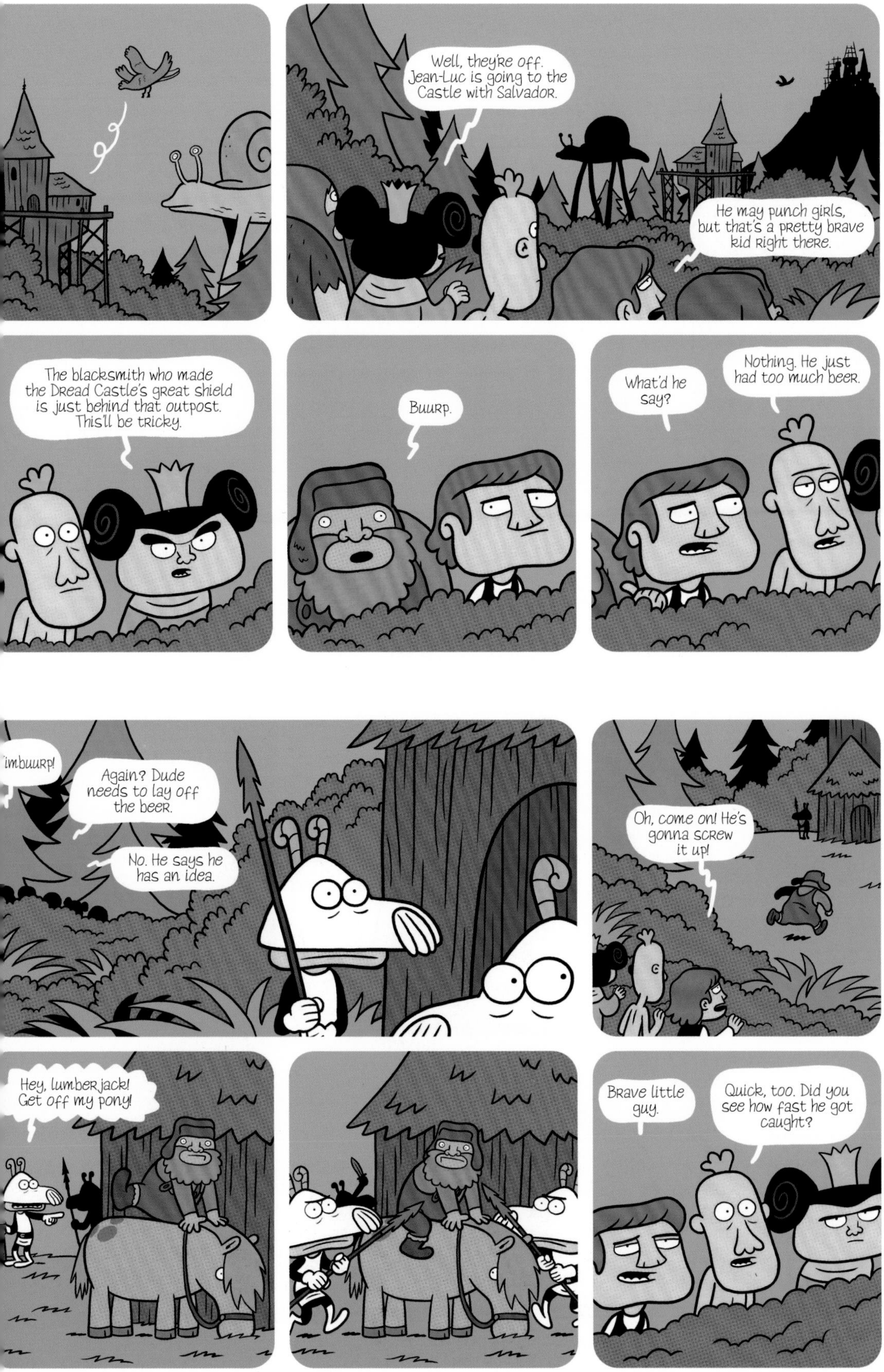
Well, they're off. Jean-Luc is going to the Castle with Salvador.
He may punch girls, but that's a pretty brave kid right there.
The blacksmith who made the Dread Castle's great shield is just behind that outpost. This'll be tricky.
Buurp.
What'd he say?
Nothing. He just had too much beer.
imbuurp!
Again? Dude needs to lay off the beer.
No. He says he has an idea.
Oh, come on! He's gonna screw it up!
Hey, lumberjack! Get off my pony!
Brave little guy.
Quick, too. Did you see how fast he got caught?

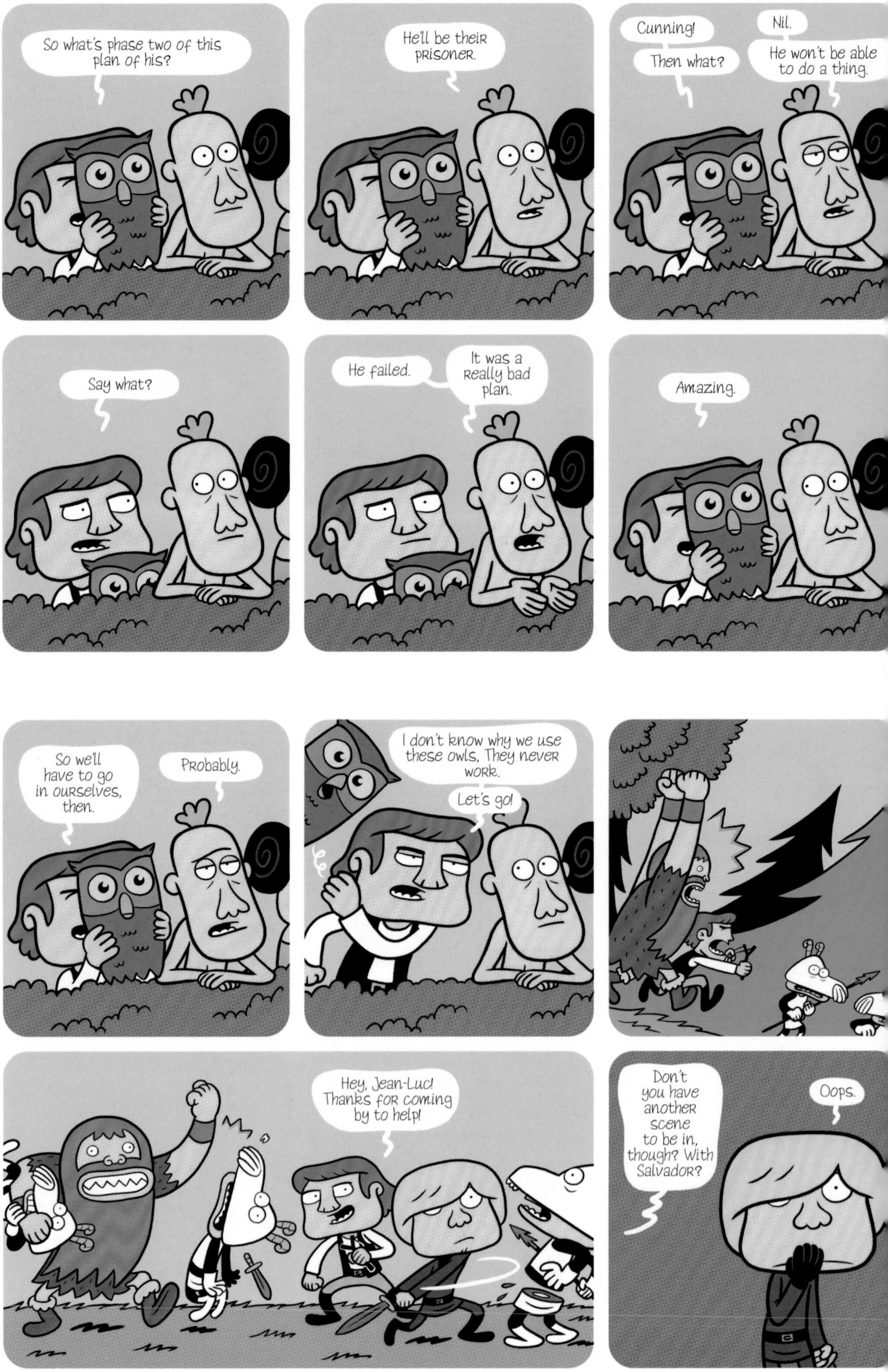
So what's phase two of this plan of his?
He'll be their prisoner.
Cunning!
Then what?
Nil.
He won't be able to do a thing.
Say what?
He failed.
It was a really bad plan.
Amazing.
So we'll have to go in ourselves, then.
Probably.
I don't know why we use these owls, They never work.
Let's go!
Hey, Jean-Luc! Thanks for coming by to help!
Don't you have another scene to be in, though? With Salvador?
Oops.

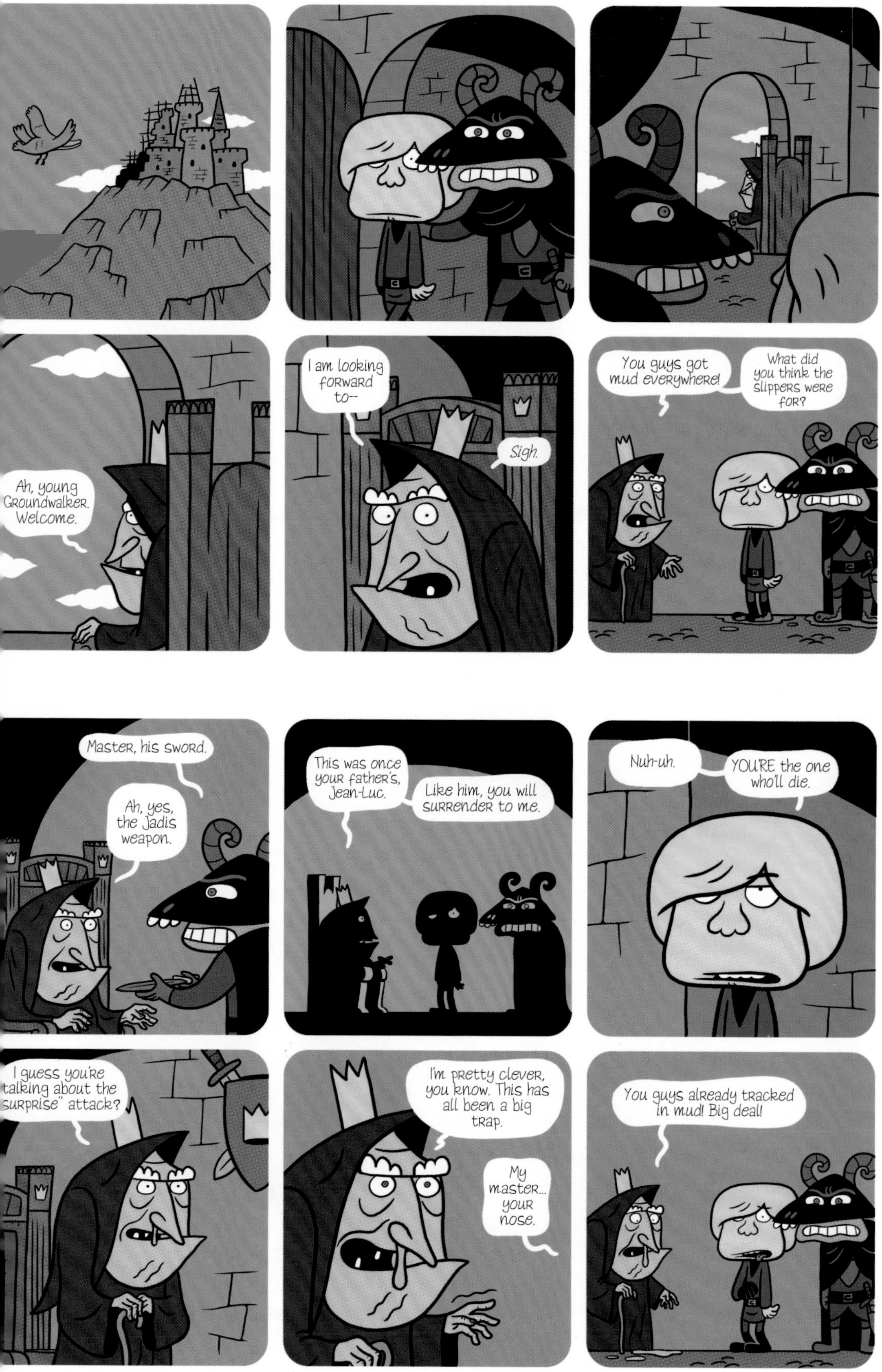

Ah, young Groundwalker. Welcome.
I am looking forward to--
Sigh.
You guys got mud everywhere!
What did you think the slippers were for?
Master, his sword.
Ah, yes, the Jadis weapon.
This was once your father's, Jean-Luc.
Like him, you will surrender to me.
Nuh-uh.
YOU'RE the one who'll die.
I guess you're talking about the "surprise" attack?
I'm pretty clever, you know. This has all been a big trap.
My master... your nose.
You guys already tracked in mud! Big deal!

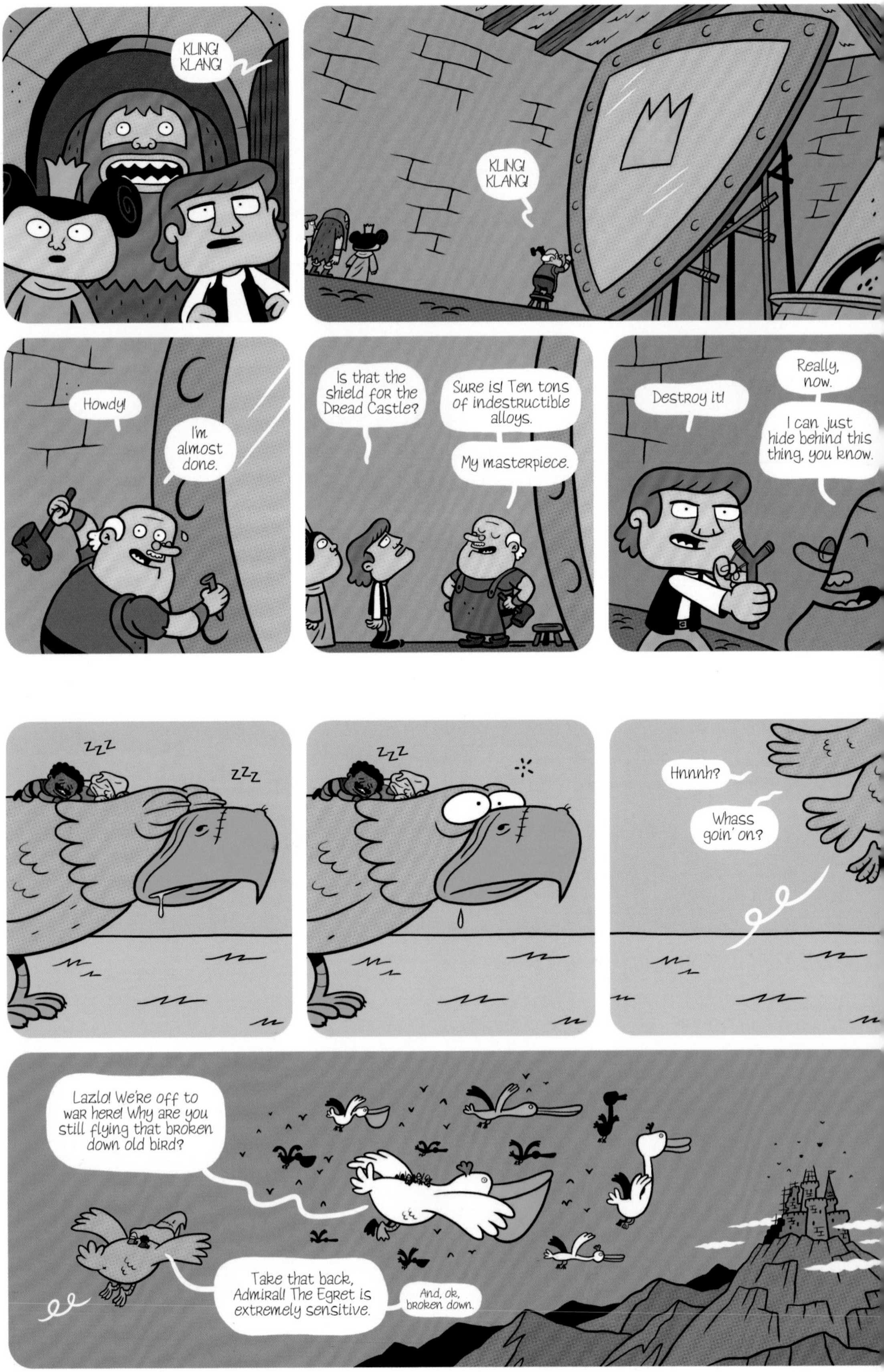
KLING! KLANG!
KLING! KLANG!
Howdy!
I'm almost done.
Is that the shield for the Dread Castle?
Sure is! Ten tons of indestructible alloys.
My masterpiece.
Destroy it!
Really, now.
I can just hide behind this thing, you know.
ZZZ
ZZZ
ZZZ
Hnnnh?
Whass goin' on?
Lazlo! We're off to war here! Why are you still flying that broken down old bird?
Take that back, Admiral! The Egret is extremely sensitive.
And, ok, broken down.

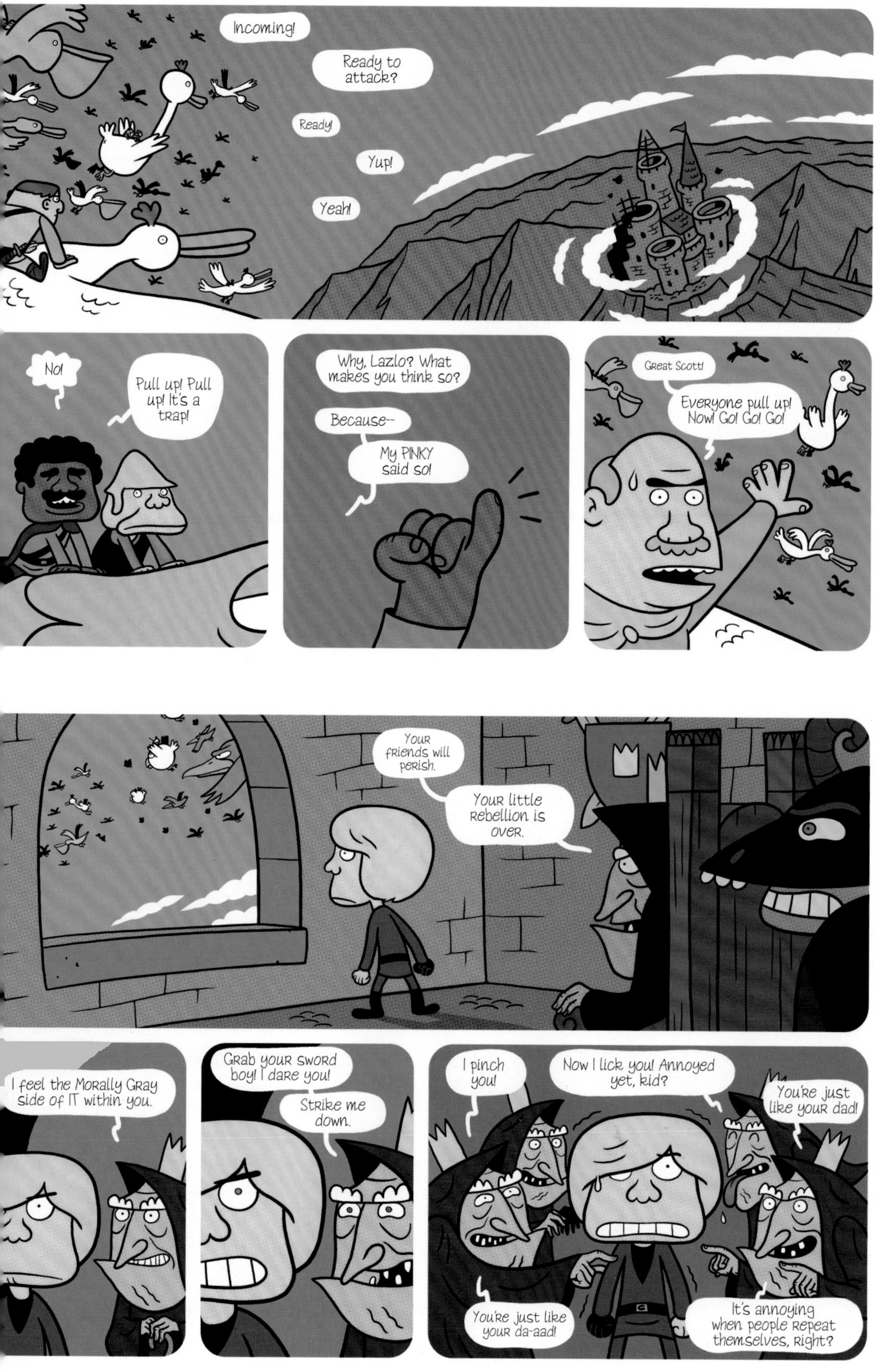
Incoming!
Ready to attack?
Ready!
Yup!
Yeah!
No!
Pull up! Pull up! It's a trap!
Why, Lazlo? What makes you think so?
Because--
My PINKY said so!
Great Scott!
Everyone pull up! Now! Go! Go! Go!
Your friends will perish.
Your little Rebellion is over.
I feel the Morally Gray side of IT within you.
Grab your sword boy! I dare you!
Strike me down.
I pinch you!
Now I lick you! Annoyed yet, kid?
You're just like your dad!
You're just like your da-aad!
It's annoying when people repeat themselves, right?

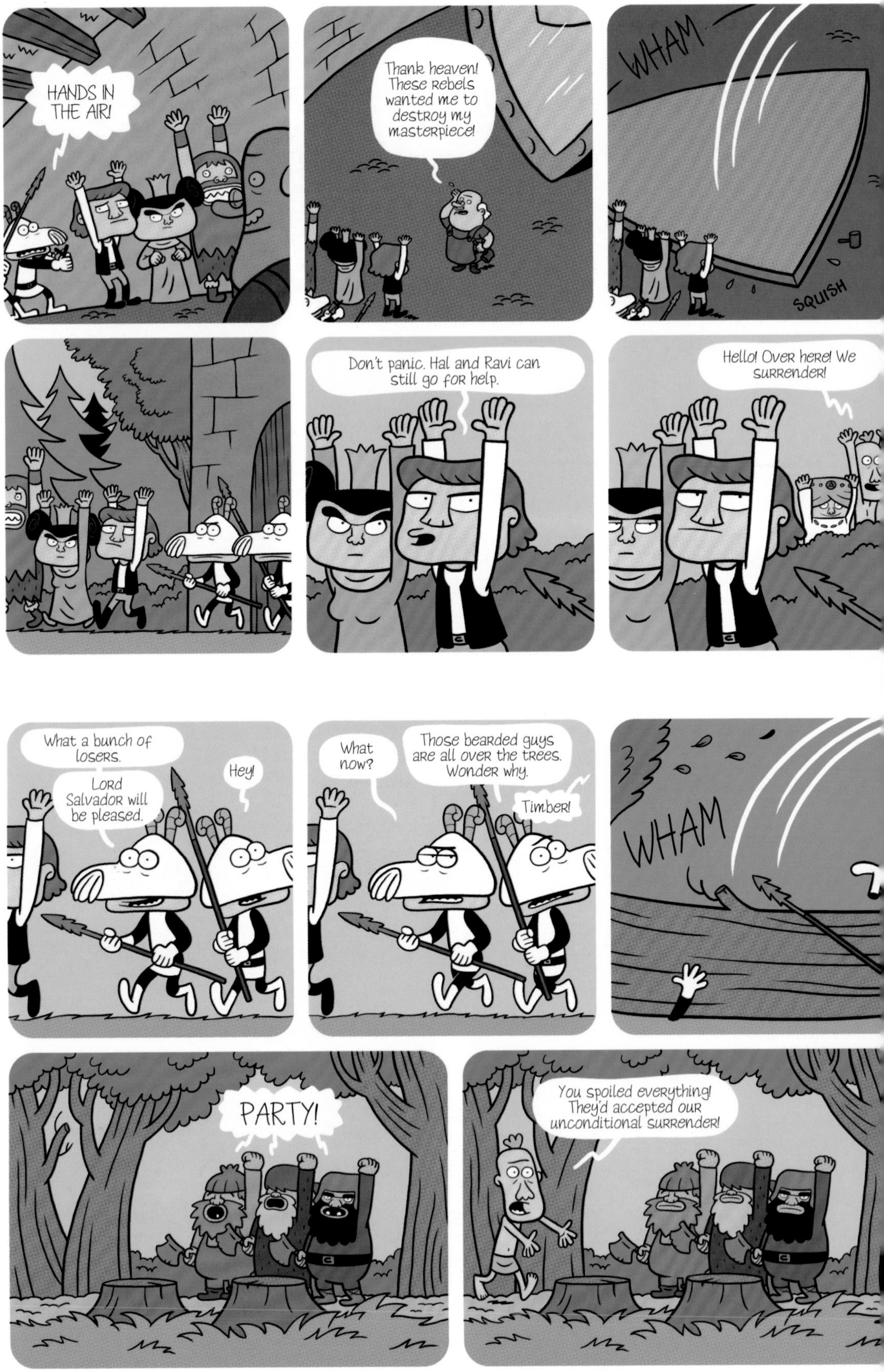
HANDS IN THE AIR!
Thank heaven! These rebels wanted me to destroy my masterpiece!
WHAM
SQUISH
Don't panic. Hal and Ravi can still go for help.
Hello! Over here! We surrender!
What a bunch of losers.
Lord Salvador will be pleased.
Hey!
What now?
Those bearded guys are all over the trees. Wonder why.
Timber!
WHAM
PARTY!
You spoiled everything! They'd accepted our unconditional surrender!

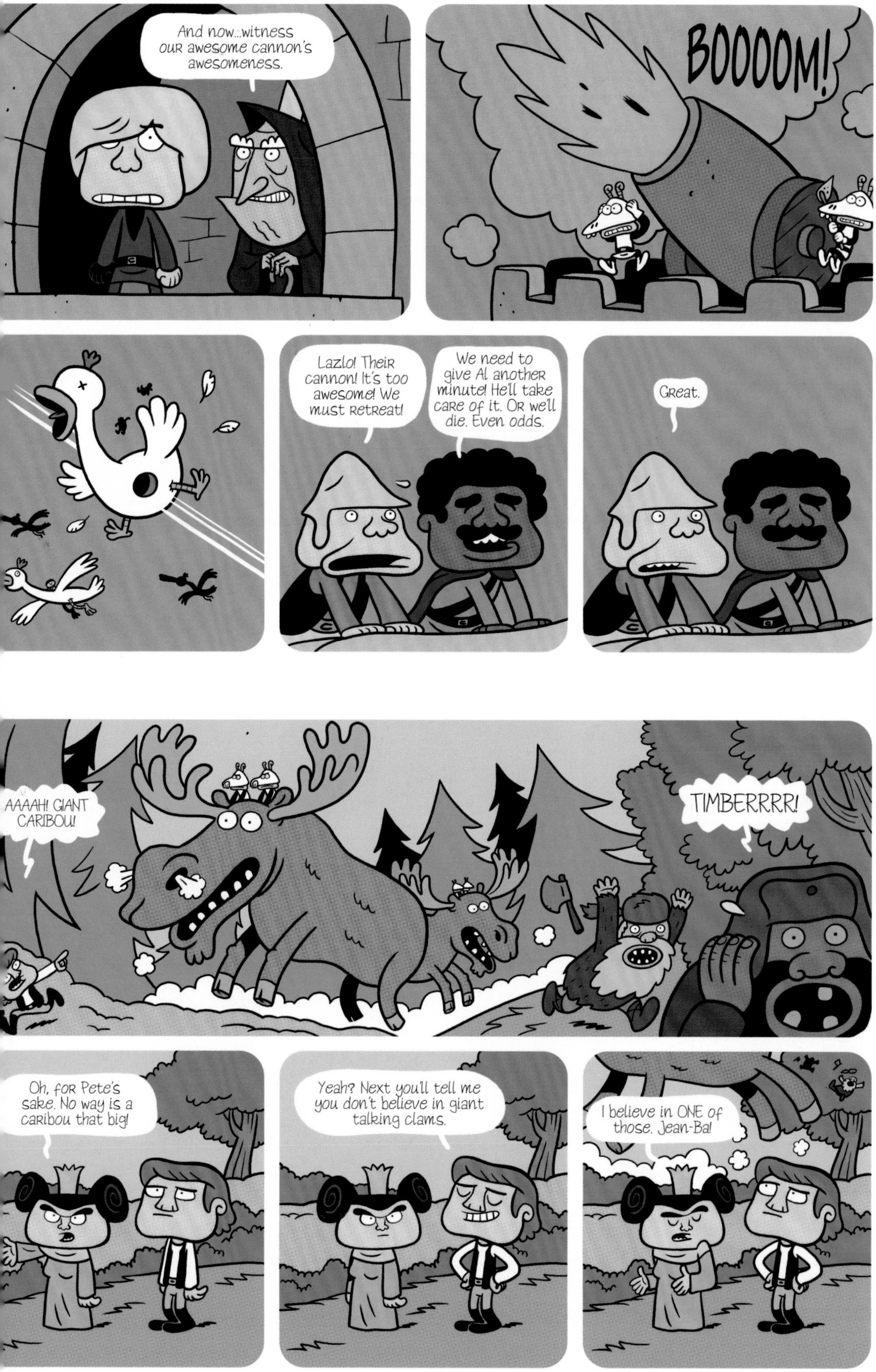
And now...witness our awesome cannon's awesomeness.
BOOOOM!
Lazlo! Their cannon! It's too awesome! We must retreat!
We need to give Al another minute! He'll take care of it. Or we'll die. Even odds.
Great.
AAAAH! GIANT CARIBOU!
TIMBERRRR!
Oh, for Pete's sake. No way is a caribou that big!
Yeah? Next you'll tell me you don't believe in giant talking clams.
I believe in ONE of those. Jean-Ba!

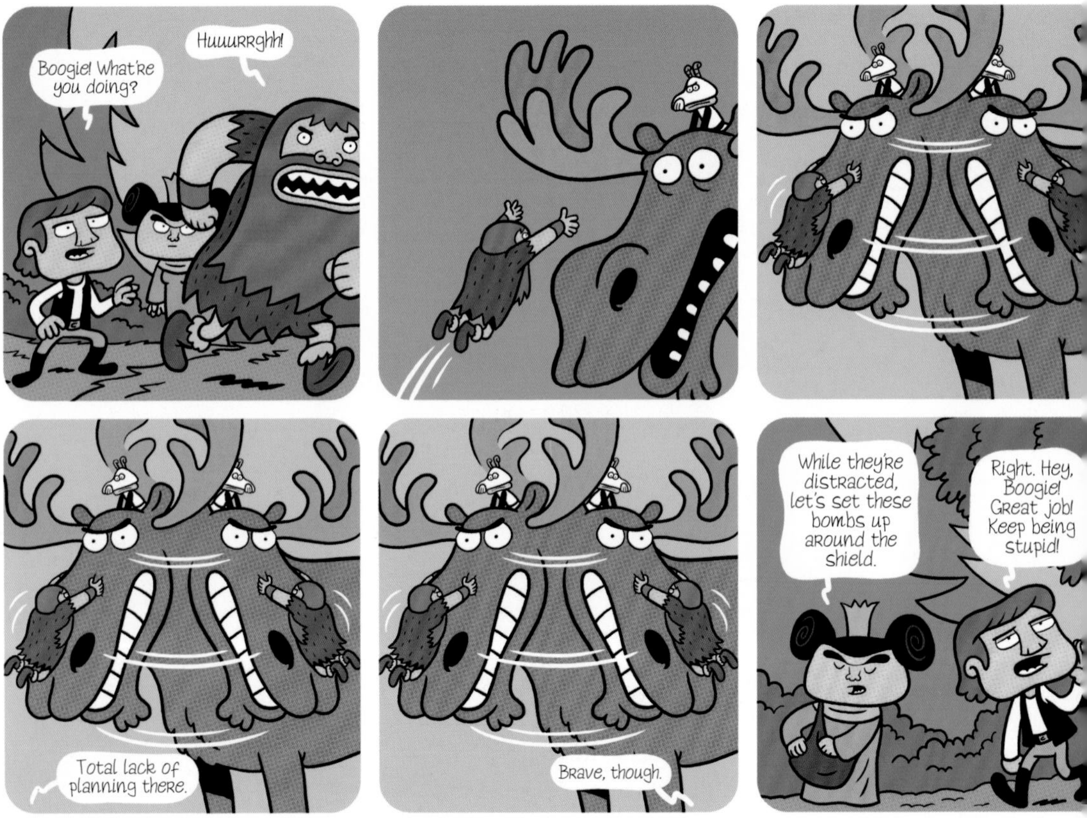
Boogie! What're you doing?
Huuurrghh!
Total lack of planning there.
Brave, though.
While they're distracted, let's set these bombs up around the shield.
Right. Hey, Boogie! Great job! Keep being stupid!

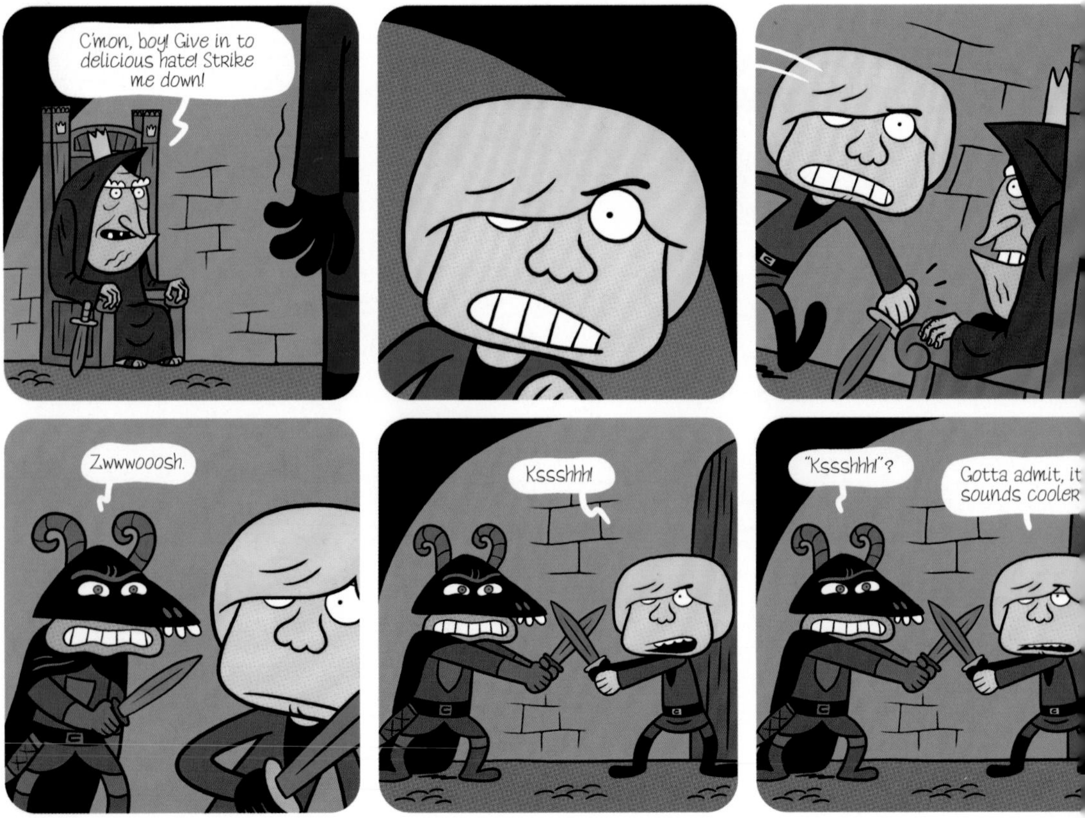
C'mon, boy! Give in to delicious hate! Strike me down!
Zwwwooosh.
Kssshhh!
"Kssshhh!"?
Gotta admit, it sounds cooler

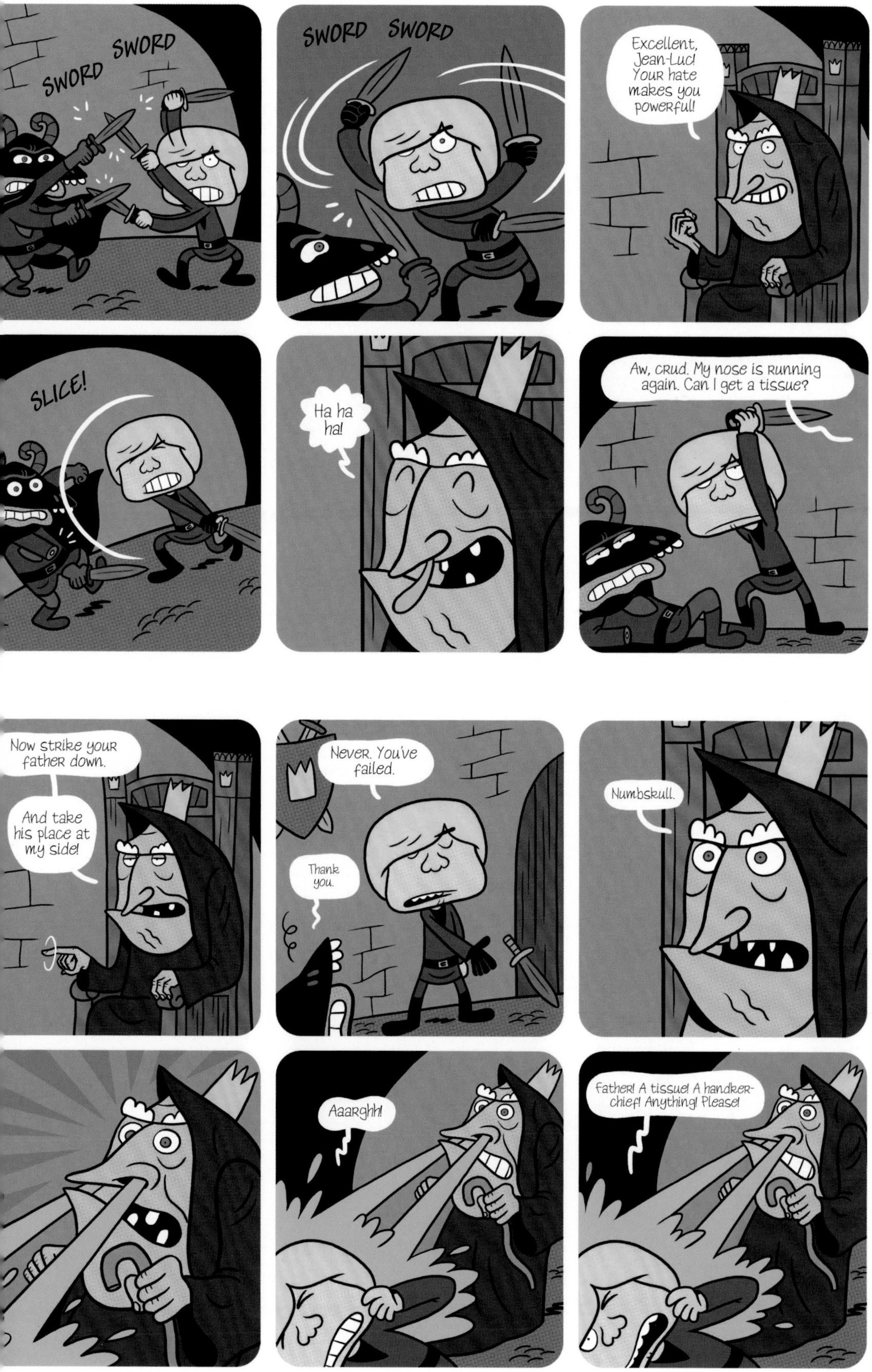
SWORD
SWORD
SWORD
SWORD
Excellent, Jean-Luc! Your hate makes you powerful!
SLICE!
Ha ha ha!
Aw, crud. My nose is running again. Can I get a tissue?
Now strike your father down.
And take his place at my side!
Never. You've failed.
Thank you.
Numbskull.
Aaarghh!
Father! A tissue! A handker-chief! Anything! Please!

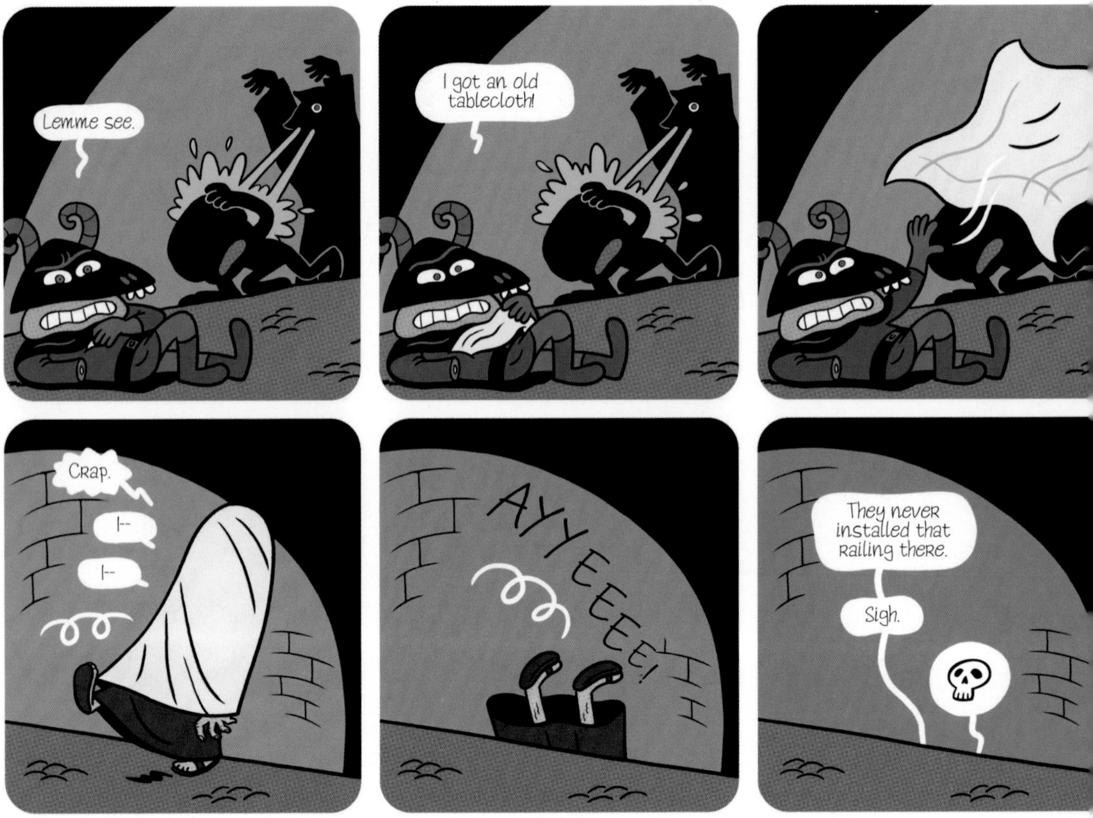
Lemme see.
I got an old tablecloth!
Crap.
I--
I--
AYYEEEE!
They never installed that Railing there.
Sigh.

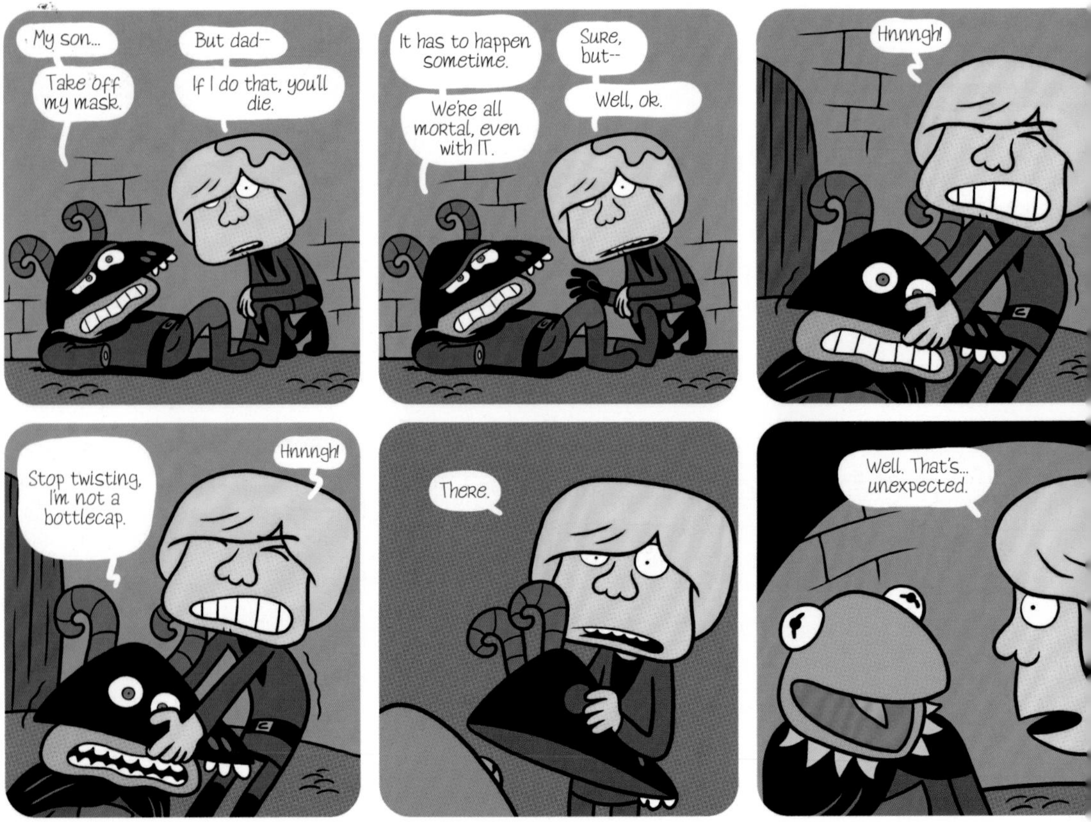
My son...
Take off my mask.
But dad--
If I do that, you'll die.
It has to happen sometime.
We're all mortal, even with IT.
Sure, but--
Well, ok.
Hnnngh!
Stop twisting, I'm not a bottlecap.
Hnnngh!
There.
Well. That's... unexpected.

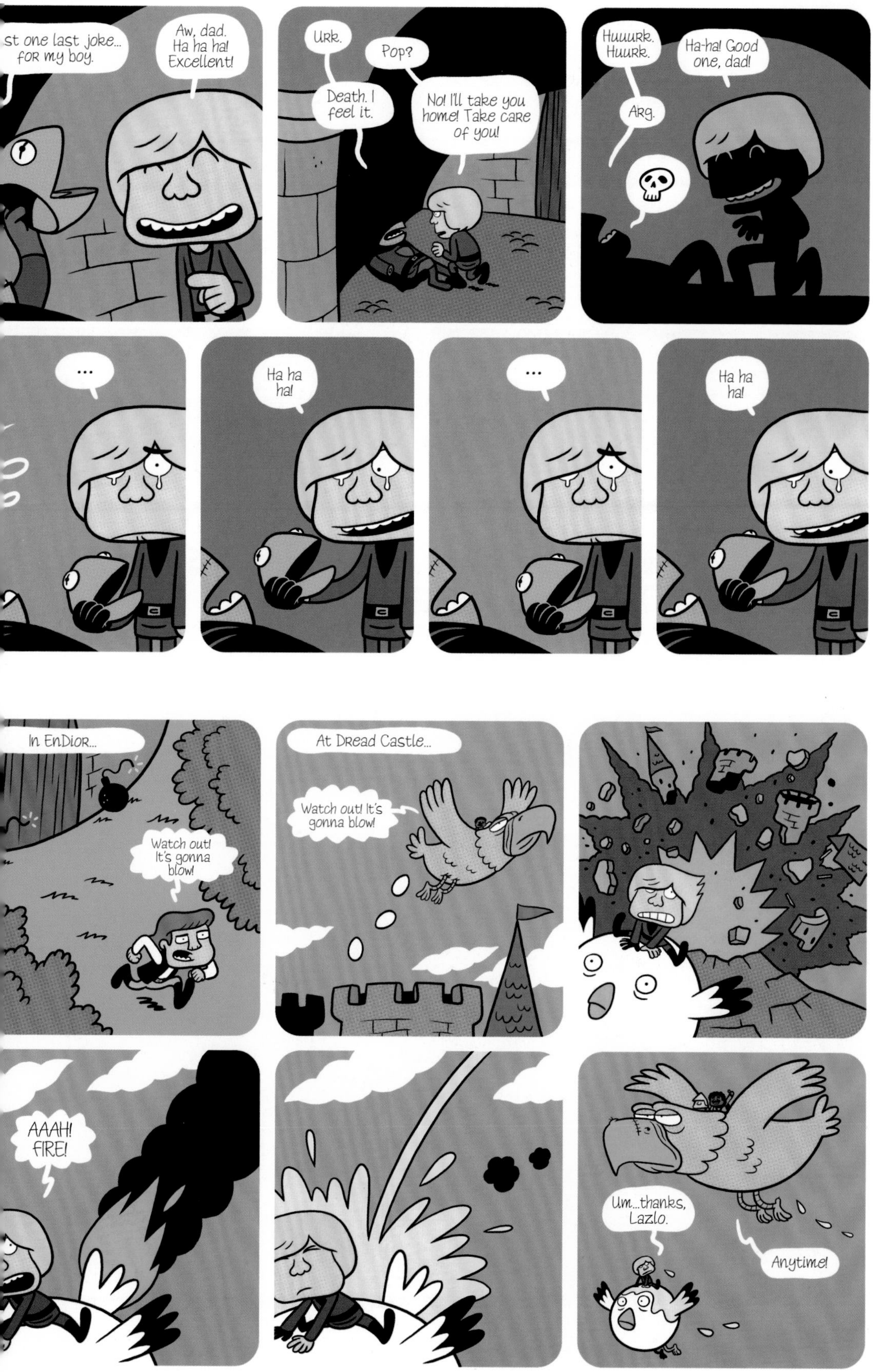
st one last joke... for my boy.
Aw, dad. Ha ha ha! Excellent!
Urk.
Pop?
Death. I feel it.
No! I'll take you home! Take care of you!
Huuurk. Huurk.
Ha-ha! Good one, dad!
Arg.
...
Ha ha ha!
...
Ha ha ha!
In EnDior...
Watch out! It's gonna blow!
At Dread Castle...
Watch out! It's gonna blow!
AAAH! FIRE!
Um...thanks, Lazlo.
Anytime!

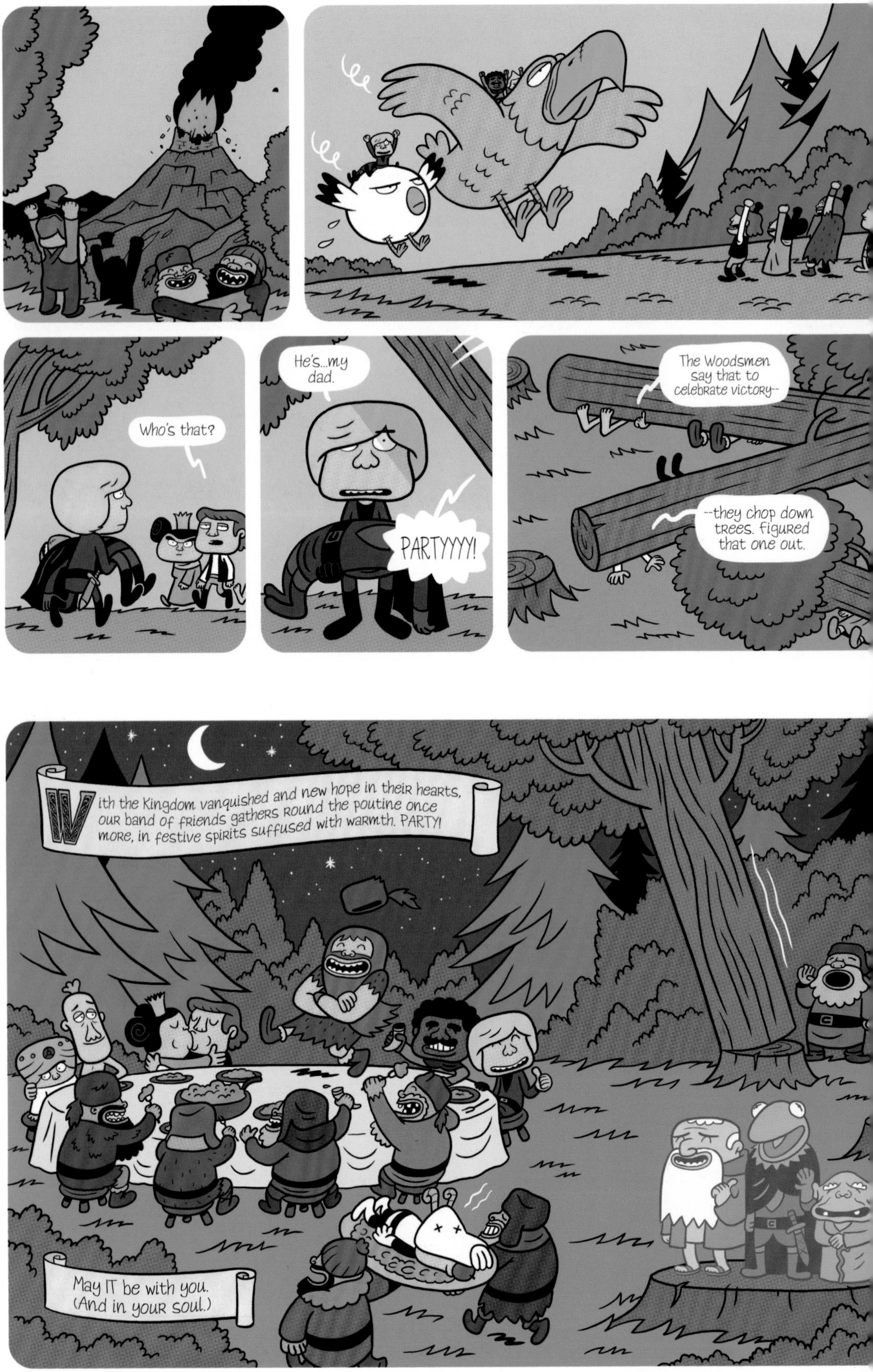
Who's that?
He's...my dad.
PARTYYYY!
The Woodsmen say that to celebrate victory--
--they chop down trees. figured that one out.
With the Kingdom vanquished and new hope in their hearts, our band of friends gathers round the poutine once more, in festive spirits suffused with warmth. PARTY!
May IT be with you. (And in your soul.)

THE

END

★

ROSS RICHIE Chief Executive Officer • **MATT GAGNON** Editor-in-Chief • **WES HARRIS** VP-Publishing • **LANCE KREITER** VP-Licensing & Merchandising • **PHIL BARBARO** Director of Finance
BRYCE CARLSON Managing Editor • **DAFNA PLEBAN** Editor • **SHANNON WATTERS** Editor • **ERIC HARBURN** Assistant Editor • **ADAM STAFFARONI** Assistant Editor • **CHRIS ROSA** Assistant Editor
STEPHANIE GONZAGA Graphic Designer • **EMILY MCGUINESS** Marketing Coordinator • **DEVIN FUNCHES** Marketing & Sales Assistant • **JASMINE AMIRI** Operations Assistant

SPACE WARPED — June 2012. Published by KaBOOM!, a division of Boom Entertainment, Inc. Naguère les étoiles, volumes 1-3, Bourhis-Spiessert Copyright © Guy Delcourt Productions 2010 - 2011. Originally published in single magazine form as SPACE WARPED 1-6. Copyright © 2011 Guy Delcourt Productions. All rights reserved. KaBOOM!™ and the KaBOOM! logo are trademarks of Boom Entertainment, Inc., registered in various countries and categories. All characters, events, and institutions depicted herein are fictional. Any similarity between any of the names, characters, persons, events, and/or institutions in this publication to actual names, characters, and persons, whether living or dead, events, and/or institutions is unintended and purely coincidental. KaBOOM! does not read or accept unsolicited submissions of ideas, stories, or artwork.

A catalog record of this book is available from OCLC and from the KaBOOM! website, www.kaboom-studios.com, on the Librarians Page.

BOOM! Studios, 6310 San Vicente Boulevard, Suite 107, Los Angeles, CA 90048-5457. Printed in China. First Printing.
ISBN: 978-1-60886-670-0

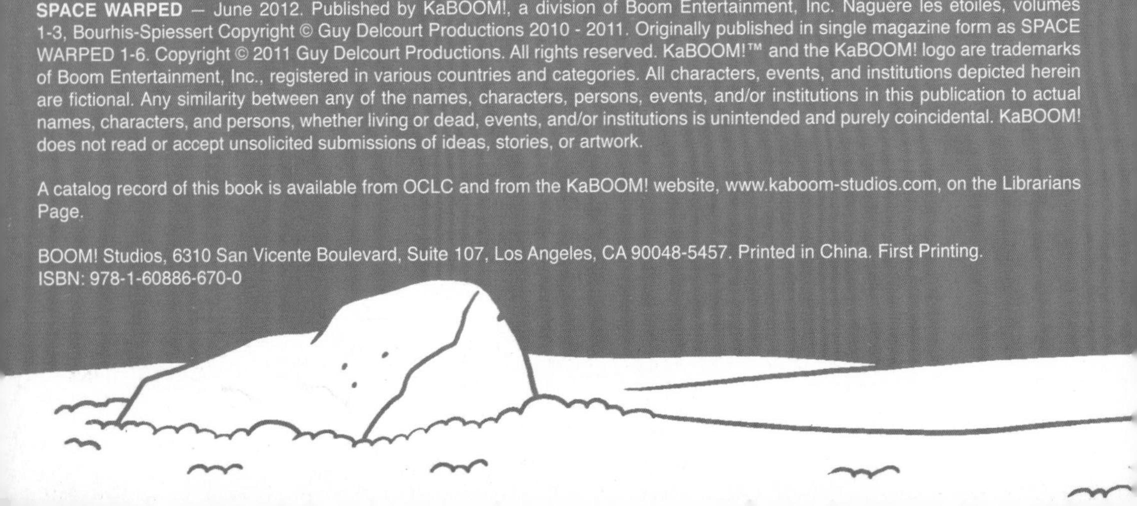